Dances
With
Whippets

by

Philip C. Wright

Published by

MELROSE BOOKS

An Imprint of Melrose Press Limited
St Thomas Place, Ely
Cambridgeshire
CB7 4GG, UK
www.melrosebooks.com

FIRST EDITION

Copyright © Philip C. Wright 1999

Cover illustration by Maggie High
Cover design by Bryan Carpenter
Author photography by Kevin Maunton LBIPP LMPA

ISBN 1 905226 03 9

Printed and bound in Great Britain by:
Bath Press Limited, Lower Bristol Road,
Bath, BA2 3BL, UK

Dances
With
Whippets

Chapter 1

The sun was bright yellow, the sky reflective blue. In many ways, it was like any other day in New York. Down below the skyline, shadows were cast onto the streets and alleys from the towering skyscrapers above. There was no peace here. It was early morning, yet the city that never stops was in the process of erupting like a dormant volcano. Traffic noise, people too busy to notice, rushing like ants to their various destinations. One such man, already late for work due to a small fire on the underground, was trying to hail a taxi. His name was Richard Waters; he was an anachronism, a man out of his time. A descendent of a once-proud North American Indian Tribe.

As he settled into the back of a familiar black and yellow cab, he thoughtfully reflected as to what was he doing there: "My name is Running Water, and all I seem to be doing is running." He continued with his private thoughts: "Wearing a suit, carrying a briefcase, breathing all the poison of this city, and for what? To get mugged one night, just trying to get home."

Looking from the cab window upwards, the sky seemed so clear. He thought of his roots. He didn't think for long, however. His carriage arrived outside our hero's place of work.

"Six bucks, mate", exclaimed the acne-faced youth with attitude.

Purporting to be a customer-caring, cab-conveying server of the community, he drove off at speed on the assumption that the four dollar balance from the ten spot tendered was in fact a tip, and not deemed change.

Hadim Gotcha & Grabit Inc. is a well-established firm of lawyers. Corporate lawyers, specialising in land purchase for the purpose of industrial development.

Richard had worked there for the past nine years. Suffocating in the all-consuming environment of the Big Apple. The many times he had wished to be out on the prairie, riding a pinto-coloured Indian pony, hunting buffalo.

"Good morning, Mr. Waters", enthused Rachel cheerfully, as Richard entered his office.

"Good morning, Rachel", he replied, with less enthusiasm. "What's on the agenda today, then?"

"Mr. Grabit wants to see you in his office the moment you get in", she answered, in a manner that gave Richard an uneasy feeling.

"What's going on?" he thought to himself, "I haven't been upstairs for at least two years ... not since I was asked, ever so politely, to take a pay cut."

"Ah, good morning, my lad", said an excited Mr. Grabit, outstretching his hand.

Richard shook hands and smiled. Mr. Grabit was a short man full of his own self-importance. Understandable really, when you are made to realise that this fifty-something was worth in excess of fifty million dollars, and was married to a twenty-something ex-centrefold who just happened to be blonde, if not by nature then by design. Who cared, she fitted the bill.

"I have an assignment for you Richard, of a delicate nature, that we here at the firm feel is ideally suited to your special talents", the boss said, in a particularly serious fashion. "Let me give you the details", he likewise continued.

Richard sat at his desk in a state of shock. He had been chosen to negotiate a very special land purchase. A theme park, for a very cash rich consortium. Millions were at stake. Sensitive issues. Public opinion. After nine years with the firm he was finally to be given the chance to prove his worth, and to leave the Big Apple. Richard was going to England. Yorkshire in fact; wild and barren, to look at and purchase suitable land in order to build a kind of Disney. It was not Disney, however, but a series of different fantasy worlds. Adult escapism. Market research had been done. People who were searching, looking to escape, to relax, to reduce stress. People with a mid-life crisis, yet with cash to spend.

"People very much like myself", he thought.

Less than twenty-four hours later Richard found himself strapped into a first-class seat of a Boeing 747. No expense spared, this had to be the big one. His brief, along with contact references, was securely locked inside his black, leather-bound briefcase: a present to him, from his father, on his twenty-first birthday. Richard smiled, more of a smirk really, as he looked at the briefcase, carrying for the first time something more important than his lunch.

"I'll look at my notes later", he muttered quietly to himself.

As the plane took off and levelled out, he reclined his seat, shut his eyes, and began to think of his father: a proud man who had been proud of his son. It was he who had given Richard his Indian name. Apparently, in the confusion during labour, shortly after his wife's waters had broken, someone had left a faucet on in the bathroom, which overflowed causing a flood, not only in that room, but also the apartment downstairs.

Hence the name 'Running Water'. His father had been proud the day his son was born, proud the day of his graduation, and proud the day when Richard had told him that he had a job in the city and would wear a suit to work. He himself had always worked with his hands. He had wanted his son to do well. Richard remembered what his father had told him on the day of his graduation.

"Remember, Richard", he said, firm and to the point, "A man can make a living with his hands, but a fortune with his head."

Richard smiled. He knew that if he played this one smart, his father's words could ring true.

"Champagne, sir?" said the stewardess sweetly.

"Yes please."

Richard was enjoying first class. Raising his glass he made a toast. "This one's for you, Dad", he said, just before he sipped.

Richard's father had passed away two years ago. He was now in his final resting place, that reservation in the sky.

Flight 739/B landed at Heathrow Airport at 1.35pm. The sky was a sickly grey, with more than just a hint of impending anger. Rain was imminent and expected; after all, this was England. Two hours and forty-three minutes later Richard was once again in the air. This time on a smaller plane, name and type unknown to him; in transit to Leeds Airport. The journey was short in time and distance, in comparison to the previous one, due to a near miss with an RAF Tornado. The excitement created by this occurrence more than made up for the lack of an in-flight movie. Apparently the Tornado was rehearsing for what might possibly be the real thing, somewhere in Europe, acting in its capacity as a NATO peacekeeper. Richard couldn't help thinking of times gone by, when soldiers in blue uniforms riding large horses entered his forefather's lands, claiming the same.

Chapter 2

Derek Arkwright parked his car, and made his way to the passenger arrivals area at Leeds Airport. As he made his way, he looked up at the sky. It was a dismal depressing black. More heavy rain to follow the previous band.

"After all", he sighed, "this is Yorkshire".

Derek was to be Richard's contact and guide. A born-again Yorkshireman. He stood five feet ten, of medium build, dark hair with brown eyes. At thirty years of age Derek showed all the signs of someone who had once been upwardly mobile, but had since reinvented himself. Derek had left Yorkshire at the age of eighteen, and gone down south, to London. Without formal qualifications he managed to secure a position in the City, and for a while he went from strength to strength. A Docklands flat, Porsche, Armani suit, mobile phone, and a Filofax. Alas, this was not to last. A downturn in the economy, a deal that went sour, and the first to go was the Docklands flat, quickly followed by the Porsche, Armani suit, and the mobile phone. He still had the Filofax.

"This is my chance to make it big", he said to himself, sounding not too dissimilar to an out-of-work aspiring actor.

He was glad to be away from the so-called rat race, but still hankered after the so-called trappings of wealth. "All I have to do is impress the Yank, razzle and dazzle him with the old Arkwright magic, and I'm in."

A brief period of introduction, and they were soon heading off to Richard's hotel.

All he wanted, after his long day, was to crash out for a few hours. He was in no mood for idle banter. Derek, after giving a barrage of verbal gunfire, sensed his passenger was not entirely receptive to conversational exchange, and decided to desist from further talk. He turned the radio on, leaving Richard snoring rhythmically to the dulcet tones of Abba.

"We're here", exclaimed Derek, gently shaking Richard by the sleeve of his jacket.

"Oh good", he replied, still sleepy.

Derek fetched the American's suitcase from the boot whilst Richard studied his temporary abode.

"The Grand, not an unusual name for a hotel", he thought, still somewhat wearily.

"Come on then … let's get you settled in."

The Grand was, in fact, quite grand. A Victorian affair, recently refurbished to a very high standard.

"No expense spared", said Richard quietly to himself, whilst admiring the plethora of crystal chandeliers that adorned the foyer.

After the usual formalities of checking-in, a porter picked up his suitcase and dutifully lead them to his room.

"Gee whiz!" proclaimed Richard upon entering the room. "This is something else."

"Wow!" was all Derek had to say, which, as far as Richard was concerned, was quite sufficient.

After tipping the porter, apologies were made to Derek for the need of an early night. The American, at last, found himself alone in his room.

Richard awoke early the next morning, due largely to the efficient Derek, who had called at reception the previous evening in order to place an early morning wake-up call to the American's room for 6am. A cooing pigeon just outside his window also played its part.

"No matter", thought Richard to himself, pulling back the curtains, whilst at the same time flicking at the glass with one of last night's discarded socks, attempting to deter the pigeon. "Gee, what a beautiful morning!" He smiled to himself: "At this hour, I'm not sure whether I'm talking to myself, or addressing the pigeon."

The pigeon must have been insulted, for he turned away from the window, took a step off the ledge, lazily flapped his wings, and disappeared.

The morning was indeed beautiful; the sun was shining, the sky pale blue and cloudless. Any sign of the previous day's rain had disappeared overnight.

Richard looked down from the sky, adjusting his thoughts from meteorological to aesthetic. The hotel may be called the Grand, indeed it may be grand, both inside and out, but the view from Richard's window was not.

Rows and rows of dilapidated terraced houses, many of which had boarding over the windows and doors. Dogs roamed in packs, scavenging. Two equally sized hairy mongrels were disputing the ownership of a discarded Kentucky Fried Chicken carton. The staple diet of stray dogs in the area, according to Richard's observations, seemed to consist of mainly leftover takeaways. MacDonalds' distinctive packaging featured quite extensively on the streets below.

"It's not MacDonalds that's to blame", said Richard rather sadly, to a different pigeon who had landed on the windowsill. "After all", he continued, in what appeared to be a friendly attempt to engage the latest pigeon in conversation, "who is to blame for death from a gun? The inventor, the manufacturer, the seller, or the person who pulls the trigger?"

The pigeon responded in an apparently understanding manner. He cooed rather loudly, defecated on the windowsill, stepped off it, flapped his wings, and disappeared.

"Oh well", said Richard, rather profoundly.

Prior to turning his back on the view, he noticed a rather large sign at the end of the street directly in front of him. It read For Sale, Land for Industrial Re-Development.

He was somewhat numbed, unsure of his feelings. Shrugging his shoulders as he walked to the bathroom, he spoke rather quietly, this time to himself: "Time to start the day." He showered, changed, and went down for breakfast.

The American didn't realise just how hungry he was until he entered the Grand's grand dining room. "More chandeliers", he thought unsurprisingly, as if by now expecting to find them in every closet.

"Good morning, sir", said the waiter brightly. "Table for one?"

"Yes please."

"Smoking or non-smoking?"

"Smoking."

As Richard was led to his table he wondered why he had said smoking. He didn't smoke. He had never smoked, except that time when he had been twelve, and decided to try out his father's peace pipe. On that occasion he had been violently sick, and as a result had not smoked since. " I suppose in the absence of real tobacco, I shouldn't have tried smoking a mixture of autumn leaves collected from the local park, and a selection of herbs from the kitchen", he thought reflectively, as he sat at his table.

The smell of food upon entering the dining room had awakened a dormant appetite within him.

"I'll have the full English breakfast please."

"Tea or coffee, sir?" asked the waiter patiently.

"Tea, please."

"Darjeeling, Earl Grey, or China?"

"Earl Grey", came the reply swiftly.

Sipping the tea a few minutes later, he wondered why he had asked for this particular beverage. He had never drunk Earl Grey before. In fact he had never drunk tea before, well, not since that time when he had been twelve, shortly after watching Mary Poppins. Miss Poppins had given him the inspiration to try a cup. However, in the absence of real tea leaves, he had tried brewing a pot using a mixture of autumn leaves collected from the local park, and a selection of herbs from the kitchen. To this day, tea had never passed his lips.

"Oh well, when in Rome", he mused nonchalantly. "It's a lot better than my efforts all those years ago." He took another sip, and then a mouthful. The tea by now had cooled. "And then again, perhaps not", he thought. Still musing nonchalantly, he replaced the half-empty cup in the saucer.

The remainder of the breakfast had been a delight. Eggs, bacon, fried bread, sausages, baked beans, hash browns, and grilled tomatoes. Toast and preserves followed.

Richard chose marmalade, requesting coffee at the same time. "Gee, I'm stuffed", he said, patting his stomach gently.

Later that day, the breakfast would come to remind him of the time his father gave him some very good advice concerning food.

"Son", he had said. "Of all the good foods there are in the world, never eat parrot."

"Why is that?" Richard had asked.

"'Cause son, it has a tendency to repeat."

As arranged, Richard was waiting in the foyer at 8.45am for Derek to arrive. At 9.10am Derek arrived.

"Hi, Derek."

"Good morning, Richard", replied Derek. "Sleep well?" he continued.

"Fine, Derek, just fine."

Richard thought it prudent not to mention a 6am early morning wake-up call, nor what was probably Derek's secondary plan, just in case the first one failed, i.e. to send the pigeon. Best not to start the day by getting off on the wrong foot.

"What's on the agenda then, Derek?"

"I've got your hire car parked outside, I thought we would take a look at the site", replied Derek, full of enthusiasm.

"What is it?"

"The land, you know, up on the moors", answered Derek rather puzzled.

"No Derek, I meant the hire car. What is it?" Richard hid his frustration, putting it down to jet lag.

11

"Jeep Cherokee, 4WD, thought it might make you feel at home", said Derek, still exuding enthusiasm.

"Gee!" thought Richard. "This guy even talks in abbreviations."

"Nice one, Derek."

Richard smiled to himself. He hadn't driven a vehicle for at least four years, preferring cabs and public transport. New York was not the best place in the world to own a vehicle, let alone drive one. Richard smiled to himself again. His Aunt Bessie's ride-on lawnmower had been the last vehicle he had driven; four years ago last June.

"Right then, let's make a start", said Richard, actually appearing to express some enthusiasm himself.

They left the hotel and approached the jeep.

"You drive, Derek", said Richard, not wishing to show himself up. "You know the area, and the roads. I'll have a go later." He immediately regretted saying the last sentence.

Derek enjoyed being behind the wheel of the jeep. It reminded him of days gone by when he had the benefit of driving similar such salubrious modes of transport. The days of the feel-good factor, now just a memory. A rather distant one at that. They left Leeds behind, and the scenery changed from urban to rural.

"This is more like it, Derek."

"Like what?"

"Out in the countryside, out in the fresh air."

"Just wait until we get up on the moors, Dick", replied Derek informally. "Is it all right to call you Dick?" he continued, not wishing to offend his American colleague.

"I prefer Richard", he answered, pausing before adding, "Dick is slang for penis, and I wouldn't want the confusion of not knowing whether someone was just being friendly, or referring to me as some kind of prick."

"Good point Dick … er … sorry, I mean Richard."

They continued on in silence for a while. Richard liked to be called Richard, or Mr. Waters. Only close friends were allowed to be more affectionate. Only close friends, and family referred to him as R.W. (short for Running Water). Although in the main he was against abbreviations, he liked the term R.W. It had a certain ring. Richard's dislike for abbreviations emanated a long time ago from the workplace. He hated corporate abbs., the kind each company seem to have for their own products, installations, practices, etc., none of which are universal, and of no use whatsoever outside that particular environment. However, he still quite liked being referred to as R.W., but only by a few people who were close to him.

"It's getting a bit more rugged now", spoke Richard, opening up the dialogue once more.

"It will get a lot more rugged than this", stated Derek, as if his reply summed up the entire contents of National Geographic's archives on the subject.

Silence once again reigned.

Some ten minutes later the silence was broken.

"We're here", spouted Derek in what seemed to be an excited frenzy.

"God, it's beautiful!" said Richard in reply, expressing a delight not apparent to date.

Both Richard and Derek got out of the 4X4. Richard walked away from the narrow, not too well-kept excuse for a road onto the moor. He hadn't got too far when a covey of small birds exploded into the air only a few yards in front of him.

"Gee, what are they, Derek?" inquired Richard, as though genuinely interested.

"Grouse, Richard", answered Derek, only to happy to expand the Yank's knowledge. "A much-prized game bird", he continued.

"Fast little critters, aren't they?"

"That's why they are so highly regarded, er … Richard", he replied, almost responding with the Dick word.

"What, so highly regarded that they're killed for it?"

"Yes, rather ironic, isn't it."

Richard understood. Hunting was in his blood, although he had never personally practised the art. Except for that time, aged twelve, when in the local park, probably gathering leaves, he attempted to creep up on what he had assumed to be a dozing grey squirrel. The 'squirrel' (for all intent and purpose) was resting on a park bench. In fact the small creature was nothing other than an impostor. A stuffed toy, left behind by some forgetful juvenile. Richard had lunged at the prey, misjudged, and upon landing caught his testicles on a broken slat. He had instantly fallen to the ground, and rolled around in agony, his hands clutching the 'family jewels'. From high in a neighbouring tree, the real McCoy looked down, frantically chattering. It appeared to be laughing its little grey head off, no doubt at the way this young human had failed to properly protect its 'nuts'.

Yes, Richard understood. He acknowledged that it was sometimes necessary to kill, as his ancestors were once obliged to do. Not only for food, and clothing, but to prevent being killed themselves, by other predators, such as bears, wolves and humans.

Yet the true hunter respected his prey, and in doing so respected the sacrifice. Life is to be valued. Death is to be respected.

Derek waited beside the car. He looked towards the visitor from overseas, and wondered what made him tick. "A fancy New York lawyer, over here, to make money for himself, his employers and their clients", he said softly to himself. Derek didn't want his private words carrying on the wind, especially in Richard's direction. "Well, I want to be in on the action. This is my chance to be where I rightfully belong. I'll pick my time, pump Dick the Prick for information, and get in quick", said Derek, by now down to a whisper. "That almost rhymes", he said lifting his voice slightly, "I'll have to work on that a tad." Derek smiled, took a mobile phone from his pocket and dialled.

Richard by now had walked several hundred yards, and was standing amongst an array of different-coloured heather. He looked back. The vehicle was only just barely visible; Derek was not. "This surely is God's country", he thought. "Wild and unspoilt, timeless, like nature had intended." Richard was impressed with what he saw. The land was indeed as it had been described.

There existed a kind of romance to those who were receptive enough to sense the emotion. Richard's own perception of the romance had obliterated the various communicational masts that were dotted here and there, albeit far in the distance. The occasional crisp packet and coke can had also gone unnoticed: probably a case of what the eye chooses not to see, the heart can't grieve over.

A screeching sound in the sky above made Richard look up. It was a buzzard, circling above, no doubt searching for food, or maybe just enjoying the thermals that this particular warm day offered. "I love this place", he shouted to the bird of prey above.

The raptor moved on as if unaware of the human's existence. In fact, with the bird's eyesight and vantage point he was totally aware of any movement beneath him.

"Hello, are you lost?"

Richard turned round sharply. "No!" he said abruptly, pausing briefly before adding, "My colleague is with the vehicle over there er … .somewhere." He pointed roughly in the direction from whence he came. The jeep could no longer be seen. "I must have wandered further than I thought", he said, looking directly at the person in front of him. "A hiker", he thought, "and a female one at that."

"I didn't think you were out for a ten-mile hike, dressed like that", the hiker replied, almost sarcastically.

Richard had dressed that morning as Derek had suggested, warm and casual. To that end, he was wearing brown brogue shoes, brown corduroy pants, and a thick brown woollen jumper.

"Quite appropriate for a drive in the country, but not a ten-mile hike", he reflected thoughtfully to himself. "I got out of the car to admire the scenery and wandered a bit far off", he answered, almost apologizing.

"Easily done, it is rather gorgeous up here at this time of year", she said, as if sensing the stranger's plight.

Richard looked at the hiker, attempting to analyse her visually. A black woollen hat, three-quarter length yellow weatherproof jacket, navy-blue waterproof pants, and brown, well-worn walking boots. And of course, the obligatory rucksack. She was holding a clipboard to which was attached a map. She stood about five feet eight inches in her boots, of slender build, with brown eyes. Some brown hair was visible from beneath her hat.

"A very pretty face", he thought, trying hard not to make his analysis apparent.

She smiled: "Would you like me to help you back to your car?"

"I sure would, Derek is probably getting a bit worried by now."

She smiled again, lifted the clipboard and began to study the map. "I'll take you to the road, come on, it's this way."

With Richard slightly behind, they began to walk in the general direction from whence he had come. With a compass in one hand, and the map in the other, she led Richard towards the waiting Derek.

"She makes for a very attractive guide", the American mused to himself, as they steadily walked. "Do you walk a lot?" he inquired, trying to start a conversation.

"When I get the chance … Actually I'm on holiday at the moment."

"Is it safe to walk alone?" he inquired, showing genuine concern.

"In this day and age probably not. I try not to think about it."

"Did you think about it before approaching me?" he asked teasingly.

"As a matter of fact I did, but you looked to me like a lost soul."

"So you thought I needed assistance?"

"Yes, something like that", she replied, appearing slightly embarrassed.

Derek was indeed getting anxious. He had been engrossed on his mobile telephone for much of Richard's absence, but after looking at his watch some fifteen minutes earlier, concern was beginning to show. Richard had been gone for nearly two hours. "Shit!" he said rather loudly, whilst looking at his watch again. "Where has that damn Yank got to?"

Just as Derek was in the process of contemplating his next move, he glimpsed something yellow in the distance. Raising a pair of binoculars to his face, Derek could make out two people heading towards him. A minute or so later he could see his colleague waving at him.

"It looks as though your lift waited for you", the girl said, acknowledging the vehicle parked ahead.

"Thanks", replied Richard, grateful for the young hiker's assistance. "Without your help I'd still be wandering."

"Don't mention it."

Her smile was infectious.

"How about lunch – you know, to kind of say thanks."

"That's very nice of you, but unnecessary", she said, still smiling. "Anyway, my lunch is in my rucksack, and I've still several miles to walk."

"Do you know of somewhere around here where we might eat?" he asked, whilst pointing towards Derek, who had just flashed the car's headlights in their direction.

They were only about two hundred yards away from where Derek was waiting.

"I can give you directions to a nice pub, it's only a couple of miles away. It's called the 'Dog and Duck', they do really nice food. In fact, that's where I'm staying", she continued, without seemingly pausing for breath.

"That sounds great", said Richard as an idea flashed into his mind. "If you have the time … I mean … if you're not doing anything better er….perhaps you could act as a guide, and show me around a bit."

"What exactly do you have in mind?" she confidently enquired.

"Well, you can see I'm a novice at this sort of thing. I'm really interested in getting to know the area better, and I don't want to get lost again."

"You had better get the right gear then." she said laughingly, her eyes focusing on Richard's apparel.

"Does that mean yes?" he asked, almost pitifully.

"Depends when you had in mind", she said, answering a question with one of her own.

"How about tomorrow?"

"OK".

Directions were given to the Dog and Duck. Arrangements were made to meet at the pub the next day at 10am.

"By the way, what's your name?"

"Richard … Richard Waters. What's yours?"

"Molly Weston."

"Pleased to meet you, Molly Weston, and thanks once again."

They parted about fifty yards away from the 4X4, just as Derek was disembarking.

Molly walked back onto the moor, leaving Richard on the road.

"See you tomorrow, Molly."

Molly turned towards him, smiled, waved, and turned away again.

"Hi there, Richard. I thought I'd lost you."

"Did a good job of that myself, Derek. Sorry to have kept you waiting, got a bit carried away."

"I can see why", teased Derek, looking in the direction of Molly, as she disappeared into the distance.

"She's a very nice girl, Derek. If it hadn't have been for Molly, you could have well been waiting a lot longer."

"Molly, is it?" he said, still teasing.

Richard decided to change the subject.

"Fancy lunch? I know of a good pub not far from here."

"You must be referring to the Dog and Duck."

"That's the one."

"Right then, let's go. I'm starved."

"So am I, Derek. So am I."

The directions Molly gave to Richard were easy to follow and accurate. Derek didn't need them, so Richard kept quiet and followed them in his head.

The Dog and Duck was indeed a fine establishment. Built in the late eighteenth century, it blended in well with its surroundings. The property was well maintained,

and deserved the current accolade of Best Kept Pub. To just what extent this title meant, Richard was unsure, so he left it at that.

"What can I get you, gents?" asked a rather rotund gentleman behind the bar.

"A pint of Badger's Water, please", said Derek longingly.

"I'll have the same", answered Richard, unsure of exactly what Badger's Water was.

"It's OK, sir", replied the landlord, observing that Richard appeared a little perplexed. "All the beer here, sir, has been passed by the management."

Richard smiled at the landlord. He was unsure as to whether the bartender's comments were meant to encourage or enlighten.

"Oh well", said Derek, "As long as it doesn't taste like badger's piss."

Richard decided on the cottage pie. Derek chose the giant Yorkshire Pudding filled with steak. They chatted at length over lunch. The ale no doubt assisted the free flow of speech. Derek seemed either interested, or inquisitive of Richard's background. Richard obliged, but with caution. He, on the other hand, appeared indifferent to his colleague's personal life, preferring to talk about England, and in particular, Yorkshire. At the end of lunch both felt a little closer to the other. No doubt the ale also had some bearing in this.

They left the pub, and walked towards the car.

"Have you a map of the area?" enquired Richard.

"Yes, in the jeep, I brought it specially for you."

"Thanks, Derek."

Inside the vehicle Derek opened up the map. It was of the Ordnance Survey kind, and it gave excellent detail of the area of land to be purchased. The land in question was owned by one Hugo Oldsworth, an artist living at present in London. A year earlier he had inherited the farm from his father. Tragically both parents had been killed during a skiing holiday in Austria. Apparently, whilst on the piste, Mr. Oldsworth Senior suddenly felt the urge to yodel. This caused a sudden avalanche, which buried both parents deep in the snow. Their son, the only child, had never been interested in farming. The farm itself, due to the type of land, was unsuitable for crop growing. Apart from the occasional shooting days, the only other real form of income was sheep. Hugo had been put off sheep as a boy. He was at a delicate age, and had the misfortune to be involved in an incident with one of his father's rams. To this day he has never once eaten lamb.

Derek, using a highlighter pen, marked out the farm on the map. It was comprised of some two thousand acres of mostly moorland. The farmhouse, now rather run down and unoccupied, lay on the western edge. The land bordered a National Park, and was serviced by a reasonable road infrastructure.

"Right, Derek!" said Richard. "I need to purchase some suitable hiking gear."

"Business or pleasure?"

"Perhaps a bit of both."

"Care to elaborate a bit?"

"Molly has very kindly offered to be my guide, and show me around."

"That's nice for you, looks like you're in there."

"You never know Derek, but just remember I am over here to do a job." Richard replied, in a more serious tone. "And what better way than to check out the area, than on foot." he added.

"Agreed, Richard … makes sense to me. When are you planning to do this hiking'?"

"Tomorrow morning. It'll give me a chance to try out this jeep."

"OK, let's go, and get you kitted out. I know just the place."

Derek started the car and drove away. Richard studied the map, asking various questions now and then. Where Derek couldn't answer, he was given the task of finding out and reporting back. Instructions were also given to Derek to set up a meeting with the planning people.

"Also tomorrow, Derek, make an appointment for me to meet Mr. Oldsworth."

"When for?"

"Well, I'll need to meet up with the planners first, and then the owner. Keep them a day apart, though, Derek."

"Righty-ho", answered Derek smartly, "I am going to be busy while you're out there with Molly communing with nature."

"I'll have my work cut out just keeping up … I guess."

Derek pulled up outside Worlds Apart, a camping and leisure shop specialising in, amongst other things, outdoor clothing. They went inside.

"Can I be of any assistance, gentlemen?" enquired a smiling young man, as they approached the counter. The shop assistant was aged around twenty, bespectacled, quite tall and athletic looking.

"Probably has every scout badge known to man, including a bronze Duke of Ed. award", muttered Derek quietly to himself.

"Yes please", answered Richard, "I'm looking for some clothes to go walking in, over the moors."

"Certainly sir", replied the young man, still smiling.

"Nothing is ever quite as simple as it first seems, is it, Derek?" said Richard some thirty-five minutes later.

Derek nodded, as if in agreement.

The shop assistant had gone to great lengths to impress the two men with his knowledge of the different garments and boots that were on offer.

"What the heck!" alerted Richard, "I'm on expenses, let's go the whole hog."

A further thirty-five minutes later, the two men left the shop. The jeep was now loaded with enough equipment to support a small party on a three-month expedition to the Himalayas, or so it seemed to Derek. The young man stood behind the counter, smiling to himself. He was looking down at the American Express slip, held in his hand. "Another couple of dozen like him this week, and the governor would probably make me a partner", he chuckled to himself.

"Did you really need a tent, sleeping bag, and cooking equipment?" asked Derek, as they approached the heavily laden vehicle. "Is the hotel too comfortable for you?" he said wryly, lapsing into a Yorkshire accent.

Richard was unsure of quite why he had purchased so much equipment. Perhaps he had just got carried away, or perhaps it was something deeper. In any event it was his concern, and not Derek's. "You never know, Derek, this project is likely to take some time. You very thoughtfully got me this 4X4, it

19

can hold the stuff, so why not use it? It might be appropriate to stay 'on site' sometime."

Derek accepted the explanation. "Where to now, Richard?"

"Back to the hotel, I need to make some calls."

Without further response, Derek started the engine and drove off.

Chapter 3

As usual, New York was busy. Everyone, everything, everywhere, it all seemed busy.

It wouldn't be the Big Apple if it wasn't, or so thought Ernest Grabit as he peered from his office window, high above the street below. "I love this place", he said out loud, albeit to himself, for he was alone in his office at the time. A knock at the door diverted his attention. "Come in."

"Good afternoon, sir, you wanted to see me."

"Good afternoon, Rachel, yes I did. Have you heard any thing from Richard yet?"

"No, sir, but I am expecting a call from him this afternoon."

"Good, good. When you do, tell him to fax me a report. Remind him from me that he's not there on vacation."

"Yes, sir."

"That'll be all, Rachel."

"Yes, sir."

Rachel turned, and left Mr. Grabit's office.

"Now, where was I?" said Ernest Grabit, turning once more toward the window.

Derek drove into the Grand's car park, and looked for a place to leave the hire car.

Finding one, he parked, and they both got out.

"Here are the keys, Richard, you'll be needing them."

"Thanks, I wouldn't get very far without them. And thanks for your help today."

"I'll give you call later", replied Derek.

"Yeah, do that Derek, see you."

They parted company. Richard proceeded towards the hotel, and his room. Derek went off in search of a taxi. He needed to return to the vehicle hire depot in order to collect his car.

"God, I hate this place", he moaned, looking at a row of dilapidated terraced houses.

Richard's intention was to go straight to his room, but as he passed reception a voice called out to him. "Mr. Waters, excuse me, Mr. Waters." The voice belonged to an attractive lady standing behind the counter at reception. He turned to face her, and approached. "Mr. Waters, I have a message for you. Could you please call a Miss Weston, I have her telephone number here." She passed a card to him on which was written a telephone number.

"Thanks very much, miss."

"You're very welcome sir", the receptionist politely replied. She then turned towards a waiting guest, a middle-aged woman, and said: "Good afternoon madam, how may I help you?"

Richard strode out, heading towards his room. He was impatient to call Molly.

"Gee, I do hope Molly hasn't called it off for tomorrow", he muttered, upon entering the lift. "Especially as I have just bought a truck-load of stuff", he said, still muttering as he exited the lift. The American hurried to his room, anxious to telephone her. "Here goes, fingers crossed." He held the telephone in one hand with fingers crossed. He dialled with the other. "Hello Molly … it's me, Richard, I got a message to call you. Is everything still all right for tomorrow?"

"Hi Richard, yes of course it is, that is if you still want me … as a guide I mean."

He could almost sense her blushing.

"I surely do", he replied, in a typical New York drawl.

"Great, I'm looking forward to it", she answered.

Talking on the telephone was not one of Molly's strong points. She considered the phone to be too impersonal. Despite the efforts of Bob Hoskins, and whoever followed him in those British Telecom adverts, she did not find it 'good to talk', leastwise not on the telephone.

"Why did you want me to call?"

"Um … I was wondering if … perhaps … if you were not doing anything this evening, but no doubt you're too busy anyway", she hesitated, waiting for a response. She got one immediately.

"No I'm not too busy, what did you have in mind?"

"Dinner!" There, she had said it; after all, this is the twenty-first century. "In this day and age it is possible to ask a guy out on a date", she suddenly thought to herself, although not entirely sure whether she was being a bit forward.

"Great idea, Molly, great".

"Great", replied Molly.

"Your place or mine?" he asked. "Or somewhere neutral?"

"Somewhere different", she answered, almost apologetic.

"Leave it up to me, I'll pick you up at seven … OK?"

"I'll be ready."

"By the way, how did you track me down?"

"That was easy", she responded. "The very large tag on your hotel key was sticking out of your trouser pocket. It has the hotel name on it. You should really leave the key at reception when you leave the hotel, you know. It's safer that way." She seemed to have mastered the art of talking on the telephone. Perhaps Bob had got through after all.

"Good idea, Molly, I'll do that in future. See you at seven then."

"Bye Richard, see you at seven."

"Bye Molly." He replaced the receiver. "Yes … yes, yes, yes", he shouted rather loudly, at the same time raising his arm and punching the air.

A pigeon landed on his windowsill to see what all the fuss was about.

Richard made a few other phone calls that afternoon, one of which was to his secretary Rachel. "Hi there, Rachel, how's it going?"

"Good afternoon, Mr. Waters, Mr. Grabit wants you to fax him a report, sooner rather than later, and to remind you, you're not on vacation."

"First thing tomorrow, Rachel."

The remainder of the telephone conversation consisted mainly of routine matters.

Richard was keen to get off the phone and get himself ready for the evening. And as yet he still had several bags to unload from his trusty steed, parked outside. "Bye Rachel, talk to you soon."

"Goodbye Mr. Waters, have a nice day."

Richard replaced the receiver. "God, I hate that phrase", he murmured to himself. It was a phrase that was said constantly, to so many people by so many people, yet it meant nothing. It had no meaning, due to the insincerity of the statement when offered.

Richard made two trips to the car in order to unload only what he was likely to need in the morning. The tent, sleeping bag, and cooking equipment could stay where it was. He left the bags beside the bed. "I'll sort them out later", he said to himself, as if in some kind of hurry.

Richard had plenty of time, it was just that his mind had focused elsewhere. It had settled on the Dog and Duck, or rather on a certain young woman who would be waiting for him there later that evening. He had dated before, many times, but had never found the right person – that special lady with whom he could settle down, and live 'happily ever after', or so the saying goes. Richard didn't expect anything different this time. He had only just met Molly. She seemed nice, but that was as far as it went. After all, he was alone in a foreign country; the company would do him good. It was a dinner date, nothing more than that. He picked up the telephone. "Hello reception, this is Richard Waters, I wonder if you can give me some information?"

"Good evening, Mr. Waters, how may I help?"

"I am taking a young lady out this evening, for dinner, nothing too formal."

"Yes, sir."

"Being new to the area, I don't know of anywhere suitable to take her. Perhaps a pub, old-world charm, with a smart restaurant. Oh yes, somewhere around Riddlesthwaite."

"Hold the line a moment, Mr. Waters, and I'll see what I can do for you", she helpfully answered.

Richard held onto the receiver with pen poised, and hotel stationery at the ready.

He waited for what seemed like an eternity, but in fact was less than a minute.

"Hello, sir!"

"Hi there, any luck?" he asked.

"Just the place sir, the 'Tart and Crumpet', full of old-world charm, excellent choice of real ales, and a separate restaurant."

"Sounds just great."

"Would you like me to book a table, Mr. Waters?"

"That would be just great, thanks a bunch."

"Just the two of you, sir?"

"Just two, say for … .eight-thirty", came the reply.

"Certainly, sir. I'll get back to you in a few moments with the confirmation."

"Great, just great."

A few minutes later Richard's phone rang. He picked up the receiver and answered: "Hello."

"All booked, Mr. Waters. If you care to pop in at reception on your way out, the details will be waiting for you."

"Excellent, thanks, you have been really helpful, have a nice day."

"You're welcome, sir."

"Shit!" said Richard, replacing the receiver. "Why did I just say that?"

Half an hour later, having showered and changed, Richard was seated at the wheel of the jeep. "Well, here goes nothing", he said, turning the key. The engine started, as expected. He drove off nervously, as expected. The jeep left the hotel car park and headed off in the general direction of the Dog and Duck. "Like water off a duck's back", he thought, not quite expressing his sentiments with the correct saying. "Just like riding a bicycle", he said proudly to himself, realising immediately that driving an automobile was actually nothing like riding a bike. What he had meant was that, once you have mastered the art of riding a bicycle, that skill is never forgotten. In Richard's case, a more appropriate description of his driving could have been, 'like a duck out of water ….riding a bicycle'. A few miles on, and he had virtually tamed his steed; however, driving on the other side of the road was a totally new experience. Fortunately, the traffic was light, and he arrived outside the Dog and Duck without incident. He looked at his watch: "Six-thirty-eight, I'm early. Good, I can have a drink to steady the nerves." He entered the pub for the second time that day, approached the bar, and ordered a scotch. "Better make that a large one, please, landlord."

"Gone off the Badger's Water, then?" the landlord enquired, as if gently mocking.

"Dutch courage."

"Oh I see, meeting a young lady, are we?"

"Well I don't know about you, but I am", the American replied, giving as good as he got.

"Good luck, then", retorted the bartender, turning to serve another customer.

"Way up then, you be an American?"

Richard turned to face the person who had addressed him. A short man, wearing a cloth cap and sporting a wax coat. At his side stood a dog. To Richard, the dog resembled a greyhound that had mistakenly climbed into a washing machine, yet somehow managed to survive a hot wash. It also appeared to be wearing pyjamas.

"'Fraid so", answered Richard, as if apologising.

"You here on holiday?"

"Kind of", he replied, not really wishing to engage in a conversation.

"Never been to the States, what's it like?"

"Big!" he answered curtly.

"Guess it must be … .judging by the atlas I've got at home."

Richard seemed unsure of whether the man was in training for a forthcoming village idiot competition, or merely taking the piss. "What type of dog is that?" he asked, in an attempt to divert the talk away from himself.

"Greyhound … .he's a bit small like, on account he got stuck in the wife's washing machine and shrunk some."

"This guy is not for real", thought the American.

"Actually, he's a whippet. Come in all sorts of colours do whippets, this one is 'brindled'. Only got the one now, used to have three." The Yorkshireman continued: "Used to call em, Whippet-In, Whippet-Out, and Wipe-It. This one's called Wipe-It … .his name's Jack really."

Richard saw the funny side and laughed. The ice was broken. He offered to buy the man with the dog a drink.

"Heck as like! Don't mind if I do", replied the Yorkshireman.

Several minutes passed and the unlikely duo were still deeply engrossed in conversation.

"Hello", said Molly rather softly, "Sorry if I'm a bit late, couldn't get the hairdryer to work properly."

Richard looked up: he appeared visibly stunned. To him a transformation had taken place. From an attractive hiker to a beautiful young woman. From Cinderella to Princess. "You look stunning, Molly."

"Thank you", she replied, adding, "I don't always wear woolly hats and walking boots, you know."

"I didn't mean …"

"That's OK, I was only teasing."

He looked relieved, and then smiled. The Yorkshireman was trying to attract Richard's attention.

"Let me introduce you to Albert, Molly, this is Albert, Albert this is Molly."

"Way up Molly, pleased to meet thy acquaintance."

"Pleased to meet you, Albert", she greeted, offering her hand.

Albert took her hand and shook it firmly.

"Have you two known each other long?" enquired Molly, looking at them both.

"Only just met the fella", replied Albert, getting in first, then adding, "And a jolly nice fella he is too."

"Gee thanks, Albert", said the American, a little embarrassed. "Anyway we had better get going", he continued, looking at his watch, "Don't want to be late for dinner."

"Nice to have met you Albert," said Molly, as if meaning it.

"It's been good talking to you Albert, see you around."

"See you around", Albert responded, raising his glass to them both as they left.

"Nice pair", said Albert to the landlord, this time raising his eyebrows.

"I thought you didn't like Americans", replied the Landlord.

"I don't particularly, I was talking about her breasts."

Molly did indeed look stunning. In the absence of a woolly hat, her medium-length, medium-brown hair hung healthy and vibrant around her shoulders. Her face, wearing only a hint of make-up and a little eyeshadow, shone radiant. She wore a medium-length, low-cut black sequinned dress, which enhanced her trim figure perfectly. The walking boots had been replaced by a pair of black court-type stilettos.

"I am indeed a lucky man", thought Richard to himself, as he crossed the pub car park. He approached the passenger side of the car, took out a key from his pocket and inserted it into the door lock. Turning it, the central locking did its electronic magic. He opened the door and Molly stepped in.

"You are a gentleman, kind sir."

"I am surely trying", he said, closing the door gently.

He walked around the vehicle and got into it.

"I hope my driving can hold up", he thought.

"Where are we going?" she asked, appearing excited. "Or is it a secret?"

"The Tart and Crumpet. Have you been there before?"

"No, but I've heard that it's supposed to be very nice", she answered, unsure of her grammar.

"Well if it isn't, don't blame me, the place was recommended."

"I'm sure it will be just fine, and if it isn't, the evening will be a success anyway, it's the company that's important."

"I agree", replied Richard, "And from where I'm sitting, the company looks just swell."

Molly blushed; sensing this, she hoped that the darkness obscured her redness.

Richard's skills at the wheel were improving with each mile. However, nearing their destination and feeling somewhat more confident, an unfortunate incident almost wrecked Richard's unblemished record whilst driving on English soil. With less than two hundred yards to go, a cat, of the domestic variety, made a decision to gamble one of its lives. In an attempt to re-enact a scene from the 'Why Did the Chicken Cross the Road' series of jokes, it darted out in front of the young couple as they approached. Molly screamed and placed her hands over her eyes. Richard swerved to avoid the mad moggie, and in doing so mounted the pavement, crashing into two wheelie-bins. Richard brought his trusty steed under control and parked it approximately fifty yards nearer to the Tart and Crumpet. "Are you all right, Molly?" he enquired, showing genuine concern.

"I'm fine … are you all right?"

"Couldn't be better", he responded, not really meaning it.

"At least you didn't hurt the cat."

His concern at this time, having established that Molly was OK, was for his pride, rather than the welfare of some less than streetwise feline. "Gave those bins a bit of a bash though", he said, looking back through the rear window.

Molly also turned back to look. They then looked at each other, she smiled, he smiled, and then she started to laugh. The rubbish bins were lying on their side at the pavement's edge. Their contents, however, had decided to evacuate shortly after impact, and were now strewn over quite a large area. Richard failed to see the funny side of these recent events, but due to the infectious nature of Molly's laughter, he soon found himself laughing also.

"Better check for damage and clear this lot up", he said, as the merriment subsided.

"I'll help", said Molly, opening her door.

"Thanks, but no thanks Molly. Remember, I'm trying hard to be a gentleman."

"Don't be so silly", she stated firmly, continuing to disembark.

"Women!" he thought, unsure of his meaning.

With Molly's assistance, the wheelie-bins were soon righted and the contents restored within.

"I think we'd better wash up."

"Good idea", replied Molly, getting back into the jeep whilst discarding a lettuce leaf that had hitherto welded itself onto her left hand.

Five minutes later they were standing in front of the lounge bar of the Tart and Crumpet, having cleaned themselves up.

"What can I get you, Molly?"

"A G & T, please."

Richard ordered Molly's drink.

"Ice and lemon?" responded the barperson effeminately.

"Yes please", replied Molly.

In an age where it is considered politically correct to describe an individual as a person, rather than as of a particular sex, this is all well and good, but for the purposes of descriptive accuracy, it is sometimes necessary to totally ignore this practice.

"What can I get for you, sir?" asked the barperson politely (gender – male, sexual orientation – doubtful).

"Nothing alcoholic, I'm driving."

The barperson made a few suggestions and Richard settled on an alcohol-free lager.

"And we have a table booked, the name's Waters."

"Someone will bring you a menu shortly, sir", said the effeminate member of staff, as he handed Richard his drink.

"Where will you be sitting?"

"Over there", replied Richard, pointing towards an unoccupied table.

They sat down and engaged in polite conversation, initially using a form that can best be described as 'hairdresser talk' – the kind of banter that hairdressers speak continuously, that somehow manages to say absolutely nothing of any relevance whatsoever. A waitress brought over the menus as promised. They pondered over the choices.

"I had a very full English breakfast this morning, and I mean full", he said, emphasising the 'full'."

"Are you not hungry, Richard?"

"On the contrary, Molly, I'm absolutely famished, it must be all that walking."

"All that walking! Just wait until tomorrow, I'll show you walking."

He laughed and then added: "It must have been the fresh air then."

"That's it", she answered, joining in the laughter.

Over dinner the conversation gradually progressed to a more intimate, personal level. Topics of discussion revolved around background, including, for example, childhood, education, and occupation. Molly asked many questions about the States. Richard was happy to answer as best he could. He, on the other hand, was keen to know more about England, and in particular, this part of Yorkshire. Molly was only too happy to oblige as far as she could. She was enjoying this evening; the food, the wine, the atmosphere, and, in particular, the company of the gentleman sitting opposite her.

"Gee, I like this place", he said, raising a glass of wine to his lips. "Tastes a lot better than that no-alcohol beer I had earlier."

"Horrible stuff", she replied, screwing up her nose, "I once drank six bottles of that one evening, and my head the next morning."

"I know … all the pain and none of the pleasure."

"Exactly", she replied.

Although Molly had assumed that Richard was referring to the Tart and Crumpet when he had said, 'Gee, I like this place', his comments were less specific and more general. Richard had reserved an open mind about England, Yorkshire, and the task at hand, but since his arrival opinions were beginning to form. As yet he was unable to see the picture in an overall light; emotions were becoming involved. The American, in the main, had liked what he had seen so far.

"Thank you for a lovely evening", said Molly sweetly, as Richard walked her to the Dog and Duck.

"It's been great, Molly, really great."

"See you tomorrow."

He leaned forward and kissed her gently on the cheek. She blushed once again.

"See you tomorrow then, at ten."

Molly turned and went into the pub. Richard turned and walked back to his car.

"Time for a night-cap back at the hotel", he said to himself, whilst looking at his watch.

The return journey went very much as one would have hoped, and judging on recent events, better than Richard had expected. As the jeep turned into the Grand's car park, he reminded himself of the need to fax his boss a report, first thing tomorrow. "Better prepare it tonight", he said, bringing the vehicle to rest, "I'll be a bit short on time in the morning." His thoughts turned to the job at hand, and what he had learned so far, since his arrival. His thoughts however, were somewhat jumbled: "Can't seem to concentrate … guess I'm tired."

He walked across the tarmac, his mind clearing a little. "Swell place", he thought, entering the foyer. He was not referring to the Grand, although the summary could have equally applied. It was a general statement; what he had seen and experienced so far today had impressed him. Approaching the bar he hailed the attendant. "Scotch please … make that a large one."

"Certainly, sir, any particular brand?"

"I'll leave that one to you, I guess you're the expert", he answered, detecting a hint of Scottish brogue.

"Tis true, I am fond of a wee dram, now and again", came the reply, only now the accent was stronger. "Perhaps you would like to try a single malt?"

"I'd prefer a double."

"A double, single malt it is then."

The man from over the border selected a suitable malt and poured a double. "Tell me what you think of that."

Richard took the glass, raised it to his lips and sipped. "Gee", he proclaimed, "This is like heaven's nectar." He took another sip. "This is great, what brand is it?"

"Talisker, it's an island whisky, distilled on the Isle of Skye. It was praised by Robert L. Stevenson in his poem, 'The Scotsman's Return from Abroad', as one of 'the King o' Drinks'."

"You sure do seem to know your scotch", the American guest added, in apparent praise of someone who had devoted their entire life to the study of such a worthwhile subject.

"It's a wee hobby of mine, care to try another brand?"

"Don't mind if I do", said Richard, once again raising his glass, only this time instead of sipping, he emptied the vessel's entire contents.

"How about Glenlivet? Very poplar in the States, and was one of the first distilleries licensed under the reforming 1823 Licensing Act, a fact which so incensed his still-illegal neighbours that its founder, George Smith, was obliged to carry pistols for his own protection."

"You're a regular mine of information", he answered, taking the Glenlivet. "Is this a large one as well?"

"I thought you might want enough to taste", the Scot replied gleefully.

"Mighty generous."

"You're welcome, sir."

Richard took notice of a badge that the knowledgeable bartender was wearing on his waistcoat lapel.

"May I call you Robert?"

"You're not trying to pick me up, are you sir?"

"Good gracious!" replied Richard, by now feeling too warm to show embarrassment.

"I meant, can I call you by your name, not like, as in, can I call you tomorrow."

"I knew what you meant, sir, just my Scottish humour coming through", answered the grinning bartender, "And yes, you may call me Robert, or Rob if you prefer."

"I think I'd better try another one of your personal recommendations, Rob", said the American, pointing in the direction of the whisky bottles stacked neatly on the shelf behind the bar.

"Happy to oblige, sir."

Forty-five minutes and several tastings later, Richard left the bar. He somehow managed to stagger to the lift, get in and stagger out on the correct floor. He had, however, gone up and down in the lift a few times before making the correct exit. "Damn elevators!" he cursed, whilst trying to extract the room key from his trouser pocket. " Damn key!" he cursed, whilst trying very hard to insert said key into the wrong door lock.

"May I help you, sir?"

Richard looked up. It was the night porter. "Glad if you could", replied Richard, with a strong hint of slur.

The night porter was very adept at deciphering slur. It was a language that many guests used late into the evening, and beyond. "Next room along, sir", he said, realising that the number on the key did not match the one on the door. The porter opened Richard's door and handed him the key. "Goodnight sir."

"Er ... goodnight ... and thanks." Richard staggered to the bed, fell onto it and promptly fell asleep.

Richard awoke the next morning to the sound of a pigeon cooing outside his bedroom window. "Oh, my head", he muttered, raising his hand to his forehead. He then proceeded to rub his eyes, and after doing so looked towards the clock, which was situated beside the bed. "Shit!" he said, jumping out of bed as if his life depended on it. The red LED display on the clock turned another digit; it now read 8.57. He rushed to the bathroom and turned on the shower. "I'm going to be late, no time for breakfast this morning."

He quickly showered and dressed himself. He looked at the carrier bags on the floor and thought for a moment. "No time to check out the gear now." He picked up the bags and moved towards the bedroom door. As he left he could still hear the pigeon going about his business. "Forgot to thank the little bugger", he proclaimed, hurrying down the hall towards the lift. "Bugger", he said to himself, seemingly somewhat surprised. "I've only been here two days and I'm already beginning to talk like a local." Struggling with the carrier bags he hastened towards the waiting jeep. "Shit! I haven't sent a report to Grabit. Sent one, I haven't even compiled one! Oh well, c'est la vie, I'll do it later", he said, apparently resigning himself to the fact.

He climbed into the vehicle, started the engine and drove off. "Shit!" It was the third time he had used that word this morning. "I've left my cellular phone in the bedroom. Bugger, bugger, bugger." If nothing else appeared to be going right that morning, at least he was making good use of the local vernacular so far learned.

Derek Arkwright had also started his day. Richard had given him his brief the previous afternoon, and Derek wanted to give a good impression. He had placed a call to Richard's room late last evening, but was unable to make contact with him.

"I'll call him later ... on his mobile", Derek thought to himself as he filled the kettle. "Must get some caffeine into me, can't start the day without it", he continued.

Derek lived in a modest flat, in a fashionable area on the outskirts of Leeds. What had once been a thriving maltings had now become, for want of a better expression, a block of flats. The building had been empty for many years, becoming sad and derelict. Changing times brought changing needs. The property had been sympathetically converted, and for the present it suited Derek's purpose.

"Where did I leave my Filofax?" He put down the partially drunk mug of coffee and began to search for the diary. Without it, Derek would be completely lost. To him it represented the last bastion of his former glory days. With it, he, like the phoenix, would once again rise. "There you are, my little beauty", he enthused, on finding his beloved Filofax underneath a pile of adult magazines. Derek had temporarily forgotten that in an attempt to go to sleep the previous evening, he had turned to the mags for a little light reading.

"Nearly 9.30, time to contact the Planning Department", he said, thumbing through the pages of the newly reunited 'little black book'. "Williams, Colin – that's it", answered Derek to himself, upon finding the appropriate entry. The born-again Yorkshireman dialled the Local Authority. "Hello, can you put me through to Mr. Williams in the Planning Department?" he answered in response to the telephonist's greeting.

"Certainly sir, who may I say is calling?"

"Derek Arkwright."

"Thank you, please hold the line."

Derek thought it refreshing to speak to a real person on the end of a telephone.

In many such situations he was frequently confronted with a taped voice, offering a telephone keypad choice of options that more often than not resulted in being cut off, but not before at least five minutes had elapsed. It didn't matter whether the call that he made was business or pleasure, a recorded message increasingly seemed to greet him.

"Good morning Derek, what can I do you for?" quipped an effervescent voice.

"Good morning Colin, long time no hear. How's the wife and kids?"

"We divorced eight months ago, but thanks for asking. Now let's put the small talk to one side, and tell me what you phoned me for."

Derek had had dealings with Colin Williams in the past, and considered him to be a no-frills, no-nonsense Yorkshireman. A firm but fair man. "You're a hard man, Colin. Right, I'll cut straight to the chase." Five minutes later and the appointment had been made. They would meet with Colin Williams tomorrow afternoon at two. Derek once more perused his Filofax.

Chapter 4

"Ah Rachel, any news from our overseas executive?" enquired Ernest Grabit upon his arrival at the office.

"Not as yet, Mr. Grabit."

"Try and get hold of him for me, would you please Rachel?"

"I have tried this morning sir, but his cellular phone is not responding. I also phoned the hotel, and apparently he has left."

"Oh well, he must be on the job then", replied Mr. Grabit.

Rachel's only response was to raise her eyebrows.

"I expect he's a bit preoccupied just now."

"Probably, sir", answered Rachel, offering a verbal response on this occasion.

"If he hasn't reported by lunch, try and get hold of him … keep trying until you do."

"Yes sir."

Ernest Grabit left Rachel to her work and proceeded to his office. "I choose Waters for very good reasons", he thought, closing his office door behind him. "This is a big one, mega-bucks involved." He continued with his thoughts. "Richard can pull this one off, he has the talent, he wants the chance to prove himself. And if he should, God forbid, fail, I have an in-built scapegoat." Reaching for the telephone, he smiled wryly.

Richard arrived at the Dog and Duck at two minutes past ten. "Made it!" He parked, got out and hurriedly approached the pub. Molly was waiting for him inside. "Hi Molly, sorry I'm a bit late."

"Only two minutes", she replied, as if apologising on his behalf. "Fancy a cup of coffee before we set off?"

"Good idea, I kinda missed breakfast this morning."

"I didn't keep you up too late last night, did I?"

"No, not at all, it was a lovely evening, it's just that I stopped off at the hotel bar for a night-cap."

"Oh yes, and I guess one thing led to another."

"Something like that, Molly. Rob, the Scottish barman, introduced me to single malt. By the way, you don't happen to have any Tylenol on you, do you?" he enquired whilst clutching his head.

"I have no sympathy for you Richard, your headache is purely self-inflicted", she answered disapprovingly, reaching into her rucksack and producing a small bottle of tablets. "Paracetamol, will they do?"

"Gee thanks, you're an angel." Richard ordered coffee for both, and toast for himself. Molly had already eaten breakfast, in preparation for the impending hike. Richard couldn't help but notice that his companion had once again attired herself in the now-familiar apparel befitting the task that lay ahead. "Don't worry, Molly, all my gear is in the car, including boots", he said, in response to her apparent observation that the pair of brogues at present adorning his feet, were, judging by the facial expression, not considered suitable.

"Sorry Richard, I didn't mean ..."

"That's all right", he said, interrupting, "after all, I am a novice at this sort of thing."

"I'll do my best to put that right ... anyway, I bet you're good at ordering a taxi."

"I can do that well enough, but just because I live in the city doesn't mean to say that I wouldn't prefer the country", he replied, as if defending himself.

Sensing this, she reached out and touched his hand.

"My roots, Molly, are in the country, after all, I am of Indian descent."

"Really, what tribe?" she asked excitedly.

"Sioux, good for a lawyer, eh?"

She laughed, and said, "Brilliant." Molly blushed a little. Perhaps the reason she found herself attracted to this man was due to a fantasy she had secretly carried for many years, which involved a North American Indian wearing full traditional dress, including warpaint. She felt a shiver going down her spine.

"I even have an Indian name."

"Are you going to tell me?" she enquired enthusiastically.

He went on to tell her, not only the name that his father had given him, but also the story that lay behind it.

"Brilliant!" she said again.

The drive to the starting point of the proposed walk did not take long.

"If you park here", said Molly, pointing to a small pull-in, "we can take a circular route and pick up the car at the end."

"Sounds good to me."

Richard pulled in as suggested. "Time to try out the boots", he thought, not wishing to alarm his guide as to the perils of hill walking in new footwear.

"I've brought some food ... just in case."

"In case of what?" he enquired, seemingly alarmed.

"Well, amongst other things ... we might get hungry", mused Molly.

"Good idea", he replied, struggling to get a boot over three pairs of socks. "Did you bring any Band-Aids, by any chance?"

"There's a first aid kit in my rucksack, why?"

"Just in case, Molly, just in case", he answered in a gasp, whilst forcing the second boot on to an uncooperative foot. Richard locked the jeep, put on his newly purchased rucksack, and declared his readiness. "Right, I'm ready."

"Well, you certainly look the part."

"Part, or prat?"

"You look great ... like a professional. Born to it."

"I'll let you know later", he responded, still unsure of the boots.

They set off, Molly in front, setting the pace. The weather ideal for the task, sunny, but not too warm. Richard soon got into his stride; time to take stock, after all, he was here to do a job. He wanted to see the land first hand, to test its suitability for the proposed development. As he continued to walk, his mind focused on the various theme parks that his firm's clients wanted to build here. He had studied the brief, given to him prior to leaving New York. Any personal opinions he had concerning the project were of no consequence. His role in this endeavour was to negotiate planning permission, and to secure the land purchase at the lowest price possible. The suitability and viability had already been previously vetted. He wanted to see the area as it was. As much background information as possible was needed, in order for him to negotiate successfully.

"What are those guys doing, Molly?" enquired Richard, pointing towards two men who, between them, had five of those pre-shrunk greyhounds, like the one he had seen the previous evening.

"They are using whippets to catch rabbits."

"Hunting with dogs, then?"

"Yes, for the pot I guess, or to sell to a local butcher. There's a lot of unemployment here", she added, "catching rabbits helps to feed the family, and puts a little extra cash in their pockets."

Richard approved; in times of economic decline the situation made sense. "If they bulldoze this land, there will be no more rabbit hunting ... but the development will at least bring employment", he thought to himself. "They sure can run."

"Extremely agile", replied Molly.

"And graceful with it", he said, admiring the dogs at work. "Not against hunting, then, Molly?"

"Not this kind", she answered, "but I am against certain so-called blood sports."

"Care to explain?"

"Hunting for the pot, as opposed to killing for profit, I guess is the difference", she answered, with reverence.

Richard understood. His father had, on many occasions, offered similar explanations, when referring to their ancestors hunting buffalo. His forefathers hunted for food, taking only what they needed in order to survive, and then along came the white man. The rest is history. His mind turned briefly to that time, aged twelve, and in the local park…"Oh well … it wasn't a real squirrel", he thought.

They continued walking, occasionally chatting to one another. Richard's feet were holding up. He was enjoying the walk. He particularly enjoyed the scenery. Wild and barren, the heather reflecting various colours in the sunshine. The fresh air and exercise cleared his head.

"Fancy a break?" asked Molly. "Sandwiches and coffee?"

"You took the words right out of my mouth, Mol." He hesitated briefly before speaking again. "I'm sorry, Molly, I didn't mean to be presumptuous."

She blushed. How sweet of her companion, she thought. "I liked it, I liked you calling me Mol."

"Great, let's have coffee!"

Molly took off her rucksack and sat down on a suitable rock. She undid the rucksack, took out a flask, and poured two cups.

"Just what the doctor ordered, thanks", Richard said, taking a cup from her.

"You're welcome: cheese and tomato, ham and cheese, tomato and cheese, or cheese and ham?"

"Big choice, what was it again?"

"Cheese and …"

"Only kidding, I'll have the ham … with cheese, please".

They both laughed. Richard enjoyed Molly's company, in his opinion she was kinda swell.

Chapter 5

"Hello."

"Is that Mr. Oldsworth?"

"Speaking."

"Good morning, Mr, Oldsworth … Derek Arkwright, we spoke a few days ago."

"Yes I remember … about the farm. What can I do for you?"

"A colleague, Richard Waters, has asked me to telephone you in order to fix up a time when we can all meet."

"Is he serious about buying the farm?" enquired Hugo Oldsworth.

"Yes, if the price is right. Will the day after tomorrow be OK?"

"That sounds fine, that is as long as you can visit me, I'm too busy to come up to Yorkshire."

"No problem", responded Derek, thinking that a trip to London would be just like old times.

"Come to my studio … two o'clock, do you know where it is?"

"I'll find it … I have the address", said Derek, with all the confidence of someone who had recently acquired a London cabbie's 'knowledge'.

"Good", said Hugo, "see you Friday at two."

"See you on Friday, bye."

"Yes, goodbye."

Hugo replaced the receiver and turned to face a naked young woman sitting on a chair. "Sorry about that Sophie … business … now where were we?"

"You were painting me, Hugo."

"I know that, Sophie, it's a figure of speech. Speaking of figures, assume the position, girl, there's work to be done."

Sophie stubbed out her cigarette, got up from the chair, and moved over to a chaise longue where she dutifully took up her pose. Hugo enjoyed his work, his particular interest being the human form. He specialised in painting nudes. To be more precise, he specialised in painting female nudes. The last time he had actually painted a naked male form was at art college, and that was twelve years ago. "I've had the farm valued", Hugo thought, as he took up his palette, and recommenced painting. "Not worth as much as I would have hoped, but there's no money in sheep these days", he thought, as a shiver went down his spine. The thought of sheep had this effect on him. Hugo did not want the farm; he enjoyed living in London. The money would be handy though, artists in the main do not make a lot of money. Very often their work can be extremely profitable, but usually for the art dealer or someone else, and even then not until the artist has died. Yes, the money would be useful, if only to allow him to continue with his work. Hugo loved his work. "Lean back, Sophie."

"I'm not a rasher of bacon, you know. All men are the same, they treat us women like pieces of meat."

"Very funny, very funny indeed, now, as I'm paying you, lean back a bit." Sophie obliged.

"That's better, your breasts look more pert now."

Yes, Hugo enjoyed his work.

"Well, that's my work done for the day, can't do any more 'til tomorrow", said Derek to himself, shortly after replacing the telephone receiver. "Appointment made with the planners for tomorrow, and off to London to see Hugo Oldsworth on Friday. I might as well go off to the golf course now. Anyway, I need to work on my handicap", he said, as if having to justify himself.

Derek Arkwright was a master of the understatement. The fact is that he had been playing golf, off and on, for the past eight years, and yet still struggled to maintain a twenty-eight handicap. "A lot of business can be done on the golf course", whispered Derek, seemingly to his golf clubs, as he loaded the bag into the boot of his Ford Mondeo. Looking like a hybrid cross of Rupert the Bear, which apparently is suitable attire for any aspiring golfer, he got into his car and drove off.

Chapter 6

Richard and Molly, having finished their refreshments, were now well into their stride once more.

"It really is great out here, Mol."

"I know what you mean", she answered in acknowledgement.

Richard was taking note of the area, constantly referring to the map Derek had given him. From time to time, he brought the newly acquired binoculars up to his dark brown eyes, and studied the landscape. On this latest occasion he spotted a man in the distance, bending over a large basket. There was a pedal cycle beside him.

"What's got your attention?"

"There's some guy over there, with what looks like a wicker basket."

"Perhaps he's having a picnic", she replied, as though not particularly interested.

"What, on his own!"

"Could be that there's a rug on the ground, with a pretty young maiden already lying on it."

"Could be … .but if so, they came on one bicycle."

Molly once more dived into her rucksack, only this time producing a pair of binoculars of her own. Putting down her bag, she proceeded to peer through the focal equipment in the general direction of her companion's attention. Suddenly, the basket opened and a flock of birds were released.

"Pigeons", she said.

"Pigeons?" he replied.

"Homing pigeons … there … that's your mystery solved."

"What, no pretty young maiden?" he joked.

"Doesn't seem that way." she answered.

"Ever since I've been in Yorkshire, I can't seem to escape pigeons."

"Pigeons and whippets are synonymous with the area", she said, by way of explanation.

"Oh", was all Richard had to say on the matter.

They continued walking.

"Are you all right?" asked Molly, showing concern at her friend's increasingly apparent limp.

"My feet hurt, Mol, but I'll be OK."

"New boots, by any chance?"

"Bought them yesterday; didn't have time to wear them in."

"I can see that", she replied, observing his pain.

"I've got three pairs of socks on, thought everything would be swell."

"Well, in your feets' case, they probably are swell, or should I say swollen."

"Very funny, can we stop a while … *please*?"

"Good idea. I'll get out the first-aid kit; sit down and get those boots off."

Richard looked around, selected a suitable rock, and sat down. "I'll never walk again", he proclaimed, on seeing his blistered feet.

"Rub some of this on", she answered, handing him a tube of antiseptic cream.

He obeyed her orders, gingerly applying the cream.

"Not too much, otherwise the plasters won't stick."

"You make a fine nurse, Molly", the American stated, watching her delicately place a plaster over a very large red and raw blister.

"I wanted to be a nurse once", she said. "Glad I didn't, though."

"Why's that, Mol?"

"Long hours, hard work, and little reward."

"I guess it's a vocation being a nurse in this country?"

"It sure is", replied Molly. "The pay is nowhere near enough for what you have to do."

"Not like the States; a fortune can be made in the medical profession."

"And in the legal profession", she added coyly, affixing the last Band-Aid.

"That's true enough, and with less risk of being sued."

"And even if you are, you must be in a better position to deal with it."

"True enough Mol, true enough", he replied, replacing the last of his second pair of socks.

"Three pairs of socks! You either were anticipating trouble, or you suffer with cold feet."

"Prevention is better than cure."

"Didn't work though, did it?" she joked.

"You never know, could have been worse", he answered, still endeavouring to secure the left boot to his foot. "Could have been a lot worse", he thought. "It's just as well that I don't suffer with smelly feet."

"Will you be able to walk?" enquired the surrogate nurse.

"I'll be fine."

"Sure?"

"Just fine, Mol … how much further?"

"About three miles."

Molly witnessed the expression on his face, a grimace, summing up the agony.

"Morale-boosting time", she thought. "Better take his mind off it."

Molly was an old hand at hiking. Walking was in her blood. As a child, she had been on many camping trips with her parents and older brother. Her father liked walking, and in particular hill walking. As young children they had no choice other than to tag along and keep up. Whereas Molly had come to enjoy this form of leisure pursuit, her brother Simon had not. Finally, desperate to avoid contact as far as possible with land, he joined the Royal Navy. Molly, enjoying this particular form of recreational activity, carried on and followed in her father's footsteps.

"How long are you here for?" she asked, in an attempt at taking his mind of the journey.

"Until my work is done, and of that I'm not yet sure. Perhaps a couple of weeks, maybe more."

"I hope it's longer", she replied softly.

Her remark caused him to pause momentarily. He looked directly at her face and, making eye contact, he took her hand in his. "So do I, Molly." He slowly leaned forward and kissed her.

Derek Arkwright, having completed a round of golf, headed towards the clubhouse. "Ninety-six, not bad", he thought, placing the clubs once more in the Mondeo's boot. "The par is seventy-two, that makes my round equvalent to a handicap of twenty-four, pretty damn good if I say so myself."

Derek, apparently pleased with himself, continued with his thoughts. "Right, a swift one in the clubhouse then it's back home to phone the Yank." He closed the boot, locked the vehicle and proceeded to the bar. "A pint of Eagle, please Bert."

"Good round?" asked Bert, standing behind the bar skilfully drying a glass.

"Not bad", answered Derek, eagerly awaiting his pint of Eagle bitter. The beer came to be so named in direct response to a local brewery, who having supplied a guest ale as part of their sponsorship of a tournament, then ran a competition to name it. In golfing parlance, an eagle is a term used to describe a two-under-par hole, par being the number of golfing strokes deemed to be appropriate for each hole.

After much deliberation, and the fact that many of the club's members rarely made a birdie, let alone anything better, the name Eagle was decided upon. This gave anyone who fancied it a chance to at least have an eagle at the nineteenth hole. The brewery presented an engraved commemorative pint mug to the originator of the beer's eventual title.

"Lovely drop of beer, Bert", said Derek, taking a sip from an engraved commemorative pint mug that bore the name 'Derek Arkwright'.

Invigorated by Molly's softly spoken words, and even softer lips, Richard had somehow managed to hobble the remaining distance, thereby completing their circular tour.

"Well done, you made it", she said sympathetically. "If you're not used to it, this kind of walk can hurt."

"I'm not used to it and it does. According to this map it looks as though we've walked nearly fifteen miles."

"We have."

"Gee, no wonder my feet are sore!"

"Think that has more to do with those new boots than anything else."

"I think maybe you're right, Mol", he replied, collapsing onto a large rock. "I'll rest here a while, if you don't mind."

"I don't mind … fancy a coffee? There should be enough left for two cups."

"In the absence of a cold beer, coffee will do just fine; thanks."

Richard took up residence seated on the large rock, his eyes fixed on the recently

acquired boots. "They don't look so new now, do they?"

Molly handed Richard a cup of coffee and sat down beside him. "Hath the man tamed the boots, or hath the boots tamed the man?" she asked dryly.

"Good question, I'll give you an answer after I've had a chance to soak my feet for a few hours."

Molly acknowledged. There had been many occasions in the past when she had suffered with blisters, and was fully aware of the misery they caused.

"Thanks for a great time, Mol. Despite the feet I really have enjoyed myself. Next time I'll wear four pairs of socks."

"Keen for a next time, then?" she asked.

"Only if you're my guide."

Molly's face began to show a little colour. Unsure of whether he was asking her a question, or merely making a statement, she did not speak.

"Would you, Molly?"

"Would I what?"

"Be my guide?"

"I'd love to be your guide", she answered, this time knowing that a question had been asked of her.

"Do you ride?"

"Pardon?"

"Can you ride a horse?"

"Yes, although I haven't ridden for years."

"Good, how about on horseback next time?"

"Sounds great … why not?" she replied.

After dropping Molly off at the pub, Richard returned to his hotel; he was desperate to have a long soak in the bath. His body ached and his feet were sore. Richard had explained to Molly that he would be busy for the next couple of days, but would phone her on Friday.

"I need to speak with Derek", thought Richard as he entered his room. "And I'd better fax the office." A familiar coo from outside the bedroom window somehow made him feel at home. He ran a hot bath, undressed and entered the water. "God, that feels so good", he said softly, as the foam bubbles engulfed his tired frame. The American's thoughts shifted between work and Molly. Tasks that needed to be done that evening, and the job overall. Perhaps he and Molly could have dinner on Friday evening. Maybe they could go out horse riding on the moors at the weekend. "I need to talk with Derek", he muttered to himself.

The hot bath had relaxed him, so much so that only a few minutes had passed and he was asleep. The pigeon, out on the bathroom window ledge, was now in the process of doing a duet, apparently competing for the lead with Richard's snoring.

Richard awoke suddenly; the phone was ringing, the bath water was cold. He quickly got out of the bath, grabbed a towel, and went to the phone. "Hello."

"I have a call for you Mr. Waters, a Derek Arkwright", answered the hotel receptionist.

"Thanks", replied the American, trying to stop his teeth from chattering.

"Putting you through."

"Thanks", replied the American, still trying to stop his teeth from chattering.

"Hi Richard, finally caught up with you."

"Yep, guess you did Derek. How are you?"

"Great, just great. Set up those meetings, as you requested."

"Swell, when for?"

"Planners, tomorrow at two, and the landowner at two on Friday. Just one problem, though."

"What's that, Derek?"

"Oldsworth lives in London and that's where he wants the meet."

"No problem, Derek, we can travel down to London after the appointment with the planners, take in a few sights, stay the night, and be fresh for Mr. Oldsworth on Friday at two."

"Fine by me, Richard ... by the way, I think there's a fault with your phone, perhaps you'd better report it, your voice sounds funny."

"It's not a phone fault, Derek, I fell asleep in the bath, the water had gone cold and then you phoned. Standing here in the buff ... apart from a towel that is."

"Sorry Richard ... how did the walk go with the lovely Molly?"

"Swell Derek, and I have the blisters to prove it. Book a hotel in London for tomorrow will you, I'll leave the choice up to you, it's your town."

"Will do."

"And can you come to the hotel in the morning at nine? There's a few things we need to go over prior to tomorrow's meeting."

"Will do."

"Thanks for calling, Derek, see you in the morning."

"Will do Richard, bye for now." Derek replaced the receiver, looked up and smiled. "Yes", he cried out loud. "Yes, yes, yes, I'm off to London for a night on the town all expenses paid", he gleefully gloated to himself. "A bloody good piss-up is just what I need." Derek reached for his beloved Filofax and searched through the index. "Ah, got it", he said to himself, his eyes lighting up as though the diary's entry had just revealed the whereabouts of Blackbeard's buried treasure. He picked up the telephone receiver and dialled.

"Prince's Palace, Soho. How may I help you?"

"I'd like to make a reservation", said Derek, still smiling.

Richard dried himself and dressed. "That's better", he said. He mulled over the contents of the recent telephone conversation with Derek Arkwright. "If all goes well I should be back in time on Friday to see Molly." His thoughts then turned to more pressing matters. "Better get a report together and send it to Grabit, otherwise I'll be in deep fertiliser."

Richard walked over to the wardrobe, opened the door and took out his briefcase. He carefully placed the briefcase on the bed, opened it and took out a laptop computer. "Right then, let's get started", he said, as if addressing the machine. The American made himself comfortable on the bed. Fluffing up the pillows and resting his back against them, he placed the computer on his lap. Richard turned on the laptop, waited a few seconds, and then began to type. "Shit! Shit, shit, shit ... the bloody battery has gone flat now. That's all I need. Bugger, bugger, bugger ... I'll have to bloody wait for it to charge. Shit!" Richard got off the bed, walked over to his briefcase, opened it and took out a charger. He plugged it in. "All I can do now is wait. I know", he said, "I'll wait in the bar." Picking up the key, Richard left the confines of the bedroom and proceeded to the bar as planned.

"Hi there, Rob", enthused Richard, addressing the bartender as though a long-lost friend.

"Good evening, sir, come to try a few more whiskys, have ye?" replied Robert.

"I don't know about a few, but I'll start with a large one. The choice is yours, Rob."

"Happy to oblige, sir."

The Scot reached for a bottle, measured a double and handed the American the glass.

"Cheers."

Richard raised the tumbler to his lips, tilted back his head and downed its contents in one go. "That hit the spot ... tell me about that one, Rob?"

"Knockando."

"I'm sorry Rob, I can see that you're busy ... tell me later."

"Knockcando, sir ... that's the name of the scotch", answered the barman, as he picked up the bottle and proceeded to point to the label.

"You got me again, Rob, just for that you can pour me another."

Forty-five minutes, and several more tastings later, Richard left the bar. "Better go in for dinner, it'll help clear my head ....anyhow, I'm absolutely ravenous." Richard found himself in the foyer. Not entirely steady on his feet, he began to look round. "Where's the God-damn dining room?" he quietly muttered to himself, his eyes trying hard to focus.

"May I help you, sir?"

Richard looked up; it was the night porter from the other evening. "Gee, you're like a real knight in shining armour ....always popping up when I need ya."

"Only to willing to help sir ... if I can", replied the porter, displaying extreme patience and courtesy, especially for one who was, as yet, not on duty.

"Er ... can you point me in the direction of the dining room?" enquired Richard, slightly slurring his words. "I seem to be having difficulty."

The as yet not on duty night porter happily obliged.

"Table for one, sir?"

"Yes, please."

"Smoking or non-smoking?"

Richard pondered for a brief moment. "Non-smoking."

"Certainly, sir, follow me."

The attendant led the American to a non-smoking table; he sat down and a waiter arrived offering him a menu. "There's à la carte if you prefer, sir."

"Er ... thanks", replied Richard, taking the menu.

"Would sir care to see the wine list?"

"Er ... no thanks ... just coffee."

Richard contemplated the choice of food, came to a decision and placed his order. Awaiting his meal, Richard sipped the hot coffee and reflected. "Important day tomorrow, better get an early night." He continued with his thoughts, the coffee helping to clear the alcohol. "At least I didn't order tea", he mused, taking another sip from the cup. "Better do that report straight after dinner."

The waiter appeared at the table. "Hope you enjoy your meal, sir."

"Yea ... thanks."

After dinner Richard went back to his room. "God, my legs ache", he said with a groan. The laptop was indeed charged. Richard, however, was not. He unplugged the charger, walked over to the telephone, lifted the receiver and dialled. "Hello reception, I'd like to book an early morning alarm call." Replacing the receiver Richard undressed, got into bed, and promptly fell sound asleep. Just prior to doing so he muttered a few words. "I'll do the report ... first ... thing ... in ... the ... zzzzzzzzz"

An owl hooted outside. It may not have been an owl, more likely a pigeon coughing.

Brrring brrring coo, brrring brrring coo, brrring brrring coo. It was 6am the following morning, the usual dawn chorus once again had been joined by the sound of a telephone ringing, only this time Derek Arkwright could not be held responsible.

Richard, from the confines of the bed, reached out a hand, lifted the phone's receiver and placed it to his right ear. "Hello."

"Your wake-up call."

"Thanks", came the sleepy response. The receiver was replaced from whence it came, and the hand that did so disappeared once more under the duvet.

Coo ... coo ... coo, coo ... coo ... coo, coo ... coo ... coo. The pigeon continued unaccompanied.

"Damn! Damn, damn, damn." The American threw back the covers and got out of bed. "Am I the only guest to get a damn pigeon, or does everyone get one?" Walking to the window he drew back the curtains. The morning skies were grey; spots of rain began to hit the glass. Despite his protests, the pigeon seemed reluctant to leave the ledge. "Must be the rain", he thought. "I know, I'll make a cup of coffee, break open a biscuit and invite the bugger in." Richard liked using the word bugger; he had heard it being used quite a lot since his arrival in Yorkshire. It seemed to fit in many situations. It seemed to fit this one. He put the kettle on, and thought of Molly. Molly had put the kettle on.

Coo..coo..coo, coo..coo..coo. The cooing appeared to have a sense of urgency about it. Perhaps it had understood the word 'biscuit', or indeed the word 'bugger'. Breaking open a complimentary packet of biscuits, he approached the window. With one hand still holding a biscuit, he struggled with the other in an attempt at opening the aperture. Upon doing so, he held out the hand still holding the now broken biscuit, and offered it to the pigeon. The bird looked briefly at the offering, even more briefly at Richard, then turned away from the window, stepped off the ledge, flapped his wings frantically and promptly disappeared.

"Must have been the word 'bugger'", he said to himself, smiling. He then proceeded to crumble the remaining biscuits, sprinkling them on the ledge before closing the window. "What a horrible morning … Oh well, at least the weather held up for yesterday's hike." Thinking of the previous day's walk reminded him of his aching limbs. "Gee! Do I ache. Another hot bath should do the trick." He moved over to the boiling kettle and once more thought of Molly. "*Molly* put the kettle on … no it wasn't, it was Polly who put the kettle on." He made coffee, ran a hot bath, placed the cup beside the receptacle and got in. "Half an hour in the tub, make another cup of coffee and settle down to write up the report."

Half an hour and another cup of coffee later Richard did indeed settle down to write his report. Some forty minutes later he had finished. "Just time to get dressed, fax the report and have breakfast before Derek arrives", he said to himself, seemingly pleased thus far with the morning's progress.

Derek Arkwright had also had an early night. It was not his original intention to do so. A few beers and a game of snooker had previously been contemplated. But in an attempt to set the forthcoming scene, anticipated in Soho on Thursday evening, a sudden change of plan had occurred to him. He left his flat at around seven p.m. and returned about twenty minutes later. In that time he had rented an adult video and purchased a six-pack of 5% lager. About two thirds of the way through the video, and about the same into the six pack, he had suddenly found the urge to go to bed.

Possibly invigorated by a good night's sleep, and maybe excited about the day ahead, Derek was also up and about in good time. At eight-fifteen he was ready to leave the flat and meet Richard at the Grand as arranged. With overnight bag packed he was all set. "Right then, all packed, let's go", he said to himself, picking up his keys. He was about to lock the door and remembered last night's video. "Sod it, I'd better drop the tape off on the way." Derek re-entered the flat, collected the video, and left again, locking the door behind him.

It was not until he had returned the source of the previous evening's entertainment, and was well on the way to see Richard, that another almost-forgotten item suddenly came to his attention. "Sod it, I've left my briefcase in the flat. Shit! I'll bloody well have to go back and get it … can't do without it. Shit!" At the first opportunity Derek turned the Mondeo round and headed back towards his home. "Shit!" he said angrily. "Now I'm going to be late. That's a bloody good impression to make, just what I didn't want to do. Sod it!"

The Yorkshireman drove as fast as conditions allowed, and then faster. As the speeding Mondeo approached a pelican crossing, a cat, for reasons probably unknown to even itself, chose this exact moment to cross. Exhausting one of its nine lives, the cat miraculously managed to escape death as the car, with Derek at the helm, swerved to the right, and then to the left, somehow avoiding the moggie and an on-coming milk float. "Jesus! that was close", said an anxious Derek, firstly checking the rear-view mirror to see if all remained well at the crossing, and secondly, his complexion for any colour change. "Phew! That was a near one", gasped Derek, as his colour turned more towards normal. "Better take it a bit steady from now on." He eased up on the vehicle's accelerator. "Oh well … no good crying over spilt milk floats."

After breakfast Richard returned to his room to await Derek's arrival. Inside the room he looked at his wristwatch. "Ten to nine … just time to phone Molly."

"Good morning, how may I help you?" spoke a cheerful receptionist.

"Hi, could I have an outside line please?"

"Certainly, sir", came the reply, and then a click, followed by a buzzing noise.

Richard dialled, heard a ringing tone, and waited. The ringing tone continued. "Must be busy", he thought. Just as the American was about to replace the receiver, the ringing tone stopped. A male voice answered. "Dog and Duck."

"Hi there … may I speak to Miss Weston?"

"I'll try her room for you. Who's calling?"

"Just tell her Richard."

"Ah, the American, from the other night."

"Er, that's right."

"Spent quite a while chatting with Albert … as I recall."

"Er … yeah", came a somewhat stunned reply.

"Miss Weston's rather sweet on you she is."

"Really", responded Richard, wondering what business it was of his.

"She's a real good lass that one, one of the best I'd say … just make sure you treat her right."

"I intend to", he answered curtly.

"Just a bit of friendly advice mind, and just to prove it, next time you come here, there'll be a drink on the house awaitin for yer."

"Er, that's very kind … thanks. May I speak to Miss Weston?"

"I'll try her room now."

"I guess the fella means well", thought Richard, as he waited to be connected.

"Hello, Richard."

"Hi Mol, thought I'd give you a call, while I had the chance."

"Glad you did ….it's nice to hear your voice."

"It's great to hear yours, too, Mol ….by the way, that guy who answered the phone."

"Who, Bill?" she replied, a little perplexed.

"On the phone just now, gave me a friendly warning, told me to take proper care of you, I think he said I had to treat you right."

"Don't worry about Bill, he's got a heart of gold", she said, trying to hide any embarrassment.

"I've heard what the Brits used to say about us during World War II, overpaid, oversexed, and over here … isn't that correct, Mol?"

"That's what they used to say, doesn't apply to you though."

"Glad to hear that. Tell Bill from me, that given the chance, I'll treat you just fine."

Molly blushed. "I'll tell him."

They continued to talk, and were still chatting, when a knock sounded on Richard's door. "It's the door Mol, probably Derek, I'd better go and see to him. Fancy a meal on me tomorrow night?"

"Love to."

"Is it OK to eat there?"

"Here will do fine", she gleefully replied.

Another knock sounded on the door, only this time louder.

"Can you reserve a table?" he asked.

"Of course I can, eight-thirty for nine all right?"

"Swell Molly, just swell."

They said their goodbyes and Richard replaced the receiver. Knock, knock, knock.

"All right, I'm coming", responded Richard, to the sound on his door.

Richard walked towards the bedroom door, glancing at his watch as he reached for the handle.

"Nine thirty-eight, he's late", he muttered, then opened the door.

"Morning Richard, sorry I'm late, bad accident held up the traffic", lied Derek convincingly.

"Anyone hurt?" enquired Richard, showing concern.

"Can't say, ambulance roared off though, lights flashing", lied Derek, as if born to it.

"Let's hope no one was badly hurt, eh?"

"Bloody cat", murmured Derek to himself.

"What was that?"

"I said hope not'", replied Derek, lying once more.

"Fancy a cup of coffee, Derek?"

"Love one", enthused the Yorkshireman.

Richard put the kettle on, this time making no reference to either a Molly or a Polly.

"Before we get down to the day's business, I need you to do something for me", said the American, looking directly at Derek.

"If I can I will."

"Knew you would, Derek, you're that kinda guy."

"Thanks", replied the guest, unsure of whether the Yank was extracting the urine, or merely taking the piss. "What is it you want me to do?" he asked.

"Enquire about some riding stables, Western preferably."

"You want to go horse riding?" asked the Yorkshireman, as though the very thought of it directly compared to taking all of one's clothes off, smothering the naked flesh with honey, and then proceeding to demolish an entire colony of beehives single-handed, with nothing more than a stick of candyfloss to defend oneself.

"Yeah, thought I'd get to see more of the land on horseback."

"Oh, I see!" said Derek, apparently enlightened. "Further reconnaissance?"

"That's right, Derek", replied Richard unconcerned.

"But we're seeing Oldsworth on Friday."

"That's right", replied Richard, handing his colleague a cup of coffee, apparently still unconcerned.

"But how will that help?"

"Two reasons – one, a further in-depth look at the area may help at a later date with negotiations, and two, it's the weekend, and I'd like to go riding."

"I see, mixing business with pleasure, eh?"

"Something like that. Now, when you've finished your drink, perhaps you could go down to reception and see what you can find out for me. I need to stay here and catch up on some paperwork." It was now Richard's turn to lie; not something he was in the habit of doing, leastwise not on a personal level. It was, however, sometimes necessary to do so in a professional capacity. After all, he was a lawyer. The fact is that Richard had an uneasy feeling about Derek. A gut feeling. A lawyer's intuition. There appeared to be something about Derek Arkwright that didn't sit right, although the American, as yet, couldn't put his finger on it.

Chapter 7

Molly left her room at the Dog and Duck and proceeded downstairs. Reaching the bottom, she spotted the landlord, who was about to disappear into the cellar. "Good morning Bill ... didn't see you at breakfast."

"Morning Molly, been busy with an early delivery. Anyhow, I spoke to you earlier, put that young fella through on the telephone."

"Yes I know, told him to treat me right, didn't you?"

"Ah ... he told you did he?"

"Yes Bill", she answered, scowling.

"Didn't mean to offend anyone", replied Bill unashamedly.

"I know you didn't, it's rather sweet of you to look out for me", said Molly smiling.

"Ah well, all right ... not off hiking today, then?" asked Bill, trying to change the subject.

"Very observant Bill; as you can see I'm not really dressed for walking."

"Let me guess then ... off to Leeds to do some shopping?"

"Got it in one", she said, still smiling.

"Well ... off you go then, and have a nice time."

"Thanks, I'll try ... Oh by the way, can you reserve a table for two, tomorrow at nine?" Molly had a sparkle in her eye that did not go unnoticed.

"If I didn't know better I'd say your eyes twinkled just then", said Bill, causing Molly to laugh.

"Bill, I think you're a bit of a romantic at heart."

"Not just a prerogative of the young", replied the jolly landlord.

"I'll see you later", said Molly grinning, as she headed towards the door.

"See you later ... table's booked."

"Thanks, bye."

Molly closed the door behind her, and walked across the pub's car park. She looked at the sky. The early morning rain had stopped. "Looks like a fine day", she thought. "Just the ticket for shopping."

The weather was indeed conducive to a day's shopping. A few fair-weather clouds, of the cumulus type, hung high in the air above. The sun shone bright; only a light breeze existed. Any signs of earlier rain had all but gone; only a few puddles remained.

"Good morning, Oscar", said Molly cheerily, addressing her bright yellow Lotus Elise. She took out the keys from her jacket pocket, unlocked the car, and got in. Molly's previous car had been a Golf GTi; that one had been called Gordon. Molly liked to give names to her things – not everything, only special things; to her it seemed the friendly, decent thing to do. She had given a name to her first bicycle. It had been a Christmas present from her father when she was seven years old. Molly had named her bike 'Walter'; apparently her father had purchased a Raleigh. The habit of naming future modes of transport became fixed at that point.

She reversed the recently purchased Lotus from its parking spot, placed the gear shift into first, and drove off. "We're off shopping", she informed Oscar. Oscar responded in the only way such a car could; leaving the pub's car park, the wheels spun, and gravel leapt into the air.

Derek Arkwright, having obtained the information that Richard requested, left reception and headed towards the lifts. "What am I, some bloody personal gopher?" muttered Derek, seemingly annoyed. The annoyance became apparent when he almost knocked an elderly gentleman to the ground, whose only crime was attempting to vacate the lift. This was not an easy task, as the elderly gentleman was using a Zimmer frame at the time. "Silly old sod", exclaimed the gopher, pressing the appropriate button, enabling him to arrive on Richard's floor.

As the lift's doors closed, Derek witnessed a bellboy giving assistance to the old gentleman. "Silly old fart", he muttered, changing the end expletive in an attempt to add variation.

"Knock, knock."

"Who's there?" said Richard, obviously familiar with 'knock, knock' jokes.

"It's me, Derek", replied Derek, upon hearing Richard's question.

"Derek who?" asked the American, keen to continue.

"Derek ... Derek Arkwright", came the answer.

Richard smiled, then opened the door. "Not a very good punchline."

"Sorry", said Derek, looking confused .

"You weren't doing a 'knock, knock' joke then?"

"Er ... ha ... very funny", responded the Yorkshireman, finally getting the picture.

"Penny dropped?"

"Yes, yes … very good … got the info you wanted", answered Derek, upon entering the room.

"Any luck?"

"Yeah, stables nearby to the lot, choice of English or Western."

"Great! Well done."

"You're welcome, my aim is to serve", replied Derek sarcastically.

"Good", was all the American could be bothered to say.

Derek handed Richard a piece of paper containing the details.

"Thanks, you're a good man", quipped the Yank.

"I know", was all the Yorkshireman could be bothered to convey.

After making more coffee for them both, Richard settled down to brief his English colleague on events soon to take place at the planning office. The American intended to keep Derek informed, but only as far as he deemed necessary. The Englishman had been engaged to act as a local liaison mediator, nothing more. Only details relevant to Derek's involvement were to be revealed. Richard would keep him strictly on a 'need-to-know' basis.

Derek, however, had different ideas. His intentions were to be as much in the front line as possible. If there were to be any Brownie points, preferably with a pound or dollar sign attached, he wanted to be there, to collect. In the pursuit of personal gain it did not matter to Derek Arkwright on whose toes he trod, nor in whose back he stabbed a knife. To Derek Arkwright, all that mattered was Derek Arkwright.

"What can you tell me about Colin Williams?" asked Richard politely.

"In what way?"

"Character, personality, family, hobbies, that kind of thing. What am I likely to be up against?"

"Don't you worry about that, Richard, I can take care of Colin Williams", came a condescending reply.

"I don't want you to take care of Mr. Williams, that's my job. I want you to furnish *me* with as much background as possible." Richard had been aware for some time that confrontation with Derek would, at some point, be inevitable. That moment had arrived.

"Why worry yourself, I'm there with you … take your lead from me, I'll have Colin eating out of your hand."

"You've finally made the connection, Derek."

"Sorry?" he enquired, unsure of what connection he had made.

"The rub is, Derek, that you will not be in on the meeting this afternoon. Get the drift?"

"You mean that I'll be sitting outside, while you're with Williams'?"

"Got it in one", answered the American, satisfied that round one belonged to him.

Derek was far from happy with current developments. This situation was one he had not allowed for. However, he did not wish to rock the boat, upset the applecart, nor put the cat among the pigeons.

Outside on the window ledge, a pigeon cooed contentedly, having recently feasted on the crumbs of a broken biscuit.

Angry that he was, Derek had no desire to convey this emotion to the man sitting opposite. Thinking for a moment, he contemplated dealing the Yank a hand off the bottom of the pack. Feed the man from overseas a pack of lies, and then watch him screw up. "Better not", he thought. "Could jeopardise the whole show." Derek swallowed his pride and relayed what background information he had on Colin Williams.

"Thanks Derek, you've been most helpful, what about an early lunch?"

"Brilliant, I'm starving", replied Derek, glad to have a break from proceedings.

"You go and sort out a table, and I'll be along in ten minutes. Got to make a phone call."

"Fine, see you later", responded Derek, quickly standing up and moving towards the door.

"Right", said Richard, as soon as the door closed. "Now to reserve a couple of horses for the weekend." He picked up the piece of paper that had been given to him earlier, and walked over to the telephone.

"Bastard", swore Derek, no sooner than the door had closed. "Bloody Yankee Doodle." The unhappy Derek entered an empty waiting lift, turned towards the door, reached out an arm and pressed a button. The door closed, and the lift began to move down. The following fading words could be heard from somewhere in its shaft. "Bastard, bastard, bastard."

Arriving on the ground floor, the lift door opened. As the Yorkshireman made his exit, an anxious, elderly gentleman, hindered by a disability, quickly manoeuvred his Zimmer frame and scurried out of the way.

Chapter 8

Ernest Grabit sat at his desk, perusing a report that had been faxed to him earlier that morning. "Good ... good, mmm ... favourable, yeah, yeah, good." He studied the fax carefully; it reported favourably thus far. Noting the salient points he continued. The location in terms of accessibility and populace scored high. The acreage and suitability of the land in question seemed good, although further investigation was considered necessary. This aspect would be personally taken care of. "Good ... the lad's done well, the next hurdle is the planners. Waters is taking care of that one this afternoon, English time of course."

He finished reading the report and considered progress. "Everyone has his or her price", he murmured. "If all goes well at this afternoon's meeting, great, if not, I'll instruct the lad to offer a brown envelope. That is on the assumption that the land purchase can be successfully negotiated", he continued. "Everyone has their price."

Grabit smiled, took out a rather large cigar from a wooden box on his desk, put it to his lips and proceeded to light it. "Good work Waters'", he said, exhaling blue smoke from his mouth.

After an alcohol-free lunch, Richard went back to his room and collected a bag containing items needed for the stay in London. He had arranged to meet Derek in the hotel's car park. Meanwhile Derek, who felt the need to relieve himself, had made his way to the nearest toilet.

"Ah, that's better", he sighed, turning away from the urinal and zipping up his flies. "Better out than in, that's what I always say", he said to a stranger who, without reply, hurried into an empty cubicle and quickly shut the door. As Derek was not required to attend the afternoon's meeting, he decided to have, in the main, a liquid lunch.

The Yorkshireman arrived at his car and waited for Richard. The American arrived a few minutes later. "Put your bag in the boot, it's unlocked."

Richard went round to the back of the Mondeo, and opened up the trunk. He placed the case inside, and closed the lid.

"You can put your briefcase on the back seat, it's unlocked."

Richard opened the vehicle's rear door and placed the briefcase on the seat. He then shut it, opened the front passenger door, and got in. "This car got central locking, Derek?"

"Sure has, and electric front windows."

"Really!" replied Richard, with a look of surprise equating to the one that Rip Van Winkle might have expressed had he been introduced to such technology, having just awoken from a hundred-year sleep.

"And it's got power steering."

"Great."

Derek started the car and drove off. The journey to the Council offices took about fifteen minutes, and was uneventful. Parking the car turned out to be another matter.

Due to maintenance taking place, there were only a limited number of parking spaces available at the Council offices, and these had already been taken.

"Can't park here, sorry", said a car park attendant, obviously pleased to exert his authority.

"Why?" replied Derek sharply, as if the attendant's refusal may have been personal.

"No spaces, we're full up, part of the car park is being resurfaced."

"Oh I see", said Derek, almost relieved. "Where's the nearest car park, then?"

"Nearest eh … .that would be Trumpet Street."

Richard sat in silence.

"Can you give me directions please?"

"Certainly. You want to turn round, then go left, turn first left, after about a hundred yards turn right, go to the bottom and turn right again, at the T junction, turn left, and it's on your left, can't miss it."

"Thanks", said Derek, grateful.

"You don't want to go there though", offered the attendant.

"Why's that?" enquired a puzzled Derek, about to drive off.

"They're full."

"Full! Full! Why the bloody hell did you give me directions to a car park that's full?"

"'Cause you asked me to."

Richard looked at his watch. It read ten to two. "Er … scuse me Derek, it's getting late, I'd better get out here, you park the car, and I'll see you later." Richard reached over to the back seat, took hold of the briefcase and got out of the car. He nodded to the car park attendant, and walked off in the general direction of the offices.

Derek firmly pressed a button causing the Mondeo's window to close. Selecting first gear, the car moved forwards. He then proceeded to turn the vehicle around.

Passing the attendant, he offered a one-finger salute, and drove off in search of a parking space. "Prat!" he muttered, driving off at speed. Ten minutes later Derek was still searching for that elusive parking space.

Richard, meanwhile, had found his way to the appropriate office. He went in, and approached a middle-aged lady sitting behind a desk.

"May I help you?" she said.

"The name is Waters, Richard Waters, I have an appointment with Mr. Williams."

"Yes … he's expecting you. Are you alone?"

"My colleague is trying to park the car, he'll be along shortly."

"Parking is a bit of a nightmare at the moment. Part of the tarmac is being taken up and replaced", she said, as if apologising.

"So I gather", replied Richard, thinking of recent events.

"If you care to take a seat, I'll let Mr. Williams know you've arrived."

"Many thanks", acknowledged the American.

He sat down and waited. A few minutes later a door opened, and a rather large, red-faced man appeared. He approached Richard.

"Mr. Waters, I presume?" asked the red-faced gentleman.

"You presume correctly", returned the American, offering out his hand. "And you must be Mr. Williams?"

"Aye lad, as it happens I am", retorted Colin Williams, in a thick local accent.

They shook hands firmly. Richard made a point of doing so, endeavouring to express sincerity.

"Come into my office; I'm rather intrigued as to what you might want to discuss." Williams gestured him towards his office. Passing the secretary Richard paused. "When my colleague, Derek Arkwright, arrives can you ask him to wait for me?"

"Certainly Mr. Waters."

Richard looked directly into the secretary's eyes. His expression went stern. "Under no circumstances is Mr. Arkwright to interrupt me", he pronounced.

She seemed to understand. "Very well", she uttered, going back to her work.

The American entered the office.

"Have a seat lad, and get to the point, I'm a busy man, and I suppose you are too", resounded the Head Planning Officer.

Colin Williams seemed to be very much as Derek had conveyed. Brash, forthright, loud; whether he was straight, firm, and fair, had yet to be tested.

"I understand from Derek Arkwright that he has intimated to you the outline of our proposals, is this correct?"

"Only insofar as you wish to develop a commercial leisure complex, on some moorland."

Richard offered a business card, which was accepted. "As you can see I represent a firm of lawyers … from New York."

"I gather from this that you're not Hadim, Gotcha, nor Grabit", recited Mr. Williams.

"You gather correct", came the American's wilful reply.

"So if you're not the organ grinder you must be the monkey?" queried Williams, trying to establish some kind of rank.

"Well if you must put it that way … I am indeed the monkey."

Colin Williams smiled. "Glad to hear it, lad, I like a man who talks straight. You do talk straight, don't you?"

"As straight as permitted … after all, I am a lawyer", parried the man from New York.

The other man's smile now widened further. "Right then, let's hear what you've got to say."

Richard reiterated the outline proposals, keeping details brief.

"Now let me see if I've got this correct", stated the Head Planning Officer. "You, representing your firm, Hadim Gotcha and Grabit Inc., who themselves are acting on behalf of a consortium, wish to purchase two thousand acres of moorland and turn it into a theme park, yes?"

"That's about the size of it", replied Richard, looking directly at the man across the desk.

"Where, exactly, is this land?"

Richard took out a map from his briefcase, opened it up on the desk, and with a finger pointed to the farm's location. "The farm's owner lives in London, he's an artist … at present the land isn't worked", informed the lawyer. "He has no interest in the land … apart from selling it, that is", he added.

"Tell me more about this consortium."

Richard could only relay what he knew, and that was very little. "I am assured, however, that the necessary funds are available to develop the project." he conveyed persuasively. The American went on. "It is possible that your Government may be involved with partial funding … but don't quote me on that, not my department." Richard had no idea whether the British

Government was involved. It had, however, sounded good. A carrot had been dangled. Would Colin Williams turn out to be a donkey, or an ass? He would have to wait and see. This particular planning officer kept his cards very close to his chest. A canny Yorkshireman indeed, thought Richard.

"What about employment?"

"Glad you asked that, Mr. Williams, I was about to cover that next."

Richard went on to describe the various types of theme centres to be incorporated on the site. He emphasised the intention not to disturb the general appearance of the countryside; any development would be strictly in keeping with the surrounding environment. The development and construction would generate considerable employment, both local and brought in. Local materials would be used where possible. Local businesses, such as shops, caterers, and those providing accommodation would benefit.

The American paused for reaction. He didn't get one. He had, however, retained his listener's attention. Richard continued. He covered development through to construction, and finally, the opening. He explained what this would mean in terms of local employment, increased revenue from tourism, and spin-off business growth.

"Aye lad, I can see the potential for the area and its community", Williams said, rubbing his chin. "Could be Leeds' answer to EuroDisney", he added. "Mind you, there will no doubt be an influx of *foreigners.*"

"There is that, I suppose", said Richard, probably thinking of the French. "Think of the prosperity it will bring, think of the money ... after all, you are part of Europe now."

Colin Williams reflected. "Well lad, my motto has always been, if you can't beat em, join em, and if you can't join em, beat em."

The American studied Colin Williams; he appeared deep in thought. Observing the pregnant pause technique, Richard waited in silence. Fortunately he didn't have to wait long.

"The committee meets in a week's time, I'll raise the matter then. If it all pans out, you have my recommendations to proceed."

Richard inwardly gave a sigh of relief. The first hurdle had been successfully negotiated. Approval in principle.

"Mind you", said the Head Planning Officer, "a full presentation will have to be made to them, at the appropriate juncture."

"When would that be?" asked the American.

"Depends ... how long would you need to prepare?"

"Couple of weeks should be fine."

"In that case, I'll fix it up for the week after next. Let's have a look at my diary." Colin Williams turned to face a computer console on his desk, tapped a few keys on the keyboard, and briefly waited. "Two weeks today, is that all right with you?"

"It'll be just fine", replied Richard with a smile.

"Ten-thirty?"

"Ten-thirty will be just fine."

They shook hands, made a few pleasantries, and then Richard left the office.

Derek, having eventually managed to find a parking space, made his way to the planning office, and waited in reception. To pass the time he browsed through several magazines, none of which were current. He was deeply engrossed in the problem page of an eighteen-month-old copy of Woman's Realm when Richard suddenly appeared. "Hi there Derek, anything good?"

Derek hurriedly replaced the magazine and stood up. "Just passing the time." He turned toward the secretary, who was busily working at her desk. "Tell me, is there some law that I've somehow missed, that prevents waiting areas – such as this, and especially doctors – from providing reading material less than twelve months old?"

The secretary looked confused. "Sorry?" she said.

"Never mind."

She didn't, and went back to her work.

The American said goodbye, the secretary looked up, smiled, replied likewise, and then went back to her work. They then left the planning office.

"It's just possible", thought Richard, "That my erstwhile colleague is a little pissed off."

"How did it go?" enquired the erstwhile colleague, as they walked down the steps outside the Council offices.

"Very well ... Williams has approved the project in principle, and will brief the committee next week."

"So he's going to recommend it, is he?"

"That's about the size of it."

"Great, that's the first major step out of the way."

"Long way to go yet", Richard responded, as they turned left out of the Council car park.

"Yes, but without planning consent, we'd be on a hiding-to-nothing."

"*We* haven't got it yet."

"Yes but ... so far so good. What's next?"

"Next?" he paused. "Next will have to wait until tomorrow."

"I didn't mean with regard to the land purchase", relayed Derek, as they took another left.

"What did you mean, then?" asked the American.

"Well, I gather that your meeting with Colin Williams was merely a preliminary one."

"Oh I see … yes, that's correct. A presentation will have to be made in two week's time … in front of the committee."

"Who's going to do that?" said Derek, raising his eyebrows in anticipation.

The Yorkshireman, walking briskly, made another turn, this time to the right. Richard followed closely behind.

"Not sure, probably a team representing the consortium."

"Yes, but we'll be involved, won't we?"

"I expect so … to some degree at least", replied Richard, not wishing to elaborate.

They continued walking in silence.

Derek used the silence to think. He desperately needed to be involved, make an impression. He would bide his time, bypass the Yank, and go straight for the chiefs. He had enough of dealing with the indian.

"Couldn't we have gotten a cab, Derek?" posed Richard, breaking the silence.

"Sorry?"

"We've been walking for fifteen minutes, just where did you park the goddamn car … Manchester?"

"Very good, I see you're getting to grips with local geography", came a sarcastic response.

"Well … ?"

"Well what?"

"How much farther?"

"No further … .we're here", jousted the Yorkshireman.

"Thank Christ for that", retorted the American, his patience, much like his blisters, wearing thin.

The drive to the railway station took about ten minutes; nothing more than idle banter passed between them. Derek steered the Mondeo into the station car park.

"Look, there's one!" said Richard quickly, pointing to a parking space. "Great, no walking." His relief was apparent. "Don't think my blisters could stand another hike", he joked.

Derek carefully manoeuvred the car into the available space, and turned off the engine. "Got to get a ticket", he said, getting out of the vehicle and walking off in the direction of a ticket machine.

Richard, having disembarked, now stood waiting for Derek, his briefcase and overnight bag in hand. What seemed like an eternity to the American, was, in actual fact, slightly less than two minutes.

"Have you got fifty pence? I haven't enough change", Derek asked politely, upon his return.

The American placed the luggage on the ground, and searched through his pockets. "Here's one."

With outstretched arm, hand forward, palm upward, Richard offered the chauffeur a choice of coinage. Derek took a fifty-pence coin, said thanks, and went off once more to apprehend a car-parking ticket.

"That guy's not having much luck today", thought Richard, as he again waited.

"Got it", said the hapless Derek, returning to the car. He firmly affixed the ticket to the inside windscreen, closed the door, and, almost in jubilant fashion said: "Right, I'll get my bags and then it's off to the smoke."

Richard picked up the luggage, shook his head a little and smiled. Proceeding towards the station, his thoughts turned somewhat to that of a casting director. Assuming that role, and with his accumulated knowledge of the man walking beside him, somehow, he couldn't envisage offering the lead role in the film 'Raiders of the Lost Ark' to Derek Arkwright. More like 'Mission Impossible', he thought.

Inside the station, the atmosphere was one of bustle. Commuters hurried to and fro. Occasional travellers, hesitant, unsure of what platform to head for, stood around, staring at timetables. Richard was accustomed to this level of human activity. He faced it each working day. Derek also took this aspect in his stride.

"What time does our train depart?" enquired the American.

"Usually about twenty minutes after it should do", replied the Yorkshireman, taking a look at his wristwatch.

Richard smiled, having previously heard that, since its privatisation, the British railway network had been experiencing a few difficulties, to say the least. "What time is it supposed to leave?"

"Two minutes ago."

"In that case, we'd better get a move on."

Derek quickened the pace; Richard followed. An announcement came over the tannoy regarding the London-bound train.

"What was that?"

"No idea", replied Derek. "They seem to have a nationwide policy of employing people with speech impediments. Been that way for as long as I can remember", he added.

Another announcement came over the tannoy. Richard strained both ears, but was still unable to decipher its content.

"Here we are … platform two."

"Well, at least the train hasn't left", pronounced Richard.

They hurried along the platform, looking for vacant seats.

"This one will do", said Derek, on spotting a likely carriage. He then embarked with obvious determination, not wishing to be deprived of a seat.

Richard followed. Yet another announcement came over the tannoy.

"Nope, didn't get that one either."

Derek had found two empty seats, and was firmly installed on one of them, his luggage on the rack above, when Richard caught up. "Saved you a seat."

"Thanks Derek." The American placed his bag and briefcase on the rack, and then sat down on the allocated seat. "That's better", he said.

"Well, we just made it", proclaimed Derek.

The tannoy once again burst into life.

"*What was that?*" asked Richard.

"Beats me", replied Derek.

"The train has been delayed, due to mechanical problems", offered a softly spoken voice from the aisle opposite.

Richard turned his head in the direction of the voice. The voice belonged to an elderly woman. She appeared smartly dressed with bluish-grey hair. To the American she seemed reminiscent of Agatha Christie's Miss Marple. "Do you know how long the delay is?" asked Richard, addressing Miss Marple.

"About another forty-five minutes ... so they said."

"Thank you." The American turned to his colleague.

"Well ... we did just make it ... with about three quarters of an hour to spare."

"Bloody British Rail ... or whoever they are now ... I'm going to get a drink ... want one?" He stood up and squeezed past Richard.

"Good idea, I'll have a lager please."

Derek walked off in search of the buffet car, mumbling something under his breath as he went.

"Derek has missed his true vocation", thought Richard. "He would have made a *pretty damn good* railway announcer. In fact, if he gives me much more trouble, I might suggest it to him." He turned again to face Miss Marple. Pointing toward the disappearing Derek he said: "He's not having a good day."

She nodded in acknowledgement, and then went back to her knitting.

Richard settled into his seat. He laid his head back and his thoughts turned to Molly. He closed his eyes and continued to think of her.

Chapter 9

Molly, having shopped till she almost dropped, was once again behind the wheel of the yellow Lotus. The car's storage space, although limited, had nevertheless been filled to capacity. Bags of shopping were crammed into every nook and cranny. Not that Oscar had many nooks or crannies. She had bought clothes and shoes for herself, presents for her family, and one very special present. "I do hope he likes it", she told Oscar. Oscar appeared nonplussed. Somehow, that did not seem important. She continued to enlighten the inanimate object. "I think red will suit him. It should fit all right. I *hope* it fits all right." Molly had guessed Richard's measurements. She had purchased an Aran-style pullover. Buying gifts for other people gave her pleasure. Buying a gift for Richard had meant more. "I'll give it to him tomorrow", she continued.

The Lotus quietly purred; it did not answer back.

"Oh gosh!" she suddenly blurted. "What if he's embarrassed?" She considered this aspect momentarily. She tutted. "I'm being silly, he'll love it." Molly changed down a gear and gently braked. A cat had caught her eye. Standing nervously on the pavement, near a pedestrian crossing, the cat seemed undecided as to whether or not it wanted to cross. Safely passing the feigning feline she changed gear upwards and accelerated. "He'd better like it", she informed Oscar.

The cat, having established that there were no imminent speeding Mondeos, crossed in comparative safety.

"Two pints of lager please", requested Derek, having found the buffet car.

"Only got cans", the steward replied.

"Two cans then."

"Don't do birds … only refreshments."

"Sorry?"

"No parrots, budgies, peacocks, eagles or toucans."

"Very good … most amusing, er, two cans of Fosters." Derek had decided that politeness and courtesy did not apply in this particular situation.

"Anything else?" asked the steward.

"Not at these prices", replied Derek, handing over a ten pound note. The Yorkshireman took the change, looked at it, and sighed. He then put it into his pocket. He picked up the lager and plastic glasses. He started to leave, but as he did so, turned back to address the steward. "Thought you said you didn't do birds."

"Yep, that's right."

"How come then, matey, you've got chicken sandwiches, Penguin bars and Kestrel lager?"

"Good point", replied the steward.

Derek turned away again, this time leaving the buffet car without further verbal exchange. "Moral victory, mine I think", he said, evidently pleased with himself.

"I've got your lager", said Derek, gently shaking Richard's arm.

"Must have dropped off." Richard raised himself from the seat to let Derek pass.

"I've only been gone about ten minutes."

"Tired I guess."

"This'll liven you up." He handed the American a can of beer, and commenced the initiation ceremony of opening his first tinnie of the day. Likewise, Richard did the same, that is, insofar as opening the can. There the similarity ended, for whilst Richard poured the liquid into the plastic receptacle, Derek, dispensing with this artificial aid, raised the can to his lips and heartily drank from it.

"A rather disturbing trend", thought the American, only too familiar with this less than civilised form of behaviour.

"Excuse me."

"Yes, sir", answered the conductor.

"Any idea when this train will leave?" enquired the American politely.

"'Bout ten minutes."

"Thanks."

"About bloody time too", butted in Derek, raising the can to his lips once again.

The conductor, ignoring the previous comment, continued his patrol.

"You seem very impatient."

"I am."

"Why?"

"Keen to get to the 'Smoke', see a bit of night life … if you get what I mean", winked Derek, at the same time nudging his colleague.

Richard, unsure of what the Yorkshireman's plans were for that evening, decided to investigate further. "What have you got in mind, Derek?"

"What, for this evening like?" Every now and then, the would-be-born-again-yuppie's control over his accent and dialect lapsed.

"Yes."

"I thought you and me could have a few beers, take in a couple of strip shows, and maybe get fixed up with a tart apiece."

It was becoming apparent to Richard that the man sitting to his left not only lacked any social graces, but also any form of refinement. "Alas, there are far too many Derek Arkwrights in this world", he privately concluded. The American was not opposed to the idea of seeing female naked flesh. However, what he was opposed to was the thought of spending an entire evening with Arkwright, and watching him gradually become more obnoxious as time went on. Richard shuddered at the thought. "Not for me, Derek."

"What!"

"I intend to have a relaxing meal, with a glass or two of good wine, and then an early night."

"What!"

"It's another big day tomorrow, Derek."

"Yes, but …"

Richard interrupted: "You can spend the evening how you like, and within reason I'll even cover expenses."

Derek's eyes lit up. "That's more like it", he thought. "All expenses paid. Anyway, why would I want that pompous Yank with me, cramping *my style*?"

"Yeah, good idea, you'd better keep fresh Richard. You're absolutely right, tomorrow is a big day."

"Thought you'd see it my way, Derek."

Arkwright yet again lifted the can to his lips. "Bugger!" he exclaimed, "The bloody can's empty."

The train began to move, and slowly it left the station. Richard leaned back in his seat and shut his eyes once more. As the train chugged out, a continual burping sound could be heard, emitting from the approximate location occupied by Derek Arkwright.

"Gee whiz, he's uncouth", thought Richard.

"Have we finished for the day?"

"Yes Sophie, I think that's enough for today, you can get dressed now."

Sophie relaxed the pose she had sustained, on and off, for the past six hours. She got off the chaise longue, stretched her limbs, and put on a dressing gown. "How's it coming on?" she enquired, referring to the painting.

"You can't look yet … not until it's finished."

"Oh come on Hugo", she pleaded.

"You know the rules", replied Hugo Oldsworth. "I never let anyone see my work until it's completed."

"Fancy a cup of coffee, then?"

"That seems like a good speech … yes please."

Sophie went off to the kitchen, lighting up a cigarette as she went.

"Very good, if I say so myself", he said, standing back to admire his work. "Another day and it'll be finished." Hugo turned the easel to face a wall, thereby denying visual access to the canvas. "There, no one can see you now, my beauty."

Sophie returned carrying two mugs.

"Thanks Soph."

"You're welcome." She carefully placed the two mugs on an occasional table, which sometimes dubbed as a prop.

"I don't know how you manage it, I really don't."

"Manage what?"

"Only you could carry two mugs, and hold a fag at the same time … and not spill either a drop of coffee or any ash. Look, the ash must be an inch long." No sooner than he had spoken, the ash from the cigarette dropped to the floor, as if, in slow motion.

"See what you made me do now", she pouted.

Hugo laughed:

"You're multi-talented, Soph … you're an absolute gem."

"Yeah, yeah."

"I mean it, what *would* I do without you?"

"Find someone else with big jugs, who'll pose naked all day, freezing her arse off for next to nothing, I guess", came the sultry reply.

"Not like you my dear, you're irreplaceable. Besides, I'd probably have to pay someone else a lot more", he jokingly responded.

"Bastard!"

"I was only joking", he said, pretending to be hurt.

"So was I", she said, pretending to be sorry. Sophie stubbed out the cigarette, and at the same time rubbed her bare foot over the ash.

"I saw that."

"It's good for the carpet", she answered defensively.

"Oh is it? Who said?"

"My mother did, apparently it keeps the moths away."

"Balls!"

"It does ... she told me years ago."

"No, I meant moth balls."

They both laughed, only it would be fair to describe Hugo's attempt as more reminiscent of the sound that an asthmatic badger might make, had he been recently gassed.

"Anyway", said Hugo, calming down. "It's a rug not a carpet."

"Same difference", she said, pouting once more.

Hugo lifted the mug, and raised it to his mouth. "Yuck ... I don't know whether to drink it or wash my brushes in it", he teased.

"Keep that up and you'll be wearing it."

Sophie was good for Hugo, she helped to breathe life into him. Continually jousting with each other, her sparring served to create stimulus for the artist. "I'd better get going", she suddenly stated, noticing the time on the wall clock. She finished her drink, replacing the vessel back on the table.

"I'll wash the mugs up later", offered Hugo.

"No, I can do it."

"I'll do it ... otherwise you'll be late."

"OK", she replied, slipping off the dressing gown.

Sophie had modelled for Hugo for the past two years; in that time they had got to know each other very well. They were friends; the relationship was more than professional, but had remained platonic. She had been twenty-five years old when they first met – a single mother, with a two-year-old son. Modelling for Hugo supplemented the state benefits she received. The cash-in-hand payments, given to her by the artist, were not declared. Sophie had no desire to be dishonest, but her choices were limited. In the grand scheme of things neither she, nor Hugo, considered the deception to be a real crime.

"After all", Hugo had often said, "there exist many people in power whose exaggerated expenses claims amount to far more than her meagre allowance."

Two years on, and two years older, her situation had remained very much the same.

Thankfully, now aged twenty-seven, her body had remained firm and her looks youthful. As her son grew, so did his requirements. In an attempt to satisfy these ever-increasing demands, she had taken on extra work. Living in London, this extra work was not difficult to come by. The work involved stripping, taking her clothes off for men's titillation, and more recently lap dancing. The latter meant dancing for just one man, at any one time. Neither allowed touching. Sophie had never had any hang-ups about being naked in front of people. To her it was just flesh, the same as anybody else's. "After all", she had often said, "it's a living."

Sophie quickly dressed, picked up her things, and headed for the door. "See you tomorrow."

"Ten o'clock sharp ... I have some people coming to see me at two."

"Does that mean I get the afternoon off?"

"Hardly, I would like to finish the painting tomorrow."

"Good, perhaps I'll be able to see it then", she jibed.

"Only if you're a good girl, now clear off."

"I can take a hint, bye, see you tomorrow."

"Bye Soph", Hugo replied, still trying to clean his brushes.

Hugo's studio basically consisted of one large room, with a small kitchen area at one end and, adjacent to that, a shower-cum-toilet. Littered with artist's materials, and strewn with paintings and props, the studio could be considered clean, if not exactly tidy. "A few more minutes clearing up, and I can get off home", he cheerfully said to himself .

Home was a modest, modern apartment, a few streets away. Although Hugo could drive, he did not possess a car. He walked or cycled to and from the studio, and when he felt the need, or desire to venture further afield, a taxi or public transport sufficed.

"I wonder what riches, if any, tomorrow will bring?" he said, thinking of the following day's meeting. His thoughts turned to Sophie: "If I can get a good enough price ..." A ringing telephone interrupted the current train of thought. "Hello."

"Hi Hugo, how's it going?"

"Good evening Rupert, nice to hear from you, should be finished tomorrow, that is, if all goes well."

"Good, good, when can I see it?" inquired the art dealer.

"When it's finished, Rupert."

"You *know* I have a prospective buyer for it?"

"So you've said ... many times", answered the artist.

"So ... can I come round tomorrow, and have a look?"

"Give me a ring later in the afternoon, see how I'm getting on."

"Will do Hugo, ciao", chortled Rupert, replacing the receiver.

"Good, he's gone ... now, turn off the lights, lock up, and go home." Hugo put on his coat, turned off the lights, locked the door, and left the building. As he proceeded to walk the short journey home, suddenly, he had a thought: "Blast ... I completely forgot to wash those mugs up. Never mind, Sophie can do it in the morning."

Derek had managed to sleep for most of the journey from Leeds to London, thanks mainly to the effects that the alcohol at lunchtime had induced. Richard, on the other hand, had remained very much awake, thanks mainly to the effects that the Yorkshireman's snoring had produced.

"Come on Derek, wake up, we're here", said Richard, shaking the other man's shoulder, possibly wishing that it was his throat.

"What, we're here?" replied Derek, gradually coming to. "Must have dozed off."

"*Dozed off*, you've been snoring your head off since Sheffield."

The train screeched to a concluding halt. Richard removed Derek's luggage from the rack above and handed it to him, then obtained his own. "Ready?"

"I was born ready", answered the still dopey one.

"Yeah, looks like it."

They joined the queue attempting to disembark, and slowly shuffled their way to the exit.

"I'd better get us a taxi", stated the man from Yorkshire.

Richard remained silent as they marched along the platform and across the station.

"Taxi, taxi", hailed Derek, upon reaching the outside world.

"Good grief", thought the American, watching the artist at work.

"Taxi, taxi", went Derek once more, only this time, waving his right arm in the air.

"Knew a chap once, in New York, who got hit by a cab that fell out of the sky", remarked Richard.

"Really?"

"Yep … apparently he'd been hailing taxis."

"God, I'd heard your winters could be rough, but that's extreme", muted Derek, obviously now fully awake.

"Where to, mate?" asked a cabby, pulling alongside.

"Soho … Prince's Palace Hotel", advised Derek, stepping into the black London cab.

Richard, remaining silent, followed suit, allowing his colleague to enjoy the moment. The taxi moved off, joined the streaming traffic.

"Out on the town then?"

"Business", retorted Derek.

"Must be a bit of pleasure as well … if you're staying at the Palace that is?" queried the cabby, his reference to the Palace being a hotel, and not the Queen's residence.

"Hoping to take in a few of the local sights", smirked Derek.

"When in Rome, guv, when in Rome'", offered the cockney cab driver.

"My learned friend here intends to have an early night", mused Derek.

"Busy schedule, guv?" asked the driver, addressing Richard.

"Important day tomorrow, need to keep my wits about me."

"You do that, it's a bleedin' rip-off anyway. Charge a bleedin' arm an' a leg, in some of them bleedin' places. Bye the way, the name's John."

"Nice to meet you, John", replied Richard, being polite.

As the modern hansom cab wheeled its way to their hotel, the taxi driver continued to engage in a localised form of dialogue exchange. This ranged from advice on where to shop, and places to visit, interspersed with a running commentary on areas of interest passed en route. It seemed to Richard that this particular cab driver's 'knowledge' extended way beyond that of merely understanding the London A to Z.

"Right lads, you're here."

"Thanks John", said Derek, stumbling out onto the pavement.

"How much?" asked the American.

"£16.80, please guv."

He took out a twenty-pound note from his wallet and gave it to the driver. "Keep the change John, thanks for the guided tour." Richard then got out of the taxi, closing the door as he did so.

"Have a good stay, lads", said John, who then drove off and rejoined the traffic.

"*£16.80*, he must have taken the scenic route just for your benefit, Richard."

"It sure does seem that way", responded the American, at the same time looking around. "A lot like parts of New York", he thought, taking in the coloured lights, smell of traffic fumes, and the general busyness the surrounding area generated.

They entered the Palace via revolving doors and stood in the foyer.

"It's a big place", informed the man of the North.

"Sure is", replied the other, accustomed to large hotels. "Let's check in."

The hotel's size from outside was deceptive; situated almost on a corner, it seemed much smaller than it actually turned out to be. Nowhere near as grand as the Grand in Leeds, it could nevertheless be described as adequate. It boasted several hundred rooms, all of which were clean and comfortable, although only a few came with en-suite facilities. Unfortunately, neither room booked by Derek had these facilities. A brief discussion with the receptionist resolved this predicament, a supplement was agreed, and rooms with bathrooms allocated. After checking-in, they proceeded to the lifts.

"Sorry about the en-suite, Richard."

"Don't you mean the lack of one?" he replied. "Anyway, it's sorted now."

"Hard to get a decent hotel in London at such short notice", said Derek, trying hard to conceal the fact that the only reason he chose this particular venue was its close proximity to Soho.

"Never mind Derek, I'm sure I could have managed to walk down the hall for a leak – if I had to, that is."

"Thanks to you, Richard, neither of us has to now." If it was Richard's intention to make his colleague feel guilty, the Yorkshireman resisted any attempt to display it.

"I do prefer attending to my ablutions in the comfort of my own bathroom, but at a push, I could have managed for one night."

"That's the spirit, Richard."

"Arsehole", thought the American.

The rooms were adjacent to each other on the fourth floor. Richard appeared relieved that he was able to close the door of his room, safe in the knowledge that Derek was somewhere on the other side of it.

"Peace at last", he murmured.

Knock, knock.

"What now?" thought the American, turning to open the door.

It was Derek Arkwright. "Fancy a drink in the bar a bit later?"

"I thought you were going out on the town."

"I am … later. I thought, perhaps, you might want some company for a little while."

At this point, it was Richard who had the guilty feelings. "Sure, why not? Seven-thirty in the bar, OK?"

"Great, see you then."

Richard closed the door for the second time, walked into the room and placed his luggage on the bed. "I need a bath, a very hot one … with bubbles. Lots of them."

Later that evening, seven-thirty-five to be precise, Richard walked into the bar area of the Prince's Palace Hotel. He proceeded to the bar, looked around, but could not visually locate his colleague. "Looks like he's late again", he thought.

"Yes sir, can I help you?"

Richard turned to face the bar. "A pint of lager please."

"Certainly, any particular brand?"

The American glanced along the bar, perusing the pumps. "Nordic Gold … please."

The lady behind the bar obliged.

"Thank you", he said, as she placed the glass in front of him. "Book it to my room, if you wouldn't mind?" Richard offered his room key, and the young lady noted the number.

"Thanks", she said smiling, and then immediately turned away to serve someone else.

"Typical transient response", he cynically thought, taking a sip from the frothy-topped glass. Although it was still quite early in the evening, already the bar seemed busy. Four people were serving: two males and two females, all in hotel uniform. Richard briefly studied the four; the one who had served him was probably the youngest, around mid-twenties, blonde, attractive, but heavily made-up. Her buxom cleavage, readily on show, seemed to be going down well with the male guests and customers alike. "Come to that", thought the American, looking about, "There don't seem to be many women around here at all." The bar area was, indeed, male dominated. Richard put that fact down to the possibility that many of the gentlemen he could see around him were presumably in London on business. Another fact had not escaped his notice: "This hotel is pretty-damn close to Soho." Richard looked at his watch. "God, it's nearly seven-forty-five, where is that son-of-a- ..." Although he was only thinking to himself, out of politeness he did not finish the sentence. Instead, he raised his glass and sipped away some more of the froth. "Gee, this beer is gassy", he thought.

While waiting for Derek to join him, he continued to analyse the bar staff. The other female had dark hair, far less make-up, smaller breasts, and was probably in her mid-thirties. "Quite attractive, very polite, and also very popular", he summarised. His attentions turned to the spotty-faced youth drying glasses, situated about midway along the bar. The young man's facial expression bore a direct contrast to his female counterparts. For while their faces were obliging and all smiles, his was sullen and moody. "Definitely a teenager", thought the American.

Richard raised his glass once again to his lips, only this time, as the froth had all but disappeared, he was able to take an unencumbered mouthful. "That's better", he said. He was about to finish his character assessment of the hotel's bar staff when an all-too-familiar voice alerted him.

"Hi there Richard, sorry I'm a bit late, been on the 'dog' trying to sort out some entertainment for a bit later this evening ... if you know what I mean?"

Richard didn't, unable to decipher Derek's verbal diatribe, especially the reference to the meaning of 'been on the dog'. His only response was to utter: "Run that by me again, would ya Derek, only slower."

Derek looked at the American with a confused expression, as if in some disbelief that anyone, with even a smattering of the English language could have any difficulty understanding what he had just said. "I've been on the phone ... you know, 'dog and bone' ... phone."

"Oh I see", replied Richard, apparently relieved in the knowledge that the term 'been on the dog' was merely cockney rhyming slang, and not a reference to any sexual practices of a bestial nature. "Can I get you a drink?"

"I'll have a lager, thanks."

"'Scuse me, miss."

"Yes sir?"

"Two pints of Nordic Gold please."

The buxom blonde went off to do his bidding.

"Nice chest", said Derek, enthusiastically leaning closer to the bar, and in the process nearly knocking Richard from his bar-stool.

"So what's the entertainment you mentioned?"

"Well, I made a few phone calls from the room, and as a result, I've sorted some company for later this evening."

"Thank you", said Richard to the barmaid, as she placed two glasses in front of him.

"Same room number?"

"Yes please."

The buxom barmaid turned away, and directed her smile towards someone else.

"I don't think the expense account will somehow entertain *your* entertainment Derek."

"Oh come on, I'm sure we can work it somehow, *can't we*?"

"You bring me legitimate receipts for no more than two hundred pounds, and I'll see that it's covered. No more, mind."

"You're a diamond Richard, a real gem."

"Yeah, yeah, twenty-four carat … fancy another drink?"

"Er, no thanks, got to run, off to see a show."

Derek quickly swallowed the remaining dregs left in his glass, and placed it on the bar. "Right then, see you later." With those final words he turned away, made a sharp exit, and promptly disappeared.

"Great", thought the man left sitting on the bar stool. "He asks me to meet *him* for a drink, agrees seven-thirty but doesn't show until eight, lets me buy him a drink, mugs me for expenses so that he can get himself laid, and then sods off. Bastard." Richard looked at his watch: "Time for a quick call to Molly before dinner."

Molly had decided that, after a busy day's shopping, she would have an early night, tucked up in bed with a good book. In the absence of a good book, she settled on one written by Jeffery Archer that had previously been left in her room.

Brrring, brrring … brrring, brrring.

"Hello."

"That young fella is on the line Molly."

"Thanks Bill, put him through."

"OK will do, Roger and out", replied Bill, seemingly assuming the role of Biggles.

"Hello Richard, how are you?"

"Fine Mol, just fine, how are you?"

"I've been shopping."

"I gather shopping equates to a 'yes, I'm fine', does it?"

"Yes, I'm fine", she said smiling. "Where are you?"

"In a hotel near Piccadilly Circus. I'm about to have dinner."

"Where's your pal?"

"Don't call him that Mol, please. He's gone off to paint the town red, but knowing him, he'll get the colour wrong."

"You sound as though you're a bit fed-up with him."

"He's OK, in small doses I guess – anyway, that's enough of him."

"I thought you'd want to see a bit of the London night life."

"Not me, I can get enough of that at home ... if I want to, that is."

"Don't you want to?" she questioned.

"Not really Mol, I'd rather spend my time in the Dog and Duck with you."

"You say the sweetest things."

"Do I?" he responded, unable for the moment to add anything further.

"Yes you do ... and I miss you", she suddenly blurted, and then wished she hadn't.

"I miss you too, Mol. By the way, can you recommend some good tourist sites for me to see tomorrow morning? I have a few hours to kill", he said, trying to lighten the conversation.

"Er, let me see, Buckingham Palace, Big Ben, the Houses of Parliament, Trafalgar Square, but watch out for the pigeons, especially if you're wearing nice clothes, if you get my drift."

"I think I need you here to be my guide Mol. You know you're good at it."

"Are you serious?" she asked, unsure of whether he was making a joke or not.

"I'd love you to Molly, but I can't ask you to come all the way to London just to show me a few sights, I've only got the morning free."

"I will if you want me to", she offered, almost pleadingly.

"It's not such a good idea Mol. Tell you what, let's do it together properly at another time. Better still, you be my London guide, and I'll fly you over to New York, and I'll be your guide."

"Sounds great Richard, I can't wait."

"Look, I'd better get off this phone, or I'll miss dinner."

"OK, have a nice meal, see you tomorrow evening."

"See you tomorrow, bye, take care Molly."

"Bye Richard, you take care as well", she said, wiping a tear from her cheek.

Richard pressed the off button on his mobile phone, and replaced it inside his pocket. "Gee, it was good to hear her voice", he reflected. The American momentarily paused, as if in a trance, and then, with a shake of his head, added: "Time for dinner, I'm starving." On his way to the dining room, he considered the various sightseeing excursions that Molly had suggested. "Might as well give Trafalgar Square a look", he reflected, "After all, I've been crapped on by so many people in my time, what's wrong with a few pigeons doing likewise? Besides, I'm beginning to miss my feathered friends."

Derek Arkwright, having left the confines of the Prince's Palace Hotel, had made his way to Soho. The evening was conducive to an open-air stroll. The weather, at least, had smiled on the Yorkshireman, for it was warm and dry. He was enjoying the many and varied sights that this small area of London had to offer. Derek had been to Soho a few times before, but not for some considerable time. He liked the atmosphere, and the buzz it gave him. He liked the people on the streets; they appeared larger than life, but what he really liked most of all was the sex, and there was plenty of that. Soho is to sex what smoke is to fire, and Derek intended to get himself burned. First, he walked along one street, gazing into shop windows as he passed, occasionally going inside to browse; then he'd walk along another, and do the same; finally, when he had covered the entire patchwork of streets and alleys, he commenced the procedure all over again.

About a third of the way into the second lap something caught Derek's eye; he paused on the pavement and studied a notice attached to a partially open black wooden door.

Suddenly a very large man, of the intimidating variety, appeared in the doorway.

"Lots of lovely girls, all strutting their stuff, specially just for you sir", said the neanderthal-type person, apparently addressing Derek.

"Really", replied the Yorkshireman.

"Only £5, and the show is about to start, you can't afford to miss it, can you sir?"

Derek did not believe for one minute that the girls would be strutting their stuff especially just for him, but for a fiver he wouldn't mind sharing the view. He took a five-pound note from his pocket, and placed it into the already outstretched hand of the big guy. Without offering a thank you, the recipient stuffed the note into his back trouser pocket. "Follow me." The doorman gestured towards Derek to follow, but instead of entering the aperture previously obscured by his body, he strode off along the pavement in the direction from whence the Yorkshireman previously came.

"Where are we going?" inquired a worried Derek.

"Just follow me, sir", replied the man in front, responding in such a manner as to deny the one behind any possibility of further confrontation.

Derek, on his previous excursions to Soho, had always been amongst a group of people. He had, on those occasions, attended such shows as those staged by the world-renowned Raymond's Revue Bar, and had thoroughly enjoyed the experience. This time things were different.

"Here we are, sir." They had arrived at another door, also black, some two-hundred-and-fifty yards away from the first. "The show's just about to start, in you go."

"Thanks", came a slightly nervous reply. He entered the doorway and proceeded to walk along a dimly lit hallway. After a few yards it curved. He could hear a female voice. Derek continued walking, when suddenly, he found himself confronted by a marginally overweight, dark-skinned woman, aged about thirty, sitting at a desk wearing little more than a pair of high heels, briefs, and a smile.

"Good evening sir, come to see the show have we?"

Derek looked around, as far as he could see there was no 'we', only he.

"Yes, that's right."

"Good, that'll be £10."

"What! I paid the other guy £5."

"That was an introduction fee sir. If you want to see the lovely girls, it'll cost you £10 to get in."

Derek stared at the woman's naked breasts: "All right, here's the tenner."

"Thank you, enjoy the show."

Encouraged by the sight of naked flesh, the man from the North scurried through what he hoped would be the final doorway.

"Table for one, sir?" said another girl, similarly dressed to the one who had greeted him a few moments earlier.

"Er, yes, please", replied the Yorkshireman, unable to take his eyes of the young lady's chest. He followed the girl to a *small* table, situated in one corner very close to a *small* stage. "Brilliant", he thought, "I'll get a good view here."

"Drink?"

"Yes please, I'll have a pint of lager." Derek watched the waitress's bottom as she walked off to fetch the beer. "Very nice", he murmured.

As soon as the bottom disappeared from view, Derek turned his attentions to the establishment that he found himself in. The table and stage were in direct proportion to the venue – small. Of the nine tables Derek counted, only two were occupied, his own and one other. A group of five men were huddled around the other table, chatting noisily. 'Dancing Queen' by Abba could be heard emitting from a sound system reminiscent of the one on Leeds railway station that he had been audibly witness to earlier that day. The room was dimly lit, only slightly brighter than the hallway outside. Red nicotine-stained flock wallpaper adorned the walls. The stage was in darkness. Red velvet curtains were hanging on both sides of the stage, and as a backdrop. They also had seen better days. "What a dump", thought Derek, "Never mind, I haven't come to buy the place." His eyes brightened as the waitress approached with the lager.

"That's ten pounds please", she said, placing the glass on the table.

"What!"

"Ten pounds."

"For one pint, you've got to be kidding", he protested.

"I'm not kidding, it's ten pounds."

"Take it back, I'm not paying."

"You ordered a drink, so bloody well pay up."

"Don't you swear at me, and no, I'm not paying ten pounds for a pint of watered-down bat's piss."

The woman who had taken Derek's ten pounds at the door approached. "What's the trouble, Susan?"

"It's this tight-fisted Yorkshire git, he's refusing to pay for his drink", the waitress replied.

"Oi, who are you calling a tight-fisted Yorkshire git, you cockney tart?"

"Now come on sir, that's no way to speak to a lady. Just pay for your drink, and then we can start the show", intervened the dark-skinned woman.

Over on the other occupied table, the five men sat in silence, huddled even closer together.

"Look, I've told you already, I'm not paying ten pounds for one lousy pint, got it." Derek stood up in preparation to leave.

"Just where do you think you're going?" asked the waitress aggressively.

"I'm outa here, you can stick your show", said Derek, responding likewise.

"Not til you pay for your drink", insisted the older one.

"Bollocks."

The Yorkshireman then made an attempt to leave; he didn't get very far. The waitress made a grab for Derek's jacket, caught it, held tight, and pulled back hard. As he went down, the older woman lashed out her right leg, and with the pointed end of a stiletto, managed to make contact with his testicles. Derek lay on the floor writhing in pain, making groaning noises, and clutching his groin area.

"Ten pounds, please, sir."

Derek removed one hand from his family jewels, reached into his back trouser pocket and took out a ten pound note. The waitress bent down and relieved him of it.

"Now sod off, and don't come back", ordered the older woman.

The Yorkshireman gingerly rose to his feet.

"Don't forget your drink", suggested the waitress.

"You can have it", he retaliated.

"No, you have it", said the waitress, picking up the glass and throwing it in his face.

The five men on the other table huddled yet closer.

"Go on, piss off, go back home to your mummy, and don't ever come back", stated the older woman, with authority.

Derek left the premises, head bowed and soaking wet. He had terrible pain in his crotch. Once outside, his pace quickened; he seemed determined to put some distance between himself and that hell-hole he had just vacated.

"Shit, I stink like a wino", he muttered, shuffling along the pavement. The Yorkshireman headed back to the hotel, pondering over recent events as he progressed: "I've just been accosted by two topless tarts, now that doesn't happen every day." This philosophical approach somehow seemed to cheer him up. His pace quickened, and his head lifted. He glanced at his watch: "Just time to get back to my room, clean myself up, and wait for the bit of skirt to arrive."

Derek had managed to enter the Prince's Palace Hotel, cross the foyer and board an empty lift without being noticed. He pressed a button for the fourth floor. "So far so good", he whispered, gazing into a mirror attached to the lift's rear wall. "Jesus … I look a mess", he said, upon realising what the reflection actually looked like.

At the appropriate floor, the lift stopped and the doors opened. "I hope no-one's waiting to get on." He vacated the lift with caution; the last person he wanted to bump into was his American colleague. Derek moved along the hall with speed; exceptional agility considering recent events, namely a swift kick to the scrotum. "Where's my bloody key?" Fortunately for him, the key had remained in his back trouser pocket, where it had been placed earlier. "Ha-ha, got it", he announced, obviously relieved that it had not departed his person at the scene of the fracas. He opened the door and went inside, quickly closing it behind him. "Phew, made it."

Derek went into the bathroom and turned on the shower. He then removed his clothes. "What a stink", he proclaimed, summing up with one phrase the state of his clothes and body. "I need a drink." He picked up his wet, beer-sodden clothes, and walked over to the wardrobe. "There, that's got rid of 'em", he said, stuffing them inside and closing the doors. The Yorkshireman then ventured over to where the mini-bar was situated and took out a bottle of lager. After removing the top with his teeth, he proceeded to drink its contents direct from the bottle. "God I needed that", he said, belching loudly. The naked man raised the bottle once more to his mouth, finished off the remaining liquid, and tossed the empty vessel into the waste-bin provided. "Good shot! Right, time for a shower, and I'd better give you an extra good scrub", he chuckled, looking downwards, apparently addressing his bare appendage.

Approximately forty-five minutes later a knock sounded on the door. During that time, Derek had showered, consumed two more bottles of lager from the mini-bar, and ensconced himself on the bed, waiting with eager anticipation. He was wearing a Japanese-style kimono dressing gown, which had been purchased for him, by him, as a birthday present that year. Derek Arkwright had prepared himself well; hair combed, teeth brushed, after-shave applied. The moment of truth had arrived. He leapt off the bed and made a move towards the door. "I hope I'm up for it", he said, hesitating for a moment. "Well, here goes." He gingerly opened the door.

"Hello, I'm Divine."

"I can see you are, come in."

"My name is *Divine*, silly."

"Oh I see, Divine by name, and divine by nature."

The young lady entered the room at the kimono-wearing man's request.

"You look very sexy", commented Divine, in a rather husky, sultry voice.

"Thank you ... you look *and* sound rather sexy yourself."

"Thank you, it's nice of you to notice."

"Can I get you a drink?"

"It's your time, sweetheart, we can spend it how you like", she answered, sitting down on the bed.

"What would you like?" he asked, opening up the mini-bar once more.

"Red wine, if you've got it."

Derek did indeed have red wine, it came in its own tiny bottle, priced six pounds.

"Bugger it", thought the Yorkshireman, "Expenses will cover it." He poured the wine into a glass and handed it to the girl.

"You're not nervous are you, sweetie?" she said, noticing Derek's hand trembling when the glass was taken.

"I am a little", he confessed.

"You don't have to be, not with me", she said, reaching out and touching his leg. "Just relax, I'm here to give you a good time."

"I hope that includes sex", he suddenly blurted.

"My God, you're a fast one."

"I'm from Yorkshire, blunt and to the point. Besides, time is money and I know your meter is running."

"In that case, what do you want?"

"The full works, darlin' … if I'm up to it that is … if you know what I mean", he replied, whilst visually admiring the young woman's body.

Divine, which in all probability was not her real name, did indeed try exceptionally hard to live up to her chosen handle. Aged about thirty, she had long auburn hair; a heavily made-up yet attractive face, her lipstick bright red. Her clothing looked expensive; a white translucent blouse covered her ample chest; a lace bra exciting the client.

"I bet she's wearing stockings", thought the man wearing the kimono. "Jesus, I'm horny", he added, getting aroused.

The escort's pencil skirt, hemline about two inches above the knee, revealed her long slender legs. She wore black patent-leather high-heeled shoes. "That'll be £250, all inclusive, sweetie. Cash or credit card, no cheque."

Derek Arkwright was beyond the point of no return: "American Express?"

"That'll do nicely", she said, leaning forward and placing a kiss on his right cheek.

The client handed over the card, and Divine organised the transaction. Meanwhile, Derek had removed his dressing gown, and was now sitting up in bed. His face beamed with anticipation.

"Good boy, I see you're ready for me", she said purringly, and then proceeded to disrobe.

The naked man watched gleefully as Divine removed her blouse, and then her skirt.

She stood before him wearing a white lace bra, with matching panties and suspender belt.

"You look gorgeous", he enthused, adding: "I love white undies … especially with black stockings."

"Yes, it's a kind of cross between the virtuous and the wicked", she replied.

"Exactly, come and get into bed … now."

She crossed the floor and got into bed alongside Derek, as he had ordered. She then leaned over him and kissed him passionately, fully on the lips. Her mouth opened, and Derek responded likewise. Their tongues touched; his excitement grew. Her hand went down in between the bedclothes. He writhed in ecstasy as her hand caressed intimate parts of his anatomy.

"Oh God, this is great", moaned the client.

"I hope you like it?"

"Like it, I love it!" His hand went in search of her breasts, he found one of them, and firmly squeezed the bra that contained the soft mound. Derek Arkwright could contain himself no longer; he had gone ten months without the carnal pleasure of female company. His hand disappeared down the bed linen; he gently stroked her stomach. Arkwright's hand progressed further downwards. He expertly guided the digits inside her silken undergarment.

"What the f … !" Derek never finished the expletive, for he leapt out of bed in apparent horror, and ran to the bathroom.

"What's the matter, sugar?" inquired the escort.

The violent sound of someone vomiting could be heard coming from the bathroom. "You did know, didn't you?"she asked.

"*No I didn't know*, you freaking freak", he echoed, his head still directed inside the lavatory bowl.

"You booked me, darling."

"No I sodding didn't … I booked a woman … that is, one without meat-and-two-veg."

He heaved once more into the bowl.

"Darling, I only advertise in TV magazines, you must have known?"

"No I bloody didn't", he screamed, still gagging, "And stop calling me darling, you *dirty rotten poof.*"

"There's no need to be like that you know, it's not my fault", *she* replied, sounding hurt.

"Well, it certainly isn't my *bloody* fault that you're a *bloody* man." Derek remained in the bathroom, too embarrassed to exit.

"If you're going to be like that I'm leaving."

"Sod off then, I don't want you here anyway, I'm *straight*, I am."

Divine put on *her* clothes and left; slamming the door as she did so.

"Oi, what about my money, I want a *bleeding* refund."

Too late, the escort had gone. Derek, who had hopefully finished yodelling into the toilet, got up and turned on the shower. "Shit, shit, shit!" he groaned, trying hard not to think of what had just transpired. He climbed into the bath, stood underneath the shower, and allowed the warm running water to cleanse his body. "Shit, shit, shit!" he said again. He took a bar of complimentary soap and commenced scrubbing his soiled flesh. "I must have picked up the wrong bloody mag in the newsagents", he snarled. "I suppose it serves me right for not buying the bloody thing."

Derek had hastily glanced through an adult-themed magazine, looking for a suitable advertisement; memorising the telephone number he had placed the mag back on the top shelf; quickly departing the newsagents.

"Shit, shit, shit! What a bloody night." He continued scrubbing.

At 7.00 a.m. the following morning Richard awoke. He had not booked an early morning alarm call. He had gone to bed quite early the previous evening, having enjoyed his meal and a bottle of good red wine. An early night and a good night's sleep had left him refreshed. He got out of bed and walked over to the window, drawing back the curtains. "My God, what a lovely morning."

The sun was indeed shining; still low in the sky, it created a bright haze across the landscape. Not that much of a landscape could be viewed from this particular window, for it looked down onto a narrow side street. This did not seem to bother our hero, for as far as he was concerned the sun shone, making the sky bright blue, and today was Friday; meaning he would be seeing Molly later that evening. He looked out of the window: "What, no pigeons?"

Glad not to be sharing a bathroom, he crossed over to it and turned on the shower. "A good night's sleep has done me the world of good", he stated, squeezing toothpaste onto a brush. "Mind you", he continued, looking into the mirror above the sink, "I did hear a commotion coming from the room next door … sounded like someone throwing-up and then a lot of shouting." He vigorously brushed his teeth and spat out the residue. Looking into the mirror once again, he said: "Hey! That's Derek's room …" Richard paused for a moment: "Na … I probably just dreamed it, just wishful thinking I guess, I couldn't be that lucky … the thought of Derek's head spending half the night down a lavatory pan … na … I couldn't be that lucky."

Some twenty minutes later, the American emerged from the bathroom, all ablutionary tasks, including shaving, completed. He was dressed and ready for breakfast.

"Good morning Derek", hailed Richard, upon entering the dining room and finding his colleague already seated.

"Morning", he replied, rather grumpily.

"Everything all right?"

"Bad night, didn't get much sleep."

"Well you're up and about nice and early."

"Starving, didn't get anything to eat last night."

"Oh I see … may I join you?"

"Yeah sure", answered Derek, scoffing into yet another piece of toast.

The American sat down, and as he did so, a waitress approached the table.

"Coffee and toast please."

"Certainly sir. If you require a full breakfast, you'll find it over there", she offered, pointing towards the self-service area.

"Thanks."

"Did you have a good night?" asked Richard, more out of politeness than curiosity.

"Fine", Derek replied, not wishing to elaborate. He then gestured to a passing waiter: "'Scuse me."

"Yes sir."

"More tea please … and toast."

"Yes sir." The waiter departed, leaving the two of them alone together.

"Are you sure you're all right?"

"Yes, I'm fine, just a bit stressed. I'll be OK … or I will be, if I ever get the tea and toast I asked for", he snapped.

Richard, sensing that something was not quite right with his friend, then said: "Fancy coming for a walk with me after breakfast, take in a few sights?"

"Seen 'em already." Derek, sensing that something he said may have offended his friend, added: "I mean, no thanks Richard … I've got some work to do, you go, and have a good time. I'll catch up with you later." He then rose from his seat in preparation to leave.

"Aren't you going to wait for your toast?"

"I'm not hungry now, see you later."

"Bye, see you later, twelve o'clock here, for lunch."

"OK." The Yorkshireman then left, no longer hungry, having eaten six rounds of toast, a bowl of cereal, two fried eggs, three sausages, four rashers of bacon, and two pieces of fried bread.

Richard stayed in the dining room awaiting his toast and coffee. It soon arrived. He ate the toast, and drank two cups of the beverage that had been provided. "That's enough for me", he declared, rising from the table. "Time to explore a little of this City." His first port of call was to be the hotel's reception; he needed directions to Trafalgar Square.

"Can I help you sir?"

"I sure hope so, I need to walk off breakfast, so I'm looking for directions to Trafalgar, I understand it isn't far?"

"It is, if you mean where the battle took place", said the receptionist, smiling.

"Er no … I'm looking for Nelson's Column?"

She resisted the obvious answer. "I can do better than that", she said, picking up a leaflet and opening it up on the counter, to reveal a map. "And you're right, it isn't too far." The receptionist, using her finger, guided Richard to his chosen destination.

"Why thank you, ma'am", he said, trying hard to remember the route.

"You can keep the map, sir", she offered politely.

"Thank you once again", he replied with a broad smile, taking the map. Richard left the hotel still clutching the leaflet. Standing outside, he witnessed the usual hustle and bustle of daily life in the city. He looked up towards the sky, it was as before; as he had first seen it that morning, clear blue. Although the day had not yet had time to warm to it's full potential, it was ideally suitable for Richard's excursion. "Right then, before I get started, time to take another quick look at the map."

He found his way the short distance to Regent Street and turned left; he continued walking until he arrived at Pall Mall. "Time to check directions", he uttered, unfolding the shiny piece of paper given to him at reception. "Ah ha, turn left again." Richard continued his route, taking in the various sights that caught his eye. He particularly enjoyed people-watching. There existed nowhere in the world quite like a big cosmopolitan city to illustrate such variation as can be found in the human being; except perhaps for a craft fair.

An all-too-familiar sound could be heard in the distance: coo … coo, coo … coo, coo … coo.

"I must be near", he thought, and then suddenly caught sight of Nelson's Column. He was indeed closing on the object of that morning's expedition; a few more paces and he arrived at Trafalgar Square. And there, standing tall and proud, was the statue of Admiral Nelson, perched high on his column. However, there were several pigeons perched on him.

"Impressive", stated the visitor, referring to the man-made structure, and not the mess made by the birds. He took time to take in the obvious scenery, but also took time to explore the ambience of where he stood. A sense of history shivered down his spine; it felt reminiscent of his own sense of history; his family background. "Gee, this is great", Richard said to himself, and then suddenly, a pigeon landed on his head.

"Hold it and smile", said a middle-aged man, holding a Polaroid camera and pointing it at the American.

The visitor dutifully smiled; the man clicked his camera, adding: "I can see you haven't got a camera with you, pity not to catch the moment."

"Ah, but I can see that *you have*", retorted the part-time tourist.

"Makes a wonderful memento you know … of your visit … something to show the family back home." The man handed Richard the now fully developed, almost instant photo.

"Thanks", said the American, waiting for the rub.

"That'll be ten pounds, if you please, sir."

He parted with the fee without fuss; thinking: "I'll give this to Molly tonight, should amuse her."

The cameraman greeted the ten-pound note like an old lost friend, said thanks, and then moved off into the crowd. The pigeon did likewise.

"Time for a boat trip", he said, looking at his watch. Richard briefly consulted the map. "OK, got it, another short walk, and I can sight-see from the river."

His reference to the river was of course, the Thames, a derivative of an old English word, 'thame', meaning river. The Romans, not happy with calling a river 'a river', renamed it 'Isis' after the Egyptian god. This resulted in it being known as Thame Isis, which in time became Thamesis, and eventually Thames. Richard had gleaned this information from the leaflet, and was reading it as he crossed the square and entered Northumberland Avenue. At the end of the avenue he turned left onto Victoria Embankment; a few yards further brought him to Charing Cross Pier. "Made it just in time", he said, upon seeing a River Bus about to depart.

Chapter 10

"I have a Derek Arkwright on the line, calling from England; he wishes to speak with you."

"Thanks Stephanie, put him through."

"Putting you through, Mr. Arkwright", replied Ernest Grabit's capable secretary, or as she preferred to be called, his personal assistant.

"Hello, Mr. Grabit, it's Derek Arkwright …"

"I know who you are, and to what do I owe this dubious pleasure?"

"Well … I don't know quite how to … er … um …"

"Spit it out man, time is money."

"I'm a bit concerned about … well, it's Richard."

"And what about *him*?" demanded Grabit, leaning forward in his leather, high-backed, executive chair.

"I'm not sure that he's entirely focused."

"Care to elaborate?"

"He's met someone … a girl."

"And how's that affecting his performance?"

"As yet … probably very little … I thought it best that you were informed, that's all … keep you up-to-date, forewarned is forearmed, that's all."

"Thank you Derek, I appreciate your concern, anything else?"

"We're meeting with the landowner this afternoon."

"Yes I know, good luck."

"I also understand that a presentation is being prepared for the planners?"

"That's correct."

"If I can be of any service with that, I am local to the area … and I have an understanding with the Head Planning Officer, having had dealings with him before", he explained, colourfully exaggerating his previous involvement.

"That's very useful to know, I'll bear that in mind."

"Thank you Mr. Grabit."

"No, thank you, Mr. Arkwright. Let me know if you are experiencing any further concerns … be vigilant … there's a lot at stake."

"Oh, I realise that sir, and yes I will, be vigilant that is; thanks for taking the time to listen", answered the man at the European end of the telephone exchange, doing his utmost best to suck up to Ernest Grabit.

"Good man", replied the New York lawyer, replacing the receiver.

"Stephanie."

"Yes Mr. Grabit."

"What do we know about Arkwright?"

The personal assistant left the confines of the outer office, and entered the one occupied by her boss. "He was very useful to the firm a few years ago, on the Docklands project in London."

"Ah yes, I remember, that was one of Peter's", he said, referring to his partner, Peter Hadim.

"That's right, sir."

"Anything else about our English friend?"

"Although he originated from Yorkshire, he lived and worked in London at the time."

"Doing what?"

"Worked for a property developer, as I recall, I'll go and get the file if you like."

"Yes, Stephanie, I would like that … Oh and bring me a cup of coffee at the same time, will you?"

"Yes Mr. Grabit", she obligingly replied, turning on her heels and leaving her boss to his thoughts.

"That was a job well done, I think I suitably impressed the old goat'", verbalised the would-be-born-again-Yorkshire-yuppie, shortly after ending his telephone call to the Big Apple. "A few seeds of doubt regarding the Yank; sowing a few more about my worth to the operation. A good morning's work."

Derek then began to sing a few words from a song that in all reality had escaped him.

He could only manage to repeat the following words: " ♪ The only way is up, Oh baby."

"Why thank you, Stephanie", said Ernest Grabit, taking a cup of coffee from her.

"I've brought you the file you asked for."

"Good girl", he responded, as she laid it on his desk.

"Is that all sir?"

"It is for now."

Stephanie smiled, turned away, and left the office, to once again resume her secretarial, or as she preferred to call it, personal assistant duties.

"Now let me see what we've got on the Englishman." The New Yorker opened the file and commenced perusing. "He certainly seems to have all the hallmarks of someone ideally suited to property development'", whispered the lawyer to himself, adding: "Aggression, tenacity, ruthlessness, could almost fit the bill for a career in the legal profession."

The file confirmed the information previously given to him by his secretar … sorry, personal assistant. Arkwright had worked for them in the late 1980s on a London Docklands development. His contacts had proved to be extremely useful in securing the project; it had however transpired that, due to the property market's decline soon after, Derek Arkwright had left the previously prosperous capital, and returned home to Yorkshire. It was to this end that he had once again been engaged in the employ of Hadim Gotcha & Grabit Inc.

"Mmmm, could be useful", expressed Grabit, leaning on the red leather inlaid oak desk, rubbing his chin.

Richard had enjoyed his boat trip on the Thames, taking in such sights as the Houses of Parliament and Big Ben, but now the time had arrived for more serious matters; it was time to liaise with Derek Arkwright. He had checked out of his room prior to breakfast that morning, leaving his luggage downstairs. Reservations for lunch had been made for both Derek and himself at that same time. The American had chosen to wear casual attire that morning, which had not only suited his earlier activities, but was also considered to be more appropriate to greet Hugo Oldsworth later that day.

"Twelve o'clock on-the-dot, and no sign of Arkwright", thought Richard, as he entered the Prince's Palace's dining room, taking a good look around. "Time to wash-up before lunch", he said, making a move to exit the food-serving hall.

"Three minutes past twelve, and no sign of the Yank'", muted Derek, upon entering the dining room, and almost colliding with a waiter.

"Ah, there you are Derek … did you get your work done?" asked the Yank, re-entering the dining room.

"Sorry?"

"You said earlier, that you had some work to do this morning."

"Er … yes, I think I achieved quite a bit", replied a hesitant Arkwright.

The American, not altogether understanding his colleague's comments, nodded as if in agreement. "Time for lunch, the fresh air has given me an appetite."

"I'm not really that hungry", replied the man from the north, still full from breakfast, and lacking in exercise.

"Does that mean you don't wish to eat? Because I need to discuss this afternoon's meet with you."

"Perhaps a light lunch, then", answered the Yorkshireman reluctantly.

"Table for two, sir?"

"Yes please, I reserved one this morning … in the name of Waters."

"Smoking or non-smoking?"

"Non-smoking."

"Follow me, gents", acknowledged the waiter.

They followed as requested; no words were spoken.

"Here we are gents", offered the staff member, pulling out a chair.

"Thanks", said the Yorkshireman, quick to sit on it.

Before the waiter had opportunity to make available a similar gesture of good service, Richard had dispensed with such formality and seated himself. "Thank you", he said, smiling in response to the waiter's assistance.

After lunch orders had been taken, the American settled down to brief his business companion on the agenda for that afternoon's meeting with Hugo Oldsworth.

"So let me get this straight … I am allowed to be in attendance this afternoon?"

"Of course you are Derek, you're the one with the experience … when it comes to property dealing."

"Is that why I'm the one wearing a suit, and you're all casual-like?"

"You certainly look the part", replied the American, wishing he could have substituted the word part for something else.

"Do you intend on changing after lunch?"

"No, I thought a more casual approach might be less intimidating to someone like Oldsworth."

"We British have certain standards to uphold, you know", quipped the Anglo Saxon, sarcastically.

"I'm sure your very expensive suit will impress Mr. Oldsworth, might even make him hold out for more money", registered the lawyer; turning from defence to attack.

"Bugger it, it's too late to change now", thought Arkwright, before adding: "Leave it to me Richard, the old Arkwright magic will win the day."

The meals arrived at that point, thereby avoiding any further constraints from being attached to their already dwindling relationship.

"So what can we go up to?" asked the Brit, proceeding to shovel a forkful of omelette into his gaping mouth.

"Good question. The answer is not so simple, however."

"Got ya, I'll rephrase the question: how much are you prepared to go up to?"

"Let's put it this way, anything under three million and that's a bonus, anything over that figure, and up to double it, and we're on a winner", he answered, trying hard not to be put off by Derek's eating habits.

"Pounds or dollars?"

"Pounds, sterling."

"Two thousand acres of moorland, and not particularly good sheep grazing at that; in this climate, £3,000,000 tops, I'd say."

"I agree with you, the only problem is, will Hugo Oldsworth?"

"It's our job to see that he does", argued Arkwright, wiping away a piece of egg with the back of his hand; apparently it was glued to his chin.

"And the secret is not to divulge the intended purpose."

"That would put the price up, all right", acknowledged the suit-wearing individual.

"Oldsworth is keen to get rid of the farm, we mustn't lose sight of that", concluded Richard.

The remainder of the meal was conducted mostly in silence, apart from an occasional belch emitting from the Yorkshireman's side of the table, much to the annoyance of Richard and other nearby surrounding guests.

"Burrrrp, sorry about that Richard, I think it's something I ate at breakfast."

"I think it could have been *all* you ate at breakfast."

"Could well be ... burrrp, sorry, burrp."

"If you're ready, that is, if you've finished eating ..."

"I've finished, burrrp."

"Good, I'll settle the lunch bill, I suggest you go in search of an indigestion remedy."

"Burrp, good idea."

"I'll meet you in reception, Oh by the way, it's OK to leave our bags here, and collect them later."

"Burrp, fine, burrrp."

"Nearly finished."

"Good, my back is killing me", moaned Sophie to the artist.

"You're always complaining", he jibed.

"No I'm not", she pouted in protest. "Anyway, what's this meeting about, you know, the one this afternoon?"

"I'm not going to tell you, it's a surprise … well it will be … if it pays off", he chuckled, dipping a brush onto his hand-held palette.

"Oh go on, tell me, please", she begged.

"No, I don't wish to count my sheep until they're hatched."

"Don't you mean chickens?"

"Not in this case, Sophie", he replied, applying the palette-dipped brush onto the canvas.

"I'm all intrigued."

"All will be revealed in due course, speaking of which, is it cold in here, or are you just pleased to see me?"

"Don't be cheeky", she smirked, looking down towards her ample chest.

"I wouldn't dream of it", retaliated Hugo, "Anyway, when these chaps arrive you can offer then a drink, then make yourself scarce."

"What, just offer them a drink, not make it then?"

"Now you're being silly, I mean make them one of course … and keep still."

"*Yes sir.*"

The time was almost two p.m.; a taxi pulled up outside a large, grey-bricked building, circa 1930, which contained the artist's studio. As in much of the area, a form of urban modernisation had taken place. Converted from a clothes manufacturing factory some twenty years ago, the building now housed various office suites and other small enterprises; one of which was about to receive a visit from a man representing the firm of Hadim Gotcha & Grabit Inc.

"That's the one", said Derek, pointing to a brown door with the number seven on it.

"Good, give it a knock then."

The man in the suit dutifully obliged: 'knock knock', he hammered. Richard resisted a further reference to any 'knock knock' jokes, and awaited a response to the physical announcement of their arrival.

"Hello", announced Hugo, holding the door wide open.

"Mr. Oldsworth?" inquired Derek, "I'm Derek Arkwright – we spoke on the phone – and this is Richard Waters."

"Well, don't just stand there, come in."

"Pleased to meet you, Mr. Oldsworth", offered the lawyer.

"Call me Hugo."

They followed the artist into the studio.

"This is Sophie, she models for me."

"I bet she does", thought Arkwright, admiring her visible form through the silken material of her dressing gown.

"Hi there", greeted the American.

"Hello", leered the Yorkshireman.

"Can I get you a drink, tea, coffee, something stronger?"

Derek was about to open his mouth to utter 'something stronger', when Richard intervened: "Coffee please, white … no sugar."

"Tea please, milk and three sugars", informed Arkwright reluctantly.

"You can have a 'drink drink', if you prefer, it might loosen your wallet", teased Hugo, watching Sophie disappear out of earshot.

"That's what I'm afraid of", laughed the lawyer.

"I'll go and give Sophie a hand, shall I?" offered Derek.

"Good idea", replied Hugo. "But don't mention why you're here", he added quietly.

"Mum's the word", whispered the Yorkshireman, heading off to the kitchen area, keen to assist.

"How long have you been an artist?" asked the American.

"Professionally, I'd say about ten years, as for making a living, well let's say I get by."

"By the look of some of these paintings", he said, looking around the studio, "I'd have thought they'd fetch a tidy sum."

"They do, that is, they do now, and have done for a couple of years; the trouble is, it takes too long to produce a decent painting. Not time efficient I'm afraid."

"Ah … I see", sympathised the listener.

"Then there's the parasites", continued Hugo.

"Ah … art dealers."

"Exactly."

"Tea's up, or coffee, in your case, Richard", said a jubilant-sounding Derek, entering the studio section.

"Thanks", said Richard, taking a mug from his colleague's left hand.

"Cheers", said Hugo, taking a mug from his other hand.

Sophie arrived, carrying a mug of tea, and handed it to her helper.

"Thank you", he said, taking the beverage, and smiling.

"Right I'm off, nice to have met you", she said, putting on a coat directly over her dressing gown.

"Bye, nice to have met you", leered Derek once again.

"He's making it a bit too obvious", thought Richard, regarding the close attention being administered by Arkwright towards Sophie, "If he blows it, I'll kill him."

Sophie opened the door to leave.

"Goodbye, thanks for the drink", said the American.

"Cheerio Sophie, see you later."

"Bye Hugo, bye everyone", she beamed, closing the door behind her.

"Does she always go out dressed like *that*?" probed the Yorkshireman.

"Another assignment", replied the artist, before adding: "Let's get down to business."

Accepting Oldsworth's invitation to make themselves comfortable, they each took a seat. Derek chose to sit on the chaise longue, leaving Richard with another model's prop, namely a stool; a tall one of the public bar variety. Hugo sat himself down upon an upturned plastic milk crate.

"Bit short of seats", he apologised, turning towards the American, "Now let's get down to the nitty-gritty. How much have you come to offer me?"

"We're taking about the entire farm, including the house."

"I gathered that, how much?"

"What would you expect to get for it?"

"As much as possible."

"You must have an idea how much the farm is worth?"

"Yes I do, I've had it valued."

"I see, you want me to start by offering you a figure, and then we can juggle?"

"Let's put it this way, you offer me a sum for the farm, and we'll discuss it upwards from there, or I'll give you an amount and we can negotiate it downwards, hopefully arriving at a set of digits that'll suit us both, what say you?"

"Well … what I say is, that from where I'm sitting, you don't appear to have lost any of your native Yorkshire monetary skills."

"Good observation laddie, especially for a foreigner."

"'Tis true I've only been in this country for a short while, but your Yorkshire countryman's reputation precedes itself."

"Good, I'm glad to hear it, now … where are we going to start?"

Richard took out his wallet, and removed a business card, handing it to the artist he said: "This is the firm I represent, we're acting on behalf of a group of property speculators. They're looking to buy land in this country, and elsewhere, for development growth in the longer term. Money *is* on the table, but if it isn't your land, then it would be someone else's, get my drift?"

Hugo thought for a moment; Derek kept quiet, he recognised the tactics being employed by his colleague. A pregnant pause was being observed. It was up to Hugo to break the silence; he did: "Go on then, bottom line, give it to me straight."

"£2,000,000."

Hugo thought briefly. He could hold out for more, but remembered what his late father had often said: "A sheep in the hand is worth two on the moors." The thought of sheep sent shivers down the artist's spine. "Is that your best offer?"

"It's the best I can do … I'd like to raise the ante, but it's just not economically viable, not for the people I represent."

"If you want to kiss this offer goodbye, Mr. Oldsworth, go ahead and try on the open market. You might … just might, make more", interjected the previously silent Arkwright. "But remember, it could take years."

Another pregnant pause ensued.

"All right, I'll take it, I hate sheep, my life is here; good riddance I say."

"Well done!" said Arkwright, jumping up to shake Oldsworth's hand.

"I'll see that a formal offer is sent to you shortly; if you wish to accept, give it to your solicitor, he or she will do the rest. Thanks for your time, Mr. Oldsworth."

"No, thank you", he gratefully replied, "and it's Hugo."

"Very nice, very nice indeed."

"Sorry?"

"The painting in the corner, is it Sophie?"

"Yes it is Derek, finished this afternoon."

"May I take a closer look?"

"Yes, now that I've finished it, be my guest."

"It's a fine painting, Hugo", remarked the lawyer.

"She's a fine-looking woman", commented Derek, his eyes taking in content, and totally ignoring composition.

"You're absolutely right Derek ….she has got a fine body."

"I don't know much about art, but I know what I like."

"If you don't mind me asking, Hugo, how much would a painting like this fetch?" Richard enquired.

"Around two thousand quid."

"Wow", replied the Yorkshireman, "that's a lot of dosh."

"Sounds a lot, I grant you."

"Not for the hours involved, I bet", indulged the American, trying to defuse a potential incendiary device from igniting.

"There's quite a lot of overheads involved as well, for example, this place, it has to be paid for", he said, gesticulating at the studio, "and there's the model fees, and of course materials."

"It all adds up", added Richard, still trying to divert the attention away from his cohort.

"And, one final thing."

"What's that, Hugo?" asked an inquisitive Derek.

"I like to try and make a profit."

"Good point."

Richard felt that this was an ideal opportunity to exit proceedings before his libidinous counterpart upset the applecart completely; as opposed to merely violently rocking it. "Come along Derek, time to leave, I'm sure Hugo has better things to do than stand here all day talking to us."

"Yes, time is money, speaking of which I'm expecting an art dealer any time now."

The 'Dynamic Duo' bade their farewell, and left Hugo to reflect on the prospect of having just become a cash millionaire.

Standing on the pavement below, they didn't have to wait long before a vacant cab pulled up in direct response to Derek's frantic arm waving.

"Where to, guv?"

"Prince's Palace Hotel, please."

"No sooner done than said, mate."

"Don't you mean, no sooner said than done?" corrected the Yorkshireman.

"Not in this traffic, mate."

The taxi slowly moved off, joining the busy stream of vehicles, all of which had somewhere to go, but were taking a long time to get there.

"Excellent job, I thought we performed well in there."

"Yes, *we* did didn't we", replied the lawyer, settling into his seat.

"Teamwork, Richard, teamwork."

"You certainly seem pleased with yourself."

"I am, we've just cracked a *very* good deal, and what about Sophie?"

"What about her?"

"Bit of all right, I'd say."

"Yes Derek, I did notice your tongue hanging out once or twice."

"What a cracker, wouldn't mind her posing for me."

"Well Derek, I think it's a good thing that we're leaving London today."

"Why's that?"

"'Cause this city is not a safe place for women, not with an amorous stud-muffin like yourself on the loose."

Derek refrained from comment, it being possible that the previous evening's events may have had a bearing on this noncommittal state.

The remainder of their journey, although convivial, consisted of little more than idle banter. Richard paid the cabbie the sum demanded, plus an expected gratuity, and then made his way into the hotel to collect his belongings; Derek followed.

"If we hurry, we can make the four o'clock train."

"Brilliant!" thought Richard, "I'll have enough time to get ready for this evening."

"I don't want to be late for Molly."

"We can take the tube, it'll be quicker at this time of day."

"You're the man Derek, lead on."

They made their way out of the hotel, and across the road to the underground. Derek briefly turned his head around, and looked back towards the Prince's Palace; he shuddered as though a shiver had crept along his spine, and then said to himself: "It'll be a cold day in hell before I stay there again."

The return journey back to Leeds went relatively smoothly, which as far as the American was concerned meant that the train went out on time, and that his travelling companion had remained congenial. Richard took time out, whilst the locomotive was in motion, to reflect on the day: it had gone well, he had enjoyed his brief sight-seeing excursion, and the meeting with Hugo Oldsworth had been a success.

Two million pounds for the farm, as a farm, was a fair price; to the people he worked for, it represented a bargain. Richard did not consider that Oldsworth was being cheated. The consortium would have been prepared to pay much more for the land, but in doing so would have paid far in excess of the market value; and it was they, after all, who carried the risk.

Derek, relieved to find the Mondeo unscathed, lifted the boot lid and placed his baggage inside. Richard did likewise.

"It's good to be home."

"I thought you liked London?"

"I did … seems to have changed though."

"We were only there for a day, what could have changed?"

"Me, I guess", replied the Yorkshireman, with a sigh.

"I'm beginning to feel that way myself, Derek."

The Mondeo drew into the Grand's car park. Richard got out and retrieved his belongings from the boot. "Thanks Derek, have a good weekend, call me Monday at ten."

"Will do … and congratulations."

"What for?"

"Securing the deal today, you did good."

"Teamwork, Derek, teamwork."

"Yeah, sure … have a good weekend, speak to you on Monday." The Yorkshireman drove off, and as he did so, the American turned away and walked towards the hotel's entrance.

"Teamwork? I'll give him teamwork", imparted Arkwright to himself, accelerating aggressively; the incident involving the cat and a milk-float merely a fading memory. "You may have performed well, Mr. Waters, but it'll be me who takes the credit." A broad grin emerged across the Yorkshireman's face; he changed down a gear and accelerated hard, swerved past a young boy of about seven who was trying to negotiate a skateboard back onto the pavement, and said: "I'm on my way back." He looked into the Mondeo's rear-view mirror; in the reflection was the same young boy, offering a one-fingered salute aimed at the disappearing Ford. "Bloody kids, they've got no respect", he said, and then started singing, "♫ The only way is up, Oh baby."

Chapter 11

Richard entered the hotel, and proceeded towards reception.

"Good evening, Mr. Waters."

"Good evening to you, may I have my room key please?"

"Certainly sir."

"Any messages?"

The receptionist retrieved the key and whilst doing so checked for messages. "None", she answered, placing the key into the guest's hand.

"Thank you", he said, taking the key.

She replied with the customary receptionist's smile. The American responded likewise, before turning away and heading directly to his room. "Better phone the office … and tell them the good news", he thought, upon entering his abode. He laid his luggage on the bed and moved over to the telephone; deliberating for a moment, he said: "I think I'll use the cellular." Richard opened up the briefcase that his father had bought for him, and took out a mobile phone. He turned it on, commenced dialling, and after a few moments could hear a ringing tone. "These things are amazing, no trouble connecting with the States, but if I tried to get through to someone just down the hall …"

His thoughts were interrupted by a voice on the other end. "Hadim Gotcha & Grabit, how may I help you?"

"Hi there Ellie, it's me, Richard."

"Hi Richard, how's it going?"

"Great, just great, I love England, especially the pubs."

"Better not tell Mr. Grabit that, he won't like it you know."

"When he gets to hear my news, he'll want to kiss me."

"You sound in a good mood."

"I am, I am."

"If you want to speak with Mr. Grabit, I'm afraid you can't, he's out of the office."

"Put me through to Rachel, will you."

"Sure thing, nice to hear from you."

"Take care, see you soon I expect." Richard held onto the receiver awaiting connection with his secretary. "Hurry up, come on, hurry!"

"Good evening, Mr. Waters. I guess it is evening there?"

"It is, and you can call me Richard, you know."

"Can I ... I mean ... is it all right? I haven't been with the firm long, and you are my boss."

"Exactly, I'm your boss, so please call me by my first name unless protocol dictates otherwise, OK?"

"OK Richard, what can I do for you?"

"Good girl, that's better. Can you relay a message to Mr. Grabit for me?"

"Go ahead."

"Tell him I've agreed a price of £2,000,000, that's pounds, not dollars."

"Will do Richard, that should please him."

"We can only hope, Rachel, we can only hope. I'll fax a full report first thing Monday morning."

"OK Richard, I'll tell him. Good luck, and have a nice weekend."

"Same to you Rachel, bye for now."

"Bye."

Richard pressed the 'call end' button on the cellular phone, and entered a fresh set of digits. "I wonder how clear the reception will be this time", he cynically whispered to himself, upon hearing a broken ringing tone.

"Hello, Dog and Du ..."

"Shit." The American redialled.

"Dog and Duck, can I help yo ..."

"Shit, shit, shit", he said, in response to getting cut off for a second time. "Bloody mobile phones, I'd have more luck trying to have a One 2 One with Elvis." He threw the redundant piece of modern technology onto the bed in apparent disgust, went over to where the land phone rested, and picked up the handset, pressing 9 for an outside line.

"Hello, Dog and Duck."

"Can I speak to Miss Weston, please?"

"Evenin' Mr. Waters, I understand we have the pleasure of your company a bit later?"

"Right first time; how are you, Bill?"

"Getting' by you know, makin' a shillin'."

"Glad to hear it, Bill", he replied, slightly bemused by Bill's lack of g's.

"Molly's not here right now, she's popped out for a while."

"Can you give her a message?"

"Of course I can, bye then, see you later."

"Whoa, hold up, I haven't given you the message yet."

"Oh I see, I thought that was it, you know, that you telephoned like."

"Just tell her I'll be over a bit earlier, about eight."

"OK, is that it?"

"Yeah, that's it."

"OK, I'll tell her."

"Bye for now, Bill."

"Goodbye."

A sudden click and the telephone had gone dead.

Richard, having showered and dressed, was once more reunited with the Cherokee. Seated behind the steering wheel, he reversed the 4X4 out of its tarmac resting space, and slowly manoeuvred it towards the hotel's exit. "I'm getting the hang of it", he said confidently. "Must remember to drive on the left, though." The American was indeed getting the hang of it; handling the vehicle like a veteran, he soon left the bright city lights behind him; he particularly liked the positional view that the 4X4 gave him. Sighting a filling station in the distance, he suddenly uttered: "I wonder if I can get some flowers for Molly? Gas stations are great places to get most things these days."

Richard pulled into the petrol station and parked to one side, away from the pumps.

He entered the shop and looked around; sure enough, there appeared for sale every non-motoring consumer durable known to man. It was possible to purchase a barbecue, kindling to light a fire, household coal to lay on top, rent a video, microwave a hamburger, choose between a selection of contraceptive devices and a plethora of cuddly toys. The selection seemed endless. He picked up a bunch of soon-to-be-wilting flowers, approached the counter, smiled at the person on the other side of it, and said: "What's the chance of getting a broken-down vehicle fixed here?"

"None whatsoever mate, but I know a man who can, you need to phone the AA."

"Thought so", replied the visitor, placing the flowers on the plinth.

Seated once more behind the jeep's steering wheel, and almost upon the Dog and Duck, he noticed the flowers lying on the passenger seat beside him. "Jesus!" he uttered in alarm, "They're dying in front of me." The off-roader turned into the car park adjoining the inn; peering around, he murmured to himself: "Busy tonight." The American parked the vehicle, picked up the flowers, looked hard at them, and pondered for a moment before throwing the bunch back onto the seat. "Oh well, it's the thought that counts; at least I've got the photo." He was, of course, referring to the Polaroid taken earlier that day. However, whether a photograph of himself with a pigeon sitting on his head would adequately console the lovely Molly in the absence of a bouquet, only time would reveal. "Bugger it, I should have bought chocolates."

"Way up there lad", greeted Albert, to the man who had just entered the bar.

"Hi there Albert, how're ya doin'?"

"Reet fine my boy … come to buy a packet of crisps for Jake, have thee?"

Richard stared at the dog standing by the Yorkshireman's left leg. "He could do with fattening up a bit."

"Aye, he could that … and mine's a pint", he said, draining the dregs from his glass, and planting it firmly onto the counter.

"Evenin' young man, what can I get you?"

"Pint of bitter, whatever Albert's drinking, and a packet of chips for Jake please, Bill."

"Badger's all right?"

"Yeah, do just fine Bill."

"What flavour crisps?"

"Rabbit, I expect", replied the American, his eyes focused on the canine below. Jake's tail wagged in anticipation; he had never eaten rabbit-flavoured crisps before, and was looking forward to the experience.

"You gotta friend for life there now, young fella."

"I guess I have, Albert", responded the newcomer, acknowledging the whippet's nose as it pressed firmly into his crotch.

The bartender leaned forward, and with one open hand shielding his speech from the pre-shrunken greyhound, whispered: "I've only got chicken, but don't let on, he'll never know the difference."

"I ain't gonna tell if you don't", answered Richard, with a grin.

Bill opened up a packet of the pseudo rabbit-flavoured snack, poured the contents into a clean ashtray, and handed it to the Yorkshireman.

"You coulda left them in the packet, he can't read you know", commented Albert, placing the ashtray onto the floor.

Laughter ensued, with the three of them seeing the funny side to this recent scenario.

Jake failed to join in with the merriment; he was too busy enjoying his rabbit-flavoured tit-bits.

"Can you add this to my bill, Bill?" asked the American, taking his pint.

"Didn't know you had a stutter."

"Neither diiiiiiid I", chuckled the visitor. Laughter reigned once more. "It's good to be back", thought Richard.

"Get that young fella another, looks like he's got a thirst on."

"Thanks, Albert."

"Next one's on the house, I already promised him that", stated Bill with authority.

"Oh bugger", he continued, "I clean forgot to tell Molly that you were going to arrive early."

"Oh well", replied Richard, beyond caring, "I can wait ... anyway the beer's good, and so's the company. Cheers chaps."

"Good health", replied the landlord.

"Bottom's up", responded the Yorkshireman.

"Woof, woof", barked the whippet, in the hope of more crisps.

Molly, unaware that her companion for later that evening was, in fact, enjoying a drink at the bar beneath her, leisurely prepared herself. She had taken a bath, washed her hair, and was now in the process of drying it. "I hope he's all right, I would have thought he'd have called by now. Perhaps he's had an accident. Don't be silly, there could be lots of reasons why he hasn't called." She continued brushing her hair with one hand, and holding a dryer with the other, compiling a mental list, she added: "Couldn't get to a phone."

"No signal on his mobile."

"Had to work late."

"Had an accident."

"Oh my God!" she screamed, turning off the hair-dryer, "He's had an accident!"

Brrrrring brrrrring ... brrrrring brrrrring; she had not heard the telephone ringing above the sound of the electric dryer.

"Oh ... my ... God, it's true!" she stammered, rushing to the phone.

"Hello Molly ..."

"Yes Bill?" she interrupted, "What is it? It's Richard, isn't it?"

"Yes ... he's here ... having a drink ... I'm sorry Molly ... he called earlier ... you were out ... I forgot ... I'm sorry."

"You mean he's here, he's all right ... he's with you now?"

"Yes Molly ... he's here ... having a drink with Albert ... he's all right ... in fact he's just fine."

"Thanks Bill, tell him I'll be down presently."

"OK Molly, see you later. I've told her you're here."

"Thanks Bill."

"That's OK, it was my fault, I forgot to give her the message."

"Is she all right?"

"She's fine; said she'll be down shortly, you know what women are like. Mind you, she did sound a bit anxious at first."

"Really?" said Richard, seemingly worried.

"Yeah, I told her you'd gone back to the States."

"That's a cruel thing to say, you old bugger", interjected a well-oiled Albert.

"I was only kidding."

"I know that … I've been drinking with him for over half-an-hour."

"You silly old sod Albert … I meant I was only joking with you lot, I never said anything like that to Molly … it'd break her heart … she's very taken with this here fella."

"Let me buy you both another drink", interrupted the American, attempting to change the subject.

"Good speech", answered the lubricated Yorkshireman.

"I'll just have a half, got to keep my wits about me, otherwise some people round here'll be after free drinks", muted the landlord, casting a wistful eye in Albert's direction.

"What about Jake, is he in for more chips?"

"Better not Richard, gotta watch his figure, thanks all the same."

Jake's tail immediately stopped wagging. He looked up at his master, then turned his head towards the visitor; realising that no crisps were forthcoming he let out a short whine, and then stretched his limbs before curling up into a ball on the floor, in what appeared to be apparent disgust.

"No good you sulking, you aren't getting any more of them crisps."

"At least he's all right", said Molly, hurriedly applying her make-up. She suddenly stopped and stared at her reflection in the mirror, adding: "I've really missed him, and yet I hardly know him."

She continued to stare into the integral reflective part of the bathroom cabinet's door, firmly affixed at eye level, on the wall above the sink. She then said: "And yet, I feel as though I've known him all my life." With this sudden revelation Molly reconvened make-up application. "Right that's that, now to get dressed."

Re-entering the bedroom, she walked over to the bed where her clothes were laid out, and removing the bath-sheet that had previously covered her, she quickly followed her own instructions.

During her shopping expedition in Leeds, Molly had purchased new clothing for herself, the purpose of which was to look attractive and feminine. The reason; that evening's date with Richard. Her slim figure accentuated the recently purchased tight, navy-blue chiffon dress, clinging to her body as though it had been assembled around her.

"Not bad, if I say so myself", she said, this time standing in front of a full-length mirror attached to the wardrobe door. Picking up her handbag and a plastic carrier bag containing Richard's gift, she made a move for the door, pausing briefly in front of the elongated reflector, saying: "I do hope he approves."

"Way up lass, you don't half look a picture, a sight for sore eyes, I'd say."

"Why thank you, Albert."

Richard, who had been facing the Yorkshireman, and unaware of Molly's entrance, spontaneously spun around. "Wow, Molly, you look great!"

"Why thank you, Richard", she beamed.

"Can I get you a drink?"

"A glass of red wine, please."

"Coming right up, the usual is it?"

"Yes please Bill."

"Gee, you sure are a sight for sore eyes, just like Albert said", declared the American, absolutely transfixed by her presence.

"That's what I said", said an inebriated, almost-out-of-touch Yorkshireman.

"That's what he said, you said", said Bill, trying to keep the conversation on an even keel.

"I know, I just said it."

Richard picked up the glass of claret and handed it to Molly.

"Thank you."

"Shall we find a table?"

"Yes please."

"That's right", observed Albert, "You two love birds need to be own your own."

"Good speech", replied Richard, picking up his own glass of half-drunk beer.

"See you later, Albert, and you, Jack."

"Name's Jake", corrected the weary whippet owner.

"Sorry, Jake."

Jake merely responded to this error by arching his back and stretching out his front legs, resulting in a raised posterior, the consequence of which was a noisy expulsion of unwanted flatulence.

"Speak to you later, Albert", stated the visitor, eager to vacate the immediate vicinity. The young couple moved off to sit at an unoccupied table at the other end of the lounge.

"Do you think it was the crisps?" asked the landlord, wafting a tea-towel in the air

above the unfortunate mutt.

"Could be … but it's more likely to be those half-dozen hard-boiled duck eggs I gave him for tea."

"Jesus Christ, Albert, I'll have no customers in here at all if he keeps that up", remonstrated the barman, at the precise moment that the four-legged-long-dog extemporaneously ejected another cloud of gas into the atmosphere.

"It sure is good to see you, Mol."

"You too … I'm sorry I didn't get your message."

"That's OK, no need to worry … anyway, I've enjoyed myself talking with those two."

"That Albert's a character … in here most nights … him and his dog."

"Oh yeah … sorry about that."

"No need for you to be sorry, it's not your fault … or was it?" she grinned.

"Don't blame me, *it was the dog*."

"Only teasing … anyway, how did you get on in London?"

"Have a look at this, Mol", he said, producing the photo from his wallet.

"What's a nice pigeon like that doing with a man like you?"

"Thanks, thanks a lot."

"I hope that's the only bird you pulled while you were away."

"Look, I'm strictly a one-guide guy."

"And am I the one-guide girl?"

"You'll do for me, Mol", he said sweetly, taking hold of her hand and gently squeezing it.

"And you for me."

"I nearly got you some flowers … well, in fact, I did get you some flowers, but they kinda died on the way over here."

"That was sweet of you, but you needn't have."

"As it turned out I didn't … you can have the photo … if you want it that is?"

"Of course I do, it's lovely, and while we're on the subject.…"

"What subject was that?" he interrupted.

"Gifts."

"Gifts?"

"Yes, you know, gifts, presents, like you get on your birthday, or at Christmas."

"I know what a gift is … but I hardly call a bunch of dead-heads, or a photo of a pigeon with me underneath it, a present."

"No, but this is", she said, reaching for the carrier bag from underneath the table, and presenting it to him. "Go on, take it … it is for you, you know, from me." Molly's face filled with excitement as he took the bag from her, and peered inside.

"I don't know what to say."

"Do you like it?" she asked, watching the man opposite taking out the pullover.

"I love it Mol, thanks a bunch … I really *am* stuck for words."

"And you being a lawyer", she teased.

"It's great Mol, just great."

"I hope it fits … I had to guess your size."

"Looks like you guessed fine."

"What about the colour?"

"Red's my favourite colour, has been ever since I was a kid. Thanks Mol, this means a lot."

"I'm really glad you like it, it means a lot to me too."

"I can wear it tomorrow, when we go riding."

"Oh, we're going riding, are we?"

"Oops, I forgot to tell you, didn't I?"

"You asked me if I could ride, and said maybe we could go out onto the moors on horseback next time, but you never said it was all fixed up."

"That's because it wasn't, then … I can cancel it if you have other plans."

"No, I want to go … I'm looking forward to it already, I mean it … honest."

"I should've let you know … I'm sorry."

"Don't be silly Richard, I am seriously looking forward to it … now that I know", she delicately jibed.

"So am I Mol, I haven't been on a horse for months."

"I haven't been on one for at least ten years", she added, slightly concerned about the prospect.

"You'll do just fine, Mol."

"It might be you, this time, who has to attend to my sore places."

The American paused for a moment; pondering on the issue; his eyes suddenly lit up. The thought of administering first aid to Molly's buttocks filled him with desire. "I'm the man for the job, and if you should happen to sit on a rattler and get bitten, I'll even suck out the poison", he said cheekily.

"We don't have rattlesnakes over here, but it's nice of you to offer."

"My pleasure."

"Yes, I guess it would be."

A waitress approached, handing each of them a menu. "I'll come back in a few minutes, shall I?" she obligingly said, and then left without waiting for a response.

"Thank you", Molly replied to the disappearing servant.

"I could eat a horse."

"Better not … you might feel terribly guilty tomorrow."

"That's a point", said her companion with a smile, "I could hardly spend all day knowing that the creature underneath me was possibly related to the one inside me."

"Doesn't bear thinking about", commented Molly, with a shudder. "Mind you, the French eat horse meat."

"What would you expect from a nation that also eats snails and frog legs?"

Molly raised her eyebrows as if in acknowledgement, and continued to study the menu.

"I make it a point myself, never to eat anything that has been domesticated, for example cats and dogs", stated Richard profoundly, also perusing his choice of gastronomic delight.

"What about cattle?"

"That's raised meat, Mol; you know, like pigs and sheep. They're reared to be eaten; a horse is so much more."

"You mean, if you were to eat horse or dog meat, that would be like cannibalism?"

"Exactly Mol ... or at least one step away."

"I see ..."

Taking his eyes and thoughts away from the menu, he suddenly looked up, turned towards Molly, and added: "Mind you ... if I were hungry enough, I'd probably eat Albert."

"I bet he'd be tough", she interjected with a laugh, raising her glass and drinking from it.

The American briefly contemplated the prospect of digesting an Albert burger before further adding: "Nah ... don't ever think I could be that hungry."

The waitress returned, took their order and once again promptly disappeared. They continued chatting. They talked about nothing in particular; idle banter, best described as hairdresser talk. Each of them enjoying the other's company. Noticing that Molly's glass had become devoid of any liquid, the American rose from his seat. "Another drink Mol?"

"Yes please."

"Same again?"

"Yes please."

He picked up her empty glass, smiled and proceeded to the bar. A few minutes later he returned, carrying Molly's red wine and another pint of bitter for himself.

"Our table's ready."

"Oh good, I'm starving."

"L'escargot?" enquired the waiter, in a foreign accent.

"That's mine", answered Molly sheepishly, remembering Richard's earlier comments regarding French cuisine.

"So you must be 'aving frogs' legs?"

"That's so I can stay one jump ahead", replied the quick-witted American.

"I am sorry … I did not mean … 'ow you say … to imply that you have froggy legs … your legs are very nice."

"Thank you", said Richard, a little embarrassed that the waiter was still staring at the area below his waist.

The waiter placed the starter on the table, winked and then departed.

"I think he fancies you", she teased.

"I think you're right", he nervously responded, wriggling his bottom firmly into the seat cushion.

"Anyway, I thought you didn't approve of eating such food?" she asked, popping a snail into her mouth.

"When in Rome."

"Ah, but we're not in Rome … not even in Paris."

"True, very true … but they didn't have tripe and onions on the menu."

Molly consumed the last of her molluscs, and placed the tongs beside the plate. "They were delicious."

"I'm glad you liked them."

"What about yours?"

"Just like chicken, but with less meat."

"Don't tell the chef that … he'd be hopping mad."

"More than I can say for these", he said, pointing his fork in the general direction of the vertebrate skeleton appendages that lay lifeless on the plate.

"Seriously though ….didn't you enjoy your starter?"

"I was only kidding, they were lovely ….and besides, I like chicken."

The waiter returned, picked up the plates and said: "I 'ope everything is to your zatisfaction?"

"Wonderful, absolutely delicious", answered Molly, beaming a broad smile.

"And what about you sir, 'ow were those leetle French frogs' legs?"

"Excellent …my compliments to the chef."

"I vill tell im … it vill … 'ow you say … brighten up 'is day." Taking the plates with him, he hurriedly headed off towards the kitchen, disappearing in a not too dissimilar fashion to the earlier waitress.

"*What is his accent?*" she whispered.

"I zink eet is a leetle beet cosmopolitan."

"Definitely European though?"

"If you say so, Mol."

"I'm asking, not telling."

"Well in that case … your guess is as good as mine."

"He's probably from Birmingham, just putting it on for the customers."

"Why's that ... is a Birmingham accent that bad?"

"That's not what I meant ... ."

"I know what you meant ... I was only kidding", he interrupted, totally without any knowledge of a Brummie dialect.

"Oh good, I think our meals are arriving", she suddenly said, witnessing the waiter's approach.

"Veggiebul lasagna?"

"That's mine", she politely answered.

"So ziss must be your rump?"

Richard hesitated before making comment: "Yes, I like to get some red meat at least three times a week."

The waiter placed the steak in front of the American, looked him directly in the eye and said: "I am razzer parshell to getting zome meet inside of me ... but I prefer mine pink."

"Rare?" offered Molly, unaware of any possible innuendo.

"I am afraid zo", he disappointedly replied, briefly lowering his head before adding: "Still, there is always ope." He lifted his head, smiled at Molly, winked at Richard, and retreated once more towards the kitchen.

"That guy worries me", said the American, picking up a steak-knife and proceeding vigorously to carve up the rump.

Molly watched the man opposite as he ate. Not once in her life had she sat before a fortune-teller; no-one had ever read her palm. Normally, under such circumstances, it would seem appropriate to be told that one day a tall, dark, handsome stranger would enter one's life; in her case this would have been true. Richard was indeed tall, about six feet, or so she had guessed. He was also dark; his hair jet black, his skin tanned bronze, although she had put this down to his heritage, rather than frequent use of a sun-bed. Molly knew his age; during their hike he had mentioned celebrating his thirtieth birthday the previous April. She looked at him again; his jaws were firm, his body athletic; a sudden thought came into her head: "If I were casting another remake of Superman, he would be the man, and being a lawyer, he must be able to act." She smiled to herself and placed another forkful of lasagna into her mouth.

"What age group do you teach, Mol?"

"Little ones ... when they first start school, why do you ask?"

"I'm trying to find out a bit more about you ... is that OK?" he asked, showing genuine interest.

"Of course it is, ask away."

"You obviously enjoy teaching?"

"Well it varies ... sometimes I enjoy it, other times I like it, and other times..."

"Don't tell me, let me guess – red-tape?"

"Your guess is correct ... bureaucracy, politics, call it what you will ... yes ... that can be the hardest part ... still ... it is very rewarding teaching four-and five-year-olds."

"You don't fancy teaching teenagers, then?"

"Good grief, no! It takes a person with a lot more grit than me ... I can still remember what I was like as a teenager."

"Me too ... that's why I'd never make a teacher."

"I think you would make an excellent teacher", she admiringly conveyed.

"It's not the teaching part, I wouldn't have the patience ... or should I say ... self-control."

"Yes ... I know what you mean, there's some you can teach, and there's others you can't discipline."

"I presume you are referring to teenagers?"

"No ... not always, I've had six- and seven-year-olds that have been impossible to do anything with."

"I can sum it up with one word."

"And what's that?"

"Respect ... or the lack of it."

"You're right, but there's more to it than just that." Then, noticing that he had not touched his food for some while, added: "Your food is getting cold."

"I'm more interested in listening to you."

"You are sweet", she replied, this time without blushing.

"Go on then ... tell me what you think is wrong with the kids today."

"Firstly, it isn't the kids, it's the system. For example, unemployment, job prospects, television, expectations, peer groups, marketing ..."

"Marketing?" he interrupted.

"Yes marketing ... pressure of it. Got to have this, got to have that, I'm worthless without this label, useless without that label. No-one will love me if I haven't got street-cred."

"Jesus, I thought it was just the States that have these kinda problems ... I can see you feel passionately about it, Mol."

"Yes I do ... this world is all we have, and it's all our children's futures at stake."

"Good point Mol, so what's the solution?"

"Now that's a tough one ... I guess we have to get back to basics, if that's at all possible. Somehow, we need to reverse the soft-option culture that has become so prevalent in today's society. I'm sorry, I don't mean this to sound like a political speech."

"You're fine Molly, it's nice to know someone who cares", he gently corroborated.

"Thank you."

"Let's eat."

"Good idea", she said, proceeding to pick up her fork.

As Molly resumed eating her meal, she reflected on the earlier conversational topic. She had taught in a primary school because she had wanted to, not because she needed to. It was important to her to make a difference.

Teaching small children, just starting out on the educational highway of life, if done right, could have a positive, everlasting effect; not only for the child concerned, but just possibly, a bearing on the way society's future is moulded. "From small acorns do mighty oaks grow", she thought, replacing the cutlery, having finished her main course. "That was delicious."

"And so was my steak", he added, wiping his lips with the napkin provided. "Fancy a dessert?"

"Not for me Richard, I'm sated."

"Me neither ... how about a liqueur?"

"An Irish coffee would be nice."

"And I think I'll have a brandy."

Richard signalled a waitress, who approached their table. The order was placed, and the conversation resumed.

"The evening", thought the American, "is turning out just fine, most convivial."

The candle on their table had burned low. Time had passed quickly; several tables had been vacated, cleared, and relaid.

"It's late", Richard reflected, looking at his wristwatch.

"Goodness, it is too, and we have to be up early in the morning."

"Better order a cab ... I've had a bit too much to drink."

"Why not stay here, it seems a bit silly to go back to Leeds now, only to come back in the morning."

"Makes sense Mol ... I'll see if there's a room that's free."

"You won't get a free one out of Bill ... he's a true Yorkshireman", she chuckled.

"How about one that's vacant then?"

"How about one that's not?"

Richard, unclear of what her remark had meant, decided to seek clarification, but not in a direct way; a subtle approach was deemed a wise precaution.

"Are you suggesting I share a duvet with Bill?" he conjectured, wishing immediately that he had been considerably more subtle.

"Bill hadn't crossed my mind ... but if you prefer ... ?"

"No thanks ... not my type."

114

"My room is a double … two single beds … you can have one … if you wish."

"Oh … I see … Er … thanks Mol, sounds great."

"Or, we can slide them both together", she whispered, and at the same time, thinking it a shame to waste her brand-new, expensive, silk lingerie.

"Oh … I see … Er … thanks Mol", he said, somewhat stuck for words.

"If I didn't know better I'd say you're blushing", she beamed, the alcohol obviously having its infamous, inhibition-reducing effect.

"Are you sure?"

"Very sure … what about you?"

"I don't want you to think … ."

"It's not the time to think … no regrets", she offered, reassuringly.

"I'll pay the check", he spluttered, jumping to his feet.

Chapter 12

The morning light quickly came; another Saturday had begun. Outside, somewhere in the grounds of the Dog and Duck, a cockerel crowed incessantly. The sun shone brightly, there were no visible clouds. Bill, in attendance within the confines of the inn's cellar, cursed a leaking beer-pipe. "Bugger it … I must've lost half a barrel, I'll have to mop the bugger up now … bugger." He went off in search of a mop and bucket. The cockerel continued to perform its sworn duty, unaware that dawn had long since passed. The sun warmed the earth, evaporating the early-morning mist. A pigeon cooed in the distance.

"Good morning, Bill", greeted a particularly cheerful Molly, bouncing down the stairs.

"Mornin' Molly", he said, returning the gesture.

"Hi Bill", said Richard, a few steps behind Molly.

The landlord raised his eyebrows, at the same time dropping his lower jaw at the sight of the American. Struggling for a response he suddenly blurted: "It's an early worm that catches the bird." With mop and bucket in hand, he hurriedly scuttled off into the cellar. His words could be heard echoing around the cool, sunken walls: "Bugger, bugger, bugger."

"I don't think he approves", surmised the American.

"Oh, he's all right, just caught him unawares, that's all."

Not feeling very hungry, breakfast consisted of coffee and toast, which was quickly consumed. Crossing the pub's car park, heading towards the jeep, Molly commented on her present to the American: "It really suits you."

"I know, you've told me already this morning, It's great Mol, I really appreciate it."

"It fits you perfectly."

"I hope the colour doesn't frighten the horses", he joked, unlocking the vehicle.

"I'm hoping the horses don't frighten me."

"You'll do swell, Mol."

"I *do* hope so", she confided to herself.

Seated in the 4X4, Richard started the engine and slowly moved off. They were soon speeding towards the stables, where hopefully their steeds were waiting as arranged; assuming that his Yorkshire colleague had not pre-booked a pair of donkeys instead.

"That guy wouldn't know his ass from his elbow'", thought the American.

Enjoying being behind the off-roader's steering wheel once more, and taking the opportunity to value the countryside, enhanced by the brilliant sunshine, his thoughts turned to Derek Arkwright. "I'd better watch that guy", he pondered, "My gut feeling tells me to watch out for my back."

"Penny for them?"

"Sorry Mol ... I was just thinking about Arkwright."

"What about him?"

"Probably nothing."

"You can share, you know."

"Thanks Mol ... it's maybe me being a bit paranoid, that's all. I don't wish to spoil the day by talking about him ... let's just enjoy it."

"OK."

Richard followed the details that had been given to him, and apart from one slight detour, they arrived at the equestrian centre on time. "So far so good", he thought, turning into the yard.

"This is pretty", said his companion, admiring the Yorkshire stone farmhouse and outbuildings.

"It sure is", he replied, in his native drawl.

The stables were situated on a traditionally built farm, circa 1870: local stone, roofed with slate. Farming, generally, in its modern history, had probably never been more precarious than it was at this present time. To survive, one had to diversify. In this part of the world, tourism had come to prevail as the most likely area of diversification. Some had gone into bed and breakfast, others had opened up their fields to campers and caravanners. Others had turned over the land to golf courses. Traditional crafts had been resurrected and developed, offering hand-made clothing, cream teas, local cheeses, and much more. This particular farm had remained entirely faithful to its past, and only in an attempt to make ends meet had started a riding facility. However, this facility, from its humble beginnings, now offered an indoor and outdoor school, catering for all ages and abilities. Various styles were now taught, including Western and dressage. Hacking was extremely popular with the tourist. It allowed him or her to ride – usually under supervision – out into the countryside. The scenery was considered stunning; both Richard and Molly thought so.

"Gee, this is swell Mol, I'm looking forward to this", he said, climbing down from the car.

Molly, doing likewise, had other considerations: "So am I … however I'm not so sure about things that begin with b."

"*B*?"

"Bones and bum."

"We *can* cancel."

"Don't be silly … I was only kidding", she said, hand behind back, fingers crossed.

Richard walked over to a stable that had a sign above the door saying 'RECEPTION'. Molly followed.

"Excuse me, my name is Waters, I believe …"

"One Western and one English", intervened a young girl of about fourteen, wearing jodhpurs and riding boots.

"That's us", said Molly, adding, "I hope mine is gentle."

"I guess you're riding traditional", observed the girl, assuming that the man with an American accent probably wanted to ride like a cowboy.

"I was taught English, although a long time ago", she nervously relayed.

"But you *can ride*?"

"Er … yes … but …"

"In that case, Thunder will do just fine", she stated, winking at Richard.

"*Thunder*!"

"I hope not, the forecast was for a cloudless sky", offered Richard at Molly's expense, joining in with the pretence.

"I meant the horse … he's called Thunder?"

"Yes, why … is that a problem?"

"It may be … that is … if his reputation matches his name."

"If you're worried, I'll put you on Pedro, he's quiet", she said, winking once more at the American.

"Good … I like the sound of him already."

"So you must be the cowboy'?"

"Indian, actually."

"Whatever … it's all the same to Lightning", she volunteered, this time quickly winking at Molly.

"Could be worse", responded the would-be cowboy.

"How's that?" enquired the stable-lass.

"I could have had one called 'Scattered Showers', now that would have worried me."

Richard, having paid for a day's hire for the two questionable nags, was then led to where they were tethered. Both he and Molly were suitably attired for the occasion.

Molly had equipped herself with an appropriate hard hat and crop, loaned by the establishment. Jogging pants, and a pair of moderately heeled calf-length boots had been put on when she had first dressed that morning. Richard, on the other hand, had refused the offer of protective headgear, preferring to wear his own cowboy hat, which he had fetched from the jeep. Wearing brown leather cowboy boots and faded blue denim jeans, he felt appropriately dressed for the day ahead, that is, apart from one thing. Just prior to encountering their mounts he suddenly uttered: "Sorry Mol, I think this sweater is going to be a little too warm, do you mind if I take it off?"

"Of course I don't."

They turned a corner to one of the out-buildings, and there, tied to post and rail, were the trusty steeds. Richard was not the first to see the animals, having, at the initial

attempt, forgotten that his hat was still in situ; the sweater now stuck over his head.

"God, they're beautiful", pronounced Molly.

"Jesus, you're right there Mol", agreed the American, having broken free from the woollen restriction.

"We aim to please", conveyed the young girl.

Richard retrieved his cranium cover, placed it on his head, and rejoined the others.

"Hi there, Thunder'", greeted the cowboy to the palomino, who had been tacked-up wearing full Western regalia.

"His name's Henry."

"Hi there Henry, you're a handsome one." Richard gently rubbed Henry's muzzle. The horse was indeed a fine specimen; standing at about fifteen-and-a-half hands, he looked majestic, dressed in his equestrian attire.

"So you must be Pedro, or is it Henrietta", said Molly, addressing the stable-lass.

"He's definitely Pedro, and he's quiet … bomb-proof."

"That's good to know, isn't it Pedro", she answered, replying to them both, and at the same time patting the horse's neck. Apparently the name Pedro referred to his character rather than his appearance; not in any way did he resemble an animal from South America. Standing at just under one hand less than Henry, he too was a fine-looking beast of burden. A Welsh cob cross, bay-coloured, and dressed in English tack, he was ready for a day's hack.

"He'll do what he's told, but you have to be firm, he can be a bit lazy. Oh yes, and he likes to have a nap in the afternoon … a sort of siesta."

"Hence Pedro", quipped the cowboy. "Better find an ale-house at lunch time … hole up for a while."

"That sounds like an excellent idea", said Molly, still a little concerned at the prospect of personal injury.

"Come on then Mol, ready to mount?"

She resisted an obvious answer, choosing instead to say: "OK, if we must."

Richard took hold of the horn, and swung himself into the saddle. Molly briefly paused, and then, as if by magic, her lapsed memory recall kick-started, and she mounted Pedro in true English fashion. "Wow", she thought, "I remembered."

"How does it feel, Mol?"

"Great … I think … at least *you* certainly look the part … even down to the check-shirt … I'm impressed … but aren't you a little out of character?"

"Surely you didn't expect me to dress up as Tonto."

"Come to think of it, that would be silly … and stop calling me Shirley."

Richard took from his back jean pocket, a map; the one that Derek had given him soon after his arrival in Yorkshire. Although the main intention was to explore further the land owned by Hugo Oldsworth, including the surrounding area, his alternative motive had been to be on horseback, enjoying the countryside and the company of Molly.

"I hope you've picked out a suitable respite for Pedro, and, of course, for my bottom?"

"Just checking the map before we set off … this time I'll be the guide … you sit back and relax."

"*Relax!*"

"Don't worry, I've brought the cream."

"Whipped?"

"Embrocation."

"In that case … lead on R.W."

Richard acknowledged Molly's comment with a smile, then, clicking his teeth, at the same time reining his mount, he gently kicked the animal's side. Henry responded by turning away from the fence and moving off at a slow walk. Pedro, urged by his rider, followed suit.

"Bye … have a nice day", waved the young girl.

"Bye."

"Thanks for your help."

"Do you ever get fed up with hearing that phrase?" she asked, settling into the saddle.

"Many times … but not in that particular case."

"Why's that?"

"'Cos she meant it."

Turning left at the farm's entrance, the American quickened the pace. "About two hundred yards, and we can turn right, there should be a bridle-path."

"We're right behind you ... aren't we Pedro."

"Whinnnnneeey", replied the equine.

"I'm really enjoying this", announced Molly, some forty minutes after first climbing aboard her four-legged-friend.

"So am I, Mol ... back to nature ... the weather is superb ... and the countryside ... spectacular."

"How does this compare to the 'Big Apple'?"

"No comparison ... except perhaps ... chalk and cheese."

"Looking forward to going home?"

Richard thought for a moment; he hadn't considered going home. A sudden sadness came over him. "I'd rather stay here, Mol."

Molly, riding alongside, could see in the American's face that he had genuinely meant what he had said. "What do you like about it?"

"The scenery, the history, the people, the pace, the pubs, this ... but most of all ...", he paused, looked directly into her eyes, and said: "Most of all Mol ... you."

The sun continued to shine bright, increasingly warming the earth, as they made their way onto the moorlands. Molly progressively gained confidence with each sure-footed step that Pedro took. The ragged terrain was made easy by well-worn paths and their experienced mounts. Skylarks sang loudly high above them, while rabbits darted here and there; occasionally a disturbed ground bird would take to the air. The horses had seen it all before, and remained calm despite such unwarranted and unintentional provocation.

"Fancy a canter ... or maybe a gallop?"

"Can't we start with a trot?" she pleaded.

"Sorry Mol, forgot that one ... Western riding only has four speeds."

"Four?"

"Walk, lope, and gallop."

"That's only three, what's the other one?"

"Park."

"Very good ... I like that one."

"Well, are you ready for it? The ground here is about as good as it gets, I guess."

Molly displayed her faith in the bay by firmly heeling the animal's side, remaining seated in the saddle and verbally urging her trusty steed. Pedro responded to her firm tones by shifting up a gear. "Good boy", she praised, as the cob cross entered into a slow canter.

"Atta boy, Henry", responded Richard, as the palomino likewise followed suit. "This is more like it", said the American, drawing alongside Pedro. "How's your butt?"

"Holding up so far."

"Glad to hear it … fancy a gallop?"

"Not *just* yet."

"OK, what about a walk then?"

"Good idea … before my confidence wanes."

"Whoa there, Henry", cried the cowboy, pulling on the rein.

Pedro responded in true fashion by pre-empting his rider's instructions, reducing his slow canter to an even slower walk. Richard waited for them to catch up.

"So that was a lope?"

"Sure was … a lope is a slow gallop, looks very much like a canter, I know."

"So, apart from park there is only walking and galloping … but gallop has two speeds … lope and flat out?"

"That's about the size of it, Mol."

The ground once again became more uneven, the path narrowing. A flock of pigeons flew overhead. One of them, possibly attempting to re-enact a certain scene from the Dambusters movie, decided to release part of its cargo.

"Sorry, Richard", laughed Molly.

"What for?"

"Laughing."

"What at?"

"Your hat."

"What about my hat?"

"Some say it's a sign of good luck."

"What is?"

"That", she answered, pointing to the offending dropping.

Richard pulled Henry into park mode, removed his hat, looked at it, and then gazed upwards at the disappearing flock of birds, saying: "That's no way to treat someone who, only the other day, shared a complimentary packet of biscuits with one of your fellow compatriots."

"I beginning to wonder about you and pigeons."

"I know what you mean", he said, whilst at the same time trying to clean off the offending material with a piece of tissue.

"There's a stream down there … you could clean your hat", she advised, pointing to a narrow flow of clear water, gently meandering its way through the landscape.

"Good idea, Mol … and the horses can have a drink."

"I could do with one myself."

"So could I … I forgot to pack …"

"I didn't think either … how far is the pub?"

Richard once more produced the map and consulted it. "About an hour … I guess."

"Oh well … I guess we'll survive 'til then."

Standing side by side, the horses took a long drink from the stream. The cool water replenished their state of partial dehydration. Richard, squatting at the water's edge, proceeded to clean the bird excrement from his hat. Molly, holding onto the animal's reins, watched the man as he attended to his laundry.

"As good as new", he proclaimed, rising to his feet and holding out the stetson for Molly to see.

"Very good … I should have brought my washing."

"No thanks Mol … I don't fancy bashing your briefs on a rock."

"There's no answer to that … are you fit?"

"Well … I try to keep in shape."

"I meant are you ready for the off?"

"I sure am", he replied, taking hold of Henry's lead with his left hand, and at the same time grabbing the horn with his other. He then placed a foot into the stirrup and with one movement swung into the saddle. "Your turn."

"I know", she answered, mounting Pedro by an entirely different method. "There, are you impressed?"

"I surely am … although I must confess, I've never witnessed John Wayne getting saddled up like that."

"And I've never seen John Wayne doing dressage", she said tauntingly.

"Touché", responded the man who was accompanying her.

The cowboy eased Henry forward and steered him back onto the path. Pedro lazily followed.

"I think he's almost ready for his nap."

"Not for a while yet, I'm afraid", he said, seemingly sympathetic to Pedro's plight. They hit the trail once more. An abundance of wildlife greeted them as they progressed. The sun, now almost directly above them, continued to shine bright. Richard, grateful to the shade afforded to him by the stetson, turned to his partner and said: "Are you OK Mol? Don't want you to get sick from the sun."

"I'm fine, thanks, this hard hat is keeping the rays at bay."

"Good phrase, I like it."

"Just made it up ... spur of the moment."

"Very good, very witty ... I s'pose there's no chance of you reining in now?"

"No, not in the 'mane', I guess."

Maintaining this equestrian banter, they slowly made their progression towards the intended hostelry; in this particular case, the Wine and Grouse. Richard had chosen this location as it was situated in close proximity to Oldsworth's farm. In actual fact, they had been on his land for some time. The American had temporarily, psychologically, discarded his cowboy hat for one that would, hypothetically, have been worn by a lawyer. As they continued to ride, Richard occasionally checked the map, making mental notes of the terrain. In the distance stood a farmhouse.

"That must be Oldsworth's", he thought. Maintaining the lead, he guided his horse in the direction of the empty dwelling.

"Sheep-Dip Farm."

"You know it?", he asked.

"Sort of, the owner lives in London, I think. He inherited the farm from his parents who were killed a year or so ago, in a terrible accident while they were on holiday." Molly, unaware of her friend's involvement, continued. "Sad really, the son's not interested in the farm, and it seems like everything his parents worked for has been wasted. Even the house is empty."

Richard reflected on her comments. The unfortunate, premature demise of Hugo's parents had indeed been tragic. However, whether they would have agreed with Molly's remarks would not now, or ever, be known, as verification in this life was no longer an option. To consider a life's work as wasteful demeans the effort and passion invested by those individuals involved. The same could be held true of most people's lives. What could be considered wasteful would be to allow the farm to die.

As Henry approached the buildings, Richard stood up in the stirrups and looked around. Taking in what he saw, and had previously seen, he mentally queried the land's intended final purpose, for which he had been sent to England to set in motion.

"You're miles away."

"Not really Mol ... I was just wondering."

"What were you wondering?"

"An observation, I guess."

"Care to divulge?" she said, trying to drag more from him.

"It just seems a pity to change all this ... alter it that is."

"No-one's going to do that, are they", she offered, more as a statement than an intended question.

"Molly, I love this land, I love being on this horse … compared to what I'm used to, this is paradise. I'd much rather be working this ranch, than be stuck in the carbon-monoxide-filled environment of New York, dealing with money-grabbing …egotistical ….back-stabbing, artificial nonentities, such as the ones I seem to deal with every day of my existence."

"Wow! What a speech, I didn't know you felt that way."

"I guess I didn't either ….not until just now."

Molly urged Pedro closer to Henry, and held out her arm. Richard reached out and took her hand. She looked into his eyes and gently squeezed his palm. He smiled in response to her apparent acknowledgement of his sentiments.

"What a lovely house."

"I love it Mol ….it's got character", he answered, and then dismounted for a better examination of the property, soon to be bulldozed to the ground.

The farmhouse had originally been erected approximately one hundred and fifty years ago. During that period, the original building had experienced many changes, including alterations and extensions. It now boasted five bedrooms, three bathrooms, a sitting room, dining room, study, games room, and a kitchen with walk-in pantry. All rooms were proportionately large. Due to sympathetic design, and use of local materials, the various improvements carried out over the years were not easily detectable. To all intents and purposes, the dwelling could have been built to its present specification at the time of conception.

"The Oldworths had taste", thought Richard, peering through the kitchen window.

"What a kitchen!" exclaimed Molly, her feet now standing on terra firma alongside her companion. "And it's got an Aga", she continued.

"I like the beams … they're in every room."

"Don't get carried away", she corrected, "Only in the rooms where you've looked through the windows."

"True … but I bet there's beams in all the rooms."

It was obvious to Richard that the house had been tastefully cared for, and had been maintained to a high standard. However, a year or so of being unlived in had taken its toll. Signs of neglect were apparent. Nature was in the process of reclamation. "God", thought the American, "It's one thing not allowing the farm to die, but to raze this property to the ground and erect a theme park all over the landscape … well … that could be deemed murder." He shuddered at the prospect.

"Are you all right?" she enquired.

"Yeah fine, it just seems a shame to see the house empty."

"Empty of people maybe … but there's still a lot of furniture."

"Yeah, covered by sheets ... a house should be lived in ... 'specially a house like this."

"I agree Richard ... I wonder if it's for sale?"

Deciding to ignore Molly's question, preferring instead to change the subject, he said: "We'd better get moving, I guess."

"Look Richard, there's stables over there, and a barn; if we lived here you could keep horses."

The words "if we lived here" had slipped innocently from Molly's mouth. Realising her Freudian slip she started to blush, and attempted to correct the mistake. "I'm sorry ... I didn't mean ..."

"Molly, I couldn't think of anything nicer", he interrupted. Smiling, he approached, placed his arms around her waist, leaned forward and gently kissed her fully on the lips.

"Ready for lunch?" he asked, breaking their lip contact.

"Yes please, I'm starving."

"Come on then, let's get off this farm and find the pub."

"Don't you mean 'ranch'", she teased, taking hold of patient Pedro's reins.

"To me it's a ranch ... I don't see sheep ... I see small white buffalo."

"Now *that's* what I call lateral thinking."

Some fifteen minutes later, and guided by the map, Richard had navigated the four of them safely to the Wine and Grouse. "Pedro looks pleased."

"He's not the only one", she replied, raising her posterior off the saddle seat and patting it.

Provision had been made available at the pub to secure horses and ponies. Many riders passed this way, and in order to attract additional custom, facilities had been afforded to allow for the tethering of four-legged modes of transportation. Drinking water had also been provided. Fortunately for the equines, the facilities had been set under a group of trees, offering shade from the sun.

"Tents!"

"Sorry?"

"Tents ... over there, in that field", informed Richard, pointing to an area apparently set aside for would-be campers.

"Oh, I see", she replied, having just ensured that Pedro's needs had been properly catered for. "What a splendid spot to camp."

Richard, having secured the palomino to the hitching-rail, had directed his attention away from the horse, and was now seemingly concentrating on events surrounding the miniature campsite. "Do you like camping, Mol?"

"Love it."

"Fancy camping here tonight … if that's possible?"

"But … we haven't got a tent."

"Oh yes we have … in the jeep … all brand new."

"You *carry* camping equipment around with you?"

"I bought it … just in case."

"In case of *what*?"

"Er … it's a kind of back-to-nature thing, I guess."

"I'll need to pick up my sleeping bag … unless you carry a selection with you?"

"Now you're being facetious."

"Only teasing … I'd love to sleep under canvas with you … it's quite romantic."

"What about nylon?"

"What about it?"

"I don't think tents are made from canvas anymore."

"Oh, I see … probably not nylon either."

"Yeah, cotton and some other man-made-fibre."

"Whatever … it'll still be romantic … as long as I'm with you."

The surrounding scenery certainly had its charm and appeal. The landscape had barely been touched by the influences of man, forged mainly by time and the elements; it appeared craggy and rugged, yet made hospitable by the glorious sunshine. The public house, now known as the Wine and Grouse, and formerly as the Sheep Shearer's Folly, was a relatively new building to the vicinity, having stood for a mere ninety years or so. It had also been built using local materials (obvious really when one considers the alternatives) and yet had a more modern appearance than its age belied.

"What would you like?" asked Richard, standing the customer side of the bar-counter.

"Lager shandy, please."

"Two lager shandies, please."

"Halves or pints?" enquired the rosy-faced rotund woman behind the counter.

"A half for me."

"And a pint for me", instructed the American.

"All right, me ducks", acknowledged the fifty-something assistant.

"Not quite the charm of the Dog and Duck'", he whispered.

"Oh, I don't know … she seems quite pleasant to me."

"I was referring to the establishment, not the staff member", he corrected.

"English levity", she said, by word of explanation.

Before Richard had an opportunity to respond, the lady had returned with the order. "Are you eating, me dears?"

"We sure are", he replied, taking hold of the smaller glass and handing it to Molly.

"Thank you", she politely said, taking the shandy and placing it to her mouth.

"In that case, I'll run you up a tab ... if you like."

"It'll do just fine", answered the cowboy, himself raising the liquid refreshment to his facial orifice.

"Come on horseback then?"

Richard, realising that his apparel somehow gave the game away, pointed to his hat, and said: "The hat ... bit of a give-away, isn't it?"

"It's not that me dear ... it's the smell."

The stout server of lager shandys, at this fortunate point, turned to serve another customer. Molly, covering her face with a hand, was trying exceptionally hard to muffle the giggles that the barmaid's comments had provoked. Richard, slightly embarrassed by the same nasal-induced remarks, tried to avoid detection by consuming two thirds of the gassy beverage at one attempt. Sensing a pending attack of unwanted wind, and remembering the effect that a similar drink had had on Derek Arkwright, he paused, placing the almost empty vessel onto the counter.

"Thirsty?" she inquired, still in the throes of stifling her chuckles.

"Very funny", he sneered, then seeing the lighter side, and the fact that his partner had found the entire incident most amusing, decided to join in with the merriment.

After lunch had been heartily consumed, and a pitch booked for the coming evening's stay, the pair exited the cool confines of the inn's thick stone walls, greeting once again the heat of the sun's rays.

"That was just what the doctor ordered", said the American, rubbing his stomach.

"Very welcome, thank you", she replied.

During their riders' absence, the horses had taken the opportunity to eat all the available grass within reach of their tethered stance. They had then drunk water from the containers provided, and with little else to distract them from the desire to rest, had settled down for a quite period of private meditation. With both tails having been switched onto automatic insect swatting mode, the four-legged creatures patiently waited; enjoying the respite, until such time as further demands were to be made upon them.

"Look, they're asleep."

"A well deserved siesta, Mol."

"Are we going back the same way?"

"Only if you want to."

"I don't mind."

"Let's take a look at the map."

Having studied the options, a different return route was mutually agreed upon; taking in additional scenery, including a promised waterfall.

"Come on then, Pedro, time to wake up."

Henry pricked up his ears, shook himself and stood alert, ready for action. Pedro, on the other hand, either didn't hear, or pretended not to, the comments made by his passenger.

"Come on, Pedro", she said, only this time directly into his left ear. With a yawn and a shrug, Pedro responded. First, by stretching forward his front legs, followed by a rearwards stretch of his back legs.

"Stand clear, Mol."

Molly, aware of Pedro's imminent actions, immediately took several backward steps. Pedro, not demonstrating any outward signs of embarrassment, proceeded to empty his urinary reservoir.

"Obviously doesn't like being disturbed during a nap."

"Apparently not", she answered, preferring not to look.

One hour later, and well into the return leg of their journey back to the stables, a sudden disturbance further along the trail, had caused a covey of partridges to break cover. The cause of the small birds' flight soon became apparent. A large brown hare, running at speed, crossed the path in front of them, about fifty yards ahead.

"Look at that jackrabbit go!"

"It's a hare, dear", she informed.

"OK ... no need to split hares."

From seemingly nowhere, a brindled dog burst onto the scene. In hot pursuit, it chased the fleeing leporine figure across the moor.

"Isn't that ... .?"

"Jake", he interrupted, "Sure looks like him."

"Way up ... it's you two."

"Hello there, Albert", responded the cowboy, turning round in the saddle.

"Good afternoon, Albert."

"Afternoon Miss Molly ... what brings you two out here then?"

"The horses, actually."

"I can see that, you daft bugger, I mean ..."

"It seemed like a good way to spend a sunny Saturday ... that's all", she said, answering what appeared to be a ludicrous question.

"And what are you up to ... you sly old dog?" enquired the American.

"After my supper, that's what", he replied, removing a furry object from a bag slung over his shoulder.

"A ferret!" gasped Molly, "I love ferrets, what's his name?"

"He's a jill."

"Strange name for a male", puzzled the man on horseback.

"He's not a he, he's a she."

"Oh I see ... I think ... hi there Jill."

"Jill's not her name", offered Molly, in an attempt to clarify the situation, "Male ferrets are called jacks, and females are called ..."

"Jill."

"That's right my boy, you're catching on, by heck."

"So what *is* her name?" she asked, hoping to resolve the matter.

"Jill."

"Jill!"

"That's right, thought I'd call her Jill, save any confusion."

At this point, Richard's attention was drawn to the course taking place to his left. "That dog of yours certainly can run."

"I'm out here after rabbits, not those long-eared buggers", informed the man on the ground. "He'll never catch that one, tough as ... my boots he is."

Both Molly and Richard were engrossed in the scene taking place on the moorland close to them. Each time the powerful whippet got near to his quarry, at the last moment the prey turned, either to the left or right. The dog then had to suddenly brake and change direction.

"Most hares are too good for a single dog ... didn't expect to come across one, he'll be knackered when he gets back. Might as well go home, or go straight to the pub."

"He's lost it."

"Good ... just hope he hasn't cut his feet too bad."

"Can I hold Jill?"

"Don't know about that ... ferocious she is ... don't want her killing that nag of yours."

"He's not a nag, his name is Pedro", she uttered defensively. Pedro pricked his ears up at the mention of his name. "Good boy Pedro ... the nasty man didn't mean it ... did you Albert?" she said, scowling at the poacher.

"I apologise, Pedro ... now that I'm lookin' properly I can see that you're a thoroughbred. Probably won races."

"No need to go that far", interjected Richard, carefully watching Albert hand Molly the polecat.

"Will he bite?"

"Handle him firm, and he'll be just fine."

Molly took the small creature and cuddled it to her chest.

"Most women would be too scared to be near a ferret, let alone hold one."

"Yeah ... but Molly's not just any woman", advised Richard, from high-on-horse.

"Thank you", she acknowledged, still stroking the unpaid rodent operative.

"Good boy, Jake", greeted his owner, reaching down to the panting long-dog. Albert made a fuss of the returned canine, whose tail was wagging vigorously, with saliva dripping from a gaping mouth.

"I'm afraid we haven't got any water."

"That's all right miss ... I've got a flask of tea in the bag."

"I *meant* for Jake."

Richard took off his hat, and still holding it in his hand, wiped his forearm across his brow. Leaning forward, and covering his face with the hat, he whispered into Henry's ear: "I'm god-dammed sure that man is a rabbit short of a stew."

"Best be off, Mol."

"Time to hit the trail", she said, winking at Albert as she handed back the jill called Jill.

"Are you in the pub tonight?"

"Not tonight Albert ... we're camping."

"See you around Albert ... look after that dog, he's a little bit special."

"By heck I'll do that young fella, I'm too old to run after my dinner."

"Bye Albert."

"Goodbye, Miss Molly", said Albert, patting the dog at his side.

The horses, sensing that they were near home, livened-up somewhat, increasing the pace at which they had been previously set by their riders. Henry pricked up his ears and whinnied; this encouraged Pedro to likewise perform.

"They know that they're nearly back at the yard."

"As long as he doesn't make a bolt for it."

"There's a joke there somewhere ... but I'm too tired to recall it."

"Tiring stuff, eh?"

"Sure is ... have you enjoyed yourself, Mol?"

"It's been lovely, really great ... and Pedro has been super", she replied, patting the animal's neck.

"Yeah", acknowledged the American, "Henry here ... he's been a real pal."

"And what about you ... have you had a good time?"

"I sure have Mol ... the best."

"Hello again … had a good day?" greeted the same stable-lass who had set them on their way earlier that day.

"Sure have."

"Pedro's been absolutely marvellous."

"Good to hear that, Pedro", said the young girl, taking hold of his bridle.

Molly dismounted and handed the reins to the appointed assistant. "Actually my bum's not as sore as I imagined."

"Mine's OK, too", said Richard, now firmly standing on the ground, rubbing his bottom.

"I'm glad you had a good time … and that these two behaved themselves."

"Most enjoyable … Henry played his part to perfection."

Molly handed back the borrowed riding-hat and crop. Richard patted his hired transport. They both said their farewells to the helpful and still very cheerful stable-hand, and also to the two animals that had been their day's companions.

"See you again, I hope", she said, then turned away, leading the two tired mounts off to be untacked, stabled, fed, watered, and rested.

"Thanks … bye."

"It's been a hoot … take care."

"That was fun", stated Molly, as they walked back to the 4X4.

"Yeah … but now it's time to set up camp."

"I'll need to pick up my sleeping bag … and have a shower."

Richard raised an arm to his face and breathed in. "Phew! Can I join you for a shower? I smell like I've spent two weeks in the saddle on some sort of cattle drive."

"Er … we did see some sheep … sorry … small white buffalo."

They got into the Cherokee, Richard once more at the wheel, and after starting the engine proceeded to drive back to the Dog and Duck.

Chapter 13

Hugo Oldsworth looked at the clock on his living-room wall: it read six o'clock. "Must get myself ready soon", he murmured to himself. He raised a glass of dry white wine to his lips and took a sip. Classical music played in the background. The artist was feeling very pleased with himself. "Not a bad couple of days. Sold the painting for a handsome sum. Sold the farm, for an much bigger, much more handsome sum. And to cap that … I'm having dinner with Sophie tonight. Not bad at all." He raised the glass once more to his mouth and swallowed. "Never did like that bloody farm."

Hugo's comments were accurate to the letter. What had been his parents' life and dreams had been his own nightmare. To maintain the business, and all that it encompassed, had meant sacrifice. Two thousand acres of mainly sheep-farming land required hard work and effort, often in extremely severe weather conditions. The winters on the moors could be very hostile. Hugo's devotion to the land and his mother's support had more often than not left him feeling lonely, isolated and deserted. Although not in a position to fully understand the predicament of the situation when he was young, he had, in later life, come to appreciate his parents' position. He now knew that he had always been loved. The problem had been that there never seemed to be any time for his father and mother to show it. As a result of his childhood memories and, in particular, the feeling of acute isolation, he now loathed the countryside vehemently.

"Wonder what taxes I'll have to pay this time", he said, referring to the sale of the farm. "Better find that one out first thing Monday morning." He drained the glass, rose from the chair, went over to where the hi-fi was situated, and turned up the volume. "There, that's better, I'll be able to hear it in the bathroom now."

Hugo went off to the bathroom to take a shower, in preparation for a social evening out with his model. He could indeed hear the classical compilation compact disc, as it boomed out Bach's 'Air on a G String'. With a toothbrush in his right hand, he attempted to conduct the reflection of himself in the bathroom cabinet mirror, as though it represented the London Symphony Orchestra. "Not a bad couple of days at all", he muttered once more.

Inheritance tax had been paid on the transference of the farm to Hugo Oldsworth out of the capital left by the Oldsworth seniors. Stock and machinery had been sold to help raise sufficient funds to achieve the Treasury's figure. Despite the pay-out of quite a large sum from an insurance policy, there had been no residue left for Hugo to make use of. The remaining value of his parents' estate was tied up solely in the farm itself.

The jeep had taken Richard and Molly, first to the Grand to collect clean clothes and toiletries, and then secondly onto the Dog and Duck to wash up and to collect her personal requirements, including a sleeping bag and bedroll. "Did you remember to tell reception that you wouldn't be there for dinner?" she asked, waving goodbye to Bill, who was in the process of giving a hanging basket some water.

"Yep."

They arrived at the Wine and Grouse at seven-fifteen exactly, made their way to the rear of the pub and located a suitable pitch.

"Will this do, Mol?"

"Looks good to me."

"Good ... let's camp."

"Let's not ... you might get arrested."

"Hardly ... not these days ... almost compulsory in some states back home."

"Surely not?"

"Only kidding ... and stop calling *me* Shirley."

"Using my own witticisms against me now, are you?"

"Only when the cap fits."

"Typical American."

"Pardon?"

"Well you mentioned it."

"Mentioned what?"

"If the cap fits."

"What about it?"

"Correct me if I'm wrong ... do Americans wear ten-gallon hats?"

"Some do."

"My point exactly."

"What point?"

"It's because of the fact that if you can wear a ten-gallon hat, you must have a ten-gallon head … in order for the cap to fit, so-to-speak. To us English, a lot of Americans do appear to have big heads, as in know-it-all."

"I'm not like *that*, am I?"

"Of course not, I was trying to be satirical."

"Very good, so you didn't mean what you said about Americans in general?"

"Well … I don't know about the Generals … but."

"So you *do* mean it?"

"Of course not … there's good and bad everywhere, generalisation is a dangerous concept."

"Molly Weston … you're one hell of a gal."

"Why thank ya pardner … now shall we get this tent up?"

"Good idea."

Richard proceeded to the rear of the off-roader and opened up the tailgate.

"Good grief, you certainly have got a lot there."

"'Fraid so", he replied, reaching into the back and grabbing hold of a bag.

"Is all this new?"

"Yep."

"But I thought you were supposed to be here on business?"

"I am", he answered, laying yet another previously unopened bag onto the ground.

"Why all the equipment?"

"I guess I got a bit carried away in the shop."

"More than a bit, I'd say."

Molly helped her 'pardner' to unload the vehicle, and then the pair commenced the onerous task of domicile erection.

"Let's start with the tent", she instructed.

"OK, Akela."

"Don't get sarky."

"No, Akela", he said, at the same time blowing her a kiss.

Following the supplied instructions, inadequate to the novice, several basic assembly misjudgments were made by both project co-workers.

"I'm sure that pole doesn't go there."

"I bet it does."

"Go on then, try it."

"You're right."

"Thought so."

"I'll tie the little metal bits to the ropes, shall I"

"OK."

"Don't think that's quite right."

"Neither do I, sod it."

"Now, now."

"Well."

However, with Molly's girl-guide experience, Richard's patience, and a lot of perseverance, the modern, igloo-shaped wigwam was soon fully upright.

"There, not a bad job I'd say … time for the pub."

"Not yet … what about bedding … have you got cooking equipment?"

"Somewhere … in one of these boxes I think."

Richard, keen to get to the pub, started on the various, still-sealed bags and boxes. Molly collected the discarded wrappings and disposed of them in the waste bins provided.

"There, that's got it."

"Hardly, but I guess it'll do for now."

"I'm worried about last orders."

"Food or drink?"

"Food."

"Ten o'clock, I noticed the time on the menu at lunch."

Richard looked at his wristwatch. Good … it's nearly nine, plenty of time."

"What for, food or drink?"

"Drink."

Richard, after hurriedly arranging their sleeping quarters, zipped up the tent. "Right then, ready."

"Come on then", she smiled, "I can see you're dying for a pint."

"Thirsty work, Mol."

"Just what the doctor ordered", he said, sipping from a pint glass some ten minutes later, and now seated at a table in the lounge bar of the Wine and Grouse.

"This is fun … I haven't camped for ages."

"I've got all the gear, Mol … just one thing though."

"What's that?"

"I forgot to get any provisions … no tea, coffee, or food."

"Don't worry … we'll manage … somehow", she said, looking around at the well-stocked contents contained within the ale-house.

"Good point", he replied, observing her observation.

"Anyway", she asked, tasting the red wine and replacing the glass onto the table, "Tell me … just *why* have you bought all that camping stuff?"

"Seemed like a good idea at the time, I guess."

"Come on, you must *know* … what *are* you doing here, or is it a secret?"

"My brief was to arrange for the purchase of some land, and secure planning consent for its change of use, that's all." Richard, reluctant to divulge too much, took another mouthful of the locally brewed beer.

"But *why* have you purchased the expeditional equipment?"

"Ulterior motive, I guess."

"You seem to be guessing quite a lot … what ulterior motive?" she further inquired.

"I bought the stuff for two, maybe three, reasons."

"Go on."

"One, I might have needed to sleep overnight … during the process of vetting the land."

"That seems a bit lame, what's the other?"

"I kinda wanted an excuse to sleep out … you know … under canvas … under the stars. Let me try and explain … I live and work in New York, very cosmopolitan, and densely populated … this seemed like a great opportunity to get back to my roots, so to speak."

"And the third?"

"I said maybe a third."

"Well?"

"Last week when we first met … you offered to be my guide."

"Yes, but only after you asked me to be your guide."

"OK, whatever. Can you remember what I was wearing?"

"Yes, brown jumper, brown trousers, and brown shoes, why?"

"Hardly appropriate for hiking?"

"No, not really", she agreed, wondering where this conversation was leading.

"I needed to see the area, including the land to be purchased. I realised that without someone to show me around, that task could be difficult."

"So you asked the first person that came along?"

"It wasn't quite like that."

"How was it then?"

"If it wasn't for your beautiful face and that lovely smile, I would think that I was under some sort of interrogation."

"Merely curious … please continue."

"Where was I?"

"About to tell me why I was chosen to be your 'scout'?"

"Because", he replied, hesitating before adding, "It was obvious by then that I was going to need help … and … I … OK, I'll say it … I was attracted to you. Would you like another drink?"

"Yes please, darling."

"You don't mind?"

"Mind, why should I mind? I'm flattered."

Richard, light on his feet, approached the counter, and placed a repeat order, thinking: "I think I love this girl."

"So … you bought all the new walking gear at the same time as the camping equipment?" she asked, almost as soon as Richard had re-seated himself.

"Yep."

"So that you could be with me?"

"Yep, that certainly had a lot to do with it. Although I'm over here to do a job, at the same time I felt a need to get out into the country … and I couldn't have met a nicer person with whom I would have rather shared the experience."

"Thank you, that's sweet."

"It's the truth, Mol."

"Are you going to tell me about this land deal?"

"It's confidential, I'm afraid."

"Who am I going to tell … you don't have to give me a detailed report, just the gist, or, if you'd prefer, don't say anything", she said, her lips now displaying an all-too-familiar pout.

"Your face, and especially your pouting lips, are hard to resist."

"Does that mean you're going to tell all?"

"I don't know about *all*, but I'll try to tell you as much as I can."

"*Lawyers.*"

"We're not that bad", he defended, raising the fresh pint to his mouth, before continuing: "A consortium of people, unknown to me, want to buy a large chunk of land around here, to develop commercially, that's all."

"In what way?"

"In what way what?"

"Commercially develop?"

"Theme parks", he offered rather reluctantly, although unsure as to why.

"What, like Disney, *here*?"

"From what I understand, more adult based."

"What … *kinky*?" she questioned, looking alarmed.

"No, not like that … more leisure-orientated adult pursuits … aimed at people with money and time on their hands. Family and children activity areas as well."

"How much land is involved?" she said, pursuing her line of questioning, seemingly showing concern.

"About two thousand acres."

"*Sheep Dip Farm*, you're referring to Sheep Dip Farm?"

"I didn't say that."

"No, but that's what it is … that's why we went riding today, so you could check out the farm in more detail", she stated, somewhat agitated.

"Not entirely Molly … I wanted to go riding … with you … it also seemed like a good opportunity to kill two birds with one stone."

"How could you?"

"Honestly … my main motive was to go riding with you."

"I'm not talking about *that*", she said angrily.

"Then what?"

"You just don't get it, do you?"

"I'm sorry, Mol", he replied, not wishing to upset her further.

"You've seen the area … it's beautiful and unspoilt. I've taken a week's holiday … to go walking … I often come here … for the peace and solitude that it affords … why on *earth* would you want to go and spoil it?"

"I don't, Mol."

"Yes you do, that's why you're here … and to think … you got me to help you with your dirty work. Damn lawyers … they're all the same, parasites, praying on other people's misery."

"But Mol, I'm a corporate lawyer."

"Personally, I can't see the distinction."

"Have you considered the jobs that this enterprise will create … why … you've told me yourself how depressed the employment situation is."

"That's as maybe, but …"

"You're letting your heart rule your head", he muted, still on the defensive.

"And you're allowing money to dictate your own terms. I'm angry, Richard, can't you see that?"

"Yes Molly, understandably …"

"You'll never get it past the planners."

"Sweetheart, there are jobs at stake."

"So, it's cut and dried is it? We'll see about that, and don't call me sweetheart."

"But Mol."

"Don't you 'but Mol' me … I'm not staying here with you … you've used me." Molly suddenly rose from the table, turned away from it, and hurriedly walked out of the bar. Standing in the pub's car park, she pondered her next move.

"Better give her a little time to cool down", he thought, assuming that she had departed to the powder room. Seeing that both glasses were empty, he stood up and once again approached the bar-counter. "Another refill, please."

"Thanks, me duck", responded the large lady, who proceeded to pull another pint.

Molly, fighting back the tears, took a mobile phone from her handbag and dialled.

Waiting only a few seconds before a ringing tone could be heard, she listened intently; and then heard: "Hello, Colin's Cabs, how may I help you?"

"I'd like a taxi, please."

Some thirty minutes had elapsed since Molly had departed. Richard had assumed, incorrectly, that she had visited the bathroom to cool down and recompose herself, before returning. However, as she had not returned, his mood had changed from

initial frustration to one of desperation. The American had become anxious. "She can't still be in the bathroom", he thought, considering the alternatives.

"If you're waiting on the young lady, I'm afraid you're out of luck, me ducks."

"Sorry", he replied, realising that the rotund lady had been addressing him personally.

"Saw her get into a taxi ... about ten minutes ago ... she seemed a bit upset."

"We had a disagreement."

"I noticed things were getting a bit fractious, m'dear ... not much escapes me, you know ... I expect it'll blow over ... fancy another pint?"

Richard paused for a moment, and then said: "Sure ... why not." He rose from his seat, took three steps and placed his empty glass on the counter.

"Got a wonderful vantage point here, m'dear", stated the landlady, placing the refilled vessel in front of him, at the same time gesturing to the area behind the bar.

"I can see that", replied the American, looking around. "If only I had sat with my back to the counter, I could have seen Molly waiting for that cab", he thought, staring out of the window and onto the floodlit car-parking area that fronted the building.

The warm and rosy bartender went off to collect empty glasses that were dead and in need of washing.

Sitting on a bar stool, devoid of Molly's company, he thoughtfully considered his options: "She's gone back to the Dog and Duck I guess, and I've had too much alcohol to go after her now ... better wait until the morning." Looking at his watch, he was made aware that the time was fast approaching ten-thirty. "Damn it, too late to order any food … Oh well … better have another drink then."

Two more pints and a double Southern Comfort later, it was time to vacate the pub.

"Time, ladies and gentlemen please", hailed the landlady, to an almost empty pub.

Richard sighed, supped the remaining fluid contained within the whisky glass, and vacated the stool, heading for the door.

"Goodnight m'dear … don't you worry … it'll be alright … just you wait and see."

"Thanks … goodnight."

Richard crossed the car-park and onto the tented area. He slowly walked over to where the wigwam had earlier been erected. Unzipping the doorway, he entered the material shelter. "Jesus, I miss that woman." Without disrobing, he climbed into the recently acquired sleeping bag, and attempted to get comfortable. Settling himself down, he focused his thoughts on the conversation that had suddenly turned things sour between himself and Molly. The alcohol muddled his brain, and it was not long before snoring could be heard emitting from the imitation canvas igloo.

Richard awoke late the next morning to the sound of heavy rain hitting the flysheet.

Warm within the sleeping bag, and still not fully awake, he struggled to gather his thoughts. Piecing together the various elements to the previous evening's events, he slowly formed a mental jigsaw of what had transpired. Molly had been angered and hurt, by several components to their conversation. He placed imaginary bullet points to the various causes.

- "She thinks I've used her."
- "She thinks I've deceived her."
- "She objects to theme parks, or at least this one."
- "Her love of the countryside, especially around here."

As he lay snug within the feather bag, the rain continued to fall hard. He tried to analyse his mental bullet-points. "I wasn't really using her, not really. I met her on the moors, I asked her to be my guide … where's the deception in that?" He thought carefully for a moment before making further comment to himself: "She *has* got a point regarding the development, though."

For the first time since arriving in the area, he had finally got in touch with his subconscious. Doubts had crept in, but had been filed away; somewhere in his brain, temporarily dismissed by the overwhelming, overriding, sense of duty to his profession. He had come to realise, thanks to Molly's intervention, that everything he had ever wanted was right here – here in Yorkshire, England. The pace of life seemed much slower than he had been used to in recent years. There was time to take stock, explore the quality, do other things. People were important. Over here, people had time for each other, or at least they did, when compared to the way life was led in the Big Apple. People such as the ones he had met during his short time in England; Rob the Scottish barman, Albert and his faithful companion Jake, Bill the landlord, the stable-lass, the rosy-cheeked large lady, and, of course, Molly. Richard was suffering; he missed Molly dreadfully, and wouldn't wish to upset her in any way whatsoever.

But he had upset her; he hadn't meant to, but he had nevertheless. The melancholy deepened, for as he lay sheltered from the rain, his thoughts turned sympathetically towards a certain Yorkshireman: "Even Derek's got his good points … .nah … don't be stupid … if he has I haven't seen them. God, I need a pee!" Richard unzipped the door and poked his head outside, and quickly popped it back again. He observed the conditions that prevailed outside. The sky was dark and dank. The ground, sodden by a night of torrential rain. Large puddles dotted the landscape. "Shit, I'll get soaked if I go out there." Not one to be easily discouraged, his eyes scanned around. "Ha ha", he said, picking up a cardboard box and opening it. The box contained a compact, lightweight yet durable, cooking stove and utensils.

Resting on his knees, he held the largest of the saucepans to his groin, and taking out his penis, proceeded to empty his swollen bladder. "God, that feels better", he said, giving his male member a shake, "That guy in the shop said the Trianga is probably the best of its type on the market … well, I can sure recommend the pan."

Fortunately for the American, the 4X4 was parked alongside the tent. A short dash, and he found himself sitting on the driver's side front seat. Taking his cellular phone he dialled the Dog and Duck. "Hello, Bill, it's me, Richard … can I speak to Molly, please?"

"Would if I could young fella, but she's gone."

"Gone?"

"Checked out … didn't you know?"

Richard paused before answering: "Yeah Bill … thought I'd catch her before she left."

"Well m'lad you've missed her … she'll be well on the way home by now."

"Have you got her home address, Bill?"

"Yes thanks, haven't you?"

"Wrote it down, but somehow can't find the piece of paper", he lied.

"You two haven't had a row, have you?"

"Nothing like that, Bill", he said, this time only stretching the truth.

"I can't give you, or anyone for that matter, a guest's personal details ... I could lose my licence."

"I see ... well thanks anyway."

"Take care, lad."

"Thanks Bill, bye", he said, and then pressed the end button on the mobile phone.

Richard stared out through the jeep's windscreen with a numb, blank expression on his face. The rain still poured hard, soaking everything it touched. He appeared oblivious to its effect. Although still staring, he had only limited vision, diminishing by the second, due to the screen and surrounding glass misting up on the inside. The continuing clattering of rain on metal somehow went unheard. "Shit, what a mess!" he finally uttered. "I need time to think." Recent events had hit the American hard. "Just when all had seemed to be going so well", he thought. "Damn. Damn. Damn", he said, only this time hitting the steering wheel with his fist.

Reasoning was something Richard had always been good at. He displayed wit and charm when necessary. He had logic and common sense; beneficial to the lawyer practising his art. Ally this to intelligence and quick thinking, and one has the ideal recipe for a career in the legal profession. Yet, probably for the first time in his life, he appeared lost, his skills having seemingly deserted him.

The yellow Lotus sped along the A1(M), heavy rain having earlier hampered its progress. The downpour was now nothing more than light drizzle. "We'll soon be home, Oscar", Molly informed the car.

Home was a two-up, two-down cottage, just outside Mansfield. Mansfield is where Molly taught. Although originally from up North, she had moved to her present location after completing her university education in Nottingham. She had applied for, and secured, a teaching post in Mansfied.

"I would've stayed the rest of the school holidays", she thought, "If only ..." Molly's stance had been based purely on emotion. In the cold light of day, the situation appeared different. Although still angry, she had, during the homeward journey, calmed a little. Applying the powers of reason, she had placed herself, hypothetically, directly into Richard's shoes. She had come to realise that, until a few days ago, he had never once stepped foot onto English soil. They had only just met.

With each mile, Molly's reasoning continued. He had not been at liberty to divulge corporate confidential information and, in any event, why should he?

He had not lied to her; in fact, he had been a complete gentleman the entire time.

"Perhaps I acted a bit hastily. I need time to think … clear my head. Anyway, one fact still remains crystal … and that's the so-called development project. It's not going ahead, Oscar … not while I can still breathe a breath."

The drizzle had ceased; blue patches appeared in the sky. Molly and Oscar had just passed Ollerton. "Only a few miles now", she said, easing off the accelerator.

"The rain's stopped at last … good. First things first", said Richard, getting out of the vehicle. "Better get this stuff packed away."

Although he didn't have the enthusiasm for the task, he nevertheless set about it as logically as his confused brain allowed. Items that had remained dry were returned to their original packaging where possible. The flysheet was removed and hung over the jeep's bonnet. The sun had broken through the clearing dark skies, and its warmth, having already dried the car's hood, now attempted to do the same to the tent's outer sheet.

"Right, what's next?" Richard asked himself. "Get everything out of the tent, I guess."

When all of the camping equipment, including Molly's belongings and his own personal effects, had been restored to the rear of the 4X4, he proceeded to take down the wigwam. "Jesus, this is wet", he uttered, referring to the groundsheet's underside. The American flipped the material upside down and threw it over the roof of his Cherokee. He then dried the bits that were still wet, as best as he could, and along with the poles disposed of them into the off-roader's tail end. "There, that's it … can't do any more for the time being." He looked at his watch; it read one thirty-eight. "I'm starving", he said, in sudden realisation that he had not eaten since lunchtime the previous day. "I'll leave these here to dry. The pub's open." Richard locked the vehicle and headed off to the Wine and Grouse, leaving the inner and outer to dry in the now warm sunshine.

"Hello m'dear", greeted the landlady, "Any news?"

"Not really … any chance of a cup of coffee?"

"Of course, m'ducks."

"And something to eat."

"That's what we're here for", she explained, handing him a menu, "And there's specials on the board."

"Thanks … you're a godsend."

"Fore!" shouted Derek Arkwright, slicing his Titleist ball perilously close to a foursome about to tee off at the twelfth. "Bugger!"

"Happens to the best of us", replied his playing partner.

"It's alright for you Gerald ... you're having a bloody good round ... my driving has been crap all day."

"Yeah, I think it started when you picked me up this morning."

"Sorry about that ... I was in a hurry", apologised Arkwright, having earlier that day tried to negotiate a roundabout by going the wrong way.

"You need Kojak's light on the top of your car."

"Look Gerald, I only ran two red lights."

"Ha, I was referring to the short-cut you took through Safeway's filling station."

"And what was wrong with that?" questioned Derek, feeling somewhat indignant.

"Attempting to save time by driving across a petrol station forecourt at forty-five miles an hour, whilst on a mobile phone, isn't considered safe, Derek."

"I needn't have bothered anyway, not the way I've been playing."

"Well at least the rain's stopped and the sun's shining", offered Derek's playing partner, as they watched Gerald's second shot to the green land within five feet of the hole.

"You jammy bastard, Gerald."

"Skill Derek, skill."

"Yeah, yeah ... now where's my sodding ball?"

The Yorkshireman, with the help of Gerald, eventually located the lost ball. It had penetrated the soil, to the point of being almost buried on the twelfth tee.

"One of them bastards trod on my ball."

"Well, if I was you, I wouldn't confront any of them."

"Why's that?"

"'Cause ... one of them is Harry the Hatchet, and that ball", said Gerald, pointing to the one in Derek's hand, "won't be the only one of yours to get trod on."

"Probably a bit miffed 'cause I nearly hit someone."

"Probably."

"Understandable really."

"Yeah ... that's what I thought."

"Seventy-eight ... not bad", said Gerald, examining his score card, whilst sitting on a bar-stool in the clubhouse. "What did you score?"

"Eighty-six."

"*Eighty-six!*"

"Yeah ... I told you I was having a crap round."

"You never were any good at maths, Derek."

"What d'ya mean?"

"You're lost without a calculator."

"Look … I did shoot eighty-four."

"Eighty-four … it was eighty-six a minute ago."

"Do you want a drink or not?"

"Yes please, a pint of lager tops."

Gerald, a tall, thin, balding, bespectacled man, aged seven months younger than Derek, had known Arkwright since childhood. They had been at school together. Derek considered his former school chum to be a friend. At best, Gerald thought of the hapless Yorkshireman as an acquaintance, and part-time golfing partner. They spent limited social time together, for if the truth be known, Derek Arkwright had always, in the cold light of day, been seen by the younger one as a full-time prat.

"So, what's this business deal you mentioned all about then?" asked Gerald, taking a mouthful of lager tops.

"Can't give it all away, but this is my chance to make some real dosh."

"You've said that before."

"*I did all right.*"

"The operative word is *did*."

"You wait and see, Gerald … when I've finished stitching up that Yank … I'll be in, and he'll be out."

"And how do you propose doing that?"

"Don't have to … he's managing to screw up all by himself."

"In what way?"

"Fallen for a girl he met over here."

"That was a bit quick, wasn't it? He's only been here for a week."

"Yeah, well … you know what they say about the oversexed Yanks."

"Remind me."

"Oversexed, overpaid …"

"And over here."

"Yep, great … for while the cat's away …"

"That rat can play", interrupted Gerald.

"I was going to say mouse."

"Yeah, but in your case rat seemed more appropriate."

"Thanks, Gerald", replied Arkwright, taking the comment as a compliment.

The American, having re-established food and beverage contact with his stomach, vacated the Wine and Grouse. Arriving back at the scene of last night's pitch, he checked the tent to see whether it had dried sufficiently.

"Seems OK", he said, giving the material a quick feel. "Ground's still a bit wet though."

He unlocked the 4X4, and once more opened up the tailgate. Gathering up the modern-day canvas he then proceeded to place it into the vehicle's rear compartment, and said: "I'll fold it up later."

During the drive back to the Grand, he contemplated his predicament. "I don't know where she lives, so I can't contact her. Perhaps she will contact me. Came here to do a job ... all seemed to be going well ... and then this."

His reasoning reflected his present state of mind. Nothing made sense. He suddenly felt isolated and alone. In an attempt to distract his thought processes he turned on the car's radio. A local FM radio station was playing a song by Simon and Garfunkel. The title of the song: 'Homeward Bound'. Richard commenced mouthing the words, loudly joining in with the chorus. When it had finished, his previous thoughts resurfaced. Oblivious to the verbal diatribe on offer by the disc jockey he said: "That's it ... if I can't straighten this thing out with Molly then so be it. I've got a job to do ... anyway ... I can't see what all the fuss is about ... it's not as though we're talking about a Brazilian rain forest."

As he turned into the hotel's car park, his thoughts turned back to the previous day. "I really did have a great time with Molly yesterday." That one comment summed up much of the confusion that he was experiencing at that present time. On the one hand, as a lawyer sent to do a job, his head could sort out the pros and cons logically. On the other, as a man subconsciously in love, his heart could see the environmental aspects of Molly's argument. His confusion extended to conflicting viewpoints regarding the way he lived his own life. Deep down, he hankered for a different existence to the one presently being occupied. All perspectives surrounding the various components that added up to the whole, he subliminally detested. Although successful, he was in a rut, a deep one. One from which there didn't appear, to Richard, to be a way out.

Having safely negotiated the only available parking space, size restricted, due to the thoughtless abandonment of a Renault Espace, the American re-entered the Grand and proceeded to reception. "Any messages?"

"I'll just check, Mr. Waters. No messages", replied the receptionist, handing him his key.

"Thanks."

"You're welcome, have a nice day."

"Yeah ... you too."

Once inside the room his attention turned to matters of personal hygiene. "Bath or shower … bath I think."

"Coo, coo. Coo, coo."

"At least I still have some friends", he said, approaching the window. Opening the glazed orifice, he leaned forward and spoke to the pigeon. "Wan'a cookie?" The tame bird, either by design or hunger, decided to take up the offer.

"Coo, coo. Coo, coo."

"I'll take that as a yes then, shall I?"

"Coo."

He opened a fresh pack of complimentary biscuits and, popping one into his own mouth, broke the others and crumbled them onto the window ledge. "There, that should keep you going 'til I can fetch you something from the dining room. How about a steak?"

The feathered friend, happily pecking at the crumbs, merely shook himself and, in doing so, ruffled his feathers, leaving them loose.

"Guess not. Cup of coffee, then?"

Content with the oatmeal offering, the winged creature continued to consume the handout without further comment.

"I'll make myself one, then", he retorted, picking up the kettle.

Richard, having bathed, now felt extremely tired. He looked at the alarm clock, marking time at his bedside. "Four twenty-eight", he noted. "Think I'll climb into bed and watch a bit of British TV."

In fact, as the hotel's facilities extended to satellite television, the choices on offer were far more extensive than he had first imagined. After perusing many of the various channels that were readily accessible, he summarised the viewing opportunities by stating: "What a load of bullcrap. Just like back home … but with subtitles." He finally settled with the BBC, a John Wayne movie; a cowboy, broadcast by terrestrial transmitters. "That's more like it", he said, dropping the towel from his waist and getting into bed.

Before the Duke had had much of a chance to express himself in his renowned Texan drawl, Richard's eyes became very weary. He struggled to keep them open long enough to at least hear one of his all-time heroes say 'OK little lady', or 'Get off of your horse'. He failed. By the time Big John had uttered one of infamous remarks, snoring could be heard emitting from under the American's duvet.

Oblivious to the sound of gunfire spilling forth from the TV, Richard slept on. Only the pigeon, resting on the ledge outside, appeared disturbed by the cracking noise venting from a Colt Peacemaker. Fearing for its life, the small warm-blooded vertebrate thrust itself forward and left the windowsill. With a frantic flapping of wings, it propelled itself skywards. Richard slept on.

Almost three hours later the American stirred, opened his eyes, and looked at the electronic timekeeper. "Shit, it's nearly seven-thirty!" He got out of bed and turned off the television. "Better get myself freshened up", he said, looking into the mirror and realising that a beard had suddenly appeared.

He went into the bathroom, turned on the taps, and started on his ablutionary tasks. Some thirty minutes later, having shaved, showered, and dressed, he felt well prepared to face the evening ahead. Richard left his room and locked the door. He walked along the corridor towards the lift, thinking: "Jesus, I miss that girl. I hope she phones soon. Don't know whether I'm hungry of not. If I don't eat now, I'll miss dinner."

He paused briefly before adding: "I'll have something light ... that's it ... a salad or something similar." He entered the lift, unaware that the telephone inside his room had commenced ringing. The doors closed and the lift descended.

"I'm sorry, there's no reply from Mr. Water's room, can I take a message?"

"No thanks ... I'll try again later", replied Molly to the hotel's telephonist. She replaced the receiver and stared out of the window. Her red eyes were not fixed on anything in particular. "I do miss him, I hope he's all right."

Molly reached for a tissue. Taking one from a box situated on the windowsill, she wiped a tear away from her cheek. Still focusing on the scenery immediately outside the window, her thoughts and attention remained firmly fixed on one Richard Waters. The visual images failed to register within her brain. The previous evening's emotional reaction to what the American had told her had now mellowed. Her initial response, with regard to Richard's stance, had somewhat softened. She had come to realise the predicament that he had found himself in. She wanted to apologise, to try and square things. Turning away from the glazed opening, she looked at the telephone and said: "I'll try again ... a bit later."

Richard, having satisfied his gastronomic needs, headed for the bar. "A little liquid refreshment to help me through the night might just do it", he muted, striding out of the dining room and thanking the waiter. "I do feel rather awake", he thought, reflecting on the three-hour sleep he had earlier taken. "Just the man."

"Good evening, sir, and how are you this evening?" enquired the barman, engaged in the process of emptying an ashtray.

"Not a good day, Rob."

"Gentleman's measures, then?"

The American appeared slightly confused.

"Doubles", offered a man, situated further along the bar, as by way of explanation.

"In that case, gentleman's measures it is. Yes please, Rob, and one for this gentleman here."

"That's very kind of you, I'll have the same again, please."

The Scot took hold of the almost empty glass being utilised by the man, and held it up to an optic. Pressing the release bar twice, he replaced it in front of the recipient.

"Thank you", he gestured to the barman. "And thank you", he said, raising his glass and looking at the American.

"Don't mention it."

"And what are you going to experiment with first, sir?"

"Sheep Dip sounds good, Rob."

"Aye ... that's a good choice."

"What do you mean by that ... it'll put hairs on my chest?"

"It'll probably prevent, kill or cure, ticks, lice, and other such unwelcome parasites", intervened the other man.

"No ... I mean it's a very nice whisky, easy on the palate."

"Go get it then, Rob", he replied, sitting on a stool adjacent to the one occupied by the tall, well-dressed man, who was now busily tasting his refilled glass.

"The name's Stanley ... Stanley Upbright", informed the stranger, thrusting out a hand.

"Richard Waters", said the American, taking hold of the proffered digits. "Glad to meet you."

"Likewise", responded Upbright, firmly shaking hands.

The Scottish barman placed the chosen scotch onto the bar and said: "There, that'll put hairs on your chest."

Richard chuckled at Rob's remarks, took the tumbler, and lifted it to his mouth. "It's bad enough shaving my face ... I don't want to include my chest as well", he uttered, and then downed the contents with one swallow. "That was too quick to taste ... I'd better have another."

"I'll get that", said Stanley Upbright, adding, "and another one for me."

"Same again for you sir?" asked the barman of Stanley.

"Not this time ... I'll try the Sheep Dip."

"Aye ... good choice ..."

"Yes Rob, we know, it'll put hairs on your chest", interrupted the American.

"No, I wasn't going to say that at all."

"Well, what were you going to say?" inquired Upbright.

"Only that it'll help prevent, kill or cure, ticks, lice and other such unwelcome parasites."

"Gee whiz, Rob", laughed Richard, "You really do know your whiskies."
"I'll drink to that", chortled Stanley.

Richard, in need of some company, continued to pass the evening away perched on a bar-stool, making light conversation with the gentleman he had earlier become
acquainted with. He had established that Stanley Upbright, a civil engineer, was also staying at the Grand, having checked in that day in preparation for a business meeting early Monday morning. Matching each other double for double, their chit-chat had degenerated into little more than typical bar-room politics. Topics of conversation included sport, state of the economy (both sides of the Atlantic), First and Second World Wars, the Vietnam, Falkland, and Gulf Wars, anorexic models, and litter on the streets.
"And what about chewing-gum?"
"Er, what about it?"
"It's everywhere, and I'm not talking about shops."
"Oh I see", slurred the American, "You mean on the sidewalks?"
"Yes … the bloody stuff is welded to the pavements everywhere."
"Same in the States."
"Do you know, I reckon there's enough of the damn stuff on the pavements of London alone to repair the hole in the ozone layer."
"Neat idea Stanley, blast a rocket full of gum up into the atmosphere, spit it out in the right place, and Bob's your uncle … ."
"Problem solved … brilliant."
"On that note, let's have another drink."
"Brilliant … Rob my boy, two more doubles of deep shit please."

Chapter 14

"Good morning Derek, and what can I do for you?"

"Good morning Mr. Grabit, thought I'd better give you a call."

"And to what, pray, do I do you this honour?"

Unsure of what was meant by Grabit's comments, Arkwright continued: "I've just had a call from Colin Williams ... at the Planning Department."

"Go on."

"The meeting has been brought forward to this Thursday ... if that's not OK then it will have to be put off till next month."

"Damn ... oh well ... I'll have to send over the team straight away, they're just about up to speed. What does Waters have to say?"

"Er ... don't know sir, haven't heard from him since before the weekend."

"It's afternoon over there ... are you telling me you haven't made contact?"

"I've tried", lied the Yorkshireman.

"Get a message to him ... tell him to call me without further delay."

"I don't quite know how to say this."

"Say it man ... time is money."

"Well ... he just doesn't seem to be focused ... I did mention it earlier ... .it's as though his heart isn't in it. His mind seems to be elsewhere."

"Does it? Is it the woman?"

"I'd rather not say."

"I see ... get him to call me ... it's *urgent*, tell him. Ted Acerrano and Dan Wolfe are the two guys coming over there to make the presentation. I'll get my secretary to liaise directly with you. Thanks for the call, Derek ... keep up the good work."

"Yes! ... Yes yes yes!" said the Yorkshireman, punching the air with his fist, after carefully replacing the telephone handset. "It's not my fault the

Yank seems to be more interested in chasing skirt." Although Arkwright's comments were far from the truth, this did not restrict him from creating a fire from what little smoke actually existed. "Better ring the sucker, I guess", he said, smiling.

Richard, having enjoyed the company of Stanley Upbright, and copious amounts of scotch, had staggered of to bed sometime after midnight. Two-fifteen a.m., to be precise. Upbright, a man accustomed to such quantities of hard liquor, had risen early and set about his allotted predetermined duties without the merest hint of a hangover.

The American, on the other hand, had not fared so well.

Brrring brrring … brrring brrring … brrring brrring.

"Shit … my head", mumbled the still sleepy one, reaching for the phone.

Brrring brrring.

"Hello."

"I have a call for you sir, a Mr. Arkwright … putting you through."

"At last, hi Richard … I've been trying to get you, problem with the line I guess."

"Sorry?"

"Are you alright? You seem dopey."

"Think he's one of the seven dwarfs, Derek", replied the American, still trying to come to.

"Very good … I was beginning to get a bit worried …"

"Got a headache, that's all, took some medicine for it last night, but I still feel rough this morning."

"As we're on the Snow White theme, I guess it's a case of going to bed feeling happy and waking up feeling grumpy."

"Yeah, something like that Derek. Have a good weekend?"

"Great, played some golf, what about you?"

"Fine Derek, just fine, that is until now", he answered, rubbing his forehead.

"Take a couple of Paracetamol."

"Good idea, I have some Tylenol in my briefcase."

"Grabit wants you to phone him, he say's it's urgent."

"You've spoken with him?"

"Yeah, a short while ago. The planning meeting has been moved forward."

"When to?"

"This Thursday, ten-thirty."

"Damn …"

"No sweat, I've got it sorted."

"Er ... good ... no problems?"

"No ... not on that front ... Grabit seemed a bit pissed though."

"With what?"

"You I guess."

"I'll give him a call and get back to you. Cheers Derek, speak to you later."

"OK, you've got my mobile number, haven't you?"

"Yeah, I'll call you later, after I've spoken to Mr. Grabit, but first I need to take those Tylenol."

"Bye for now."

"Thanks Derek, bye."

Richard replaced the receiver and went over to where his briefcase lay. He placed it on the bed, opened it up and took out a packet of tablets. "Shit, my head hurts", he stated, and then proceeded to the bathroom. Taking a glass tumbler, he filled it with water and popped two of the acetaminophen derivatives into his mouth. He then raised the receptacle to his lips and swallowed. "I wonder what Grabit is upset about? Better yet, I wonder what Arkwright has been saying?" He refilled the tumbler twice more and drank its contents. "I think I'm a bit dehydrated. In fact, I think I'm a lot dehydrated", he said, filling the glass once more.

Richard, having made himself a cup of coffee, telephoned room service. "Hi, could you send me up some sandwiches, I kinda overslept and missed breakfast."

"Certainly sir, what would you like in them?"

"I'm not fussed, whatever's going ... beef or ham ... with mayo."

"Certainly sir, what room number?"

The American hesitated, trying hard to recall the number of the room that he had been staying in for the past week. It suddenly came to him, and he conveyed this information to the person on the other end of the line.

"Thank you sir, the food will be brought up shortly."

"You may be right there", he thought, before answering: "Thanks."

Disregarding the poor signal shown on his cellular phone, he attempted to dial his office in New York.

"Good morning, Hadim Gotcha and Grabit, how may I help you?"

"Hi Ellie, it's me, Richard."

"Hello ... who did you say was calling?"

"It's me, Richard ... Richard Waters."

"How may I help, Mr. Walters?"

"Waters ... can you hear me?"

"I'm sorry, I can't hear you."

The American moved closer to the window, adjusting his stance in an attempt to obtain a stronger signal. "Is that any better?"

"Hello, hello."

"Shit!" he shouted, and then threw the handset onto the bed. "Bloody thing!"

Remembering to press end, he picked up the mobile and turned it off. He walked over to the hotel's land telephone, picked up the handpiece and obtained an outside line, lobbing the portable once more onto the mattress.

"Good morning, Hadim Gotcha and Grabit, how may I help you?"

"Good morning Ellie, how are you?"

"Good morning Richard, or should I say good afternoon? I'm fine, how are you?"

"I'm well ... apart from a sore head that is."

"How's the weather?"

"Great ... overall, some rain yesterday, but otherwise it's been nice."

"Well, that's the pleasantries dispensed with, what can I do for you?"

"Ernest Grabit, if you please."

"OK Richard, talk to you soon."

"Bye for now."

A few moments passed, and Ellie's voice was once more heard emitting from the phone's earpiece: "Putting you through."

"Well my lad, what have you got to say for yourself?"

"About?"

"Well, for a start, I'm here and you're there, update me."

"I understand you already know that the meeting with the planners has been brought forward to this Thursday?"

"Yes, thanks to Derek Arkwright. Tell me something I don't know."

Richard resisted the obvious attempt at sarcasm, like informing his boss of the colour decor of his hotel room. "I'm not so sure now whether this land is a suitable site for the proposed development", he suddenly blurted.

"*What*, you can't be serious. Have you any idea how much money is riding on this?"

"Millions, lots of them I guess."

"You guess right, have you flipped?"

"I've taken the weekend to re-evaluate the proposals ... I'm not convinced that this particular site is suitable."

"You worry me, Waters, you really do. We have the planning permission virtually signed, sealed and delivered, the land purchase agreed, just what is your problem?"

"I think we need to take another look, that's all."

"Son, let me explain, the big bucks are in the deal going through, get it?"

"But ..."

"But nothing. If these theme parks fail, not our problem. The responsibility of making the venture viable falls outside of our remit. Not our concern."

Richard, realising that this particular tack was un-navigable, decided to change course. "You're the boss. When will Ted and Dan arrive?"

"Stephanie has all the details ... but that's not really your concern right now", answered Grabit, lowering his voice. "I want you back here on the first available plane."

"Sorry?"

"Just get back to the office, we need to talk."

"But ..."

"No buts, everything is being taken care of. See you back in the Big Apple."

The telephone went silent. Richard, still holding the handset, remained motionless, puzzled by Ernest Grabit's words.

Several minutes passed. The American, sitting on the bed, tried to reason the situation. "Something's amiss", he suddenly declared out loud, adding: "Arkwright's behind this, I'm sure. Sod it, at this moment I couldn't give a damn about Derek Arkwright, Ernest Grabit, or the bloody project." He was thinking of Molly. He had no way of contacting her, and of all things he had just been summoned back to the States.

"I guess I'd better do what I've been told ... I need to get this sorted." He reached over to where the telephone rested and lifted the receiver.

"Reception, Tina speaking, how may I help you?"

"Hi there Tina, I need to book an airline ticket."

"Certainly sir, let me take down some details."

Having arranged a flight to New York for later that afternoon, he then proceeded to dial another number. He soon heard a ringing tone.

"Hello, Dog and Duck."

"Hi Bill, it's me, Richard."

"Good afternoon lad, what can I do for you?"

"I've been called back to the States ... on business."

"That's nice, thanks for letting me know."

"Woah ... I can't get hold of Molly ... I was wondering ... can you do me a favour?"

"If I can, what is it?"

"Can you get a message to Molly for me please?"

"I guess I can do that for you ... I just can't give you her address, you understand that, don't you my boy?"

"A message will do fine Bill, thanks."

"Fire away, I've got a pen."

"Tell her that …"

"Hold your horses", interrupted the innkeeper, "Bloody pen don't work, hang on I'll get another."

A few seconds later and the publican was once more in dictation mode. "I'm ready now, you can start when you like."

"Thanks, tell her that I've had to go back to New York …"

"Bugger me backwards with a feather, this bugger don't work either."

Richard's patience was close to expiration. Several more seemingly eternal seconds lapsed.

"I'm back and this one works, mind you it's red, you don't mind red, do you?"

"I couldn't care if it was aubergine, as long as it works."

"Right then, I'm ready when you are."

"I'm leaving for New York this afternoon, but I'll be back …"

"Cor, you sound like that Arnold fella, you know in that film 'Terminator'."

"Schwarzenegger."

"Bless you."

The American decided that to explain would only seek to further confuse, better to get back on track. "Thanks."

"You're welcome, sounds like the start of a nasty cold."

"Probably."

"Now where were we, let me see … that's right, you're going to New York this afternoon but you're coming back."

"Tell her I'm sorry, and that if she wants to speak to me, leave a number with you so that I can get in touch."

"Got it, anything else?"

"Yeah, tell her that I love her."

"Will do."

"Thanks Bill, you're a brick."

"Look after yourself, lad."

"And you, bye."

Richard replaced the handset and commenced packing. When this task had been completed, he picked up a plate containing the remnants of the food that had been brought to his room earlier. He approached the window, opened it, and placed the offerings onto the window ledge. A flock of pigeons soon began circling above the scraps. "I'll miss you", he said, as if meaning it. He closed the window, picked up his luggage, and headed for the door. "I'll have to hurry if I'm going to catch that plane", he thought, quickening the pace.

After checking out of the hotel, he was soon sitting in the back of a taxi, heading towards Leeds airport. He turned his neck and glanced rearwards, just managing to catch a glimpse of the Grand before his carriage turned the corner.

Chapter 15

"Hello Molly, it's me, Bill."

"Hello Bill, to what do I owe this pleasure? I didn't take any towels you know."

"I should hope not … they're not worth stealing, mostly all worn out. Got a message for you, from your young fella … that is, if he is your young fella?"

"I don't really know Bill, I think I may have blown it."

"Don't think you have, my dear … he thinks he's blown it."

Molly swallowed. Clearing the lump in her throat, she continued: "What's the message, Bill?"

"He said he's got to go back to America, work or something."

"When?"

"Gone already I expect, he said he'll be back though", answered Bill, still trying to recall that actor's surname.

"When?"

"When what?"

"When is he coming back?"

"I don't know … he says that in all his films."

"Who does?" she asked, wondering what on earth he was alluding to.

"That Arnold fella, big guy with muscles, says 'I'll be back'."

"I want to know about Richard, Bill. When is Richard coming back?"

"Don't know, he didn't say. He said, if you wanted him to speak to you, leave a number with me, and he'll call me, and then be able to call you. I wrote it all down … in red ink."

"Of course I want to speak with him, I love him", she said without hesitation, and at the same time confounded by Bill's reference to red ink.

"Oh yes, and another thing …"

"Yes."

"I'm trying to read my writing. Oh yes … he says he loves you too."

Upon hearing these words, although not in the least romantically portrayed by the message conveyor, tears welled in her eyes. "You've got my number, Bill, and my address, when he calls please give them to him."

"I'll do that for you Molly. Keep your chin up, and remember these words next time, never let the sun go down on an argument. Got that?"

"Got it … thanks Bill."

"Gotta go, work to be done, see you later."

"Bye Bill, thanks again."

"I have an appointment with Mr. Gledhill."

"Ah yes Mr. Oldsworth, take a seat and I'll let him know you've arrived."

"Thank you."

Hugo Oldsworth sat down on one of the chairs provided. Having made an appointment first thing that morning to see his solicitor, he now found himself in the offices of Robert Gledhill and Son. Hugo picked up a magazine, and after noticing that it was almost two years old, replaced it. He looked around; the offices were of the old school: dark, dismal, stuffy. Old furniture, and even older oil paintings on the walls. They depicted scenes of an era long departed. Mostly nautical; sailing ships and raging seas. Client files were scattered on almost every conceivable flat surface. The secretary's desk was piled high with them. There was no sign of a computer. An electric typewriter could be heard clicking away under the skilful fingertips of the middle-aged, tweed-skirted, cardigan-wearing employee. The room could have been, with only very minor adjustments, an ideal setting for one of Charles Dickens' plays.

Dark, dismal, and stuffy summed up the offices of Robert Gledhill and Son. "I like it", thought Hugo, approvingly.

A door opened, and a man of medium height, ruddy complexion, white hair (thin on top), and wearing gold-rimmed half glasses perched on the end of his nose, entered, and announced loudly: "Hugo old chap, good to see you again. Come into my office. Margaret, tea for Mr. Oldsworth … and for me of course." Chortling, he turned towards Hugo and said: "Is tea alright for you, you're not one of these confounded coffee drinkers, are you?"

"Tea's fine Robert, thanks."

"Good girl, Margaret, tea it is then … and some biscuits … digestives. Digestives alright for you?"

Hugo nodded.

"Righty-ho then, walk this way", he said, pointing towards the same door that he had only a few seconds earlier appeared through.

Hugo, resisting any attempt at assimilating Gledhill's stride, followed the man into the office. The room was of similar style and adornment to the outer office, although brighter, thanks to being recently redecorated; the wall colouring was pale lemon.

"Sit yourself down."

Hugo sat. Robert Gledhill walked around the rather large, rosewood desk, and sat himself down behind it. Leaning back in the green leather-backed chair, he stared directly at the man opposite. "Good sale, Hugo, two million, not bad for a day's work."

"It's not sold yet."

"True, but from what you've told me, it's as good as. What are they going to do with the farm?"

"Don't know, didn't ask … some future development apparently."

"Any ideas?"

"Oh, I see, got your solicitor's hat on, have you?"

Gledhill chortled fervently. "Is it that obvious?"

"To a blind man, Robert. I'm not really concerned, just glad to get rid."

"There might be more money in it for you."

"And you, you mean."

"I was thinking of you", responded the solicitor, trying to appear sincere.

"If I got more then so would the Government; I think they've already had enough."

"True, death duties … I mean inheritance tax was paid on a value of £1,750,000."

"Does that mean I've got to pay *more*?" asked Hugo, sitting upright.

"I'm afraid so, but only on the balance."

"That's £250,000."

"Less the capital gains allowance."

"And what's that?"

"Currently £7,100."

"So I've got to pay tax on £242,900?"

"You haven't got a problem with your arithmetic, old chap."

"Not when there's a pound sign attached I haven't. What rate do I have to pay?"

"Scaled to a maximum forty per cent."

"So what's the good news?"

"The good news is that there's no more bad news."

"So I've got to pay another hundred grand in tax?"

"Not quite, but almost."

At that moment a knock sounded on the door. It opened and in came the secretary carrying a tray.

"Thank you Margaret, you're an angel. Don't know what I'd do without her, don't you know", he said, adding another chortle.

Chapter 16

Richard stepped out of the familiar black and yellow cab, paid the driver, and, after picking up his bags, walked towards his apartment building. He paused, turned around and shaking his head said: "It's good to be back … I don't think. The traffic, the noise, the people. Oh well … life goes on." He sighed as he recommenced walking. With a heavy heart he entered the building.

"Good evening Mr. Waters, good to see you back."

"Hi George, how's it with you?"

"Looking good, had a good win on the gee-gees", answered the janitor, smiling.

"Enough to retire and move to Florida?"

"Not quite, but enough for me and the old gal to take a vacation at least."

"Good for you George. How's Felix?"

"He's been just fine … you know Felix, gets it where he can."

"Yeah sure, I know a few people like that."

"Me too", replied the elder, expressing scorn, and then cheerfully added: "He's been purring outside your door a few times this past week."

"Yeah, he's one of the few things I've missed while away."

Felix was a cat of the semi-domestic variety. He had sort of moved in a few years ago.

Although he had not signed any kind of tenancy agreement, no-one seemed to have minded too much. George tended to look out for the neutered ginger tom, but everyone in the apartment building had, at one time or another, offered food and shelter to him. Felix was the kind of cat who demanded the best and usually got it; an up-market, latter-day version of the infamous 'Top Cat'.

"How was England?"

"Great George, just great, met some really nice people, very friendly", he commented, his thoughts flashing to those that he had been become aquatinted with, finally settling on Molly.

"Get the job done?"

"I'd like to think so, George, but between you and me, I'm not sure that getting the job done is necessarily the right and proper thing."

"Ah I see ... a lawyer with a conscious ... that's rare", said George, with a hint of sarcasm, probably born out of personal experience.

Richard laughed lightly, in apparent acknowledgement of the irony contained within the other man's words. "I concur, George. It's a rare occurrence in these days of continual enlightenment", offered the lawyer somewhat philosophically.

George, unsure of the other man's meaning, merely added: "Personally Mr. Waters, I couldn't care less either."

"See you later, George."

"And you", replied the janitor, and, as Richard walked toward the elevator, raising his voice to be heard, he said: "Sometimes the right thing is to follow your heart and not your head."

"Thanks George ... I'll remember that", he said, stepping into the lift.

"Difficult concept for a lawyer, I guess", he thought, referring to the notion of a person involved in the legal profession actually acting upon emotion. He exited the elevator and progressed along the corridor towards his permanent place of residence.

"Well hi there, fella", he said, warmly greeting the feline Felix, who was patiently purring outside the door of the apartment. "Have you missed me?"

The cat rubbed himself around Richard's legs.

"Come on in ... I think there's an unopened can of tuna in the cupboard." He opened the door, and went inside. Felix followed, drooling with anticipation of tasty morsels yet to come. The motivated moggie knew that he could always rely on this particular tenant for first-class cuisine.

"I'd like to say it's good to be home puss", he said, putting down his luggage and then stroking the cat's neck. "It's good to see you, though."

Richard's residence was identical in construction to all the others in the building; individualised only by the personal possessions of each occupant. This particular dwelling showed all the hallmarks of one belonging to a professional male bachelor: functional, yet untidy. Books and magazines lay seemingly everywhere. In fact, on closer inspection, the reading material had been organised into various categories according to definition. There were more books than the allotted space really allowed for; much like an imagined public library that also had to double as a family home that included a number of teenagers. The lawyer's abode was kept clean and tidy due to one Mrs. Marino; a middle-aged lady of Italian descent. She charred for many of the building's residents and, as a result of her efficiency, was revered almost as highly as Felix. Furniture of good quality adorned the property, as did Indian mementos. One fact remained blatantly obvious throughout; it lacked any feminine touches. For the first time since he had lived there, Richard had only now noticed this aspect. He was missing Molly. In this land that was his home, and in this home that was his, there was nothing that reminded him of her. Nothing feminine.

"Wha'd'ya say, puss. Time for the tuna?"

"Meow", replied the furry one, who then resumed drooling.

Richard fed the cat, unpacked his bags, made himself a sandwich, ate it, and then prepared himself for an early night. Unable to sleep on the aeroplane, and suffering from the transatlantic time difference, he felt tired and in need of a decent night's sleep.

He considered it prudent to rest properly, preparing himself for the following day's meet with Ernest Grabit.

"Are you in or out, Felix? I'm going to bed, it's up to you."

"Meow."

"Out it is, then." Richard moved over to the door and opened it. Without hesitation the cat left. "Bye Felix … see you soon."

The feline creature strutted down the hallway in a majestic fashion; synonymous with its breed, it never looked back, or answered in any way.

"I said goodbye, Felix, nice of you to drop in and eat my fish."

Felix disappeared around a corner and headed off down the stairs.

"Oh well, that's my company gone for the evening", he thought, closing the door to the outside world. "Time for bed."

On the other side of the Atlantic, in another such dwelling, (only smaller and more cluttered) sat a man with a glass in hand. The place: Leeds, England. The man: Derek Arkwright. The occasion: Derek's private celebration at his apparent rise, and his overseas colleague's demise. "Good day, if I say so myself. That Yank has been called back to the States, and I'm looking good." He raised the glass containing a blended scotch to his lips and sipped. "Things have gone better than even I had hoped for. I've just got to make myself appear the kingpin in this deal, and then it'll be time to open up negotiations on my fee." He raised the glass once more to his lips. "I don't dislike him", he uttered, referring to Richard. "It's just that this is my chance to get back on top."

Derek refilled his glass from the three-quarter full bottle, and again drank from it. "It's not my fault the guy's a naive jerk." Continuing to consume the whisky, and at the same time enjoying his new-found status, his words, albeit spoken only to himself, became increasingly less decipherable. "I'll soon be driving a new porch … Er … did I say porch … portch … Porsche … that's better … at least I stink so." He rose from the chair and staggered over to the window. Looking out, he slurringly said: "No more bloody Mondeos for me."

His gloating, self-centred, celebratory smile abruptly disappeared. "Oi, what you little fuckers playing at?"

Down below at ground level, where Arkwright's vehicle was parked, three youths were in the process of liberating resaleable parts from it. The Yorkshireman attempted to open the window, and in doing so dropped the part-full glass. "Sod it", he muttered, when suddenly the window gave way and burst open. Derek, still holding on to the handle, was now pivoting on the window ledge, half in and half out. In a confused and unbalanced state, there he rocked, attempting to regain the knowledge as to why he had opened the man-made orifice in the first place. It rapidly returned. "Get away from that car", he screamed.

"Go on mate, jump", responded one of the youths, greeting Arkwright's perceived attempt at suicide with a one-fingered salute.

"Leave my car alone, you little shits. When I get down there I'll bloody kill you", he shouted, the fresh air and circumstances helping to improve both diction and delivery.

"You and whose army, grandad", added another of them, holding a car stereo under his left arm.

Derek eased the window toward the closed position. Allowing for momentum, his weight, and gravity to do the rest, he fell to the floor with a heavy thud. "Shit. Shit, shit, shit. That hurt." He raised himself to his feet and ran to the flat's entrance door. With balance still alcohol-affected, he zig-zagged his way to where the Mondeo rested. "My car, my bloody car ... those bastards have taken the wheels", he shouted, staring at the car perched on a platform of building bricks.

The youths had long gone, and with them, they had taken not only the wheels, but the vehicle's stereo system, a leather jacket, and a set of golf clubs.

"My golf clubs, my bloody golf clubs ... those greedy, thieving, grubby, spot-faced fuckers have taken my golf clubs." He strode round the automobile thumping various parts of the metalwork. "If I get my hands on them, I'll throttle the ..."

"Anything wrong sir?" intervened a voice from behind him.

"What are you, fucking blind?" replied the Yorkshireman, who fisted the car's boot once more, before turning to face the person from whom the voice had come. "Er ... sorry, officer."

"This your car, sir?"

"Er ... yes ... what's left of it."

"Have you been drinking?" inquired the man in blue.

"Yes ... up there." He pointed to his apartment, adding: "That's my flat. I was having a quiet drink ... that is I was ... 'til I looked out of the window. These three hooligans were robbing my car blind. I mean, look at it."

"Have you got the keys, sir?"

"It was locked, the keys are in my pocket."

Derek removed the set of keys from his trouser pocket and dangled them in front of the policeman's face. "See, I've got them", he sneered.

"I'd like you to blow into this bag, sir."

"Bag ... what bag?"

"This one, sir."

"*You expect me to take a breath test?*"

"That's the idea, sir."

"But I haven't done anything."

"Just blow in the bag, if you would, sir."

"You can stuff your bag, I'm not blowing in it. I haven't done anything ... get it ... it's me that's been robbed. What are you, *thick*?"

At this point, the unfortunate Derek found himself being arrested on the grounds of refusing to take a breathalyser, and on suspicion of being drunk in charge of a motor vehicle.

Chapter 17

The following morning, after a good night's rest, Richard found himself making his way to the offices of Hadim Gotcha & Grabit. He had been summoned by his boss, Ernest Grabit. It was Richard's intention to face the man at the earliest possible moment. Traffic above ground was particularly heavy, so the lawyer had decided to make the journey on the subway. Emerging once more into the light, he donned a pair of sunglasses and proceeded on foot to his allotted appointment. The morning was already warm, and the sun shone bright.

"It may be warm and sunny, but it's not England", he thought, jostling with the many others who were also pursuant of their daily objectives. This comment, although an obvious one, did not quite summarise his observations. However, what he had referred to was that the Big Apple, on a Tuesday morning during rush-hour, could in no way be compared to rural parts of Yorkshire, England.

There existed closer comparisons to where he was; namely any big city at their busy times. Essentially, Richard had identified himself with certain parts of the Yorkshire countryside, the people he had met, and with Molly; the one he had fallen in love with.

"Good morning Rachel, how are you?"

"I'm well, it's good to have you back Mr. Waters ... I mean Richard."

"That's better. Is he ready to see me?" he asked, pointing upstairs.

"He said he'll see you at nine-thirty."

"Fine, I'm looking forward to it. So what's been happening while I've been away?"

Rachel proceeded to alert her boss to events that had taken place during his absence. This included not only work-related items, but also local gossip. Who had done what, where, and to whom.

"Gee, a lot can happen in just over a week, can't it?"

"It can around here."

"Well, it is a big office."

"I blame Ally McBeal."

"What, personally?"

"No not her … it's the programme … gives this lot ideas."

"You may have a point there."

"Ah, Stephanie", greeted Ernest Grabit, upon his secretary's entrance, "have you sent the information I requested over to Derek Arkwright?"

"I have, yesterday afternoon."

"Good girl."

Stephanie placed some papers on the desk in front of her employer, and smiled. "These need your signature."

"What about Dan and Ted?"

"They're flying out this afternoon."

"Good, good", replied Grabit, puffing on a fat Cuban cigar. He finished signing the papers that Stephanie had brought to him. "Thanks, Steph."

"Is that all sir?"

"Tell Waters I'm ready to see him … that's if he's arrived."

"Oh, he's here sir … saw him first thing."

"Good, good … that'll be all", he said dismissively, taking another long draw on the tobacco stick.

Without touching her forelock, the secretary picked up the documents and left the office. Ernest Grabit, leaning back in his chair, exhaled a blue smoke cloud.

"The wanderer returns", said Grabit, as Richard entered his boss's office.

"Good morning", he replied curtly.

"Well … sit down."

Richard sat.

"What have you got to tell me?"

"Why have I been called back?"

"You don't know?"

"Should I?"

"We're not going to get very far if every time a question is asked, it is answered with another, are we?"

"No, probably not. So why have I been called back?"

"From information I've been privy to, it appears that you have become somewhat of a liability."

"*Liability?* I take it Arkwright is your source?"

Ernest Grabit, declining to answer the question, decided to ask one instead. "This project is a big one, lots of money involved. Do you expect me to jeopardise the firm's position?"

"Of course not, it's just seems to me that you've acted a bit hastily. I don't know what Arkwright has told you, but it's a fair guess it's all lies."

"*You're* not involved with a women you met there?"

"Personally, I don't see where that's any of your business."

"It is, if it affects the firm."

"But it hasn't … I've achieved what you sent me there to do. That is, so far, but now I'm not there to see it through."

"Let's clarify that, shall we. The last time we spoke you seemed to have a change of heart … ring any bells?"

Richard, not wishing to discuss the project's merits at this time, pressed on. "So who's running the show now?"

"It seems to me that Derek Arkwright is more than capable of pulling this one together."

"Says who … Derek Arkwright, I presume?"

"I'm not entirely stupid, Richard, the guy has worked for us in the past. We do have a file on him, and he was recently vetted."

The younger man thought for a moment, conjuring images of the Yorkshireman's trip to a veterinarian, he said: "Yes, castration would seem appropriate in his case."

"*Sorry?*"

"I know you're not stupid, but you don't know Arkwright like I do. The man's devious; he can't be trusted. He's only in it for himself … seemingly at my expense."

"You really don't like him, do you?"

"In a word, no. Look, he's placed a knife in between my shoulder blades, and he's hoping you're going to twist it in. His plan appears to be working."

"I've known you for a long time, Richard. I didn't call you back because I didn't think you could do the job. I made a judgement call; you seemed to have gone sentimental on me. I can't have that. This is business. It's a dog-eat-dog world out there."

"Yeah, and I guess I'm the bone."

"Take a couple of days off. Come back in on Thursday. I'll put you on another case."

"So, I'm off this one then?"

"It's too big to risk, sorry", said Grabit patronisingly, and then, re-lighting his cigar, he added: "Get this girl out of your system. No good can come of it. You need to get yourself re-focused. You have a good future with this firm, don't do anything that would make me think otherwise."

The hairs were standing up on the back of the young American's neck. He was furious, but this was not the right time to let it show. "OK, I'll take the two days. In the meantime, a word of advice: watch Derek Arkwright." Without waiting for a response, Richard stood up, turned, and left Ernest Grabit's office.

Some twenty minutes later the disillusioned lawyer stood alone in Central Park.

Alone, except for the abundance of wildlife making the most of this oasis within a desert of concrete and sky-rise. And, of course, the hundreds of people milling about.

Joggers with headsets, skateboarders with headsets, rollerskaters and rollerbladers with headsets. Little old ladies, feeding ducks with pieces of stale bread, also wearing headsets; the ducks, that is, not the little old ladies. Policemen on horseback. Children playing. Children on horseback. Policemen playing.

"Gee, this is a strange town", thought Richard, sitting on a park bench and observing life as it went before him. Joggers and jugglers. Mimers and muggers. The city that never sleeps, cosmopolitan extremes. Anything and everything happened here. He continued with his thoughts: "This is not the place to come and write a thesis on defining normal."

Richard had gone to the park to think. He needed time and space to do so. On the surface things did not seem to be working out as originally anticipated. Below the surface the situation appeared worse. "I need to talk with Molly, try and straighten things out. I wonder if Bill has managed to get her number. Will she want to talk with me? God knows."

A pigeon flew overhead and deposited what Richard interpreted as a critical comment on his present predicament. He stared at the dropping lying on the grass between his feet. "A narrow miss", he said to himself smiling. "Perhaps it's an omen."

At that moment, either the same pigeon on a re-run, or another from the same squadron, released yet another rectal bomb, this time resulting in a direct hit.

"Shit!" exclaimed the recipient of the bird's cargo. Taking a tissue from his jacket pocket he wiped away the faeces from his forehead.

Chapter 18

"I should bloody well think so."

"No need to take that attitude, Mr. Arkwright", informed the officer-in-charge.

"It's all right for you … you weren't locked up in a cell all night."

"You've been released without charge."

"That's because I was the bloody victim."

"You were also drunk … with keys to your car on your person … and you refused to give a breath test. You were also abusive to the attending constable."

"Well that's hardly surprising, is it? My car had just been raped by three louts, and it's *me* that gets arrested."

"We have your statement; sir, the matter is under investigation."

"You've not heard the last of this … not by a long way."

"I'm sure we haven't, sir. Anything else?"

"Yes, as a matter of fact. What chance have I got of getting my belongings back? I suppose these entrepreneurs have got away with it?"

"We're doing what we can, Mr. Arkwright. You'll be kept informed."

"So in other words my chances are slim and bugger all?"

"Have a nice day sir", replied the sergeant, turning away from the station counter and moving over to a filing cabinet.

"Bastards", muttered Arkwright as he left the building.

He stood on the pavement, placed his left hand into his trouser pocket and took out a set of keys. "Bastards, bastards, bastards", he said again, upon realising that although he had his car keys, he didn't, in fact, have his car. "I suppose I'll have to find a bloody taxi." He looked up and down the street. He could do that because the street inclined to his right. He looked up and down the street again. No sign of a horseless carriage. "Bugger it, I'll have to walk." A few drops of rain fell to the ground. "Jesus, now it's started to rain." In the absence of a coat, Derek raised the jacket collar around his neck, and placed his hands inside the pockets. "Things just can't get worse." No sooner than he had finished speaking those words, he immediately regretted saying them. For, at that precise moment, the heavens opened.

Brrring brrring, brrring brrring.

"Now what! That phone'll be the death of me."

The landlord of the Dog and Duck had been engaged in watering the various plants that occupied borders, tubs, hanging baskets, and other such horticultural containers, adorning the inn's exterior. Keen to complete this onerous task prior to the onslaught of the lunch-time trade, he expressed irritation at being disturbed for the eighth time in less than one hour.

"Bugger me, if that's another rep I'll … .Hello, Dog and Duck."

"It's me, Molly. Has he called yet?"

"No, not yet, said he would mind."

"All right … sorry to disturb you Bill."

"Don't you worry about that. Anything for you."

"You're a sweetie."

"What, like a humbug, you mean?"

"I didn't mean like that … mind you I bet you are a bit of a humbug sometimes."

"Well you know what they say."

"What's that?"

"It takes all sorts."

"Very good Bill. Bassett's 'Liquorice All Sorts'."

"*Bugger me,* I've left the tap running again. That's the third time this morning. My flowers will be flooded. Gotta go, bye Molly."

"Bye Bill … thanks", she said, as the telephone went dead.

Molly had time on her hands; school was out for the summer. She waited in anticipation for a call from Richard. She needed desperately to apologise for her actions, and to explain the reasoning behind them. She needed his forgiveness. She needed him.

Brrring brrring, brrring brrring, brrring brrring.

"I'll bury that bugger", said Bill, upon hearing the telephone ring. "Cor, I would be on my own today, bugger it!"

Brrring brrring, brrring brrring.

"All right, I'm coming." Out of breath, the landlord and part-time gardener picked up the telephone. "Dog … and … Duck."

"Are you all right Bill? You sound breathless."

"I am ... I ... just ... ran ... in ... from ... the garden. Good ... job I ... gotta ... bell."

"I'm sorry."

"That's all right, Molly", replied the landlord, his lungs up to capacity. "What can I do you for this time? Coming to stay for another week? We'd love to see you."

"My goodness, you have got your breath back."

"Not dead yet."

"Sheep Dip Farm, do you know the name of the person who owns it?"

"Yes I do. Hugo Oldsworth, haven't seen him since the funeral."

"His parents' funeral?"

"Yes, tragic it was, skiing accident, tragic."

"Do you happen to have his number or address, Bill?"

"As a matter of fact ... I don't. Lives in London."

"Yes, I know."

"Wha'da ya want him for then?"

"Personal, can't say."

"Women ... they do like their bit of mystery."

"Men ... they do like their bit of gossip."

"Toupee."

"Touché."

"Bless you."

"It's touché, not toupee, means an indication of an opponent's success."

"All right ... keep your hair on. Hang on, I think I've got one of Hugo's business cards here somewhere."

Molly stared at the piece of paper on which she had written Hugo Oldsworth's address and telephone number. Bill had kindly given her this information. Now that she had it, she seemed unsure as to what she was going to do with it. "If only Richard would phone", she thought, "I don't want to jeopardise his position by interfering, but how else can I ..."

A knock sounded at the door, interrupting her thoughts. Molly went to answer it.

Opening the front door she found herself confronted by a man holding a briefcase.

She eyed the individual as he commenced speaking. "Good morning madam, my name's Mark Biggs, and I represent a company called Homeprove, I wonder if I could interest you in ... ."

"No thanks", she replied, shutting the door on the greasy haired-man in his early twenties, wearing a black suit with brown shoes and Bart Simpson socks.

The deflated salesman turned away from the door and walked along the path to the front gate. On his way, using his right hand, he decapitated five foxgloves, two delphiniums, and a particularly attractive kniphofia. Tossing the red-hot poker onto the garden, he opened the gate and entered the street. Without shutting it, he turned to his left, and proceeded along the road. "This is a shitty job", he said, opening Molly's nearest neighbour's gate and entering the opening. Lifting his head, and quickening the pace, he strode along the path to the bungalow's front door. About to knock, he noticed a doorbell button. He raised his right arm, and using his index finger, pressed it firmly. Letting it ring for several seconds, he removed the digit and waited.

"All right, all right, I'm coming", came a voice from the inside. The door opened and an elderly gentleman appeared.

The salesman started his pitch: "Good morning, my name's Mark Biggs…"

"I'm not interested."

"And I represent a company called Homeprove …"

"I'm not interested … really."

"I wonder if I could interest you in …"

"Look sonny, I said I'm not interested, which means, that I'm not interested, so sod off."

"But you haven't heard what it is that I've come to talk to you about."

"No, and I don't want to, so piss off and don't come back."

"All right, calm down, no need to get abusive."

"*Abusive*, you think I've been abusive. This is my property. You're intruding on it, and my time. I told you I'm not interested, and I told you that politely. If you want to *hear* abuse, I can oblige. Fuck off."

The man, still standing on the doorstep, decided at that moment to cut his losses and leave. Walking towards the road, he heard the property owner say loudly: "And don't touch those flowers."

"This really is a shitty job", said the salesman, as he walked along the street in search of a potential customer.

Brrring brrring, brrring brrring, brrring brrring.

"Who is it this time? Well at least I'm not watering the plants."

Brrring brrring, brrring brrring.

The landlord of the Dog and Duck was in the process of drinking a deserved cup of tea when the telephone sounded. He had, by now lost count of the number of times it had rung that day. His plants and flowers had been well watered earlier that morning, despite the many interruptions. He had successfully dealt with the lunchtime trade, and, with the public bar now closed for the afternoon, he could, for a little while at least, relax.

Brrring brrring, brrring brrring.

He walked over to the phone and lifted the receiver. "Dog and Duck."

"Hi, Bill, it's me, Richard."

174

"Richard my boy, where are you?"

"At home Bill, why?"

"What … in America?"

"Yes, in my apartment."

"You sound as if you're in the next room."

"The wonders of modern technology, eh Bill?"

"You can say that again. People keep saying I should go on the World Wide Web."

"The Internet … why not Bill, it can bring the world to your doorstep."

"Well … I'm a bit worried about all that surfing lark."

"Why's that?"

"Can't swim."

Richard, unsure as to whether the Englishman was joking or not, changed the subject. "Have you spoken with Molly?"

"Yes."

"And?"

"Got her telephone number, and her address for you."

Richard's heart lifted. "Really, that's great news Bill, thanks. That's brilliant. So she wants me to contact her."

"Richard my lad, she loves you. Phone her right away. She's been waiting on your call."

"Thanks Bill, I owe you."

"Happy to help young love blossom."

"That reminds me, how are the flowers? They looked good last time I saw them."

"They're looking good … the secret is to make sure they don't get too thirsty", said the Englishman, adding: "Plenty of water … and, occasionally, beer out of the drip trays. Real ale mind, not lager."

"Badger's Water?"

"No, beer."

The American, puzzled either by the British sense of humour, or Bill's failure to grasp conversational context, decided to bring the communication to a close. "All right Bill, I'll speak to you soon."

"All right then, goodbye."

"Goodbye Bill, thanks again."

The telephone went silent, and the Englishman replaced the handset. "That fella's always thanking me", he said to himself, picking up the partially drunk cup of tea. "Yuck, the bugger's gone cold", he blurted, spitting the beverage back into the receptacle.

"What'da'ya mean my policy doesn't cover me if the vehicle is left unattended at night? What am I supposed to do, bring it upstairs and keep it the spare bedroom?" argued Derek Arkwright.

"Hardly, but when you completed the proposal, you did state that the vehicle would be kept in a locked garage whilst at your home address", retaliated the female voice on the other end of the telephone line.

"But I don't even have a garage", smirked Arkwright, thinking, "that's got em."

"Really, then why did you tick the box that said that it would be kept in a locked garage?"

"Did I?"

"Yes, you did."

"Well it must have been a mistake."

"In that case it's a costly one … for you."

"So you're not going to pay out then?"

"I'll send you a claim form. Fill it in, and return it as soon as you can."

"And what, you'll refute it?"

"Each case is looked at on its merits."

"I'm not concerned about other cases, only this one", fumed the Yorkshireman.

"All I am prepared to say, sir, is that it doesn't look good."

"You're right there, my car has been vandalised, items have been stolen, and you and your company couldn't give a toss."

"That's not fair sir, our customer care policy is second to none."

"So it may be, but your bloody insurance policies stink."

"There's no need to take that attitude. You advised us that your vehicle is kept at your address in a locked garage, but, in actual fact, you don't even have a garage. If you had had one, then a more sympathetic view might have been shown."

"It looks like I've already been found guilty without ever having had a trial."

"What I'm trying to say, sir, is this: if someone has a garage and usually keeps his or her vehicle locked in it at night, but on the odd occasion leaves it parked outside, and a potential claim occurred, then my company would take a sympathetic overview."

"Yeah yeah, and pigs may fly", answered Arkwright, not helping his cause.

"Complete the claim form, get it back to us, and our claims department will look at it."

"OK … send the bloody form."

"Thank you for calling Penurious Assurance, have a nice day."

"Bollocks."

"I've got to get some transport. Those Yanks will need picking up from the airport tomorrow", thought the despondent Arkwright.

Ted Acerrano and Dan Wolfe were due to arrive at Gatwick Airport in the early hours of Wednesday morning. They had been booked into the Gatwick Hilton for the night, or rather what remained of it, and would then take a connecting flight to Leeds later that same morning.

"Suppose I'd better hire a car. I know, I'll get something decent and charge it to expenses", he said to himself, his spirits already showing positive signs of having lifted. "I wonder if Waters returned the jeep?"

The American had indeed parted company with the Cherokee, having restituted it to the original hirer prior to his departure back to the States. He had also placed the various walking and camping equipment, purchased earlier at Worlds Apart, in storage at the Grand Hotel.

"A Range Rover, now that sounds about right. Yes, that's it, I'll hire a Range Rover." The thought of driving this particular prestigious vehicle excited the inimitable Yorkshireman. "Create a good impression, that's my motto", he uttered. Taking hold of his Filofax, Derek flicked through the pages until he found the entry that he had been searching for. "Got it!" He picked up the telephone and dialled.

"Good afternoon, Hertz, how may I help you?"

"I'd like a Range Rover please … a.s.a.p."

"The earliest would be Friday."

"Shit!"

"Sorry?" replied the female representative, not quite catching Arkwright's salacious comments.

"I really would like a Range Rover … or a big Merc."

"Ah, you're in luck sir, we do have a Range Rover. A cancellation, it's only got four hundred miles on the clock."

"Excellent. Good girl, I'll take it. I'll want it at least for seven days, maybe longer", said an exuberant, if not grammatically correct, Arkwright. Finalising the details he replaced the receiver, saying out loud: "Yes … .yes, yes, yes."

He then started to sing: "The only way is up, oh baby."

Chapter 19

Molly could hear the telephone ringing as she fought with her handbag in an attempt to find her front door key. "Come on", she said to herself, her hand delving deep into the bag. "At last", she uttered, her hand successfully emerging with the key. She hurriedly inserted it into the lock and opened the door. Leaving the aperture open, she ran to the telephone.

Brrring brrring.

Thankfully, it was still ringing when she picked up the handset. "Hello!"

"Good afternoon, my name is Mark Biggs and I represent a company called Homeprove, I wonder if you would be interested in …?"

"No, I would not!" Molly angrily replaced the receiver, and marched towards the front door. "Damn salesmen", she muttered, removing her grocery shopping from Oscar. She entered the cottage, closed the door with her right foot, and proceeded to carry the bags into the kitchen. Just as she was about to place them onto the table, the phone rang again.

Brrring brrring.

"If that's that salesman, I'll … Hello!"

"Molly … it's me, Richard."

Her face lit up, her smile radiant. "Hi, I've missed you, I'm sorry", she blurted, tears welling.

"What for? It's me that should apologise."

"Don't be silly, I over-reacted. It was my fault."

"Gee, it's great to hear your voice. I've missed you too. And it's not your fault."

"I shouldn't have acted that way."

"I agree, you did kinda go for the jugular", he said, softly laughing.

"Do you forgive me?"

"Nothing to forgive."

"Thank you. Why did you back to the States?"

"I was summonsed …"

"Because of me?" she interrupted.

"Partly … Derek Arkwright has been causing trouble. He used you to get to me, that's all."

"I'm sorry."

"Don't be, it's not your fault. In a way … I'm glad."

"*Glad!*"

"I've been doing a lot of thinking, Mol. Perhaps it's time for a change. I have some leave due. Thinking of taking a vacation."

"Where are you going?"

"England … that's if you want to see me."

"Of course I do … you can stay here, with me. Did Bill give you the address?"

"Yes."

"When are you coming?" she said, sounding excited.

"I could fly out tomorrow."

"Great, what about your bosses?"

"I've been taken off the Yorkshire project. They've given me 'til Thursday to sort myself out. I'll phone them tomorrow and tell them I'm taking a vacation. That will give me time to discuss the matter with you. I'm considering quitting the firm, but I need to talk to you."

"Don't do anything you're likely to regret."

Richard momentarily reflected on Grabit's advice concerning Molly; a woman he had never met, and then said: "My only regret is that I didn't somehow meet you years ago."

"That's sweet."

"So are you, Mol."

Molly could feel her heart pound. "I've still got three weeks before term starts. How long can you stay for?"

"I was kinda hoping for, forever."

Molly could now hear her heart pound. "What, and raise small white buffalo?"

"I'd love nothing better, except perhaps for raising some kids."

Molly could now see her heart pound. "Are you serious?" she asked tentatively.

"Deadly. What about you?"

"Raising sheep … and children … with you?"

"Yes", he answered tentatively.

"Well, that depends."

"On what?"

"How many."

"How many what, sheep or children?"

"Children."

"Oh I don't know, about a dozen?"

"I was thinking two, maybe three."

"I see … one of each."

"Is this a proposal or a proposition?"

The American thought for a moment before responding. "Before I contemplate any kind of proposal, I have to sort things first. No job, no money. Anyhow, what does a farm cost over there?"

"I don't know, how long is a piece of string?"

"Good point. I'd better hang up now Mol … I've got airline tickets to arrange. Do you have an e-mail address?"

"Yes, it's MollyWeston@Bigfoot.com."

"I'll mail you with my flight details."

"I'll pick you up from the airport. Gatwick or Heathrow?"

"Not sure yet, I'll let you know."

"OK Richard, I'll speak to you soon."

"Bye for now Mol, I love you."

Molly could feel, hear and see her heart pound. "Bye, I love you too."

Richard, heartened by his conversation with Molly, reflected on her words. Was it possible to change direction? Did he want to? Could he live in England, and find suitable employment? Would he be allowed to? "I wonder if Molly would like the States?" he asked himself. He thought about the previous Saturday spent on horseback. That's where he wanted to be. He no longer wanted to be a lawyer. He was now not sure if he had ever wanted to be a lawyer. "That's not true", he murmured, "I did once, but not anymore."

Richard's thoughts turned to his professional beginnings. Original hopes, dreams, and aspirations, inspired by his father's support and guidance, had been eroded over the years; due in part to man's greed, and lust for power and possession. He reflected on his roots. Thinking out loud, he said: "Time for a change, before it's too late."

Chapter 20

The sun shone brightly the following morning. Derek Arkwright prepared himself for the day ahead. He showered and shaved. He dressed, finally deciding upon the grey designer two-piece suit, with a complementary white shirt. His choice of necktie somewhat altering the otherwise acceptable image. It sported a Disney character – Mickey Mouse to be precise – in fact, several of them. The time was nine-thirty, and it was time for the Yorkshireman to leave his flat. His first task, to collect the all expenses (yet-to-be) paid for hire-car. A hooter sounded outside. "That'll be the taxi", he said, looking into a hand-held mirror, and combing his hair with the other. He picked up his briefcase and left the flat.

"Hertz."
"What does?" inquired the cab driver.
"Hertz Rentals, Leeds City Station", replied Derek, stepping into the vehicle.
"Nice tie", said the cabbie, turning away and grinning.
"Thanks. It was birthday present from a friend."
"I had a friend like that once."
"What happened to him? Or should I say her?"
"Nothing much … except that we're not friends anymore."
The Yorkshireman, sitting in the rear of the taxi as it made its way to Leeds City Station, pondered over the driver's remarks. "What's my tie got to do with him losing a friend?" he silently asked himself.
"Picking up a car?"
"Sorry?" replied Arkwright, still deliberating.
"Hertz."
"What does?"
"They rent out cars, Hertz."

"Oh yes, I see. Yes, a Range Rover", answered Derek, endeavouring to impress.

"Really, what a coincidence, I've got one of them at home. Use it for towing the boat."

"Sod it", thought the man in the back, adding: "Bet it's an old one."

"Bit extravagant though, it's six months old, and only done two thousand miles", said the driver.

"Sod it", thought Arkwright, deciding not to reply.

"Do you have a car?"

"If I did, I wouldn't be sitting in here, and getting you to take me to a car rental company to hire one, now would I?"

"Good point."

"As a matter of fact, I do have a car, but thanks to three rotten bastards on some government-sponsored self-employed initiative scheme, namely, unemployment benefit, it doesn't have any wheels."

"I think it's called Job Seeker's Allowance now."

"Whatever. In any case, it's a good bet that their nocturnal thieving is, no doubt, supported by the DSS."

"I don't think the Social would condone car theft", offered the one behind the wheel.

"I mean fiscal, not physical."

"You're probably right", agreed the taxi driver, remembering that he only declared, to the Inland Revenue, a small percentage of the tips he received.

The cab pulled up outside Derek's chosen destination. He got out and paid the driver.

"Thanks mate."

"Keep the change."

"Thanks, another ten customers like you and I'll be able to buy myself a pint."

"If you're looking for a tip then I'll give you one. I should get that meter fixed if I were you, it's been stuck for the last ten minutes."

The Yorkshireman walked off smiling. The cabbie tapped the cab's meter. He then tapped it again, only this time harder. Sticking his right arm out of the vehicle's window, and raising two fingers upwards, he shouted: "Twat!"

Arkwright did not turn around as the taxi drove off. Still smiling, he entered the vehicle rental office.

"Good morning, how may I help you?"

"The name's Arkwright, Derek Arkwright."

"And you're looking for an Aston Martin DB5, with a few extras?"

"Pardon?"

"The Range Rover?"

"Er, yes", replied Derek, somewhat puzzled. "Perhaps he's on something", he thought, and then said: "It is ready, isn't it?"

"Of course it is sir", answered the assistant, producing the paperwork.

With the formalities completed, Derek was handed the keys.

"It's parked over there", said the helpful young man, as he looked out of the office window and pointed to where the vehicle was stationed.

"Thanks, you've been most helpful", responded the Yorkshireman, clutching the car keys.

"We aim to please sir ... by the way, I like your tie."

"It was a present from a friend."

"Probably taking the mickey."

"Sorry?"

"Mickey", he answered, pointing to the tie. "Mickey Mouse", he reiterated.

Derek, in a moment of realisation, returned the quip. "Not so much taking the Mickey, more like giving it", he laughed.

The assistant acknowledged the pun with a nod and a forced smile. Derek picked up his briefcase and proceeded to the door, opened it and left.

"More like taking than giving, I'd say", whispered the clerk, this time shaking his head, and then added: "I wouldn't wear that for a bet."

Derek, a little reticent, cautiously approached the Range Rover. "With my luck of late, the bloody thing probably won't start. Even if it does, it'll more than likely break down within a mile." Arkwright's eyes widened, and then brightened, as he viewed the automobile close up. The car, having been recently cleaned, shone in the sunlight. A deep metallic blue gave the vehicle a majestic appearance. "What a handsome piece of kit", he said to himself, temporarily forgetting his earlier fears.

Opening the Rover's door, he climbed in, placed the briefcase on the front passenger seat, and inserted the ignition key into the lock. With one turn of the key the engine fired. Ticking over, the drive unit could hardly be heard. "This is more like it", he softly said, driving off. "Bugger it, I could have brought some CDs", he muttered, noticing that the vehicle came with a fitted compact disc player. He turned left out of the car park and headed towards the airport. "Just time to pick up Terminal Ted and Desperate Dan", he thought, looking at the on-board clock.

"What's the guy's name again?"

"Derek Arkwright", replied Dan Wolfe, a tall thick-set man, with blonde hair; his facial features not unlike the rather descriptive possibilities of his surname. The two Americans had arrived at Leeds Airport, and were in the process of disembarkation.

"Do you know him?" asked Ted Acerrano, a slim man of medium height, with short dark hair, and wearing round, gold-rimmed glasses.

"No, but I'm told he's on the ball."

"From what I hear he's on both of them ... Richard's."

"Yeah, poor guy, it does seem like he's been shafted."

"Not our problem Dan, we're here to make a presentation ... that's all. I have no desire to get caught up in internal politics."

"Me neither", replied Dan, picking up a case from the carousel.

"This little baby drives like a dream. I might get one of these instead of a Porsche", concluded Arkwright, as he brought the Range Rover to a halt, and turned off the engine.

He looked at the car's clock, and then at his wristwatch. "Bugger it, I'm late", he murmured, hurriedly exiting the English 4X4. He walked briskly as he made his way across the car park. A few minutes later and he had reached the arrival lounge. "Shit, how will I know them?" He looked around. "No-one's off the flight yet", deduced Derek. He looked around again. "That's it, I need a piece of paper", he proclaimed, upon seeing someone holding an A4-sized sheet of card, with the name 'Beryl Watkins' on it. "Shit ... I left my briefcase in the car." The Yorkshireman scratched his chin and thought hard.

"'Scuse me Miss, would you happen to have a piece of paper I could use?" asked Derek of the young women he had just accosted. "I'm rather desperate", he urgently stated.

"Oh I see ... ran out have they ... I think I have some tissue in my handbag."

"Not bog paper, you silly bitch, I need some to write on."

"*You rude bastard!*"

"That's as maybe, darlin'", replied the Yorkshireman, lapsing into cockney brogue, adding: "But I can also be charming. You, on the other hand, will always be ugly."

With her face depicting a flared redness, reminiscent of a bull whose parentage had just been called into question, she swiftly raised her right arm and hit Derek firmly around the head with her handbag, sending him crashing to the floor.

"And you've got no fashion sense, you arrogant prat, *just look at that tie*", she angrily retorted, turning away and storming off.

The man on the ground rubbed his head and said to himself: "What's wrong with my tie? Everybody else likes it. I got it from a friend."

Picking himself up from the floor, Derek re-focused. Turning towards a passing male art student, he said: "Can I have a sheet of that paper, please?"

The ginger-haired youth obliged; tearing a blank page from his sketchpad, he handed it to the impatient Arkwright.

"Thanks, can I borrow one of those felt-tips?"

"What colour?"

"I don't care … any colour … red. Quick, I'm in a hurry."

The young man took out a red felt-tip pen, and handed it to Derek, who virtually wrenched it from the other man's hand, and then hurriedly wrote something on the piece of paper. "Thanks, you're a life-saver", he said, returning the pen.

"Glad to help", answered the art student, taking the pen, and, at the same time, intently staring at Derek's tie.

"It was a present", offered the Yorkshireman, as if by way of explanation.

"Had to have been, I guess", replied the other, walking away.

"Ginger tosser", muttered Arkwright to himself.

At that moment, passengers began entering the arrival lounge. Among them were the two Americans.

"I guess that must be Arkwright'", said Ted Acerrano.

"Where?"

"Over there", he nodded, his hands occupied in the execution of luggage carrying.

"You mean that guy holding a piece of paper with the words 'Tan and Ded' written on it?"

"Yeah … the one with the shitty tie."

"Looks like our man all right", responded Dan Wolfe, adding: "Good thing our names are not Buck and Frank."

Chapter 21

It was Wednesday morning in New York, and Richard Waters was airborne once more. The Boeing 747 that carried him had left terra firma behind. The Statue of Liberty, a diminishing dot in the distance, soon faded out of sight. To the people beneath it, it remained the same size. To those on the ground who had noticed, it was the plane that became a decreasing object in the sky, until it too, disappeared.

"All things are relative", thought the lawyer, looking out of the window at the clouds below, with no obvious mental connection to Albert Einstein. Still staring into the clouds, he reflected on events that had taken place earlier that morning. Ernest Grabit had thought it a marvellous idea to take a three-week sabbatical.

"Just what you need, my boy", he had said. "A vacation will do you the world of good."

Grabit had not asked Richard where he had intended spending this suddenly requested leave; the American had considered it prudent not to divulge this particular piece of information.

"Just wants me out'a the way", he thought. "Still, suits me." He had electronically mailed Molly with the flight details. Molly had electronically acknowledged receipt of them. She would be waiting at Gatwick Airport later that day for his arrival. Richard was looking forward to seeing her. "I've only known her for less than two weeks. Talk about love at first sight, and whirlwind romances", he thought, still staring out of the window.

"Drink, sir?" inquired the stewardess politely.

"Er ... sorry, I was miles away."

"That's the idea sir, we're in an airplane."

"Very good ... I'll have a coffee."

"Certainly sir, black or white?"

"White."

"With or without?"

"Without."

"Certainly sir", replied the beaming stewardess, wearing a tag on her chest bearing the name Angela.

"Thank you", he said, taking the cup.

In an aisle seat, adjacent to the row where Richard was sitting, sat an American look-a-like equivalent, in appearance and manner, to Derek Arkwright. Open-neck expensive shirt. Brash gold jewellery around throat and right wrist. A gold Rolex watch on the left arm. His dark, short hair slicked back with gel.

"Double bourbon, Angela, on the rocks."

"Certainly sir."

"You sure are a pretty little thing, Angela."

"Thank you sir."

"Is it all right to call you Angela?"

"Yes sir, of course."

"How about tomorrow?" he said, laughing out loud.

"Very funny sir, I haven't heard that line before."

"Spending a coupl'a days in London on business. Fancy having dinner with me?"

She leant towards the passenger's right ear and whispered: "I'd love to, but I still haven't completely recovered from my sex-change operation yet. I'm booked into a Harley Street clinic tonight to have some pus drained off." Angela stood up and resumed her stewarding duties, having never once relinquished her muscular grip on the compulsory air hostess smile.

"Not my type", shuddered the gold-sporting extrovert to no-one in particular. He raised the spirit-containing receptacle to his mouth and downed its contents in one motion, almost swallowing an ice-cube in the process. "Not my type. Her feet are too big", he uttered, to anyone that might be listening.

"Mr. Arkwright, I presume", stated Ted Acerrano, sure in the knowledge that the man in front of him was indeed the one who had come to meet them.

"Call me Derek", he replied, thrusting his right hand forward.

"I'm Ded, and this is Tan."

"*Sorry?*"

Ted pointed to the piece of paper held in Derek's left hand.

"Oh I see, sorry, wrote it in a hurry."

"Hi Derek, pleased to meet you", said Dan Wolfe, taking hold of the Yorkshireman's hand and firmly shaking it.

"Likewise", he replied, glad to have his hand back with fingers intact. "What do you want to do first?"

"Check into the hotel, I guess", answered the taller American.

The smaller man nodded in agreement, adjusting his glasses in the process.

"Right then, to the car", said Derek, screwing up the piece of paper and depositing it onto the ground.

The two recent arrivals followed their English contact in silence. Arkwright, on the other hand, full of his own self-importance, pratled away continuously. His topic of one-way conversation mostly consisted of exaggerated enhancements as to his personal involvement in bringing the project to a potentially successful climax. His rate of exaggeration far outstripped the Government's massaged rate of inflation.

"Jesus", thought Dan Wolfe, "Is this guy on an ego-trip or what?"

The trio approached the Range Rover. Ted Acerrano, visibly reeling from Arkwright's barrage, shook his head, and then re-adjusted his glasses.

"This is it!" pronounced the Yorkshireman, on a par with the image of Archimedes extolling his famous cry 'Eureka', whilst in the process of bathing. The main difference between the mathematician and inventor and the Yorkshireman being that the former had at least one principle, whereas the latter did not.

"Eureka", thought Ted, "Perhaps he'll shut up now that he's got to drive."

"Blast, I didn't lock it", said the Englishman, realising that in his eagerness to be there at the arrivals lounge to greet the Americans, he had forgotten to secure the 4X4.

"Wouldn't be a wise to do that in New York."

"You can say that again, Dan."

"I could do, Ted, but what would be the point?"

"*Shit*, my briefcase has gone."

"You're lucky, if this was New York the whole thing would have been gone", offered the one with wolf-like features.

"Well this isn't bleedin' New York, and I don't consider myself to be fucking lucky", corrected a red-faced, teeth-gritting, nostril-flaring Arkwright.

"Is it insured?" asked Ted.

"*No.*"

"Was it expensive?" queried Dan.

"*Yes.*"

"Are you sure it was in there?"

"Of course I'm sure, it was on the front seat … I think. Yes, it was on the front seat, the passenger seat. I can clearly remember putting it there."

"Anything important inside?"

A dawning suddenly came over the beleaguered one. "My Filofax, my Filofax, I've lost my Filofax." It was at this point that Derek almost burst into tears. His beloved diary not only contained important information and references, but it also was his last link to his days of former glory. To him, being without his Filofax was akin to a priest being without a bible. He felt lost and alone.

"Perhaps it'll turn up", consoled Ted.

"Yeah, you never know. Better ring the cops."

"Can't", replied Derek, regaining some composure before adding: "My mobile phone was in the bloody case!"

Oscar purred as he sped along the highway; the M1 to be precise, just past South Normanton. The yellow Lotus gleamed in the sunshine. Molly gleamed inside the Elise. She was happy. Excited at the prospect of seeing Richard. She had missed him. Moving into the outside lane, she swiftly passed a stream of articulated lorries. "I wonder what he meant by 'how much is a farm over there'", she pondered, returning to the nearside carriageway. "I hope he didn't pack too much luggage. There isn't much room in here for suitcases ... is there, Oscar?"

The car, indifferent to such comments, sweetly purred on.

"In fact, there's hardly any room for anything when there's two people inside", she softly lamented. "Oh well, least of our worries. We can put any excess baggage on the rail, can't we Oscar?" The Lotus, built for speed and looks, appeared unconcerned about such irrelevancies as stowage space.

Richard, who had been soundly asleep aboard the 747, was awoken by the sound of a food trolley approaching. The brash American snored loudly.

"That should have been enough to wake me up", he thought, referring to the snorting sounds being exhaled from the gold jewellery-wearing individual.

The stewardess handed Richard a tray containing an in-flight meal. "What would you like to drink, sir?"

"Coffee, please."

"Black or white?"

"White."

"With or without?"

"I'll have it inside the plane", he replied, in an attempt at levity.

"Good idea, it's a bit cold out."

"Where have I heard that before ... without please", he said smiling.

She handed him the beverage as ordered, leaned towards him and whispered: "At a nudist club, on a winter's morning." Angela stood up, and looked at him briefly. They exchanged smiles, acknowledging the joke. She then picked up another tray and handed it to a passenger. "Would you like a drink madam?"

"Yes please, coffee, black, without."

Richard picked up the plastic fork, and commenced eating the plastic ham salad. "It's food", he philosophically murmured.

Derek Arkwright, having regained his composure, had delivered the two Americans to the Grand Hotel. They had agreed to meet again at 3.30 p.m. in Dan's room, to discuss the following day's presentation at the offices of the Local Authority Planning Department. This interval would give time for Ted and Dan to settle into their respective rooms, and to enjoy a leisurely luncheon, without the annoyances and irritations of their English operative.

"Gee, he sure does go on some", said Dan, entering the elevator.

"What do you make of him?"

"Not sure Ted, reserving judgement."

"If he's as half as good as he says he is, this thing is as good as in the bag."

"Could be a bit of a Dolly Parton, Ted."

"How's that?"

"All up front."

"Good one, Dan", said the other with a grin.

The lift's doors closed and the moving cubicle began to rise.

The Yorkshireman had derived no further pleasure from driving the Range Rover since the incident involving the theft of his briefcase. In fact, he had not displayed any pleasure whatsoever towards anything since the disappearance of his diary. Displaying a face more befitting the rear end of an over-excited baboon during the height of ritual mating, he pulled into a police station car park. It was the same station that he had frequented late Monday evening.

"God, what a dump", he said, looking at the building which had afforded him the opportunity of an overnight stay. He climbed out of the vehicle and, on this occasion, remembered to lock it. "A bloody victim … twice in one week … it isn't bloody fair", he muttered to himself as he entered the premises.

"Good afternoon sir … yes it is afternoon … just. Didn't expect to see you so soon. Liked our hospitality so much you've come back for more ….eh sir? What can I do for you? Assault with a deadly tie, perhaps?"

"The tie was a present. Anyway, what's wrong with the bloody thing?"

"Nothing sir, all a question of taste. My four year-old daughter loves Mickey Mouse."

"I didn't come here to discuss neckties."

"What are you here for then, sir?"

"Some bastard has nicked my briefcase."

"Would this be the same bastard or bastards who broke into your car the other evening?"

"I doubt it. I was over at the airport, and some git took it from my hire car."

"And how was entry gained?" questioned the officer.

"Through the doors, I assume."

"Has the vehicle been damaged?"

"No."

"Doors not damaged?"

"No."

"Sunroof?"

"No."

"Was the car locked?"

Arkwright hesitated.

"I said, was the vehicle locked, sir?"

"No, I forgot, all right?"

"You're not having a particularly good week, are you, sir?"

"You can say that again", answered a demoralised Derek.

"I'll need to take some details."

"That's what I'm here for."

"Let's get started then, I'm sure you're a busy man."

Chapter 22

The Jumbo jet, carrying amongst its passengers Richard Waters, touched down a few minutes ahead of schedule, its tyres screeching loudly as they met with the tarmac at London's Gatwick airport. Molly, sitting on a high stool in the arrivals area, was partaking of a cup of filtered ground coffee. It tasted bitter, she thought, but continued consuming the muddy beverage as she waited for the American to appear. Some twenty minutes later, the first of the disembarked travellers from flight 407 began filtering through to the lounge where she waited. Excited at the prospect of being reunited with her horse-riding companion, her head stretched up and down, and from side to side, eliminating the people who passed by her. More and more weary passengers entered via the customs section, but still not the one that she had come to collect. Then finally, "Richard", she called, her peach-soft, clear-complexioned face beaming.

He moved as quick as he could through the masses of humans and luggage to where she stood. She moved towards him. They met. Richard gently dropped his suitcase to the ground and flung his arms around her. Molly reciprocated and they locked in a passionate embrace. Their lips met.

"Gee, it's good to see you Mol."

"You too."

They kissed again.

"What do you want to do now?" she asked, after their lips had parted.

"Now *that's* a leading question."

Her eyes widened and her face smiled. "You know what I mean", she grinned.

"To your car Mol, and if you want to we can stop on the way for a bite to eat."

"And some real ale?"

"Now you're speaking my language", he said, his own face smiling widely.

"Um … might be a problem with the case", she muted, sizing up the carrier's dimensions.

"Sorry?"

"Fitting it in the car."

"What have you got, a toy?"

"Sort of. It's a Lotus."

"Girl racer, eh?"

"Only sometimes", she said cheekily.

Richard picked up the suitcase and they walked towards the exit, chatting continuously as they walked.

"Say hello to Oscar", asked Molly, as they approached the yellow Elise.

"*Oscar!*"

"My car … it's his name."

"Hi Oscar, how are you today?"

The Lotus remained silent.

"Shy type, I guess", commented the American.

"He's a bit of a snob", she interjected.

"That explains it", he added, maintaining the pretence. "Oscar's a really great car Mol, but I see what you mean about the luggage."

"Do you mind having it on your lap?" she asked, almost apologetically.

"Do I have a choice?"

"Not really."

"Then no … I don't mind a bit. I'm just glad to be back, and to be with you again. It's great to see you Mol, I've missed that pretty face, and that wonderful smile of yours."

"Me too", she replied, a lump coming to her throat.

Richard climbed into the vehicle's passenger seat and struggled with the suitcase until it somehow positioned itself in front of him.

"You're not going to get much of a view", she conjectured, settling into the driving seat.

"I am … I can see you."

"You are sweet."

"I mean it, Mol."

"I know you do, that's why you're sweet."

"And you're a sweetie."

Oscar responded with a throaty growl upon one single turn of the ignition key. Molly steered him away from the parked position.

"She sure sounds good."

"He."

"Sorry … he."

"It's no good apologising to me, it's Oscar's feelings that are hurt."

"Sorry, Oscar. Do you always talk to inanimate objects?" he said, his question directed at the driver.

"No, not always", she defensively replied.

"That's one of the things I love about you, Mol."

"And what's that?" she inquired, accelerating quickly along the dual carriageway.

"Your quirkiness."

"I don't think I'm quirky, and neither does Oscar."

"And what about the toaster?"

"Ah … you have a point there … .now he *does* think I'm a little odd."

They laughed in unison. The Lotus joined the M25.

"Teachers' salaries must be good."

"Why's that?"

"Aren't automobiles expensive in this country?"

"Oh I see", said Molly, "Oscar was a present. I couldn't have afforded to buy him on the pay I get."

"A secret admirer?"

"No secret."

Richard's face visibly altered; concern was being expressed. "You have a lover?"

"Yes, I do as a matter of fact", she offered, maintaining the charade.

"Then …"

Looking pained, Molly decided to end Richard's apparent misery.

"You … you're my lover … and it's no secret. I want the world to know."

Relief replaced pain.

"But … what about the admirer … I guess it's over now then?"

"*I hope not* … he's my father."

"*Jesus*, you had me right wound-up there for a while."

"Don't jump to conclusions, then."

"Your dad must love you a lot … although it's easy to see why."

"He does, and I love him dearly. Until now he's been the only real man in my life."

"*What*, a gorgeous looking girl like you? I don't believe it."

"I've had boyfriends, but they never last long. No-one's been special enough to hold my heart … not until now, that is."

"Same here Mol, same here. Tell me more about your family."

"Where do you want me to begin?"

"At the beginning."

"Well, I was born at a very young age."

"Very funny, you don't have to go that far back."

"Well, my mum died when I was twelve …"

"I'm sorry, Mol", he interrupted.

"Don't be, it's not your fault. Anyway, that's a long time ago now."

"But still, all the same ..."

It was Molly's turn to interrupt. She continued speaking: "Her death, and the loss, really hurt at the time, and for a long time after, but time really does heal. Of course it still does hurt, but I've had plenty of time to adjust."

"Go on."

"Anyway, I have an older brother, Simon, although I didn't see too much of him after he joined the Navy, but I've got some wonderful memories of my family when we were young. Especially the camping holidays. My father likes to walk, still does."

"Is that where you get the hiking from?"

"Yes ... my dad, we all tagged along. Mum used to enjoy it, but Simon was never too keen. I think that's why he joined the Navy. To get away from land."

"Seems a bit radical."

"Probably ... but that's Simon."

"So your father raised you?"

"I've always been a daddy's girl, but he took charge after mum died. Not easy at any time, especially when you have a business to run."

"What business is your father in?"

"He was in milling, retired a few years ago. Sold the factory for redevelopment ... not like your so-called project."

"We're not going to get into that right now, are we?"

"No ... not *right* now."

"Good. So where does your dad live?"

"After he retired he moved to Whitby, on the East Yorkshire coast. I don't see him as often as I should ... or would like. The last time I saw him was a few days before I met you. He travels a lot, abroad mostly. He never really had the opportunity when he had the business, he's a hands-on sort of person."

The yellow sports car continued to speed along the motorway. Richard continued to clutch the suitcase. "Wish I'd packed a smaller case", he announced, trying to get as comfortable as the available space allowed.

"Do you want me to stop so that you can stretch your legs?"

"First decent pub you see, Mol."

The time approached three-thirty. Derek Arkwright made his way to Dan Acerano's room at the Grand Hotel.

"A McSoggy burger and cold fries, that's all I've had for lunch. I bet them Yanks have stuffed themselves", he moaned, then knocked on Dan's door.

"Hi there Derek, did you get any joy regarding your briefcase?" greeted Ted, after opening the door.

Derek entered the room, saying: "I've reported it to the police, and the mobile phone company. And that's the last I'll hear about it. The cops are more interested with catching people who commit minor motoring offences than they are at arresting *real* criminals."

"Resources, I guess, Derek", offered Ted.

"That's one of the excuses *they* use", he replied, referring to the police.

"Great hotel, Derek, that lunch was terrific, thanks", praised Dan, adding: "The pigeons tend to grate a tad, though."

"Pigeons?" queried the Yorkshireman, unsure of whether the American made

reference to what he had eaten for lunch.

"The ones on the ledge outside. They make quite a racket."

"Yeah, and there's bird crap all over the sill", interjected Ted.

"Good job they're on the outside, then", said Arkwright, still smarting over his lack of lunch.

"OK then Derek, what's the form for tomorrow?"

"I was hoping you'd tell me."

"I mean, what time, and to how many people?" said Dan, attempting to clarify his previous question.

"Ten-thirty, I'm not sure about the numbers. Several I'd say, knowing the council. How are you going to deliver the presentation?" queried the Yorkshireman.

"A videotape has been prepared along with a quality brochure."

"Only the one?"

"We have brought two copies of the tape ... just in case."

"I meant the brochure."

"No Derek ... we have several copies of that", replied a rather desperate-sounding Dan.

"Good."

"We'll need a TV and VCR."

"How big do you want the television?"

"The bigger the better, we want these people to be able to see the visual side of the show. They need to be impressed."

"OK, I'll get it organised this afternoon."

"Good man, Derek."

"Just one thing, Dan."

"What's that, Derek?"

"Do you mind if I have those biscuits?" he said, pointing towards the complimentary packet. "I didn't have time to get a proper lunch."

"Sure Derek, go ahead. I was only going to feed them to the pigeons anyhow."

"Thanks", said the Yorkshireman, ripping at the packet with both hands.

The bright yellow Lotus turned into the car park of a public house called the Globe Inn; it boasted real ale and good food.

"What's this about 'Good Food'?" said Richard, as the car pulled to a halt.

"Good food?" questioned Molly.

"Yes", replied the American, peering from behind the suitcase and looking towards the sign which stated the words 'Good Food'. "That board over there", he said, pointing out the notice, and then adding: "Have you ever seen a sign outside an eating establishment that said 'Bad Food'?"

"You have a point. We'll let them know afterwards, shall we?"

"Seems reasonable", he responded.

Molly got out of the vehicle, went around to the other side, and opened the passenger door. "Need a hand?"

"Yes please", he grinned.

Molly took hold of the case and removed it from the roadster. Richard got out, and then helped her to replace the luggage. "We'll need something bigger when the children come along", he said smiling, looking into her eyes for a reaction.

"I think we'll need something bigger way before then", she retorted, seemingly testing the water, or in this particular case the Waters.

"So we're still on for three, then?"

"Eventually, if you're in agreement."

"Of course ... eventually."

"And just *what* do you mean by 'eventually'?"

"Well ... I thought that perhaps we ought to get married first."

"There you go again. Is this a proposal?"

"Let's discuss it over lunch."

"Good", she said, as he took her by the hand.

As they walked towards the inn's entrance, Richard's face broke out into a wide smile. He was happy to be back.

The pub was of the designer type; new, but made to look old. The Globe was only one of a nationwide chain. Recently erected, it contained many ornaments and bric-a-brac from a long-gone era. The inn gave the overall appearance that it had been there for many years. The ceiling was smoked-stained, in colour and effect only. The look had been artificially created to appear that way. The fireplace seemed genuine, but that was also fake. The whole place was fake; a sham, but it didn't matter. Manufactured to a very high standard, the finished product delivered the necessary ambience, which was conducive to an enjoyable experience.

"I like this place, Mol. It's not the Dog and Duck, nor the Tart and Crumpet, but it works."

"I agree, I've been into of a few of these", she said, referring to others in the chain, "and the standard has always been good. You know what you're going to get, and usually you're not disappointed."

"This would go down well in the States."

"Not thinking of starting a chain of your own, are you?"

"Now there's a thought, Mol."

Richard approached the bar, and asked Molly what she would like to drink.

"Half a lager shandy please."

"What, no red wine?"

"I'm driving … anyway, I thought I'd save that for later."

"Good girl, that's the spirit, or not in this case."

A tall, rather thin man in his early twenties, situated on the staff side of the counter, approached. "What can I get you?"

"A half of lager shandy, and a pint of 'Granny Wouldn't Like It', please", ordered the American.

"Coming right up", replied the barman obligingly.

"I do hope not", thought R.W., turning towards Molly. "Anything to eat?"

"Yes please, I'm starving."

"So am I." Richard moved along the bar, obtained two menus and handed one to Molly.

"That'll be three pounds thirty", said the young man, returning with the drinks and placing the glasses on the counter in front of the American.

"Can we order food from you?"

"Certainly, I'll get a pad." He returned a few seconds later, pad and pencil in hand. Richard placed the order, and the waiter dutifully wrote it down. "I'll put it all on the one bill, shall I?"

"That'll do just fine", he responded, his accent coming across strong.

"Where will you be sitting?" he asked.

Richard looked around. "Over there", he answered, pointing to a spare table.

"Thank you, your food will be with you shortly."

"Thanks."

"Thank you", said Molly.

The lawyer picked up his glass. "Let's sit, we need to talk."

"That's sounds ominous", she stated.

"Not really, but we *do* need to talk." They walked over to the vacant table and sat down.

"Gee it *is* good to be back, and to see you Mol. I've missed you."

"Me too."

"About what we discussed earlier, you know the marriage proposal thing."

"Thing?"

"I didn't mean it like that."

"I'm only teasing."

"Yes … you're good at that", he grinned.

"It's a talent."

"Yes well that's as maybe, but…aren't we rushing things a bit too fast?"

"I know we've only known each other for a short while, but I feel as though I've known you all my life."

"It's the same way with me, Mol."

"Then what are you worried about? I haven't said 'yes' yet."

"I haven't asked yet."

"Are you going to?"

"I'm getting there. There's things to sort out."

"For instance?"

"For starters, where will we live? I've got no job …"

"*Have you quit already?*"

"No, not yet, does it matter?"

"I want you to be sure, that's all", she said softly, touching his hand with her fingers.

"I'm sure Mol, I've had enough of the wheeling and dealing, the back-stabbing, and of city life", he passionately replied. "Having said that, I've got to work."

"Do you still want to be a lawyer?"

"Not in my heart."

"What *do* you want?"

"I have a dream … but whether that can be turned into reality remains to be seen."

"And what's that?"

"I guess it's my roots, you know, part Indian. I have never really settled to an urban environment, but didn't really appreciate that until I came over here. I love the Yorkshire countryside. I really like the people I've met. Compared to what I'm used to everyone is so friendly."

"Not everyone", she added.

"Rose-coloured spectacles, I guess, but I don't think so. The pace is slower. There seems to be time to take stock. And I'm in agreement with you."

"Over what?"

"The development. I can't let them spoil that beautiful land."

"Still want to raise sheep?"

"I'd like to give it a go."

"So you'd be willing to leave the States."

199

"In a heartbeat."

"Are you sure?"

"There's a hell of a lot of good that comes out'a the States, but there's also a lot of bad aspects as well. It's not so much America that I want to leave, it's my life as it stands."

"What about regrets? Your roots?"

"My dad died two years ago, my mother two years before that. I have nothing to stay for. My roots are within me, not where I live."

"I love you", she whispered, her eyes welling with tears.

"And I love you dearly. Come on, the food will be here soon."

"OK, go on, tell me what you're thinking", she said, taking a tissue, and wiping her eyes.

"Well, with various investments, I reckon I'm worth about $400,000. What will that buy over here?"

"In London, not very much, probably a broom cupboard, but in Yorkshire that kind of money would go a lot further."

"It'll still not purchase Oldsworth's farm", he muted, shrugging his shoulders. "What about you, Mol? What do you want?"

"You Richard, just you."

"That's great Mol, but …"

She interrupted, saying: "It doesn't matter whether I teach in Mansfield, around Ilkley, Riddlesthwaite, or not at all. I could help raise sheep with you."

"Really?"

"Yes, really."

"Great Mol, just great. Can I live in this country? Don't I need a permit, or something?"

"I'm not sure about the permit, but I believe if you marry a British citizen, you can live here."

"In that case Mol, will you consider …"

At that moment the waitress arrived with their meals. "Cajun chicken?"

"That's me", said Molly.

"You look nothing like a chicken", defended the lawyer.

"Thank you", she giggled.

"So yours, hopefully, must be the lamb chops?"

"Got it in one."

The waitress politely placed the plates down on the table, and momentarily before departing, said: "Enjoy your meals." She then swiftly departed, without either of them knowing whether their response of gratitude had been heard.

"She's quick off the mark."

"Sure is, Mol. Still, good service, and the food looks good."

"I'm starving. Now, what were you about to say before we were not-so-rudely interrupted?"

"Oh yes, I intend to do this properly, so for now, I'm going to do it provisionally."

"Do what?"

"Ask you to marry me … provisionally."

"Go on then, ask, and you don't have to wait to do it properly, or make it provisional."

"But I haven't got a ring."

"We can sort that later, I might turn you down yet."

"In that case", he said, getting off the chair and going down on one knee in front of her, "will you marry me?"

"Yes … yes, yes, yes", she rapidly replied.

He stood up, leaned over her, and kissed her fully on the lips.

"Wow", was all she could say as their lips parted.

"You've made me a very happy man, Mol."

"Me too … let's eat."

Some thirty minutes later, the Elise was once again northbound. Once again, Richard suffered the discomfort of having his luggage positioned uncomfortably in front of him.

"Are you OK?"

"I'll live", he groaned.

"Not too long now."

"I hope not. Mol …?"

"Yes, darling."

"Things will be all right, won't they?"

"What's troubling you?"

"All of a sudden my life's taken a complete full circle, or at least it's about to."

"Second thoughts?"

"About us?"

She nodded to the affirmative.

"Good grief, no … but all the same."

"Come on … talk to me."

"It's just that … I need to do things right. I want to look after you properly."

"You will, and I'll look after you."

"You are a sweet one, that's for sure."

"Richard, you'll just have to trust me. It'll work out."

"OK Mol ... I'll change the subject. What am I to do about Sheep Dip Farm? I, like you, do not want to see bulldozers all over it. The presentation for the project takes place tomorrow in front of the Planning Department."

"It might not get approval, and even if it does we can lodge some sort of appeal against it. You know, start a campaign."

"We'll be dealing with some very big boys."

"I'm a big girl."

"I can see that", he cheekily responded, looking directly at her chest.

"It's my Wonderbra."

"I seem to recall that they were pretty wonderful without the bra", he said suddenly without thinking, and then wished he hadn't.

Molly could feel her face reddening. Temporarily stuck for words, she merely said: "Thank you."

"I'm sorry, have I embarrassed you?"

"No, of course not ... I just wasn't expecting it, that's all. My thoughts have been side-tracked now. Where was I?"

"Big boys."

"Boasting, or are you just pleased to see me?" she teased.

"Now I'm getting side-tracked."

"Calm down ... there's not enough room in here to get up to much ... not even if we ditch your case. Wait 'til we get home."

At that particular moment, Richard wished that he had packed more into the suitcase.

"Would you mind if I went to see Mr. Oldsworth?" she asked gently.

"Of course not, why?"

"With my powers of persuasion I might get him to reconsider."

"You mean, turn on the feminine charms."

"Would you mind?"

"What, you turning on the charm?"

"No silly, me going to see him."

"No, not at all, if you think it might help. Mind you, he's pretty keen on selling. Anyway, I'm off the case."

"From where I'm sitting it looks as though the case is not off you."

"Very good. I wish it was though, my butt's getting sore."

"Not long now, darling."

"Let your fingers do the walking. Let your bloody fingers do the walking. I'll give them 'let your fingers do the walking'. Bloody Yellow Pages. If I had my bloody Filofax they could damn well stuff their 'let your fingers do the walking' slogan", swore the Yorkshireman to himself, flicking through the custard-coloured directory. "Got it!" he proclaimed, placing his right-hand index finger underneath an entry for a commercial television rental company.

Derek Arkwright was back at home; the Range Rover, securely locked, had been left parked outside. With both eyes staring at the vehicle through his living room window, he picked up the land-line receiver and dialled.

"Hello, 'TVs 4U', how may we help?"

Derek paused for a moment. A shiver went down his spine. For a brief moment his thoughts turned to that particular evening, spent in his room the previous week, at the Prince's Palace Hotel in Soho.

"Yes, my name is Arkwright, and I'd like to hire a television and video for tomorrow."

"What format VCR?"

"Normal, VHS I guess, and a big TV."

"How big?"

"I dunno … like they have in clubs, about five times the size of a portable. Something like that."

"What do you want to use it for?"

"That's *my* business, isn't it?"

"As far as I'm concerned sir, you can set it up in the privacy of your own personal bedroom and watch porno flicks until parts of your anatomy drop off. I'm more interested in offering you the most appropriate equipment for your audience number."

Arkwright thought for a few seconds: "Maybe I could keep it for the night."

"How many?" enquired the television hirer.

"One of each."

"Sorry?"

"ONE … TELEVISION, AND ONE … VIDEO … PLAYER", said the Yorkshireman, speaking slow and deliberate, and at the same time raising his voice.

"I want to know how many people are going to watch at any one time, and what kind of venue, in order for me to offer you equipment that's right for the job."

"Perhaps I'd better come and see you. What time are you open 'til?"

"Six."

"OK, see you shortly."

Derek replaced the handset, saying: "Jesus, that guy's a bit slow. Now where's my Filofax? Shit, shit, shit. I haven't got it, have I? It's bloody well been stolen, hasn't it?" he said, questioning himself, and then adding: "I must have Hugo Oldsworth's number here somewhere."

"Well, this is it", stated Molly, as the Lotus slowed down and turned into a gravelled drive.

"So this is where you live, Mol, it's great."

"It's small, but I like it."

"It's real pretty, like a proper English … what's the word?"

"Cottage."

"Yeah, cottage, roses an all."

"Come on, let's get you inside. You must be stiff."

"Good plan … I do seem to ache a bit", he replied, avoiding further attempts at smutty innuendoes.

Molly got out of the car and walked around to the other side. She opened the passenger door, and then assisted Richard by helping him to offload the suitcase.

"Thanks Mol, that feels great. I'll have to introduce you to the merits of an RV."

"RV?"

"Recreational vehicle."

"You'll hurt Oscar's feelings again."

"Don't get me wrong, Oscar's a great fun car, goes like the wind, it's just that he's not very big."

"Good things come in small packages."

"Just like you, Mol", he said, taking hold of the case.

She smiled and said: "Come on, I'll make you a cup of tea."

"It's not Earl Grey, is it?"

"Why, do you want Earl Grey?"

"I prefer coffee. I'm not really a tea drinker."

"When in Rome."

"Coffee."

"Tea."

"But I'm not in Rome."

"That's why you're going to try a cup of English tea, made in a pot."

"English tea from China?"

"You're catching on already", she said, turning the front door key and opening the lock.

The grey-stone property, on the right-hand side of a pair of semi-detached cottages, did indeed look attractive. Standing some thirty feet from the road, it gave the illusion of being smaller than it actually was. Although basically two up and two down, the rooms were quite large. Molly had maintained her home to a very high standard. The red roses growing against the front wall gave it a picturesque appearance. Once inside, Molly put the kettle on. "No jokes about nursery rhymes'", she said, seeing that her partner had been watching her every move.

"As if I would", he grinned.

"Sugar?"

"Yes dear?"

"Would you like sugar in your tea?"

"Will it improve the taste?"

"Depends on whether you like sweet things."

"You're the only sweet thing that I like."

"Thank you. I'll take that as a 'no' to sugar then?"

"Correct. This sure is a pretty home, Mol", he commented, diverting the conversation away from hot beverages.

"I'll show you around in a few minutes."

"Great, can't wait to see the bedroom."

"Yours or mine?"

Richard's previously smiling face altered instantly.

"Only kidding", she said, pouring a small amount of hot water from the kettle into a pot. "Mind you", she added, "Don't know how we are both going to fit comfortably into a single bed."

Richard's smile returned. "Oh, I don't know Mol, at least we'll be close."

"Kidding again. I do have a double bed, it came with the cottage", she said, holding the teapot and gently moving it around in a orbital motion, then emptying the vessel's contents down the kitchen sink.

"Why're you doing that?"

"Warming the pot."

"Does that help?"

"Keeps the tea hotter for longer."

"Makes sense."

Molly made the tea, and while waiting for it to brew gave her companion a guided tour of the cottage. Two and a half minutes later they were back in the kitchen.

"Well, that didn't take long, did it?"

"It's a great home, Mol, I just love those feminine touches", he said, referring to the abundant usage of lace and other such materials.

"Are you teasing? 'Cos if you are, this very hot pot of tea could accidentally on purpose find its way to your genitalia."

"Ouch! I mean it, Mol, all that frilly stuff, it makes a house a home. Anyway, I'm a nineteen-nineties man ... I'm in touch with my feminine side."

"What does that mean, you shave with a pink razor?"

"I don't know *what* it's supposed to mean, I guess it's one of those modern media- induced myths. Seriously though, it's hard for a lot of guys these days. We men are having a hard time defining our role in society."

"Western society", added Molly, pouring the tea from the pot into a cup.

"Traditional roles have changed, Mol. Women want careers, and good luck to them."

Molly moved the teapot towards another cup and commenced filling it.

Richard continued speaking: "Men stay at home and look after the house, and good luck to *them*."

"I think I know what you're trying to say", said Molly, handing a cup and saucer to her man.

"Go on then, help me out."

"Thousands of years of evolution, and then BANG. It all changed this century … when emancipation came along for women."

"Surely that's a good thing", he interrupted.

"Of course, like a lot of other changes."

"Such as?"

"It's not just a man-woman thing; prejudices in general. Abolition of the slave trade, for example. Sending children up chimneys to sweep them. Badger baiting, and so on.

The list is endless … but I'm getting away from the point."

"Me shaving with a pink razor?"

"Exactly … and why not. It's just a colour."

"Whatever next … men in skirts?"

"What about kilts? And why shouldn't men wear skirts?"

"That's my argument", he said, jumping straight in, "Women now wear what they like."

"Can't they?"

"That's not what I meant", he said, taking a sip from the cup, "What I meant to say was, women *can* wear what they like, which is fine. Except that a lot of their choices appear to be very masculine."

"I agree, a lot of the young teenage girls do dress that way, and they act much more aggressively."

"So girls wear the pants. Where does that leave the boys?"

"Confused", she answered sympathetically, picking up her own cup and then taking a drink.

"Exactly. Women can't expect to have it all their own way. If they want to behave like macho men then go for it. It's freedom of choice. I firmly believe in equality. That's why men need to fight back. Where *can* I get hold of a pink razor?"

"Is it for your face, or your legs?"

"One step at a time, Mol, one step at a time. Anyway, call me old-fashioned, but I like women who also know how to be feminine."

"So do I, from walking boots to silk stockings and high heels, that's me."

The mention of the latter stirred Richard to further comment, saying: "I really do like your bedroom, can't wait to see it again."

"Later, drink your tea."

"I've drunk it."

"And?"

"It was rather pleasant", he said, realising that the liquid that was in the cup was now inside his stomach, "I think I like tea. Must have been the way you made it, Mol."

"I'll teach you", she quipped, not wishing to be the only one responsible for making a pot.

"And I'll teach you how to make *real* coffee."

"Have you ever heard of the expression, teaching your grandmother to suck eggs?"

"Point taken. Anyway ... you wouldn't do that, would you?"

"Do what?"

"Pour hot tea over my lap."

"What, and spoil my pleasure?" she asked rhetorically.

"Boy, am I pleased about that. May I have another cup of tea?"

"Of course, help yourself", she winked.

Richard helped himself to another cup, and at the same time poured one for Molly.

They continued chatting, changing topics frequently. Their conversational exchange went back and forth in equal measure. They joked and laughed with each other, and the time passed swiftly. The remains in the teapot had long since gone cold.

"Crikey, is that the time?" Molly suddenly blurted. "What do you want to do this evening? I had planned to stay in and cook a meal for us, if that's all right with you."

"Gee Mol, that's great. Can't think of anything I'd rather be doing right now."

"I've got you a rather nice bottle of single malt scotch."

"That's swell Mol, thanks. I hope you got some red wine for yourself?"

"Of course. I hope you like beef?"

"Love it."

"In red wine?"

"What else?"

"Exactly. Right then, I'd better get started."

"Wanna hand?"

"OK, you can prepare the veg."

"Anything to assist."

"It'll save time, we'll be able to have an early night … you must be tired?"

"Not *too* tired Mol", he said, with a wink of his own.

"Good", she beamed.

Chapter 23

The following morning found Derek Arkwright displaying an air of jubilant anticipation. Although the weather immediately outside his flat was dull and overcast, offering a hint of rain, the mood inside was one of brightness and light. The Yorkshireman, having risen at seven-thirty, had shaved, showered, and was now dressed, ready to embark on the day ahead. He exhibited a sunny disposition. The time was eight forty-five, time to leave. "If all goes well this morning, I'm up and running", he said to himself, as he closed the flat's door behind him.

Part of the reason for Derek's upsurge towards a more cheerful nature came as a direct result of a phone call from the police, stating that his briefcase had been found. The only thing that remained missing was the mobile phone. Everything else had been found intact, that is, apart from the Filofax. Although found apparently lying beside the briefcase; abandoned on a piece of wasteland awaiting redevelopment, someone had inscribed the words 'YOU SAD BASTARD' on the leather-bound cover. "Pity about the phone", he muttered, climbing into the Range Rover and settling into the driver's seat, "and why would anybody want to scratch 'you sad bastard' onto my Filofax? *And in capital letters.* God, there's some sad bastards about."

Some twenty minutes later the intrepid entrepreneurial property negotiator drew to a halt outside the Grand Hotel. Dan Wolfe and Ted Acerrano were waiting.

"Good morning", said Derek, after the Rover's electrically operated front window opened.

"Hi Derek, how are you today?"

"Great Ted."

"Hi there", greeted Dan, somewhat less enthusiastically.

"Morning Dan, jump in, today is a big day."

Ted Acerrano opened the front passenger door and boarded the 4X4. His colleague opened a rear door and climbed into the back.

"My briefcase has been returned."

"Great, anything missing?"

"Only the phone, Ted."

"I guess there was nothing of importance to anyone else", replied the Wolfe man.

"Only the phone, Dan."

"Did you get the TV and VCR?"

"Sure did, went down to the shop and selected them myself. The television is a big one, just like you wanted."

"Good, have we got to pick them up?"

"No, the hire people should have had them delivered and set up by now."

"Great Derek, well done."

"No sweat, that's what I'm here for."

"From what I hear, you're here for a lot more than that", said Dan, from the back.

"Yeah", added Ted, "Without you, this whole project may have been a non-starter."

"As I said, gentleman, that's what I'm here for."

"You surely do seem in a good mood this morning."

"I am, I've got my Filofax back, and that's an omen."

"So was the movie", muted Dan, attempting to harness the rear seat-belt.

"Sorry?" asked the driver.

"'The Omen', it was a movie", answered Ted.

"*Jesus* ... that's not the kind of omen I had in mind."

"I hope not", replied Dan, glad to be finally secured.

"Do you always drive this fast, Derek?"

"No, not always ... sometimes I drive faster."

Both Ted and Dan simultaneously checked their restraints.

By the time the Yorkshireman and the two Americans arrived at the Leeds Local Authority offices, the meeting room in the Planning Department had been prepared for the proposed presentation, the hired television and video cassette player fully installed, and ready for use. A Nobbo flip-chart stood alongside the TV. The room, modern in design and appearance, seemed well equipped to handle the occasion. Many planning applications had been decided upon in this room. It was soon to be Ted and Dan's turn to make sure that the next one would be positive.

"Good morning, Derek", greeted Colin Williams, as Arkwright and the two Americans entered the Planning Department offices. "Just about to fetch a cup of coffee, would you like one?"

"Good morning, Colin, sounds like a great idea. Let me introduce you to these two gentlemen who will be giving the presentation. This is Dan Wolfe."

"I hope you don't bite", joked the Planning Officer, taking hold of Dan's hand and firmly shaking it.

"Only when I'm real hungry", he retorted, offering a broad smile.

"And this is Ted Acerrano."

"Pleased to meet you both", said Williams, proffering his right hand.

"You too sir", replied Ted, taking hold of the outstretched collection of digits.

"Where's Mr. Waters?" inquired Colin.

"Had to go back to the States on business", answered the younger Yorkshireman, not allowing time for either of his colleagues to comment.

"By heck lad, that's a shame, I liked that young fella. Seemed straight, a rare commodity these days. Rarer than a three-legged chicken, when you consider what profession he's in."

"Neat observation, Mr. Williams, Richard is as honest as the day is long", stated Ted, displaying sincerity.

"That aside", added Dan, "there are times when even Richard has to bend the truth."

"Way up lad, we all have to do that on occasions", replied Colin, with a wink to Derek. "Richard Waters won my approval, I trust you two lads can do the same?"

"We'd like to think so, sir", said Ted confidently.

"You're in store for a very professional demonstration, Colin", confided Arkwright, returning the wink.

"Well it's not just me that you've got to impress, there's eight others in attendance today. Now let's get that coffee." The Head of the Planning Department led them out of the reception area, and along a narrow corridor where stood a hot drinks vending machine. "Right lads, this is it. I'll just get mine; time's money, can't afford to waste it. Ask at reception and you'll be shown where the room is." He placed a coin into the machine, pressed the appropriate button, then waited for a plastic cup containing hot liquid that purported to be white coffee with white sugar. Williams picked up the container, saying: "Right lads, see you in ten minutes."

"I thought the old skinflint was going to provide us with drinks; now I suppose I'll have to get them", thought Derek, his right hand diving into his jacket pocket for change.

"Seems like a nice guy", said Ted.

"Don't be fooled, he's a canny old sod", said Arkwright, placing some change into the machine's slot. "What do you want?"

"Black coffee for me, no sugar, please Derek."

"And white without for me", said Ted.

"I'm putting this on expenses."

"Do that Derek, wouldn't want you to lose out", replied Dan, with a hint of sarcasm.

With beverages in hand, they made their way back to reception. Derek approached a middle-aged woman sitting behind a desk, and asked directions to the meeting room. Two minutes later and they found themselves in that very room.

"Great TV, Derek."

"You like it then."

"I meant *great* TV, as in big."

"Is it too big?"

"Let's put it this way, providing everyone sits at the back they'll see just fine."

"Better too big than too small", offered Ted, trying to defuse the situation.

"Said the actress to the bishop."

"*Sorry?*" said Dan, inserting the video cassette into the VCR.

"Better too big than too small, said the actress to the bishop", responded the Yorkshireman, attempting to clarify the quip.

Ted Acerrano moved quickly, arranging chairs a suitable distance from the television in theatre style. Derek, sipping from the plastic container, looked on as the two Americans prepared for the show.

"I think that's it", said Dan, placing the ninth brochure on a chair.

"Good", replied his partner, noticing that people had begun filtering into the room.

Colin Williams entered and approached the Englishman. "All set then, Derek?"

"Just about, Colin."

"I'll take a seat then lad … that is, unless you want me to do an introduction."

"Ted", said Derek, looking over to where the visitor stood perusing some papers, "Do you want Mr. Williams to do an intro?"

"No thanks", he answered, his head still directed towards the paperwork, "I can manage."

"Right then, me lad, I'll sit myself down."

"So will I", replied the Yorkshireman, depositing his empty drink vessel into a waste-paper bin.

The committee were now all seated; some were quietly talking, while a few others had chosen to view the brochure.

"Good morning, ladies and gentlemen", said Ted Acerrano in a louder than normal voice; his accent coming over strong.

"My name is Ted Acerrano, and this is Dan Wolfe." The wolf man smiled at the audience, his features softening slightly with the smile. "We represent a legal firm called Hadim Gotcha and Grabit. As I understand it, you've all been briefed on the outline proposals of the project."

Affirmative nods could be seen around the room.

"On your seat you will find a booklet giving details of what is being proposed. I can see that some of you have already found it", he said, noticing that a middle-aged, balding man, sitting to the left of Derek Arkwight, was peering into his copy, seemingly oblivious to the speaker's spoken word. Arkwight nudged the man with his elbow. The man suddenly looked up, and at the same time closed the article.

"The booklet acts as an aide memoir, in so much that it summarises the presentation. The presentation comes to you in the form of a carefully prepared, professionally filmed video. The film contains computer-generated graphical enhancements … a kinda Star Wars special effects mini-movie. So, without further ado, sit back and see for yourselves what this development will bring to the area."

Ted turned towards his colleague, saying: "It's over to you, Dan." With blinds previously lowered, Ted moved over to the light switches and dimmed the room's lighting. With the ambience set, Dan turned on the television. He then pressed play on the VCR's remote. The television's tube flickered into life. It continued flickering. Dan checked that the TV had been tuned to the correct channel. It had.

"What's wrong?" whispered Ted.

"I'm not sure", replied Dan, pressing the remote's stop button, and then play.

A few of the audience began shifting in their seats. The balding man recommenced reading the brochure, straining his eyes in the dimmed light. Derek Arkwright appeared uncomfortable. Colin Williams rose from his seat and approached the Americans.

"Is there a problem, lad?"

"The video doesn't seem to work properly", answered Ted, as his countryman continued to fault find.

Derek walked over. "What's the problem?"

"What format did you get?"

"Sorry?"

"The VCR, what format did you get?" reiterated Dan, gritting his teeth, and in doing so, expressing his canine qualities.

"*Format?*"

"Yes format … you Europeans operate on the PAL system. In the States it's different. Didn't you know that, Derek?"

"Er … no."

"There's your answer", offered a rather all-too-familiar desperate Dan. "Arkwright's cocked up."

"That's not fair", replied the Yorkshireman defensively, "How the hell was I to know?"

"Because you should, you prat", argued the other.

"Come on, this is getting us nowhere", interjected Ted, "What can we do about it?"

"Get rid of him for a start", said Dan displaying a predatory glare, pointing towards Derek.

"It's not my fucking fault", uttered Arkwight.

"We'll have none of that sort of language here Derek, there are ladies present", intercepted the Head Planning Officer.

"Sorry."

"Good. Now, let me get this straight. The basis of your presentation is on film, but the tape won't play on this machine?"

"Correct", said Ted.

"We need another machine. One that will work with this tape", said Dan Wolfe, ejecting the cassette from the PAL system VCR.

"But that'll take time", stated Arkwright.

"And time is what we you don't have, gentleman. The film show will have to be postponed."

"When for?" said Ted, obviously alarmed.

"I'm afraid it won't be until next month", replied Williams.

"What!"

"Can't be helped, I guess", said Derek, noticing the audience showing signs of restlessness.

"It could have been helped … if you had done your job properly", muttered Dan, glaring at the belittled Yorkshireman.

"I'd better make an announcement", said the Planning Officer, assuming his role as Head of Department. He turned to face the fidgeting participants. "Ladies and gentlemen, due to a technical hitch …"

"More like a technical cock-up", muttered the wolf-man.

"… we can not proceed with the presentation. I'm sorry for wasting yours and my time, but these things happen."

With the lights and blinds raised, the committee left the room one by one.

"Kindly leave the brochures", said Ted, seeing that the balding man had his copy in his hand as he was about to depart the room.

"Sorry ... I thought we could keep it", he replied, placing it on a table near the door.

"Don't want any leaks", murmured the man of medium height, with short dark hair, and sporting a pair of gold-rimmed glasses.

The Americans collected their things. Derek Arkwright collected his composure.

"Try to get it right next time, eh lads", offered Mr. Williams.

"Sorry about that", answered Dan, seemingly embarrassed, and at the same time inwardly angry.

"Bye for now, thanks for your co-operation", said Ted, trying not to show any adverse emotion.

"Shit happens", said the hapless Yorkshireman, taking hold of Colin's hand and shaking it.

"Seems to with you, Derek", muted Williams, firmly squeezing the other's palm in an attempt to vent frustration.

"What now?" asked Arkwright, sitting behind the Range Rover's steering wheel.

"Back to the hotel", replied Dan.

"We need to contact the office and put them in the picture", added Ted.

"How do you think Grabit will react, Ted?"

"With displeasure, Derek."

"Heads will roll", commented Dan, still smarting.

"Whose?"

"Probably ours", said Ted.

"What about me?" asked the driver.

"Don't worry Derek, it won't be *your* head that'll roll", prophesied the tall, thick-set man with blonde hair.

"Good", said Derek, sounding relieved.

"No ... in your particular case ... it'll be your balls."

Chapter 24

"Miss Weston, I presume?" greeted Hugo Oldsworth upon opening the door to his studio.

"Good morning, Mr. Oldsworth, it's good of you to see me."

"I'm intrigued, do come in."

Molly followed the artist into the studio.

"May I get you a drink?"

"Tea please."

"Take a seat, Miss Weston."

"Thank you." Molly sat down and looked around the studio. It appeared much as she would have expected. A kind of organised chaos. Paintings in various stages of completion. Artist's materials seemingly strewn everywhere. "A romantic mess", she thought, as she waited for the hot beverage to arrive.

"Milk and sugar?" asked the painter, calling from the kitchen area at the other end of the room.

"Milk please, no sugar."

A few seconds later the man appeared carrying two mugs. He placed one down in front of her.

"Thank you."

"You're welcome. Now tell me more, your telephone call didn't give too much away ... just enough to tease."

"Good, that's what it was meant to do."

"At least you're honest", Hugo replied, taking a sip from the mug, and almost burning his mouth. "It's rather hot", he said, returning the vessel to a coffee table.

"That's what I'm here for really ..."

"*Sorry?*"

"To stop you from getting burned ....or at least to try."

"And what do you know about it?" asked the artist, a little agitated.

"I know that you have had an offer for the farm, and no doubt it's a reasonable offer …"

At that moment the door opened and in walked Sophie.

"Morning Huggy, I'm back", she said, not noticing Molly.

"This is Miss Weston, she's come to talk to me about the farm. Miss Weston, this is Sophie."

"Hello", said Molly, offering the newcomer a broad smile.

"Hi", replied Sophie, "We're getting married."

This sudden announcement from a total stranger momentarily took Molly aback. Hugo, witnessing this, intervened. "I've finally plucked up the courage to ask Sophie to marry me. She's been my model and inspiration for a long time. Now that I'm about to come into money, I can look after her in the manner that she would like to become accustomed", he said grinning.

"Oh Huggy, you are a sweetie", commented the artist's model.

"Congratulations. When's the wedding?" enquired Molly, directing her question to the bride.

"As soon as Hugo gets the dosh."

"I want to make sure that the sale is going to go through before we make firm plans", he clarified, then added: "But even if it doesn't I'll still marry her. That is, if she'll still have me."

"Of course I will, silly. Money isn't everything."

"That is true, unfortunately it's hard to get by without it. Which leads me back to the farm."

"Do you want me to go?" asked Sophie, looking at Hugo.

"Of course not, make yourself a drink and join us."

"OK, I'll be back in a tick."

Sophie scurried off to the far end of the studio. Hugo and Molly sat down.

"She seem very nice, I hope you'll both be happy together."

"Thank you Miss Weston, I'm sure we will."

"Call me Molly."

"OK Molly, what's on your mind? How do you know so much about me?"

Molly then went on to explain the circumstances that had brought her there to see him face to face. She covered her chance meeting with Richard, and her subsequent falling in love. She briefly spoke about her time with him on the moors, including the horse-riding expedition, and how she had casually discovered the American's purpose for being in England. Sophie, having made herself a mug of black coffee, had re-joined them. She listened intently. "I liked him, he was nice", said the model, referring to her earlier meeting with the American, "I didn't go a bundle on that other man though. Gave me the willies."

"Derek Arkwright", elucidated Molly, "I'm afraid he's not everyone's cup of tea."

"You weren't the only one who telephoned me this morning regarding the farm."

"I wasn't?"

"Mr. Arkwright rang ... a few minutes before you did. A very interesting proposition."

"Care to elaborate?"

"Not yet, Miss Weston ... I mean Molly, I want to hear more from you first."

"Do you know what they want to do with Sheep Dip Farm?"

"For some future development."

Sophie remained silent, preferring to keep quiet unless she had something poignant to add. She sipped coffee from her mug, and continued to listen.

"Any ideas as to what and when?" asked Molly.

"No, haven't really thought about it. My only interest is to sell."

"But you grew up there?"

"Yes, and I hated it."

"But what about your parents?"

"They're dead."

"Yes I know, I'm sorry ... I didn't mean ..."

"That's all right ... it's not your fault."

"Look, the house will be razed to the ground, the landscape will be changed beyond recognition, and a massive series of theme parks erected. Is that what you want? What kind of legacy is that for your mum and dad? They devoted their lives to that farm."

"She's got a point, Hugo."

Oldsworth pretended not to hear. "Does Mr. Waters know you're here?"

"Yes, he's having a cup of coffee at a nearby cafe."

"But you're here trying to jeopardise the sale?"

"No I'm not. I just don't want to see a beautiful piece of this country's heritage ruined forever."

"What does he think?" asked Hugo, making reference to Richard.

"When I first found out about the so-called project, I was livid. How dare they. How dare he. Richard feels the same way as I do, he just didn't realise it at the time ... that's all. We're getting married, and he's leaving the States to live here with me. He's prepared to leave his employers over a matter of principle. To change his life for what he believes. What are you prepared to do about it?"

"But I don't want the farm."

"Then sell it."

"Buyers offering millions don't come along every day, you know. And besides, I'd be turning down another two-hundred and fifty thousand on top of what has already been offered."

"How's that?" puzzled Molly, "If you don't mind me asking."

"That Arkwright chappie, on the telephone this morning, offering to up the ante. That is, providing I split the difference with him."

"Sounds illegal", interjected Hugo's intended.

"Positively dangerous, but not out of character", added Molly, disgusted at the property developer's most recent antics.

"I agree, it's dodgy and I don't like it. I don't like him either. The man has no ethics", stated the artist.

"So, you're not going to take him up on the proposal?"

"If I had any intentions of doing so Molly, I wouldn't be telling you about it now. Believe it or not, I do have some principles."

"I'm sure you have lots. So ... what about the farm? Think of your parents. Please don't allow what they have worked for most of their lives to be erased for good. Sheep Dip Farm is a living testimony to their memories."

"She's got a point, Hugo."

This time he didn't pretend not to hear Sophie's observations. Instead, he reacted to them. "OK then, Molly, what do you suggest?"

"There are other alternatives, Mr. Oldsworth ..."

"Call me Hugo."

"In that case, Hugo, let me make a few suggestions."

Richard, having started on his fourth cup of coffee, pondered over the challenges that lay before him. "What have I got to lose?" he thought, taking an unwanted sip from his mug. "Fresh start. A new way of life." The would-be sheep farmer paused momentarily. The thought processes continued to rotate in his head. "Jesus, I'm scared. What if it doesn't work out and I lose Molly? That's what I've got to lose ... Molly." The American had got himself into panic mode. He again raised the mug, and sipped from it. "It's got to work ... I love that girl."

At that moment Molly entered the cafe, her face beamed radiantly. "Sorry I've been so long", she said, sitting beside him.

"That's all right Mol, the place is clean and the coffee is good. Mind you, I've had four cups."

"You'll be wanting the little boy's room soon."

"Hey, not so much of the little", he said teasingly, and in the same breath added: "How did you get on?"

"Fine ... Sophie's nice. I like her."

"Do you want a drink, or something?"

"No thanks, I've had enough for now. What about you, do you want another coffee?"

"No thanks, I'm swimming. So, you haven't wasted your time then?"

"Guess what?"

"What … without any clues. Er … Michael Jackson's really an android."

"No silly … Derek Arkwright has been up to no good." Her eyes widened. She waited for a reaction from her partner. She didn't wait long. Richard leaned across the small round table resting his hands on the plastic red gingham tablecloth and gently kissed her lips.

"Gee, you're lovely", he said, sitting down again.

"What was that for?"

"Because you make me melt."

Her smile widened. Her full lips reddened. "Don't you want to know about Arkwright'?

"Only if I must."

"I think you must." She then went on to explain what had transpired over the telephone, earlier that morning, between the Yorkshireman and the artist.

"Jesus, that guy's a creep. Out to make a few bucks for himself. What a bastard! Sorry, Mol."

"That's OK … my sentiments exactly. Anyway, that kind of approach didn't cut any ice with Mr. Oldsworth."

"Good. Is he still selling?"

"Yes … but not to your people."

"They're not my people … well, not any longer. Who's he selling to then? Has he found another buyer?"

"Possibly … I know somebody who might be interested."

"Who?"

"Well it's a bit hush-hush at the moment. I can't say any more at the moment."

"You're a woman of hidden depths, Mol."

"I like to think so."

"So, I guess this *somebody* doesn't plan to build theme parks?"

"No … he plans to preserve the land, not destroy it."

"Private buyer?"

"You're fishing … well, I'm not taking the bait."

"I'm the one that's hooked, Mol."

"Really … in what way?"

"I'm hooked on you."

"You say the sweetest things."

"I wish I could say that I had enough dollars to buy Sheep Dip Farm." The American thought for a moment, then looking directly into his companion's eyes posed the following question: "This buyer wouldn't consider selling me a part of it, would he?"

It was Molly's turn to think. "I don't know, it's all in the air at the moment. Anyway, I know he particularly wants the house."

"Damn."

"Come on, let's go. We can see some sights while we're here. Make a day of it."

Richard looked at her, and a broad smile appeared on his face. He then stood up and said:

"Great ... let's go ... after all, I am on vacation."

Chapter 25

"What a cock-up", uttered the disillusioned property developer, as he entered his humble abode. "Those fucking Yanks. What prats ... they should have told me what type of equipment to get. How the fuck was I supposed to know?" he mumbled, throwing the Range Rover's keys onto the sofa and depositing his briefcase on top of them in similar fashion. "If this fucking sale falls through I'll lose the £250,000 bonus. Bastards. I need a fucking drink."

He walked into the kitchen and over to where a whisky bottle was kept. It was half full, or, in Derek's present state of mind, half empty. He poured some of the golden alcoholic liquid into a lead crystal tumbler. He raised the glass to his mouth and tipped the contents into it. "Bastards", he muttered, swallowing the scotch. Lifting the bottle once more, he re-filled the crystal container, and, at the same time, growled out the following verbal exclamation: "Bastard fucking bastard Yanks."

"It's Ted on the line for you, Mr. Grabit."

"Thanks Stephanie, put him through."

A click could be heard over the telephone line and then Ted Acerrano's voice. "Good afternoon sir."

"How did it go?" replied the New York lawyer, dispensing with the need for any formal politeness; instead getting straight to the point.

"'Fraid I've got some bad news to report."

"You know I don't like bad news, Ted."

"The presentation had to be cancelled."

"You mean it *didn't* take place?"

"No ... it will have to be re-scheduled for next month."

"God ... damn it, *why*?"

"In a nutshell ... Arkwright."

"*Arkwright*?"

"He hired the wrong equipment. Wouldn't play the tape."

"Damn!"

"Made us look rather foolish."

"Damn!"

"What do you want us to do?"

Ernest Grabit thought for a moment. "Set up a new date, and then come home. I'm not pleased, not pleased at all", he growled, taking a puff on a cigar. "Time is money; this could cost us dear."

"I'm sorry sir, but that Arkwright guy has been leading us all on. He's taking the credit for Richard's work."

"In what way?" demanded Grabit.

"By all accounts he's gone down rather well over here. It was he who got the ball rolling and set things up. He did a good job."

"Are you saying I shouldn't have pulled him out'a there?"

"In hindsight, no. Arkwright has done the dirty on him. With respect sir, he fooled you. The man's full of crap. Bullshit is what he does best."

"What does Dan think?"

"Put it this way, I wouldn't let him phone you."

"That bad, eh?"

"You know how emotional Dan can be", offered Ted calmly.

"Well Ted, thanks for putting me in the picture. We'll talk further when you get back."

"OK ... sorry to be the bearer of bad tidings."

"Yeah, yeah, I'm sorry too." The lawyer replaced the telephone handset and, placing the cigar to his mouth, drew a large breath. A few seconds later the smoke exhaled, forming a large blue cloud that slowly dissipated across Ernest Grabit's office. As the smoke cleared, with his right hand he reached across to where the intercom was situated and pressed a button.

"Yes, Mr. Grabit?"

"Ah Stephanie, see if you can locate Richard Waters for me."

"But ... isn't he on vacation?"

"Yeah, have a word with Rachel, she might know where he is."

"Yes sir."

The short fifty-something lawyer leaned back in his chair and once more drew on the cigar. Letting it out, he flicked ash into the wastebasket beside his desk. As he did so he uttered one word: "Damn!"

"Will you still want to paint me after we're married?" asked Sophie, reclining naked on top of a lilac silk sheet, underneath which had been placed an array of cushions.

"Of course", replied Hugo, almost hidden behind an easel. "What makes you say that?"

"Marriage can change things."

"I hope so, but it won't change how I feel about you."

"So you're not going to mind images of my nude body hanging on people's walls?"

"Of course not. You have a beautiful figure, and I'm privileged to capture it on canvas."

"Thank you, Huggie."

"Please don't call me by that reference in front of anyone."

"Don't you like me calling you Huggie?" inquired the model, shifting her commissioned pose slightly.

"It's a bit soppy, and keep still."

"I think it's rather sweet."

"The name reminds me of that television character. You know, the American cop duo?"

"Batman and Robin?"

"*Not them,* I think it's a seventies, or early eighties series. Got it! Starsky and Crotch."

"Hutch."

"Whatever."

"Huggie Bear."

"That's the fellow."

"I was right then."

"About what?"

"Calling you Huggie."

"How's that?"

"'Cause you're Huggie and I'm bare."

At that moment the telephone began ringing. "I'll get it", said Sophie, "I need to stretch my legs." She rose from the floor and walked the four paces to where the telephone was sited. She lifted the receiver and answered: "Hello."

Sophie had her back towards the artist. He stared at her nakedness. The sunshine from the roof-light above directly illuminated her shape. Hugo had seen her without clothes many times before, and yet, he had never become too accustomed as to take the vision for granted. "She is beautiful", he thought, as the object of his focal attention turned to face him.

"It's for you … it's that Derek Arkwright creature."

Hugo moved away from the easel and towards Sophie. He took the handset from her as she passed it to him. He placed it to his right ear. "Hello, Hugo Oldsworth here, what can I do for you today, Mr. Arkwright?" said the artist, his tone intentionally curt.

"Good morning, I'm ringing you about the proposition I put to you yesterday."

"Yes?"

"Have you given it further thought?"

"Yes I have … a quarter of a million is worth further consideration."

"So you want me to negotiate then?"

"No I don't. I may be many things, Mr. Arkwright, but being dishonest is not one of them."

"It's not dishonest, it's business. Look, you've got land to sell, my people want to buy. If I can get you a better price, and they're prepared to pay, where's the harm?"

"Correct me if I'm wrong, but don't you work for the people who want to buy?"

"Strictly freelance, that's me."

"Hence the £250,000 bonus?"

"Business … merely business. Everyone can come out of this a winner."

"If there are winners there are always losers, Mr. Arkwright."

"Call me Derek, Hugo."

"Call me Mr. Oldsworth, Derek."

Sophie, still in a state of undress, entered the artist's working area carrying two mugs of coffee. She placed one of them in front of her man, and, in a low voice, said: "Good one."

Hugo smiled.

"You can't really be serious", stated the Yorkshireman, as if in disbelief.

"About what, you calling me by my surname?"

"About not wanting to make another two hundred and fifty grand?"

"Oh, don't get me wrong, I'd like to make another two hundred and fifty K, but the trouble is, I'm a man of principle."

"Over matters of money isn't it better to set principles aside?"

"Maybe for you, but then I'm not you; besides, there's another reason."

"And what's that?"

"I don't like you, and I wouldn't want you to get rich out of me."

"But it wouldn't be your money."

"Oh yes it would."

"No it wouldn't."

"Yes it would."

"How come?"

"Because now that I know that the buyers are prepared to pay even more for the land I can approach Hadim Gotcha & Grabit directly. I don't need you."

There existed an eerie silence. Hugo Oldsworth looked at his naked model and smiled. She acknowledged his handling of the irksome Arkwright by raising her right thumb upwards. Hugo's smile broadened. "Are you there, Derek?"

"Sorry?"

"I said, are you there? I thought we'd been cut off or something."

225

"I was thinking."

"Not your strong suit, is it?"

"There's no need to be like that, I was only thinking of you. I didn't want to see you ripped off."

"That's very commendable of you, and I suppose you were going to give your share to charity?" The artist, still holding the telephone's hand-piece to his ear, thought he could hear the property negotiator's brain cells whirring.

"As a matter of fact, yes."

"The Derek Arkwright Foundation, perhaps?"

"So, what are you going to do?"

"Consider my options … carefully … very carefully."

"You won't mention our discussion to anyone, will you?"

"As I said, Derek, I'll consider my options very carefully. Goodbye." Hugo replaced the receiver.

"You really had him squirming, Huggie. Well done, he needed putting in his place."

"Yes I did, didn't I? And I see you're still bare. Let's get back to work."

"Drink your coffee first, otherwise it'll get cold."

"Yes dear."

"Shit", shouted Derek Arkwright, having first remembered to replace the communicational handset to its rightful resting place. "This isn't going well. I can't believe it. Shit … what am I going to do now? What if that bastard goes direct? Shit, what if he drops me right in it?"

The Yorkshireman moved around his humble abode like a man possessed. Thoughts flitted through his irksome mind. The thought process was reminiscent of a beleaguered bat in a belfry suffering from a particularly nasty hearing disorder. Derek was correct in his analysis of the current situation; things were not going well. As far as he was concerned, the planning meeting had been re-scheduled for the following month. Although he did not consider himself to blame, he knew those damn Yanks would gang up on him, and that he would be made to be the scapegoat. On top of this, if Hugo Oldsworth decided to spill the beans on his recent entrepreneurial enterprise, the chances of him remaining in the employ of Hadim Gotcha & Grabit were nil.

"I'll have to sit tight and see what happens", he muttered, inserting a Meatloaf CD into the hi-fi as a means of distraction. The introduction to 'Bat Out of Hell', played at around eighty watts per channel, erupted from the stereo speakers. Derek Arkwright assumed the role of lead guitarist, and began accompanying the song on air-guitar.

"This is more like it", he shouted, parading around the furniture in the manner of a latent rock performer. "Like a bat out of he … ll. Like a bat out of he … ll."

♪♫♪♫♪♪

Music filled the air ... the flat, the building, the car park, and the street.

Chapter 26

"I'm nervous", said Richard, entering the lounge carrying two cups of coffee.

"Don't be, you'll like my dad … and he'll just love you", replied Molly reassuringly.

"I hope so. When is he getting here?"

"About twelve-thirty. We can take him for a pub lunch."

"My favourite bit about England … apart from you that is."

"Don't they have pubs in the States?"

"Not really, mostly bars with gassy beer. I like the real ale."

"Yes, I've noticed," she said, a teasing smirk appearing on her face.

"Don't you approve?"

"Of course I do, in moderation. A little of what you fancy does you good. My father likes his pint. He's a real ale drinker too."

"Is that why you think he'll like me?"

"One of the reasons; there are many more."

Richard, who did not want to go into his virtues at this precise moment in time, decided on a conversational diversion, saying: "I really enjoyed the sightseeing with you yesterday, it was fun."

"Me too, and thanks for the wonderful meal last night. After that experience I think you can do the cooking from now on."

"Hold on there, I can do a mean stir-fry, but that's about it."

"I'll have to teach you then."

"OK, you've got me licked, but I'll need my own apron."

"Darling, you can have as many as you like, if the meals are anything like last night's."

"I enjoy cooking; mind you, as I've been living on my own I mostly eat out, or grab a take-away."

"Junk food?"

"Yuck … sometimes, but I do try and eat healthy."

"Me too, something else we have in common."

"♪ I'll do the cooking honey, you pay the rent."

"Very good … and you can sing too."

"I was only kidding about the rent … I feel pretty bad about not having a job right now."

"Don't be silly, you're on holiday. Anyway, you do have a job."

"Yeah, but not for long."

"Things will work out, wait and see."

Richard suddenly stood up. "I think I heard a car."

"Don't panic, he won't eat you."

"I'm nervous."

"Come on then, let's get it over with", she said, taking hold of his hand and leading him to the front door.

"Hello Daddy", greeted Molly to the man exiting a large silver BMW, which had been parked behind the Elise.

"Ay up lass", responded the well-dressed, upright gentleman. Molly's father appeared to Richard much as she had described. Tall, about six feet, maybe an inch or so less. Although in his sixties, he stood erect. A full head of hair, with no obvious signs of thinning, had in recent years turned grey. The colour suited his overall appearance, considering age and stature. With back straight, he approached the young couple. "Well lass, aren't you going to introduce me?"

Molly entered his outstretched arms, and he closed them around her. He turned his head towards Richard and winked, saying: "She always did like a hug."

Richard smiled.

"You are a tease, Dad."

The man with grey hair released his grip.

"Dad, this is Richard. Richard, this is Dad."

"Pleased to meet you sir", acknowledged the American, offering his right hand.

"Pleased to meet you, lad. Call me Arthur."

The two men firmly shook hands.

"Nice automobile sir."

"Arthur."

"Sorry, nice car, Arthur."

"My pride and joy, children apart that is. I need a bit of comfort at my age, lad."

"But Daddy, you've always had nice cars."

"Not always, lass."

Molly smiled, and turned to face Richard. "He likes to remind people, from time to time, that he's a working-class lad that's done good."

"Nothing wrong with that", commented the younger male. "The States was founded on such ethos."

"Exactly", added Arthur, "I'm from working-class stock, and I've been working class all my life."

"No need to get on your soap-box, Dad."

"That's as maybe, but you'd do well never to forget it."

"How could I, you're always reminding me", she answered, her smile bright and wide.

"She's a canny lass that one, m'lad", retorted the Yorshireman, with accent prevalent.

"She sure is sir, I mean Arthur."

"Come on, let's go inside. There's lots to talk about", said Molly, herding her men-folk like sheep.

"Can't we do some of this here talking in the pub?"

"Yes Dad, we're taking you out for lunch … and a few pints."

"That's my girl. Do you drink beer, lad?" asked Arthur, looking directly at the American as if the young man's life depended upon the correct answer.

"I'm rather partial to English real ale."

"That's m'boy. Do you know what, lass?"

"What's that, father?"

"I like this lad of yours already."

"Thought you would", she replied, smiling at Richard, and closing the door behind them.

Ernest Grabit leaned back in his prestigious office chair. He appeared to be a worried man. The New York lawyer leaned forward; he then pressed a button on the internal intercom.

"Yes Mr. Grabit?"

"Any news on Waters?"

"I'm afraid not sir", replied the ever-efficient Stephanie, only on this occasion, seemingly less so. "I've spoken to Rachel, she has no idea where he's gone."

"Damn! What about his cell phone?"

"No reply sir, it's switched off."

"Damn! Send someone round to his apartment, see if anyone there knows something."

"Already done so sir, no luck. I've also left a message with his answering service, should he care to access it."

"Good girl … not a lot else we can do then." Grabit relaxed into the leather high-backed executive chair. Stephanie went about her secretarial duties. She was in the process of typing a letter on her word processor when the telephone rang. She momentarily arrested exercising her digits, and lifted the receiver. She listened to the switchboard operator, and then said: "OK, put him through."

A brief pause, a series of clicking sounds, and Stephanie was once more engaged in a telephone conversation. "Mr. Grabit's personal assistant, how may I help you?"

"I'd like to speak with Mr. Grabit, the name's Robert Gledhill."

"I'll just see if he's free. What's it in connection with?"

"I'm acting for Hugo Oldsworth, the sale of Sheep Dip Farm, don't you know."

"Just a moment, Mr. Gledhill." Stephanie placed the solicitor on hold, and then buzzed her employer.

"Yes Stephanie, what is it?"

"I have a *very* English-sounding gentleman on the line, presumably calling from England. Robert Gledhill, he's acting for Oldsworth."

"Put him through."

The dutiful Stephanie obeyed her employer's instruction.

"Ernest Grabit speaking, what can I do for you, Mr. Gledhill?"

"Thought it better to speak in person, old chap. Too much of this faxing to and fro. Something like this is better dealt with using a more personal approach, don't you think?"

"I'm not sure I understand, please elaborate", answered the New Yorker, somewhat bemused.

"Hugo's decided to call the whole thing orfe."

"*What?*"

"I'm afraid he's not going to sell to you after all."

"Oh I get it, wants more money. How much?"

"No, it's not like that, just doesn't want to sell the farm to you. That's all, old chap. Can't be persuaded, so it's no use trying. I'll confirm in writing. Nice talking with you. Cheerio."

The telephone went silent.

"Damn", muttered Grabit, reaching for the intercom once more.

"Yes sir."

"Stephanie, get hold of Arkwright. It's urgent."

"Yes sir, right away."

Ernest Grabit reached across his desk and removed a large cigar from a carved wooden box. As he raised the light brown object to his lips, he murmured: "Damn, damn ... damn."

"Another pint, Arthur?"

"Why not, m'lad?"

231

"Mol?"

"Red wine, please darling."

Richard rose from his seat, and crossed the Tappit Inn's lounge floor, heading towards the bar counter. Lunch had been eaten. General conversation had taken place. Molly had arranged the lunch-date so that her father could meet the man who had proposed to her. Arthur Weston could get to know his future son-in-law under convivial surroundings. Convivial, in the sense that Molly's father enjoyed the hospitality of a good ale house. Molly had wanted the interview, for in reality that's what it was, to turn out well. To that end, while Richard was in the process of ordering another round, she took the opportunity to question her pater.

"Well?"

"Well what?" replied Arthur, pretending not to understand.

"Richard, of course. What do you think?"

"You're my girl all right."

"And?"

"I mean you're a good judge of character, lass."

"So … you like him?"

"Yes lass, I do. You have my approval. not that you need it. You're old enough to make up your own mind."

"I know I am, but that's not the point. I do want your approval. I want you to like him, and besides, it's important, bearing in mind our discussion the other evening."

"Oh, *that*."

"Yes, you know?"

"One glass of red wine", said the American, placing the receptacle on the table in front of Molly, "And one pint of Hops's Revenge."

"Thank you", said Molly, reaching for the glass.

"Thankya lad", said Arthur, taking the mug from Richard, and raising it immediately to his lips.

"Fancy a day on the moors tomorrow?" asked Molly, turning to face her intended. "I could book a room at the Dog and Duck."

"Swell Mol, I'll need to collect my equipment anyway."

Molly looked at him, expressing puzzlement.

"When I last left for the States I kinda knew I'd be coming back … or at least I hoped I would … .so I stored the tent and the rest of the stuff at the Grand."

"We'll never get all that gear in Oscar'", offered Molly.

"Borrow my car", suggested Arthur.

"I don't think you want to go home in the Lotus, dad."

"You have a point there lass, I like my comfort."

"I'll hire a bigger automobile; better yet, maybe I can try out a suitable demonstrator for a coupl'a days. After all, we'll need something a bit bigger than Oscar."

"Good idea", said Molly, "We can sort that out later."

"Come on then lad, sup up, it's my shout. Oh yes, by the way", said the older man, looking directly into his daughter's eyes, "That other *matter.*"

"Yes", interrupted Molly, in obvious anticipation.

"Seems fine by me."

She jumped up and kissed him, saying: "Thanks Daddy, you're a real sweetie."

Three hours later, and after a period of considerably more than forty winks, Arthur Weston prepared himself for departure. "Your couch is rather comfortable, lass."

"I would guess it is, especially after a few pints of beer and a good meal."

"You wouldn't expect me to drive home without sobering up first, now would you?"

"Of course not dad, anyway at your time of life you need to rest."

"No need to be cheeky, I'm as fit as a fiddle. What do you reckon, lad?"

"Picture of health, sir", answered the American, acknowledging the fact that the older man did indeed appear extremely healthy for his age.

"Richard recognises it. He can see how fit I am."

"He didn't say you looked fit, dad", replied Molly, teasing her father.

"Picture of health ... means the same thing."

"If you say so. Are you still playing golf?"

"Of course, handicap is down to thirteen. Do you play, lad?"

"Not really Arthur, I don't seem to get the time."

"Can you play?"

"I used to."

"That's all I need to know. We can have a game together. Get you back in the swing."

"Sure thing Arthur, I'd appreciate that."

"Good man ... anyway, enough of this idle chit-chat, I'd better get going."

Molly opened the front door and the three of them went outside. Together, they walked to where the BMW was parked. Unlocking the vehicle, Molly's father got in. He started the engine, and at the same time unwound the electrically operated, front driver's-side window. Molly leaned across the opening and kissed him. "Bye daddy, see you soon."

"Bye lass, take care of yourself. Speak with you soon."

"Goodbye sir ... Arthur", said Richard correcting himself, offering an outstretched arm as a token of friendship and respect.

The older man took hold of Richard's hand and shook it firmly. "Take care of my daughter for me, she's a good lass, and you", he said directing his conversation towards Molly, "you take good care of him. He's all right."

Richard and Molly both smiled.

"I will dad, take care."

The BMW reversed away from the drive, and onto the road. Arthur Weston placed the automatic transmission into drive. "Bye Richard, bye lass."

"Goodbye sir, nice to have met you."

"Bye dad, see you soon."

With one last wave, the German piece of engineering excellence moved off, and soon disappeared out of sight.

"Well, what do you think?" enquired Molly, as they returned to the cottage.

"I like your dad, he's swell."

"He likes you."

"That's good."

"How about a cup of tea?"

"Coffee?"

"Tea, it's better for you."

"OK, tea it is."

"Relieved?" asked Molly, entering the property.

Richard followed, and once inside closed the door, saying: "You bet."

Molly went straight to the kitchen, and lifting the kettle to test whether there was enough water inside, she then switched it on; having ascertained that the electrical device for boiling H2O did indeed contain enough of the stuff to provide for two cups of china tea.

"At least you won't have to go through that", said Richard, calling from the lounge.

"I'm sorry, I would have liked to have known your family", she answered, her raised voiced carrying from kitchen to lounge.

"And they would have liked to have known you, Mol", he said softly, having approached from behind, and placed his strong arms around her small waist. She turned, and his head lowered slightly. Her mouth moved towards his. His lips met hers. They kissed passionately.

Reluctantly breaking away from the embrace, Molly's attention focused upon matters of a more practical nature, saying: "What kind of car are you looking for?"

"What, to buy?"

Molly nodded in the affirmative.

"An off-roader, you know, 4X4."

"Like the one you had when I first met you?"

"Yeah, that kinda thing. What are my choices?"

"Probably quite extensive, judging by the number you see on the road these days. Apparently they've become very fashionable. The strange thing is, hardly any of them seem to have mud on them."

Richard, although aware of what Molly's remarks referred to – the fact that many

newly purchased off-roaders never experienced anything other than tarmac under their tyres – remained unfazed.

"We need something a little bit bigger than Oscar, Mol."

"Yes, and quick. Mary's husband Paul – she's one of my colleagues at work – works for a local Ford dealership. Perhaps I could give him a call and see whether he can arrange a demonstrator for tomorrow?"

"Good idea Mol, worth a shot."

Molly walked over to where the telephone was situated, and reached for her personal telephone directory; a small black book resting on top of the Yellow Pages. She turned the pages to the section marked 'H, I, & J', picked up the receiver, and dialled. She briefly waited, and then a female voice was heard.

"Good afternoon, Hamiltons for Ford, how may I help you?"

"Hello, may I speak to Paul Seager?"

"Who may I say is calling?"

"Molly Weston."

A click, and the female voice was replaced by classical music.

"Bach's 'Air on a G String'", she whispered to Richard.

"Sounds more like 'Air on a Shoe String', by Meow", he replied, catching the inferior sound quality emitting from the telephone's handset.

Molly again nodded in the affirmative.

"Hello Molly, long time no hear. To what do I owe this pleasure?"

"Hello Paul, is Mary enjoying the summer break?"

"She sure is. We've only just got back from two weeks in Brittany."

"How was it?"

"Great, what about you? You've been on one of your walking holidays, haven't you?"

"Yes, and I've got some great news."

"Go on."

"You'll be one of the very first to know."

"Go on … you've got me in suspenders."

"I'm getting married", she excitedly blurted.

"Great … does Mary know?"

"Not yet … haven't had the time."

"You didn't phone me just to tell me that, did you?"

"No, sorry, I need a favour."

"Go on."

"We need a bigger car …"

"You're not thinking of trading the Lotus?" interrupted the salesman.

"No way, I love Oscar, he's special."

"Are you talking about your intended, or the Elise?"

"Do you mind, Oscar's my car, Richard's my intended."

"Glad we cleared that one up. Wouldn't want to misinform Mary. More than my life's worth. By the way, can I tell her the good news?"

"Of course you can, and you'll shortly be receiving the wedding invitations."

Richard sat close by, listening intently to the telephone conversational exchanges that had, so far all but missed the relevancy of the initial call.

"Thanks Molly, wouldn't miss it for the world. Is it a white wedding?" he added teasingly.

"Of course, I'm a traditional girl", she replied, her bottom lip forming an attractive pout.

Her partner looked at her and winked.

"Not that traditional, I'll bet?" inquired the salesman.

Molly declined to answer; instead she decided, metaphorically speaking, to steer the conversation back on track. "Richard wants a four-wheel drive, something big. He's used to big cars."

"Got just the thing, an Explorer. Superb vehicle. Good value too."

"Would you like to speak to him? He's here."

"Great, put him on."

Molly handed the handset to the man beside her.

"Hi there Paul … can you help?"

"Congratulations Richard, Molly just told me", said the salesman, detecting the American's accent.

"Thanks, I'm a lucky guy."

"You sure are, she's a great girl. Anyway, I understand you're looking for a 4X4?"

"I sure am."

"In that case, I got just the one for you, the Explorer. Should make you feel at home."

"How's that?"

"Come and have a look, you'll know what I mean as soon as you see it. Better still, you can have it for a couple of days."

Richard broadly smiled. He raised his right thumb upwards towards Molly. She repeated the gesture back to him, aware of its significance. "This afternoon?" asked the possible purchaser.

"Great, come on over."

"OK, see you soon Paul."

"Thank you Richard, see you soon."

"Seems like a nice guy", said Richard, replacing the receiver.

"He's fine. Mary's nice, you'd like her", responded Molly, handing him the promised cup of tea.

"That worked out swell, thanks Mol. At least we'll have something big enough to collect my camping equipment."

"Don't you mean your employer's camping equipment?"

"They wouldn't want to pay the shipping costs. Anyhow, you owe me a camping trip", he said, raising the cup to his lips.

"I'm sorry."

"Don't be … perhaps we can pitch the tent at the Dog and Duck? I'm sure Bill wouldn't mind."

"I've already booked a room … while you were talking with dad. It's got old-fashioned beams."

"Yeah, I know, *remember*?"

"Remember! How could I ever forget", she said, a wide smile forming on her face, adding, "This one's a double … with a four-poster bed."

"We'll do the tent thing another time."

"Thought you'd see it like that. Come on, let's go get your 4X4."

The Elise pulled to a halt on the premises of Hamiltons, a Ford dealership in Mansfield. Richard climbed out of the car. Molly did the same, trying her best to dignify her sex. The fact that she was wearing a short black lycra skirt, four inches above the knee, did not help.

"Not easy, is it, Mol." offered Richard, who had walked round to Molly's side of the vehicle and, very gentlemanly, opened the door.

"Can you see my knickers?"

"Sure can … thanks."

"And I thought you were being a gentleman", she uttered, locking the car.

"I was, not my fault there's an added perk. Anyway, why lock the car when there's no top on?"

"Force of habit. In this country, the top's usually on a lot more than it's off. A lot, lot more."

Richard watched in apparent amusement as Molly tugged at her hemline. "Like Dolly Parton said, 'It's hard to be a woman'", he muted, following her into the showroom.

"Well … you don't want everyone seeing my knickers, do you?"

The American didn't have time to answer, for at that precise moment a man strode towards them. "Hello Molly, it's good to see you", greeted the man. He leaned forward and kissed her on the right cheek. She reciprocated by simultaneously doing likewise, the only difference being she kissed him on his left side. "This must be Richard", he said confidently, offering his outstretched right hand.

237

"Phew ... for a moment I thought you were going to kiss me", replied the American, taking the proffered hand.

"I thought you Americans did that sort of thing?"

"Only after we get to know each other a bit better first", spoke the man from across the Atlantic, a wide grin acknowledging the greeting.

Paul Seager stood about five feet nine inches tall, aged twenty-seven; of medium build with blonde hair, and piercing blue eyes. Wearing a grey double-breasted two-piece suit, he represented his employers well. This was one car salesman who had evolved beyond the fictional Arthur Daley and Delboy Trotter school of sales personnel.

"Hello Paul, what do you think of my man?"

"You look good together. Mary'll be pleased, she worries that you'll be left on the shelf."

"*Thanks!*"

"I didn't mean it like that ... it's just that you're rather fussy when it comes to men. You're gorgeous, a real gem, a pearl, a jewel in the crown ..."

"OK, I get the message, no need to cite Captain Bluebeard's entire buried treasure."

"That's it exactly, you're a treasure, a real treasure. Isn't she, Richard?"

"She is Paul ... a diamond ... twenty-four carat ..."

"Now, don't you start. Come on, let's get to business, where's this truck."

"*Truck*", said the salesman vehemently. "You wait 'til you see it." He stared at Molly, piercing her with his steel blue eyes, adding: "Philistine. Truck indeed, ha, if you want a truck I can show you trucks", he teasingly muttered, directing the pair to where the Explorer awaited.

"We have them in the States'", said Richard, upon seeing the dark blue off-roader.

"It's big", commented the American's companion.

"Five-speed automatic transmission, air-con, cruise control, anti-lock brakes, airbags both sides. What else?" asked the salesman of himself, "oh yes, there's remote locking, electric sunroof, power front seats, power windows and mirrors. Impressive, isn't it?"

"It sure is Paul, I like it. What about you Mol?"

"It's big."

"Yeah, but do you like it?"

"Yes, if you do."

"That's no answer."

"Then yes, I like it. I just love the colour."

"The colour's great, Mol. How much, Paul?"

"The Montana is a shade under twenty-three thousand, but this one has metallic paint and leather trim at extra cost."

"*Pounds or dollars?*"

"Er, pounds", replied the salesman.

"Jesus, I'd pay dollars for it in the States."

"Of course you would, sweetheart, that's your currency."

"I mean, I'd pay the same number of dollars as I would have to pay pounds, making it a lot cheaper back home."

"It's still very good value", offered Paul.

"That's as maybe", interjected Molly, "But we still pay far higher prices for cars in this country than in most of Europe."

"It's getting better, anyway as a kind of early wedding present I can do you a very special deal."

"That's more like it, Paul. Tell you what, you work out some figures, and if in a coupl'a days I still love it as much as I do now, we're in business."

"The keys are in it … but before you drive off I'd better just check on the insurance … you being a foreigner", remarked Paul to Richard, without intending offence.

"Swell Paul, I appreciate your assistance", responded the American, showing that no offence was taken.

Some fifteen minutes later, Richard was behind the wheel of the Ford Explorer Montana; once more driving on English soil or, on this particular occasion, tarmac. He followed behind the bright yellow Lotus as it manoeuvred its way back to Molly's cottage. Allowing for Richard's unfamiliarity with the vehicle, and his newness to driving on the left, she kept the speed well within the legal limits. The American was enjoying the experience.

Later that same day, as the sun sat lower in the sky, yet still burning hot, an impatient Ernest Grabit, who had risen from his office chair and was now frantically pacing up and down, contemplated the current position. Occasionally muttering to himself, he mentally reviewed recent developments. Representatives of the consortium interested in developing parts of rural England into designer theme parks had personally contacted him that afternoon expressing their concerns. They had become restless, having been made aware of the re-scheduled presentation with the planners, and, more recently, Hugo Oldsworth's decision not to sell; added to the fact that market conditions were changing, a further feasibility study was being considered. Considering the light of changing circumstances, it now seemed prudent to re-evaluate. The New York lawyer's mood was one of panic. "God, it seems that the plug is being pulled from both sides of the Atlantic", he muttered, still striding the allotted space between desk and window.

He continued the review. "Oldsworth's not selling. Why? Can it be money? That's it, he's holding out for more. Where's Waters? I need him." At that moment the telephone rang. He stopped pacing and lifted the receiver.

"I have Derek Arkwright on the line, sir."

"Thanks Stephanie. Any news of Waters?"

"No sir, he may be out of the country."

"OK, put Arkwright through."

"Hello Mr. Grabit. What can I do for you?" grovelled the Yorkshireman, hoping that his entrepreneurial cash-making enterprise had not been made obvious to the other man.

"Ah Derek, just the man. Your services are required."

Arkwright's ears pricked. "Only too glad to be of service. What is it you want me to do?"

"We have a problem, I've received communication from Oldsworth's lawyer, or solicitor as you people call them …"

"And", interrupted the Englishman nervously.

"The guy's not selling …"

"*What?*"

"If you'll let me finish I'll tell you …"

"Sorry, go on", interrupted Derek, obviously not thinking straight.

"Personally, I believe this to be a ploy to up the ante."

"Shit", thought the Yorkshireman, "The bastard *is* after more cash. That's why he hasn't said anything about me."

"I want you to go and see him."

"What, in London?" said Derek, a sudden shiver shooting along his spine at the thought of recent experiences in England's capital.

"If that's where he is …"

"Divine."

"*What?*"

"I said that's fine, I'll go see him."

"Good, sound him out. If it's dollars, get back to me."

"Pounds."

"*What?*"

"Sterling."

"Yeah, capital, or whatever you English say. Just get it done."

"Hopefully I'll touch base soon with good news."

"Just do it", uttered Grabit, picking up a fountain pen and marking a piece of note-paper with a tick.

"Yes … yes, yes, yes", shouted Derek Arkwright, after he had replaced the telephone handset, adding: "I'm still in. It's got to be about money. This time I'll negotiate my commission from the buyer's end. A fee, added on top of the price agreed with that bastard Oldsworth." He opened up his briefcase and peered into it. "I must get another mobile phone", he said, realising that he hadn't replaced the one recently stolen.

After a few hours of overnight rain, the following morning brought clear skies, and with it, warm sunshine. The Explorer, with Richard at the helm and Molly by his side, had left Mansfield several miles behind. The vehicle's on-board timepiece read ten-thirty precisely.

"First stop, the Grand."

"Well at least you've got room to store your stuff."

"I need it, what with all the clothes you've brought."

"A girl's got to be prepared."

"So's a cub-scout, but they don't carry the amount you do."

"You want me to look nice, don't you?"

"Mol, you'd look nice in a sack-cloth."

"You say the sweetest things. Will you continue to do so after we're married?"

"'Til the day I die."

Molly reclined into the ample 4X4's seat, happy in the knowledge that the man beside her was the same person that she wanted to spend the rest of her life with. "I love you", she said sweetly.

"And I love you", came an affectionate response.

Molly wriggled herself further into the soft leather seat, saying: "What do you think of the car now that you've had a chance to drive it?"

"Love it, want it."

"Then have it."

"But I shouldn't go around spending this kinda money on an automobile when I haven't got myself a job yet."

"Go on, live a little, I've told you before, things'll work out."

"I wish I shared your optimism."

"You're not a pessimist, are you?"

"No, more of a realist I'd say."

"Look Richard, it's only been a few days, don't get paranoid."

"I'm not. Just being cautious, that's all."

She smiled her smile, melting the man who witnessed it.

"OK, I'll stop worrying."

"Good, that's better."

The remainder of the journey to Leeds passed uneventfully. The young couple continued to engage in good-humoured conversation. Wedding arrangements were discussed. Guest list invitations mulled over. As far as Richard was concerned, the day belonged to the bride. Whatever she wanted to make the day special for her, was fine by him. Her father would want to play a prominent part, he had thought, and this was how it should be. It was his privilege and his right. They clearly loved each other very much. Richard approved of Arthur Weston.

The Ford Explorer Montana cruised into the Grand's car park, and pulled to a silent stop.

"Jesus, this engine's quiet."

"Shouldn't it be?" enquired Molly, unfamilar with most mechanical, working operational systems.

"Yeah, great, isn't it?"

"Oscar growls."

"Oscar's meant to."

"Oh, I see", said Molly, not really any the wiser. "Do you want a hand?"

"Yes please, there's quite a lot of the stuff."

Twenty-three minutes later, and they were back on the road again.

"Next stop, the Dog and Duck. I wonder if Albert will be there with Jake, I like that dog", said Richard, seemingly homesick for his Yorkshire aquaintances.

"That dog, or whippets in general?"

"Both, I guess."

"What about Albert?"

"What about him?"

"You mentioned Albert and Jake, and then went on to say you like the dog. Don't you like Albert?"

"Sure, he's a hoot. And Bill, he's a blast. I think they're all great."

"Anyone you don't like?"

"I can think of one."

"Let me guess, Derek Arkwright."

"Got it in one, Mol."

Chapter 27

Brrring, brrring … brrring, brrring … brrring, brrring.

"Hold on, I'm coming", said Hugo Oldsworth, crossing the studio floor, to either the telephone or the person who had rung him. "Hello, Hugo Oldsworth."

"Good morning Mr. Oldsworth, it's Derek Arkwright."

"Yes Derek, offering me more money to sell, are you?"

"Funny you should say that … only this time it's official. I wonder if I could make an appointment to come and see you?"

"I don't really see the point, Derek."

"I've been asked to discuss an increased offer with you. If it's all right with your good self, I'd like to come along and talk it over."

"That's very charming of you, I'm sure, but I've decided not to sell the farm to your people. Haven't they informed you?"

"Yes of course, but I … that is we … thought you were holding out for more dosh. That is the case, isn't it?"

"Money isn't everything, Derek."

"*It isn't?*"

"It may be in your particular case, but not in mine."

"So what are you going to do … raise sheep?"

"That's my business."

"Look, we need to sit down and talk about this logically. You won't get a better offer than this. I can be there this afternoon."

"Let me explain, Derek. One, I have something you appear to be lacking in … and that's principles. Two, I do not wish to have my parents' farm, to which they devoted their entire adult lives, turned into some artificial playground. Three, I don't like you. You're rude, obnoxious, and potentially dishonest, and if I ever hear from you again your employers will be made aware of the five hundred thousand pound scam you so cleverly devised. Have you got the message, you conniving little toad?"

"FUCK OFF."

"Be nice, Derek, I hold the cards … four aces actually."

"Er, sorry, I didn't mean you … er … a wasp came in through the window. I thought I was going to get stung."

"Derek, you have been, and now I suggest that you take the same advice as you gave to the wasp. Good day."

"Bastard. Shit. What am I going to do now?" questioned the Yorkshireman, somewhat distraught. "It's blown. The whole bloody thing. That's it. I can't go back to Grabit with *that*. That fucking shit."

Derek Arkwright's luck was running out. The fact that his so-called luck had much to do with his own making was not an obvious consideration in the mind of the would-be property developer. Whatever else Derek perceived to be the reasons why events had not turned out too well for him, his own failings were not one of them.

"Let's evaluate", said Arkwright, taking a note-pad and ball-point pen from his briefcase. "One, Oldsworth isn't going to sell. Fine, I can deal with that. Just tell Grabit that he doesn't want the farm turned into a theme park. It's the truth. But where does that leave me? A small fee. Fuck it. Two, find more land. That's the answer. Find more land, and I can write my own cheque. *Yes*. Yes, yes, yes."

He placed the pen on the dining table, without actually having written anything down, apart that is, from the number 1. "Right, find some land, that's my next task. Then get back to that New York lawyer, convince him it's for the best, and I'm in the money." The Yorkshireman's zest had once more returned. The light was shining brightly. Derek Arkwright had regained a purpose. A goal. A reason to fight on. The reason: to take care of number one. He stared at the piece of paper. Without taking his eyes off it, he reached for the ball-point, found it, and then used it to circle the single-figure digit that he had written. Subconsciously and without conscience, he had highlighted his sole reason for living, and that was … Derek Arkwright.

"Nearly there, Mol."

"We're in good time, can we take a detour?"

"Sure Mol, where do you want to go?"

"Well, the last time we were here it ended sour …"

"Yeah, but we've made up since then", interjected Richard.

"I know, but I just thought that if we could go back to before it went bad that would set the scene for our time here."

"Kinda like rewind on a VCR?"

"That's it, rewrite the script."

"The workings of a woman are beyond me", he murmured, shaking his head from side to side. "OK, where do you want to go, the Wine and Grouse I presume?"

"No … that's a bit close to where it all went wrong."

"You are being silly, Mol."

"No I'm not, indulge me", she pouted.

Richard could not resist the face that, in his eyes, could launch a thousand ships. "OK, where then?"

Molly thought for a moment, and then suddenly blurted: "Sheep Dip Farm, the house."

Richard looked at her and felt his heart flutter. "Sure thing Mol, Sheep Dip Farm it is. Do you know …?"

"Know what?"

"You have a face that could launch a thousand ships."

"Why thank you sweetheart, you do say the nicest things."

"Not always."

"To me you do."

"That's cause you're special."

"What about if I was weighed fifteen stone and was all bloated?"

"Let me see, that's about how many pounds?"

Molly performed a quick mathematical calculation and came up with an approximate answer, saying: "Two hundred."

"That's not you, Mol."

"But if it were, say in a few years?"

"That still wouldn't be you."

"But if it were?" she insisted, pressing for an answer.

"Then I'd probably say, You have the face that launched a thousand chips."

"Very witty, aren't you supposed to say French fries?"

"Look Mol, I'm getting the hang of your English humour, it wouldn't have been funny with 'the face that launched a thousand French fries', now would it?"

"No, I guess not. A play on words. Have you tried fish and chips?"

"Real traditional English fish and chips … no, can't say I have."

"Then we'll have to correct that one. Anyway, how did you know what chips are?"

"Cause back home Mol, we call 'crisps', chips."

"The face that launched a thousand crisps. Still doesn't work, does it?"

"No, has to be chips, rhymes with ships. That's the whole point. Play on words."

Molly's faced beamed.

"You're having me on", he grinned, realising that his future bride had, in fact, been stringing him along.

Molly's face continued to express personal delight at teasing the man that she had so deeply, fallen in love with.

The scenery began to change as the Ford made its way to Hugo Oldsworth's farm. The landscape became rugged and barren, a collage of colours that only nature could design. Richard's thoughts turned to the land in question, and to what nearly might have been, if not for Molly's intervention. As the 4X4 continued its progression, his mind mulled over recent events. A persuasive woman is a formidable foe, and Hugo Oldsworth would have been no match for Molly's charm. Her natural beauty and sophisticated style were enough to melt the hearts of most red-blooded males. She had won his. As they approached Sheep Dip Farm he wondered what would become of it. "At least there won't be a theme park", he thought, turning off the road and onto the lane that led to farm house.

"Penny for them?"

"Sorry?"

"Your thoughts … you were miles away."

"I'm sorry Mol, I was just thinking about the farm. What will become of it now? It's beautiful, I wish I had enough money to buy it for us, Mol. Perhaps I could get a loan?"

"You'd need a big one, and remember, banks will lend you an umbrella when the sun is shining, but they have a tendency to ask for it back when it rains."

"Good one Mol, that about sums it up. Even so", he said, in response to thinking wishfully, "If only, eh Mol?"

"You love it here, don't you?"

"Sure Mol, don't you?" he replied, braking the car to a halt directly outside the house.

"I do, let's get out and take a look."

"We've already done that."

"Yes, but not from the inside", she said, stepping down from the off-roader.

Richard also disembarked, saying: "But we can't just break in."

"I don't intend to."

"Then how?"

"I have the key", she said, dangling a set of keys in front of him.

"Where did you get them?" he asked, following close behind her as she walked to the front door.

"Hugo Oldsworth, of course."

"Molly, you didn't …"

"Of course not, what kind of girl do you think I am? He very kindly gave them to me."

"But … why?"

"So that we could have a look inside, silly."

"But … why?"

Molly bubbled with excitement. She handed the bunch of keys to Richard, and said: "Don't you want to see where we're going to live for the rest of our lives?"

Richard stepped back. Had he heard her correctly? What was she saying? What did it mean? Molly reached up, flung her arms around his neck and kissed him gently on the mouth. Their lips parted.

"It's ours, darling", she said, her arms still entwined around Richard's shoulders.

"But …?"

"Come on, unlock the door. We can go inside, and I'll tell you all about it."

She removed her arms. Richard, uncertain as to what had just transpired, did as he was bade. He unlocked the front door, but only after nervously inserting the wrong key and almost getting it stuck. Molly amusingly observed his efforts in silence. He opened the door, and gestured Molly to enter before him. She did not move.

"Well?" she said, tilting her head slightly to one side.

"Well what?"

"Aren't you going to carry me over the threshold?"

Richard grinned, scooped her up in one single movement, and entered the property.

"You'll have to do this again after we're married", she uttered, her feet returning to terra firma.

"Come on Mol, spill the beans. What's this all about?"

"It's simple really. Let's sit down." Molly led Richard into the sitting room. Much of the contents, with regard to furniture, remained. Valuables had been disposed off soon after Hugo had inherited the property. There existed nothing to interest would-be burglars. Richard sat on a chair that had a dustcover to protect it. Molly did likewise.

"What are we *really* doing here, Mol?"

"I wanted it to be a surprise."

"If it's true, it is. A *big* one."

"It's true … the farm's ours."

"The farm … not just the house?"

"All of it."

"But how, why?"

"Because I have the money, and, as to the why, that's easy. You loved this house as soon as you saw it. I love it. You need to get back to your roots. Here we can raise small white buffalo, and … it's a great place to bring up children."

"But Mol … I don't know what to say. I'm overwhelmed."

"Are you pleased?" she asked, hopefully knowing the answer.

"I sure am. It's a dream come true. I can't take it all in yet. But you're a schoolteacher?"

"Yes, and a rich one too", she muted, her face beaming.

"But how? Have you won on the lottery? You do have a lottery in this country, don't you?"

"Yes we do, and no I didn't. I have a very large trust fund … set up for me by my father. I was a shareholder in dad's business. When he sold, I got even richer."

"Gee, I don't know what to say. Beautiful, intelligent, humorous … and you come with money. What more could a guy want? I can't take your money, Mol. It isn't right."

"Why not? I know you love me. I love you, why shouldn't my money help make a few dreams come true?"

"'Cause I didn't earn it, I guess."

"Neither did I. Forget Richard Waters, think of Running Water."

"If I think of running water it makes me want to go to the lavatory", he mused, trying to make light of the present situation.

"You know what I mean. No more legal wheeling and dealing. No more big cities. From now on it's hard work and nature. Can you cope?"

"I sure can Mol. I love you. You amaze me, " he said, getting up from the chair and moving over towards her.

Molly stood up. He placed his arms around her waist. She reciprocated. He bent forward and kissed her. Several seconds later their mouths parted.

"Wow!"

"You can say that again, Mol."

"Wow!"

Some forty minutes later, and on the way to the Dog and Duck, Richard found himself still in a state of complete shock. It would take time to adjust. They had looked around the house, and yes, he had been correct in his earlier assumption that was made on his first visit to the farmhouse; all the rooms did, in fact, have beams. For Richard a dream had come true. He had found Molly. And boy, did she come gift-wrapped. Apparently, so Richard had discovered, Molly had offered Hugo Oldsworth a viable solution for all concerned. After seeking her father's approval, she had offered to buy the farm. It would be kept intact. No theme parks. No demolition of the farmhouse. With Sophie's assistance, Molly had persuaded Hugo to sell the farm to her, and, at a lower figure than originally agreed upon during the negotiations with Richard. Oldsworth would retain five hundred acres, for which a yearly rent would be paid. This would supply the artist with a regular income, and, as a result of a reduced purchase price, lower the Capital Gains Tax liability. This aspect had appealed to the vendor. Approaching the Dog and Duck, Richard looked across at her and said: "Molly, you're amazing."

She smiled back at him, saying: "Yes, I know."

The Explorer Montana pulled onto the car park appertaining to the Dog and Duck public house. The American manoeuvred the vehicle into an available parking space, applied the handbrake, and switched off the engine. "I still can't believe it, Mol, I must be the luckiest guy in the world."

"And I'm the luckiest gal."

"You're beginning to sound like a cowboy."

"Cowgirl, if you don't mind."

"Sure, that's what I meant. Looks like there's several people here, judging by the car park."

"At least we've got a room booked", commented Molly, noticing the number of parked vehicles.

"Good, I'm looking forward to that four-poster", said the American, locking the 4X4 by remote.

"I bet you are."

"Aren't you?"

"Of course I am ... I'm tired."

Richard's face noticeably dropped. Molly made a decision to end her teasing of him, adding: "But not *too* tired."

Richard's face noticeably lifted. A pigeon flew low overhead. "You're winding me up again, aren't you?"

"Only a little ... anyway, let's see what you're like after a few pints of real ale."

Having crossed the car park, the young couple reached the door that was marked by a sign saying 'PUBLIC ENTRANCE'. Richard opened it, and gestured his future bride into the establishment. Molly entered, closely followed by her future groom.

"Way up lass, you're a sight for sore eyes", greeted Albert, from his customary bar-side position. "And you lad, it's good to have you back."

"Hello Albert", said Molly, returning the greeting with her infectious smile.

"Hi there Albert, how are you?" said the American, his right hand moving forward in friendship.

"Doin' good", replied the other, taking hold of the proffered set of human digits.

"How's that dog of yours? I've kinda missed him."

"He's about here somewhere, gone off with the landlord. Bill's got some out-of-date crisps out back. I won't need to feed the bugger when I get him home."

"I hope for your sake that they aren't cheese and onion", mused Richard, displaying his understanding of crisps, and the connotations contained within.

"Can I tell him?" asked Molly, looking at her partner.

"Sure, go ahead Mol."

"Tell me what? Do you want me to …?"

"We've got some exciting news", she interrupted. "We're going to be your neighbours."

"Way up, that's great lass. Where?"

"Sheep Dip Farm."

"What, the Oldsworth place?."

"Yep", added the American.

"You renting or buying?" enquired the poacher.

"Buying", said Molly.

"Cor, you lawyer types don't half get good pay", offered the Yorkshireman, turning his attention to his empty glass.

"Would you like another drink, Albert?"

"Don't mind if I do lad. That bugger Bill'll be back in a minute … I hope. A man could die of thirst here."

"Anyway, I'm no longer a lawyer type."

"How's that then?"

"From now on he's a sheep farmer", chirped the American's bride-to-be.

"Know a lot about sheep then, young fella?"

"No, but I'm willing to learn."

"You'll need my help then?"

"Are you a shepherd as well?"

"As well as what?"

"I should say the list is endless."

"You're not far wrong, m'lad."

At that moment the landlord entered the bar. "You've arrived, then?" he said, mastering the art of stating the obvious.

"Hi Bill, it's great to see you."

"And you laddie, but it's much better to see that pretty face again", he stated, smiling directly towards Molly. "Hello lass, it's good to have you back, both of you. Your room's ready, but first, what can I get you?"

"That sounds like an excellent idea", chipped Albert. "We've been waiting for you to tend this bar."

"Hold your horses, you old bugger, I've been feeding that dog of yours."

"Well, now it's our turn."

"I'll get to you in a moment." Bill focused on the young couple, saying: "What'll it be, then, and this one's on the house. Celebrate your pending marriage."

"I'll drink to that", added Albert, his throat assimilating a three-day trek across the Sahara desert without the merest hint of sustenance.

"Keep your shirt on", replied the landlord.

"A pint of bitter and a glass of red wine please Bill, and thanks. And I'm paying for Albert's drink."

Bill frowned at the last remark as he proceeded to fulfil the alcoholic order.

"This young couple are moving into the Oldsworth's place, buying the farm, lock stock and that better be a fresh barrel, that last pint tasted a bit off."

Bill chose to ignore Albert's remarks as to the condition of his ale; instead the topic of conversation centred on the first part of the Yorkshireman's earlier comments. "That's great news", he said, placing the vessel containing grape residue in front of Molly.

"Thanks Bill ... we're going to raise sheep", she said, in a matter-of-fact fashion.

"Most young couples get married and contemplate having kids, these want to raise sheep", stated Albert, still deprived of liquid refreshment.

Bill placed a pint glass containing his best bitter in front of the American. "Know much about sheep?" he inquired.

"Not much", said Richard, adding: "But I'm considering placing Albert on the payroll."

"Not a bad idea, you'll be able to keep an eye on him. Sheep Dip's one of his poaching playgrounds."

"I deny it, where's my pint?"

"Get that down yer", replied the bartender, placing a pint of stout in front of the alleged taker-of-game.

"'Bout time an'all."

"Gee, it's good to be home", uttered Richard, wiping his lips; having replaced the part-drunk glass onto the counter.

"Do you really mean that?" asked Molly, taking hold of his hand.

"I sure do Mol ... I surely do."

"In that case, I have another surprise for you ..."

At that moment, a foul smell filled the air. Albert had temporarily vacated his bar-stool. Blame could not be apportioned in that area. Molly brought

Philip C. Wright

a finger up to her nose, and at the same time backed away. Richard's eyes searched for the offender. "Jake's back", he said, noticing the whippet underneath Albert's empty stool, adding: "He sure is cute, I might just get me one of those."

"Bloody dog", muttered Bill, "He needs a cork."

Albert re-entered the bar area carrying a cardboard box. He approached Molly and handed over the container.

"This is for you", said a smiling Molly, stretching her arms out towards the would-be sheep farmer. "Your other surprise."

Richard, looking puzzled, took the box and placed it onto the counter. He peered inside.

"It's a pup ... *for me?*"

"Yes darling, for you."

Richard reached into the carton, and took out a small black object. He cuddled it to his chest, and, almost in tears, said: "A black whippet pup, for me, I can't believe it. What a day. Thanks Mol, you're the greatest." He lifted the puppy to his mouth and kissed it on the head. The little dog responded by licking the American's face. "Gee Mol, I don't know what to say."

"Jake's the father, he sired a black bitch belonging to an acquaintance of mine", said Albert, once more situated on his bar-stool, "She's going to be a good'un. In a year's time, her and Jake'll have those rabbits on that farm of yours well under control."

"Thanks Albert", said the man, cuddling the pup.

"Thank you, Albert."

"No need to thank me, miss, I've been paid. Mind you, my glass is *empty.*"

"Another round, Bill", said Richard, unable to take his eyes of the minute canine.

"He's gone again", added Albert, picking up a newspaper.

A few seconds later the landlord returned, carrying an iced cake. Several lit candles burned brightly. "Come on then, you two, blow the buggers out."

"Oh Bill, this is sweet."

"Bill, you're one in a million."

"I know lad, now blow."

They both took simultaneous deep breaths, directing their exhalation towards the celebratory cake. The lighted wax sticks were soon extinguished. The inscription on the cake read, **Richard & Molly Forever**.

"What a nice thought. Thanks again Bill."

"For you Molly, anything."

"Gee thanks, Bill, let me buy you a drink."

"Now you're talking", said Albert, lifting his head from the local rag.

"Anything good?" asked the man clutching the tiny black bundle of fluff.

252

"I's just reading bout this Yorkshireman, who got caught by a policeman, performing a lewd act in a public toilet with another man. 'Appened in London."

"Funny people about", offered the landlord, reaching for a fresh glass.

"You might know him." stated Albert.

"I hope not. What's his name?"

"A fella called Derek Arkwright."

"Never heard of him", replied the innkeeper.

Richard looked at Molly. Molly looked at Richard. They both grinned at each other, yet made no comment.

"Rum goin's on", offered Albert.

"You can say that again", added Bill.

Richard, with one hand still firmly holding the now sleeping pup, placed his other arm around Molly, drawing her close. Molly placed her right arm around him and squeezed gently. Richard looked at her, then the whippet. He then raised his head, looked at Bill and said: "The drinks are on me, for everyone."

A pigeon landed on the Dog and Duck's rooftop. It commenced cooing.

The End